WILD AND free

WENDY HOLDEN

headline
review

First published in Great Britain in 2015
by HEADLINE REVIEW
An imprint of HEADLINE PUBLISHING GROUP

1

Cataloguing in Publication Data is available from the British Library

ISBN 978 0 7553 8531 7

Typeset in Adobe Garamond by Avon DataSet Ltd,
Bidford on Avon, Warwickshire

Printed and bound in Great Britain by Clays Ltd, St Ives plc

Headline's policy is to use papers that are natural, renewable and recyclable
products and made from wood grown in well-managed forests and other
controlled sources. The logging and manufacturing processes are expected to
conform to the environmental regulations of the country of origin.

HEADLINE PUBLISHING GROUP
An Hachette UK Company
338 Euston Road
London NW1 3BH

www.headline.co.uk
www.hachette.co.uk

CHAPTER 1

HM Prison Folgate
January

The massive prison door slammed behind Jude. Its mighty metallic clang filled his ears and boomed in his head.

His first thought was that he was out.

His second, that it was bloody freezing.

And so, what now?

That was the third.

A car was parked nearby. Jude's first deliberate act of freedom was to bend and look in its wing mirror. He had not seen a proper reflection for years; mirrors were banned inside, for obvious reasons. You got those metal ones nailed to the bog walls, but they were scratched and usually vandalised; the reflection was distorted.

The wing mirror, between wipes with his sleeve as it steamed up with his breath, confirmed that he was as devilishly handsome as ever. A weak winter sun bounced off his bright blond hair, a tad too long. His skin and teeth looked fine, lousy prison diet notwithstanding. They had always been excellent; the former firm and glowing, the latter strong and white. Genes, he would

1

tell people. Having a Seventies supermodel as a mum. It wasn't true, but it sounded good. In his line of work, a bit of glamour didn't hurt.

If anything, Jude decided, chokey had made him better-looking. Bitter experience had firmed his jaw, hardened his mouth, given a new, flinty depth to the long, tawny eyes. He straightened to his full willowy six foot two and pushed his fraying wristbands deep in the pockets of the scabby black anorak.

He'd always been a natty dresser, but the style he'd affected on the outside had no place in prison. Snowy Jermyn Street cuffs to show the expensively plain gold links and the discreet glint of an even more expensive watch. Savile Row suits, single-breasted, held by one button; closely fitting round the shoulders. He'd always had taste, bought the best he could afford. Good stuff didn't date.

God only knew where all that was now. In storage some-where, possibly, along with his silk boxer shorts and cashmere overcoats. Or maybe they'd all been nicked by the cops who had ransacked his rented flat at the time of his arrest.

Inside, it had just been prison overalls. He would not have wanted to stand out anyway; that was obviously something you did at your peril. He'd kept his head down and kept in with the right people, both screws and lags. Jude had always been a diplomat. In another life, with another background, he might have ended up as Her Majesty's Ambassador. Not lounging at Her Majesty's Pleasure. But you could only play the cards you were dealt and sometimes, as had happened, you lost the game.

When he'd lost his and been jailed it was summer. Six and a half years ago. Now the city was in the very depths of winter and as warm welcomes went, it lacked something.

Jude glanced up to the high, cold blue sky stretching above

the bare black branches of the trees. He produced a packet of cigarettes, slipped one out and tapped it on the box. He narrowed his eyes as he lit it. Exuding plumes of smoke and warm breath, he walked off.

'Coo-ee! Jude!'

A woman's voice. He twisted round.

A beautiful blonde girl was waving from a car on the other side of the road. Curvy, sexy, expensive and with a beautiful body. And that, Jude thought, was just the gleaming scarlet Ferrari with the famous yellow badge on the door. He identified it instantly as a 1955 750 Monza and felt his heart turn over.

Classic cars were Jude's passion. Even inside, he'd followed the market; you were allowed magazines, if not books, not that he wanted those anyway. This beautiful low-slung baby, with her swooping lines and her big black tyres with the cross-hatched silver spokes, called to him. With every nerve of his being, he answered.

The girl was getting out with the knees-together ease of the debutante she certainly wasn't. For all that her voice and poise were pure Kensington, she hailed, Jude knew, from Neasden.

'Nice schmutter,' she said ironically.

'Wasn't expecting you,' Jude replied dryly. 'Would have put on my white tie and tails if I'd known.'

'Well, that'd be more your style.' She probed the anorak's grubby cuff with a polished fingernail. 'Man at C&A, is it?'

'All the rage inside. Height of fashion, believe me.'

'I must say, I've always loved a stonewashed jean.' She examined the clinging pair Jude had on. As well as being too tight, they were far too short; the crotch stopped only a few inches above his knees.

'Great, aren't they?' Jude agreed. 'Especially with the white trainers.'

'White-ish,' she said, wrinkling her nose.

'And I've got on a lovely nylon polo shirt in a really fabulous petrol blue.' He unzipped the anorak and showed her.

'Woah!' She shaded her eyes, as if from the dazzle. 'You're working a serious look there.'

'HMP Folgate Charity Clothes Store chic,' Jude told her. 'When you're leaving you get to choose an outfit. You should have seen what I left.'

She giggled.

'You look good, though,' Jude told her, dropping the irony. Frankie was a stylish bird, always had been. Today she wore a simple-yet-expensive, close-fitting white shirt and no bra that he could see; also a very short tweed skirt. Emphasising long and coltish legs were a pair of tight-fitting, low-heeled knee-boots. She had high cheekbones and full lips and her shoulder blade-length hair lifted in the breeze. Jude felt a wave of desire. It had been a very long time.

But there was, he knew, no point looking to Frankie. She was his best friend's girl and therefore untouchable. Jude may be a thief, but there was honour involved; besides, Rich was not a man to cross. People who crossed him wound up under crosses themselves. Six feet under.

But if Frankie had noticed, she gave no sign. He was relieved when she indicated the Ferrari's passenger door. 'Come on. Get in.'

After the cold street the car was deliciously warm. It smelt cedary and expensive and the low-slung seat fitted him like a glove. To be in something like this after those white crim vans with the row of black squares along the top! At his trial there had been banging on the sides, hysterical shouting and cameras. Some groping old DJ was being tried in a neighbouring court for historic abuse; the crowd thought Jude's van contained him.

Running down the ramp amid a hail of violent invective, Jude had been glad to be a mere armed robber on a murder rap.

He adjusted his seat to an exaggeratedly relaxed angle. The engine purred richly into life and the car glided down the road. He watched as, in the red-framed side mirror, the prison receded.

'Thanks for the reception committee,' he remarked conversationally to Frankie.

'You're welcome.' Frankie smiled at him again from the wheel. There was, he felt, a cryptic edge to the curve of those full lips. He did not ask where they were going; he did not much care. He supposed it was to Rich's Surrey mansion.

It was, frankly, high time Rich stepped in to help. Jude had heard nothing from his mentor and gang leader the entire time he'd been inside. Not even a postcard, let alone a file inside a cake. Rich, always a jammy git, had avoided arrest. He'd been in the right place at the right time as opposed to the wrong place at the wrong time like Jude.

Rich's silence was for a reason, Jude guessed. The obvious one was that communication with the prison was risky. Rich was doubtless under suspicion still, and presumably this was why Frankie had been sent to pick him up. But under the banter about the clothes had been relief. Rich's other possible reason for not being in touch, Jude knew, was that he had forgotten all about him.

It would be good to see the bastard, Jude thought. And to see his cars especially. Rich's pride and joy, the fruits of all his labours as he liked to call it, was the colossal uber-garage under the Surrey mansion. It had a heated marble floor, a surround-sound system, spotlights and viewing platforms offering vistas of, among other stunners, Rich's 1973 Porsche 911 and pre-war Bentley. You could see them from the huge sitting room too;

glass panels in the floor afforded an extra view of the glories below.

'Got any plans?' Frankie asked.

Jude shrugged. 'Considering a few options.' Admitting he was desperate, homeless and without prospects might, he knew, considerably reduce what market value he had.

They were driving through South London now, along one of those long streets typical of the area. Shops along the bottom, crummy flats along the top; the shops a mixture of betting emporia, convenience stores, dry cleaners, cafés, off-licences with grilles over the windows. There were newsagents with lottery signs outside and the odd ethnic food store with old men in white robes picking dubiously through boxes of suggestive-looking vegetables.

'I might have something for you,' Lorna said, smiling at him.

Jude did not reply. He did not want to sound too keen. He registered the 'I' and slotted it with the fact she was at the wheel of Rich's most beloved car, the pride of his collection. If he let Frankie drive it, things had obviously got serious during the last few years.

Jude guessed that, since he last saw her, Frankie had risen in Rich's affections and within the organisation. She had become the Bonnie to Rich's Clyde. The only female member of the famous Diamond Geezers.

This moniker had been bestowed on Rich's gang by a press keen to emphasise and cartoonise their East London roots. Coverage tended to concentrate on the daring aspect of their work – an audacious series of raids netting hauls of at least $100 million a time – rather than the part that involved shooting people or leaving them maimed.

The Diamond Geezers' stamping ground – or, more precisely, their shooting, threatening and stealing ground – had been the foyers of the great hotels of the world. Twenty metres in, to be specific, where the glass cases of necklaces and fine watches were. Preferably at two in the morning, with sledgehammers and getaway motorbikes revving outside.

It unnerved Jude, the way Frankie drove while looking at him, not the road. Not for his sake, but for the car's. Only thirty-three Monzas had ever been made and this one, Jude knew, was worth something north of five million.

They were coming up to a pedestrian crossing with a crowd of schoolkids jostling each other off the kerb. They spotted the Ferrari and started shouting. Frankie lowered the window.

'How do you get one of these then, lady?' A small black boy with longing eyes, his face pinched with cold, was bouncing a football by her driver door.

'Be good, work hard and get a good job,' Frankie called, laughing, over her shoulder as the car zoomed away.

'Just like Rich, eh?' Jude remarked dryly.

As Frankie did not answer Jude remembered that Rich wasn't someone you joked about. He'd better watch his step.

He stared through the windscreen as the long road of shops gave way to a huge roundabout. It had come up in the world since he'd been inside. The centre of it had been a clump of benighted flats but these seemed to have been razed to the ground and replaced with smarter ones. There were balconies equipped, not with dismembered bicycles, washing and general rubbish, but trendy outdoor furniture. At ground level there was that reliable bellwether of extraneous cash, a flower shop.

Jude felt a tug of apprehension. He had heard London property was going through the roof. He was going to need a lot of money to live in the manner to which he had become accustomed before he had had to accustom himself to HMP Folgate.

The Ferrari was crossing Lambeth Bridge. Jude looked out at the sparkling wintry water and the graceful stone tiara of the Palace of Westminster ranged along its side. That tall glass thing way down the river, that was the Shard, right?

'Look, Jude,' Frankie said suddenly. Her bantering tone had gone; she sounded serious. 'Do you want a job or not?'

Jude continued to stare ahead, as if he had not heard. There was no way he was taking instructions from Frankie. Not without seeing Rich first.

From the wheel, she continued to urge him. 'Come on, Jude. It's a great job. One of the best we've done.'

Jude's well-formed lip curled sceptically. The bar was set pretty high for that. Take the famous Handbags and Gladrags raid on Monaco, when he, Rich and the other Geezers had arrived in blond wigs, Hermes scarves and crocodile totes in which .357 Magnums were concealed. They had departed with $150 million in assorted jewels, including the celebrated Vicomtesse de Chabron necklace with its centrepiece 150 carat diamond.

They were driving through Westminster now, packed with tourists despite the chill. Hundreds of mobile-phone cameras flashed at the Ferrari. Lots of people, Jude reflected, were recording the fact that his first act on release was to jump into a conspicuous car. Bought with conspicuously ill-gotten gains.

She was changing lanes by Westminster Abbey now. Jude, for all his consternation, could not resist a glance at it. He'd watched the royal wedding; along with many of Her Majesty's other guests at Folgate. The sight of all those sparklers had made his fingers itch.

'Let me talk to Rich about it,' he said.

It had struck him that Frankie was following an odd route if she intended to go to Surrey, heading west rather than south. She was driving up the red-topped tarmac of the Mall now. Up ahead, atop the grey spread of Buckingham Palace, the Royal Standard fluttered in the freezing breeze. Her Majesty, at whose pleasure he had been languishing, was at home. Should he pop in and thank her?

'I'm afraid that's not possible,' Frankie said.

'What isn't?' Jude's tone was tight with suspicion.

'You can't talk to Rich.'

'Why not?' So this was it. A schism. He'd known something was up. Had Rich and Frankie split and were now setting up rival gangs? Was this why she had met him, to swoop in first and claim his loyalty?

But he was not on her side. Never would be. Rich may have left him high and dry in prison, but they went back a long way. All the way to the children's home.

Frankie did not look at Jude as she skirted the Victoria Memorial. More tourists, snapping the Palace, captured them as they zoomed past. 'Because he's dead, Jude,' she said in a low voice.

For a moment, Jude was too surprised to react. Time stopped and a singing silence filled his head. As always when experiencing extreme emotion, Jude shrank into himself, was still, betrayed by no flicker of a muscle what he felt.

Dead? Rich was dead? Not such a jammy git then, after all. Jesus.

'What happened?' he muttered, when he was able to speak, by which time they were way beyond Victoria station and going round Hyde Park Corner.

Frankie reached out over the gearstick and took Jude's hand. A great stone was spitting light on her middle finger. He had always wondered what had happened to the Vicomtesse de Chabron diamond.

'What happened? *They* happened.' She felt in the door pocket and passed over a copy of the *Evening Standard*.

Five Star Heist, read the headline. *Sledgehammer-wielding robbers stage smash-and-grab at prestigious Park Lane hotel*, screamed the subhead.

'On our turf!' Jude exclaimed, stung into violent expression at last. 'Who are these jerks?'

'The head man's an ex-Balkan general, with all that implies.'

'He needs to be taught a lesson,' Jude said grimly.

'That's what Rich thought,' Frankie sighed, 'and look what happened to him.'

'What did happen to him?' Jude asked, then wished he hadn't, as Frankie described how Rich had been met outside the Royal Automobile Club by iron-bar-wielding thugs in motorcycle helmets. The remains had had to be identified by dental records.

'It was planned,' Frankie told him. 'The Balkan wanted Rich out of the way.'

'And you want me to take him on now?' Jude slid her a look.

'It's not a hotel job,' Frankie said quickly. 'Rich realised before he died that he couldn't compete with these psychos. He knew he had to find another market. Think outside the jewel box, as it were.'

Jude surveyed her doubtfully. His every nerve end was telling him to bail out. But this car, as Frankie had possibly realised, was hellish hard to bail out of.

'He had a plan,' she continued urgently. 'But only you can make it work, Jude.'

As she talked she piloted the Ferrari down a cobbled Knightsbridge mews street and pulled into a narrow space defined by black-painted chains. The Ferrari's red door was right by the house entrance; a sage-painted door with a gleaming gold knocker. Her place, Jude assumed.

The low purr of the engine now ceased. Frankie sat still for a moment, as if making up her mind about something. Then she turned to him and traced his cheek with her finger.

The thought roared through Jude's mind that now Rich was dead, Frankie might not be unavailable after all. It was an ill wind that blew nobody any good.

'What is it?' he heard himself muttering. 'This plan?'

He was aware he was playing into her hands but her hands were on his groin now. The nerve ends screaming at him to bail out were drowned out by the clamour of another, equally urgent need. This became deafening as Frankie leant over and pressed her parted lips to his.

'Festivals,' Frankie said, pulling away with tantalising gentleness.

'Festivals?' Aflame with lust, Jude strained to control his rioting senses. Hippies and burger vans ran through his mind. Glastonbury and mud.

Frankie flopped back against the driving seat and slowly undid the top two buttons of her shirt. 'Festivals,' she pronounced, 'are a gold mine.'

Jude was struggling now. On the one hand he ached to possess Frankie. On the other hand, what the hell did she mean? Festivals were all warm beer in plastic glasses, horrible Portaloos and skint teenagers. He'd done a bit of festival business in the past. On the narcotics side. But the takings had hardly justified the effort or the risk.

Frankie undid the remaining buttons of her shirt and opened it just enough for him to glimpse, rather than see. 'The point is, in the last few years while you've been inside, festivals have changed out of all recognition.'

Jude felt that the point was something else entirely. One agonisingly constricted by his tight trousers.

'You get these posh ones now,' Frankie went on, placing her hands behind her head so the shirt opened a little more. 'Boutique festivals, they're called. Very select. They're held at stately homes. Rich kids go to them. Famous people. Super-models. And the thing is, their guard's right down. They reckon they're roughing it, they're full of love and peace. They shove their diamond rings in their tent pockets. Rich pickings,' she added, leaning over towards him with a smile.

He didn't dare look. If he did, he would lose himself. Promise her anything, anything. He stared violently out of the window trying to control himself. He felt he still didn't buy it.

'I haven't convinced you,' Frankie sighed.

He shook his head.

'So what's the problem?' Her long-nailed fingers were walking towards his trousers again. He folded his hands primly over his pelvis and decided to be straight with her.

'Why do you want me to organise it?'

Frankie's eyes sparkled. 'Because you're smart, you sound posh and you're good-looking. Perfect boutique festival material.'

Jude inclined his head. 'Flattery will get you everywhere.'

'I do hope so. But you still don't look too sure.'

'Who would I be working with?'

'That,' Frankie said, 'would be up to you.'

This, Jude decided, was the deal-breaker. 'I've been out of the scene for a while,' he objected. 'I wouldn't know who to trust.'

'Pity,' Frankie said. She rippled her elegant fingers on the steering wheel of the car. 'This would be your fee, if you do the job.'

Jude felt as if his head might explode. He stared at Frankie with the wide eyes of a dazzled child. '*This* car?' he croaked, looking wildly around the interior.

'Rich once said you were the only other person on the planet who loved it like he did.'

True. He and Rich shared a contempt for 'expert' collectors who didn't even know how to open their car hoods. 'Which festival?' he asked. He was in, no question. He was off to buy a tent and a bloody CND T-shirt before you could say portable toilet.

'That's up to you as well.' Her smile flashed. 'Look,' she said, 'let's go inside and, um, discuss it further.'

Never had Jude moved so fast.

CHAPTER 2

February

One hundred and forty miles north of London, in the Midlands town of Chestlock, the phone rang in the office of head teacher Mark Birch. He picked up reluctantly. He had been expecting this call and he had not been looking forward to it.

'Mate?'

Mark was briefly confused. He had been expecting a particularly forceful female on the line but this voice was male and casually friendly.

'It's Spencer, mate.'

'Spencer!' Mark's ear burned against the receiver. 'Spencer? *Spencer*?' Spencer from *Branston*? From *university*?

'Blast from the past, mate, eh?'

Over twenty years in the past, in fact.

'How's it going, mate?' Spencer asked.

'OK,' Mark said, adding hurriedly, 'how about you?'

'Oh, cool. Still at the agency.'

Mark remembered now that Spencer had gone into advertising. 'Board member now, mate, proper grown-up stuff,' the other end added. 'Garlanded with awards, trailing clouds of glory sorta-thing.'

'Good for you.' None of the awards was for modesty, Mark assumed.

'Took me ages to track you down. Didn't realise you'd left London.' Spencer sounded slightly incredulous about the latter.

'Yes, just last year. It was a bit . . .' Mark hesitated. 'Sudden.'

Memories were slowly breaking the surface. Mark could picture Spencer now – forceful; piratically handsome with thick black hair, dark eyes popping with excitement and huge, infectious grin. He didn't remember him saying 'mate' all the time before, however.

'So,' Spencer said, 'I'm guessing you've moved north with the BBC, mate?'

'No, I got made redundant.'

'Bad luck, mate.'

'Well, yes and no. I retrained as a teacher. I'm a primary school head now,' Mark said with a touch of pride.

'And how hilarious is that?' snorted the other end.

'Why hilarious?' Mark asked stiffly. He'd done exceptionally well in all his exams and had passed his interview with flying colours. The obvious leader in a very good field, the Head of Governors had said.

'Because you're called Birch. As in Bring Back The Birch. Perfect name for a headmaster. Nominative determinism or what?' Spencer explained mirthfully.

Mark, who'd heard it all before, felt irritated as well as patronised. 'Actually, we don't use corporal punishment in primary schools any more.' Although more was the pity in some cases. 'Look, if you've just rung up to laugh at my job . . .'

'Nah, nah, mate. No offence, yeah? So how's the old love life?' asked Spencer, abruptly changing tack.

The question came at Mark like a bomb. It sat on his lap,

round and black, lit end fizzing away. He stared at it, unable to answer.

Spencer, oblivious, pressed on. 'Claire, wasn't it? At the Beeb too, wasn't she?'

'On Woman's Hour, yes.' And how ironic was that? Claire had worked in a highly moral, feminist atmosphere yet had run off with a hedge fund manager invited on the programme to defend financial sharp practice. Not that Mark intended to tell Spencer any of this.

He took a fortifying breath to summon the few self-deprecating sentences in which he habitually packaged the horror of Claire's betrayal. But did he need to bother? Spencer had never met Claire. 'It's kind of over,' he elided, amazed at how casual he could sound.

'Shame. Divorced, are you, mate?'

'We never married.' He would have liked to, but Claire had been firmly against. She had used the 'why bother, it's only a piece of paper' argument. He had thought that was the independent woman talking but it turned out that she had other reasons.

'That's a relief then,' Spencer remarked, reminding Mark that sensitivity hadn't been one of his virtues any more than modesty had.

'But *you* got married, didn't you?' Mark said slowly. 'Yes, I remember your stag night.'

Mark had been one of the stags who had ended up being chained naked to lamp posts in Leicester Square before being force-fed laxatives. Held in a police cell, he had missed the actual wedding. The reasons why he had not seen Spencer for so long now came back to him.

'Great, wasn't it?' Spencer's tone was warmly nostalgic. 'But me and Sadie, we've split up now. Commitment issues, you know?'

So he'd gone through all that and Spencer had not even lasted the distance! 'Well, it's been great to catch up,' Mark said tersely. 'But I've got to go.'

'Whoa, mate!' cried the other end. 'Not so fast. I rang for a reason. My fiftieth.'

Spencer was fifty? 'Oh my God,' Mark exclaimed involuntarily. Because if Spencer was fifty, so was he. Practically, anyway.

'Bummer, yeah? We're all so bloody ancient, aren't we? But anyway, mate. I wanted you to help me celebrate. I've got something I really want to do. You're not gonna believe it, mate.'

Mark felt his insides tense. Celebrating with Spencer was a dangerous business, as Leicester Square illustrated. What his idea of a landmark birthday celebration was did not bear thinking about. Some testosterone-fuelled mayhem, that was for sure.

'Don't tell me,' Mark said ironically. 'Getting pissed in Prague. Strip billiards in Las Vegas in a bunga bungalow with mohair walls and a wet bar. Rally-driving with glamour models.'

Someone cleared their throat near his ear. Mrs Garland, the school secretary, eyes boggling, was placing a cup of tea down on his desk. She hurried out, radiating disapproval.

'What did you say?' Mark asked, distracted. He had missed Spencer's last few sentences. Or perhaps he had imagined them.

'That I want to get the band back together, mate.'

'What band?'

'The Snakes, of course. It'll be great, won't it? The four of us, back on stage. Woo hoo!' said Spencer.

Mark screwed his eyes shut then opened them again. 'Hang on. You want to get the Mascara Snakes back together? Our old band, from college?'

'Our ad hoc neo-ambient proto-prog-rock combo? Sure, why not?'

'We weren't prog rock,' Mark rebutted indignantly. 'We were New Wave.'

'Course we were!' crowed Spencer. 'That was a joke. But it proved my point. You still care!'

'No I don't!'

'Now you're backtracking. Come on, mate. It'll be reem.'

'Be what?'

'Reem. As in, jolly good fun,' Spencer cackled. 'Contemporary slang. Honestly, mate, get with the programme. Don't be a fuddy-duddy.'

'I'm not a fuddy-duddy,' Mark objected.

'OK, so tell me this. Who are the Kardashians?'

'I don't know and I don't care.'

'Mate, come on,' Spencer urged. 'Don't slip into your dotage without a final last blast on life's amp.'

'I'm quite happy as I am, thanks.'

'Old and boring, you mean,' Spencer mocked. 'Tell me this. In recent years have you had an uncontrollable urge to wax the car, edge the lawn and write to the council about recycling?'

'Sod off.'

'Looked at ads for stairlifts with more than the usual interest? Is your hair going grey and your legs going bald?'

'Fuck off!' shouted Mark, realising too late that Mrs Garland, possibly on purpose, was tidying a bookshelf right outside the door. 'The answer is no to all those things. Including the band thing. Especially the band thing. I don't want to relive my youth, OK?'

He crashed down the phone, but just as soon it rang again. He ignored it, but then heard footsteps descending the stairs. A few seconds later, the line from Mrs Garland's office buzzed through.

'Call for you, Head Teacher.'

Spencer again, obviously. 'It's still eff off,' Mark growled, aware that the school secretary was back at the shelf outside the door.

There was a shocked exclamation from the other end, then 'Is that the headmaster?'

Mark groaned and sank his head into his free hand. Oh God. He'd forgotten about this call. The one he had been waiting for in the first place.

He had been in charge at St Stephen's C of E Primary a mere few months and in most respects was still learning the ropes. But he already knew more than he wanted to about the rope called Lorna Newman.

'Good morning, Mrs Newman,' he said resignedly. 'I must apologise. I'm afraid you caught me at a bad moment.'

'So it seems,' Lorna Newman replied tightly. 'I must say, I'm both surprised and disgusted,' she added, with obvious glee.

He had played right into her hands, Mark knew. Given her something to object to. Something else, that was. Because she would have been ringing to complain in the first place, there was no doubt about that. What would it be this time?

Not the school Christmas production of *Joseph and the Amazing Technicolour Dreamcoat* again? It had played to packed houses and raised an unprecedented amount for the PTA. The only parent who had found fault with it was Lorna Newman.

At first she had complained because her son, Alfie had failed to land the main role. After that she had gone on the offensive, attacking the musical on moral grounds. Jacob, she claimed, was the ultimate feckless father. His twelve sons were evidence of his sexual incontinence. Spoiling Joseph outrageously at the expense of the others was irresponsible. Jacob's rightful place was not as a hero in the Bible but in local-authority-sponsored parenting classes.

Lorna was one of the permanently offended. She kicked about the football of political incorrectness with a Ronaldo-like skill and moved with brazen impunity the goalposts on the moral high ground. As Mark had learnt, you were always in the wrong with Lorna. And Lorna was always right.

Forcing himself to put the swearing incident behind him, he did his best to sound brisk and dignified. 'How can I help you, Mrs Newman?'

'You can stop calling me Mrs for a start,' came the acid retort. 'It's Ms. And while I'm on the subject of names, you should know that I'm changing mine.'

'Again?'

Lorna Newman had changed her name once already. She was recently-divorced; her married name had been Lintle. Alfie had entered the school as Alfie Lintle; this had changed to Alfie Newman when his mother reverted to her maiden name. What further alteration could possibly be necessary?

'I'm Lorna Newwoman from now on,' the voice at the other end stridently announced. 'To celebrate my freedom from the prison of marriage and the start of the rest of my life.'

Mark was temporarily speechless. 'I see,' he said eventually, although in fact he didn't. Not only was calling yourself Newwoman ridiculous, it had implications for poor Alfie. Having a mother with that name would be horribly embarrassing.

'I'm imagining that Alfie's name remains the same,' he said, just to make sure. You never knew, with Lorna Newman. *Newwoman.*

'You imagine wrong,' Lorna snapped. 'He's Alfie Newwoman from now on.'

Exasperation swept Mark. He roused himself to fight Alfie's corner. The boy certainly wasn't capable of fighting it for himself. Alfie was tiny, skinny, bespectacled and had ginger hair into the bargain. Being called Newwoman would finish him off completely.

'Do you really think—'

But Lorna butted straight in. 'I wasn't ringing you about that anyway.' As if, Mark thought, condemning her son to a lifetime of playground ridicule was a mere side issue. What could possibly supersede it?

He was about to find out.

'I was ringing you because Alfie brought a Roald Dahl book home last night. I object to the school making my son read Roald Dahl books.'

'He would have chosen it, Mrs Newman, I mean . . .' Mark forced himself to go on. '*Ms Newwoman*. The children always get a say in their reading material.'

The other end sniffed dismissively. 'Children are hardly in a position to make the right choices for themselves. They need to be guided by responsible adults.'

Mark moved to defend Alfie's teacher. 'Miss Blossom is a very responsible adult.' Unlike some people he could think of. 'Why exactly do you object to Roald Dahl?' he asked. 'Most people think of his books as modern classics. Take *Matilda*, which besides being a wonderful story has been made into a musical by the RSC.' Mark remembered that that wonderful story was about a little girl with unbearable parents.

'Elitist tripe,' bulldozed Lorna. 'And Dahl is a complete throwback. Affairs left, right and centre. Patrician, outdated attitudes completely out of touch with our inclusive contemporary society. The problem with children's literature today,' she snorted, 'is that there are so few truly inclusive books around.'

Mark resisted the temptation – if that was the word – to argue. 'Perhaps,' he suggested tartly, 'you might consider writing something yourself, Ms Newwoman.'

He braced himself for a blistering riposte. Instead, a thoughtful silence greeted his words. 'Hmm,' she said eventually. 'You know, I might just do that.'

Having got Lorna off the phone, Mark dialled Mrs Garland on the internal system. He wanted her to send up Miss Blossom. The sooner Ginnie knew, the better. They needed to concoct a Save Alfie plan.

As he waited he saw himself in the mirror on the shelf above the computer. His own reflection these days always caught him by surprise. It was like looking at someone else.

He had always looked young for his age. So much so that some of the mothers at his last school had been a bit giggly and blushy around him. No longer.

Spencer was right. He was getting old. The traumas of nine months ago had added years. Threads of grey had appeared in his once-dark hair, and his skin, previously peachy and line-free, now looked drained and colourless. His smile, once so quick, so wide, so ever-hovering, now had to be dragged up like a draw-bridge. His large eyes still had shock in their depths, hanging around like the last patches of snow in spring.

Following the agony of the split he had left his school in London to make a new start in the country. He had intended to begin again with a clean slate, to restore his professional and especially his emotional strength. But never had he felt so weak, in both body and mind.

He had been here in the country six months and had expected, vaguely, to have found a nice cottage by now. But after a week at the educational coalface the last thing he felt like doing with his weekend was trailing around after an estate agent. He was still renting, albeit not very satisfactorily. The cottage had damp walls and swollen windows that would not open. Mark had written to his landlord about it. And – not that he was going to admit as much to Spencer – he had been in touch with the council about rubbish as well.

While the council was yet to resolve the problems with the recycling collection, the landlord, eventually, had countered with the information that the cottage had only been purchased recently so redecoration had not been possible. He added, in self-congratulatory fashion, that he had bought it at a knockdown price at auction after the cottage had languished for years on various estate agents' books.

Only the other day, Mark had come across a possible reason for this. Attempting a spot of gardening in the wasteland before the cottage, he had unearthed a battered nameplate in the raggedy long grass. It was split and broken, but had evidently been fairly recently wrenched out. By his landlord, Mark immediately suspected; the screws in the back exactly fitted the holes in the battered gate. 'Hangman's Cottage', the sign said.

He was living in Hangman's Cottage.

Mark told himself that the living were more to be feared than the dead. If he was haunted by anything it was Claire's betrayal. But knowledge of the cottage's provenance did not increase its appeal.

A soft knock interrupted his reverie. A woman had appeared at the door.

'Ah. Miss Blossom.' Hastily, Mark got to his feet. 'So sorry. Do come in.'

Nervously tucking her hair behind her ear, Alfie's form teacher walked into the room. The mere sight of him sent a powerful rush of self-consciousness through her and the constricted space made her feel enormous. Ginnie reminded herself that Mr Birch had asked her up here for professional reasons and not because he had the remotest interest in her personally.

Ginnie, on the other hand, had a strong personal interest in Mr Birch.

'Hot? *Him*?' Kay Green, the Juniors teacher, had snorted when Ginnie inadvertently blurted this out. 'Looks like a creased paper bag to me. Have you seen his shirt collars?'

Ginnie had noticed that the new headmaster was a little crumpled. But eco-activist Kay, with her low-carbon-emission wardrobe and oversized purple glasses made of recycled plastic, was a fine one to talk. There was something almost mediaeval about her hand-weft linens, lumpy knits and vegetarian shoes.

Besides, Mark's slightly battered air only increased his attraction so far as Ginnie was concerned. The mild neglect of his appearance appealed strongly to her caring instincts. Independent woman though she was, she wanted to iron his shirts.

Not to mention his soul, which she sensed was crumpled too. He looked so sad sometimes it twisted her heart. He was tall and thin and slightly stooping, as if he shouldered some heavy, unhappy burden. Or was a starved or scorched plant moved into the shade just in time. Ginnie liked gardening too.

Whenever her own eyebeam fused with his her heart fizzed like a firework. Whenever she glanced at his long, pale hands – devoid of any wedding ring, she had noticed – she imagined them touching her. And that made her feel giddy, palpitating, nervous.

'Bit old for you, isn't he?' Kay would tease.

Ginnie never dignified this with an answer. She had no intention of confiding anything to spiky Kay, least of all that she liked older men. Ginnie also liked Mark Birch's slightly dry, exasperated air; it spoke of high intelligence and high expectations. He was not the eager-to-please sort while Ginnie was, excessively. She wished she wasn't, but suspected it went with the territory of being plump and single. Whether the new head-master was single was only one of many unanswered questions.

Kay Green's theory was that Mark Birch was scared of women. 'Or maybe he just doesn't like *us*. He's from the Big Smoke, after all,' Kay added with an eco-activist's contempt for fossil fuel consumption. 'Probably thinks we're all country bumpkins.'

Kay had, Ginnie knew, an axe to grind. Last week Mark Birch had asked her to tone down some of her more alarmist lessons about climate change on the grounds that some of the Juniors now thought the world was about to end. According to their mothers, they were having nightmares. Ginnie privately thought Mark had taken exactly the right action, but knew eco-zealot Kay disagreed.

She blushed as, now, Mark smiled at her and gestured to a chair. 'Sit down.'

Ginnie tucked her skirt beneath her ample rear and lowered it on to the square red pad of the seat. She clasped her plump white hands together and waited.

Perhaps it was the light up here, Mark Birch was thinking, but Miss Blossom was looking unusually attractive today. Her skin had a fresh, dewy quality and was flushed a lovely pink. She had soft green eyes. He knew he was staring, but suddenly he could not help himself. How had he not noticed before how lovely she was? A curvy beauty with thick, shining, milk-chocolate-coloured hair and freckles scattered across her face like cinnamon powder on cream.

'You wanted to see me?' Ginnie prompted, stuttering slightly under his scrutiny. Inside she was swirling hot and cold. Was he about to sack her? She knew the school was short of money and she, despite her youth the longest-serving teacher, was the most expensive.

'I'm afraid,' Mark said, 'I've got some rather bad news.'

Ginnie only just stopped herself crying out. Then Mark broke the news about Lorna Newwoman and she wanted to cry out for a different reason altogether.

He watched Miss Blossom's face drain of all colour.

'No! Oh that *ridiculous* woman! Poor, *poor* Alfie!'

Mark was rather relishing watching her clear eyes widen in horror and her mouth open to reveal a pink tongue and a row of small white teeth. Now he realised she had finished exclaiming and hurried to fill the gap. 'I agree. It is ridiculous, isn't it?'

'It's more than that. It's . . . it's *cruel*.' Ginnie's brows had knitted and the green eyes glittered angrily.

He had not realised Miss Blossom had such passionate depths. He felt something within him twist in answer, and not entirely because of Alfie either. He was filled with the sudden urge to clasp her soft hand and feed deep on her peerless eyes.

But he knew he could not. It would be unprofessional in the extreme.

Ginnie Blossom, in addition, was a good two decades his junior. She was sure to have a boyfriend, how could she not have? But even if she was free, he would be of no interest or use to her. His heart had been broken; it did not work any more.

Ginnie stood up abruptly. She had felt suddenly too angry to remain sitting down. Mark looked up to the magnificent breasts jutting out into the confined space above him and rose slowly and carefully. Brushing gently against her embonpoint made politeness a pleasure.

He had almost forgotten about the circumstances that had brought about the encounter and was temporarily at a loss when Ginnie said, her chin raised determinedly, 'We'll just have to help him through it, that's all.' He was grateful for the orientation when she added, 'We mustn't let Alfie suffer.'

CHAPTER 3

March

Some hundred miles south-east of Chestlock, spring had, once again, come to the ancient university town. A low sun warmed the flowers in the Fellows' Gardens and made coloured fire from the dewdrops in the grass. It flashed on the gold finials and lead-paned stained-glass windows. It sparkled on the river under the balustraded stone bridges and followed the water curving round banks of glossy green.

Any of the recently returned birds passing overhead might have looked down at two girls on one of the bridges. Rosie, thirteen, was out with her best friend, Shanna-Mae, four years her senior. They were walking into the town centre and had paused on one of the elaborate stone bridges overlooking the river. Rosie wanted to see whether her newly pink hair showed up in the water and was bending over to look.

'It's come out well,' Shanna-Mae assured her. They had spent the previous evening doing it. 'Looks totally festival.'

Rosie peered into the water below. Hit by a sudden sunbeam, her reflected hair showed as a patch of swirling rose. She hoped that it wasn't the nearest to a festival she was going to get. Her heart was set on Wild & Free but her mother was distinctly reluctant. 'You're too young, Rosie,' Diana had insisted. 'You won't know anyone there. What happens if you get into trouble?'

In vain had Rosie argued that she *wouldn't* get into trouble. She wasn't interested in drugs and drink and boys, or whatever else her mother was worrying about. Rosie's interest was fashion, and fashion was why she wanted to go.

Festivals were fashion central these days. All the actresses and supermodels went there, carefully prepped by their stylists to look as spontaneous as possible. They didn't fool Rosie. What she loved about festival fashion was how hard it was to get right. There was more to it than slinging on a vintage floral dress with wellies, or teaming some tiny shorts with huge sunglasses and a big floppy hat. That was entry-level stuff. What made the difference were the witty touches; the beads, the bags, the scarves, the funny T-shirts, the bold, eccentric gestures. DMs with neon tutus. Tailcoats with crowns. Whatever. Rosie itched to get there and experiment herself. Go wild. But only with clothes, not in the way her mother feared.

'What's up?' Shanna-Mae looked up from her celebrity magazine. She had been studying a famous actress's new hair-style. Bad move, Shanna felt, but her eyebrows looked amazing. Whoever had threaded those had serious skill. Shanna could thread, but not as well as that. Not yet, anyway.

Rosie jerked her head up from the river – it made her feel slightly dizzy – and looked at her friend in despair. 'Just, you know. My mum. Not letting me go to Wild and Free and that.'

Shanna blinked her false lashes sympathetically. 'Definite bummer. Might change her mind, though. She's all right, your mum is.'

Rosie rolled her eyes and tucked her thumbs behind the braces holding up her baggy jeans. She dressed to please herself and some combinations, while always striking, were more successful than others. She shook out her short, pink-tinged fringed bob. Her gamine outfit, pointed pixie face and blunt hair gave her the look of a 1930s Ernest Shepard illustration. Shanna surveyed her admiringly. Even at thirteen, Rosie had enormous style. It was, Shanna thought, what made the four-year age gap between them almost irrelevant. Their mutual passion for fashion was what mattered.

They interpreted it differently, even so. While Shanna adopted a swirly, layered, goddessy look appropriate for her curvy figure, Rosie was a complete one-off. The long-haired, mini-skirted, twang-toed look common to every other teenage girl was not for her. She dressed like a boy and looked the more feminine because of it. Her fairy face helped; thick, straight brows above huge green eyes and a mouth like a pink rose. There would be cheekbones too, eventually, Shanna could see. The sort you could abseil up, or climb under in rainstorms.

The sort, Shanna-Mae knew, that she would never have herself. But so what – she was clever enough at make-up to give her own plump face the hills and hollows of Angelina Jolie's anytime. Most days, in fact; Shanna-Mae was rarely less than fully made-up. To add height to her bulky frame she wore her shining toffee-coloured hair in a pile atop her head from which fetching tendrils descended here and there. Shanna planned to be a beautician and knew she was her own best advertisement.

'Don't worry, Ro,' she said comfortingly. 'We'll come up with something.' Shanna had boundless confidence in her own resourcefulness. It hadn't let her down yet and it was going to help her build a retail empire.

Shanna had known her direction in life ever since trying on her first lipstick. That had been at about the age of five. It was the moment, she planned to tell future biographers, when first she realised the power of make-up to transform. After that, school had been a mere waiting game until she could leave and go to technical college. Shanna was now approaching the end of her first year there and had won every accolade going. She knew far more than the instructors, in some cases.

'But what if all the tickets get sold?' Rosie wailed. 'I've been on the website. The family tickets have all gone already.'

'We're not a family, though,' Shanna-Mae pointed out sensibly. 'And it's, like, massive, Wild and Free. The park is huge. They're never going to run out of space.'

Rosie hoped she was right. She monitored the online fashion community exhaustively, and all the leading British fashion bloggers would be at Wild & Free, as well as her favourite designer. 'Koo Chua,' Rosie groaned to Shanna. 'His stuff's seriously amazing.'

Shanna looked unconvinced. Koo Chua's clothes were incredibly tight and suited only stick insects like Rosie. Who, incidentally, Shanna felt sure, was going to be one of the world's great models. Rosie always laughed when she said so and pointed out that she ate like a horse, but Shanna felt both the laughter and the eating were all part of Rosie's charm. She loved fashion yet was not the least self-conscious or vain. It was possibly a unique combination.

'You might have to go on your own,' Rosie grumbled. 'You and the Beauty Bus.'

Shanna's exquisitely made-up face fell. The Beauty Bus was her pride and joy. A rusting twentieth-hand VW van acquired for a song with savings from her Saturday job at Pizza Express, it had been put back on the road by Shanna's mechanic father. Shanna had been in charge of all the design aspects. As ever, she had a strong vision and had eschewed the flowing retro letters one might have expected.

A smitten art student at her technical college was currently spending happy Sundays in the garage painting the outside of the van a shiny cream under Shanna's direction. 'The Beauty Bus' was then to be stencilled on the sides, back and front in black Chanel font. A reversed-out version with cream lettering on black was to go over the spare tyre cover. An adoring textiles student was helping with that, and the cream awning to extend out at the sides.

She had persuaded yet another of her college admirers, this time studying carpentry, to help her fit out the inside. The result, still in progress but most encouraging, was a masterpiece of tiny drawers, shelves and cabinets that would contain her own Beauty Bus brand of lotions and cosmetics. There was a pull-out table for manicures and illuminated mirrors were already fixed to walls. It was all in the same cream and black palette; the textiles student was supplying black banquette seating. He was also, at Shanna's request, designing some witty eyelashes to fit around the circular headlights at the front.

It was a thing of beauty, the Beauty Bus, and Shanna already adored it.

It would represent in miniature the salons she planned to open once she was qualified and had the backing. However, its success depended on there being more than just her to run it. The plan was, while Shanna performed treatments ranging from facials to waxings to pedicures, Rosie would man the front desk, take bookings and sell the various creams and lotions that were Shanna's own invention and which she made up herself in pots labelled Beauty Bus and bought cheaply from eBay.

In particular she needed someone to run things while she operated the spray tan tent. This was the centrepiece of her offer and would, she was certain, draw the crowds. 'People who get spray tans for the festival will be desperate for top-ups,' she had explained to a Rosie eager to be convinced. 'I'll make *loads*.' The pop-up black tent, stencilled with the Beauty Bus logo in cream, was currently on a shelf in her father's garage, as were gallons of brown tanning liquid from an internet supplier. Shanna had not yet cracked the problem of operating the spray machine without an electricity point, but an engineering student was working on the possibility of it running from the van's engine.

All that remained now was to pass her driving test, but Shanna had no serious worries about that. She had never yet failed at anything she'd set her mind on.

And she would not fail at this either. Rosie would be with her at Wild & Free, come hell or high water.

She pushed herself away from the bridge wall and grinned at Rosie. 'You'll get there, don't worry. We'll think of something.'

They mooched on towards the shopping centre, kicking the old leaves on the path. Shanna wanted to check out the make-up hall in Debenhams, see if anything new had come in. Rosie wanted to go to Topshop.

'Hey,' Shanna exclaimed, as a sudden thought struck her. 'You could get your mum to ask Isabel. Get her to come to Wild and Free.'

Rosie's freckled pixie face radiated doubt. Isabel was her mother's best friend. She had been a student when she had met Diana and now she was a Junior Fellow at Branston, the college where Rosie's stepfather was Master. 'Maybe,' Rosie allowed. 'But I dunno if festivals are her thing. She might agree with my mum that I shouldn't go. And she's not really the boho type.'

'She might be, underneath all that lecturer stuff,' Shanna countered. 'And she's lovely. Really nice. Not stuck up or anything.'

Rosie had to agree. Next to her mother, Isabel was the kindest woman in the world. All the same, it was hard to imagine her roughing it in a tent.

'You don't have to rough it now,' Shanna reminded her.

'There's glamping and sushi stalls. People bring their food from Waitrose.'

'Isabel might be a bit old,' Rosie demurred.

'How old? Twenty-five is nothing,' Shanna argued. 'Seriously ancient people go to festivals these days. Like, parents with their kids.'

Rosie scrunched up her face. 'How embarrassing is that?'

'And Isabel's boyfriend's a writer, isn't he?' Shanna steered the subject back. She had, Rosie recognised, got the bit firmly between her whitened teeth. 'Wild and Free's full of writers and stuff. Olly'd love it. Maybe's he's going anyway,' Shanna added, warming to her theme. 'That book of his did really well, didn't it? What was it called again? Smashing something.'

'*Smashed Windows*,' corrected Rosie. The title had been much bandied about in her home on the book's publication six months ago.

'And what was it about again? Olly being a student and stuff?' Shanna, too, was recalling the now-distant drama surrounding the book. Her own mother Debs, also a friend of Diana's, had been vociferous in her criticism. 'He was at that really snobby college, wasn't he? The one with the club full of total yahs where they tore tenners up in front of tramps and drank washing-up liquid or whatever. And smashed windows of restaurants and stuff.'

'Yeah. And Isabel was going out with the yah club's president. He was totally lush and she was crazy about him . . .'

'Yeah, now I remember!' Shanna chimed in. 'Until he tried to get her blamed for him selling drugs or whatever. And there was that posh girl, that socialite or whatever, who took an overdose and nearly died.'

'Amber Piggott,' supplied Rosie. 'She's fine now. She was on the last series of *Strictly*.'

'Oh yeah. With that guy from TOWIE. They did a really good tango.' Both girls were devotees of the show.

They were getting close to the centre of town now and passing an imposing carved college gateway. 'This was the one,' Rosie said. 'St Wino's. Where Olly was.'

Before the two girls could walk across the cobbled front of St Alwine's College, a couple strode imperiously out of the gateway and barged past them, seemingly oblivious to their presence. The male was a short, strutty, standard-issue Sloane with side-parted hair, tweed jacket, red cords and brogues whose solid heels crashed on the stone pavement. The girl had a frosted blond mane, wobbly eyebrows, a miniskirt and black tights. Rosie slid a look to Shanna-Mae, who was examining both eyebrows and heart-attack pale pearlised lipstick more in sorrow than in anger.

'How rude was that?' exclaimed Rosie, once they had gone.

'Omigod.' Shanna was looking crossly after the pair. 'I can see why Olly wrote a book about that place. You'd want to vent. Get it out of your system.'

'I wonder what Isabel thinks, though,' Rosie mused, remembering that this had been Diana's concern. 'I mean, it's fine for Olly. He writes the book, it does well, he gets the glory. But for Isabel it's just embarrassing. All that really really personal stuff about her and that buff president guy coming out. I'd be totally pissed off if I was her.'

Shanna considered. 'But she might be cool with it.'

'Howd'you figure that out?' That had certainly not been Rosie's mother's view.

'Well, you know what they say. The only thing worse than being talked about is not being talked about. So,' Shanna finished, 'are you going to get your mum to ask Isabel or not?'

They were at Topshop now. Rosie's eyes narrowed as she

assessed the window display. 'OK,' she said, accepting the inevitable. 'I will.'

A mile north of the girls, and quite unaware she was the subject of their debate, Isabel was emerging from Branston's gateway. Built in the 1960s by a cutting-edge Scandinavian architect, the college was a Brutalist challenge to the town's prevailing ornate mediaevalism. It was daring both inside and out. While the other university colleges might boast a beautiful tower, a Tudor chapel or a dining hall with a minstrels' gallery, Branston's main feature was a large concrete dome bristling with silver pipes. Within its red brick walls were an egg-shaped chapel, a futuristic dining hall popularly known as 'the Incinerator' and a subterranean round-walled concrete bar which had been known as 'the Turd' to generations of students.

When the college's current Master, a celebrated American neuroscientist, had first begun to live in the shoebox-shaped Master's Lodge, the light from the one thin horizontal window had been almost entirely blocked off by a thick fringe of ivy hanging down from the roof. This had been helpfully removed by Rosie's mother Diana, the college gardener, with whom the Master had fallen in love and married. Shortly afterwards another daughter, Violet, had come along to join Rosie.

Isabel swung along through Diana's garden, the unexpectedly warm spring sun lighting up her streaming red hair. Isabel was a Scot and had the pale skin and auburn mane of the Celtic race. When Olly had first seen her, on the train at the start of her very first term, he had thought her straight out of Walter Scott. But with a small rucksack instead of a wind-rippled plaid cloak and sitting in a crowded carriage instead of striding amidst the heather.

Amazing, Isabel now reflected, to think that was six years

ago. She could remember their first date as if it were yesterday. Writing was more or less all Olly had talked about. They'd met in a pub called the Duchess of Cambridge. As Olly drank a beer called Pippa's Bottom Isabel had sipped a white wine called Château Carole and listened as he explained how he was forever starting new books. On any number of subjects and in any amount of genres. But never finishing them. Of course, he had finished one since: *Smashed Windows*, that source of pain and pleasure in equal parts.

Isabel sighed. She had tried to be happy for Olly. But for her the success of his book was marred with complication. Oh, why had she believed him when he had said that it would sink without trace?

Primed by tales of hard times and publishing woe, they had been steeling themselves for failure at the very first hurdle, publication. And although she had never – could never – admit it to Olly, failure was what Isabel most wanted; for the whole tale to remain buried.

And the portents had been excellent. Or terrible, depending on how you looked at it. Tarquin Squint of the Old Laundry Press wasn't planning a promotion or even an advertising budget. And then, disaster. Against all the odds *Smashed Windows* had become a word-of-mouth smash hit.

People had recommended it to each other, it had started to creep into newspaper articles, into the lower reaches of the bestseller lists. And then, having submitted *Smashed Windows* to a number of literary prize-giving bodies, Tarquin had called with the news that Olly had 'managed to land one of them, old chap'. In consequence, Olly had been photographed for several newspaper lists of the 'Faces to Watch' and 'Hot Young Writers' variety. He'd appeared on the radio, on a late-night television art show . . .

'Sorry! So sorry!' Lost in thought, she had collided with someone, quite hard. A tall youth with dark hair in a sweep of fringe over his eyes was staring at her in an affronted fashion.

Branston was doing interviews at the moment, so she assumed he was a hopeful sixth-former in pursuit of a university place. Although it had to be said that he didn't look all that hopeful.

'Is this, like, Branston?' asked the youth.

As Isabel confirmed that it was, he raised his head – he was very handsome, she noted – and looked critically at the college buildings from under his fringe. 'It's horrible,' he concluded.

Isabel felt simultaneously indignant and amused. She was very loyal to Branston; it was her alma mater as well as her employer. But there was no denying it scored low in the attractiveness stakes. 'It's a *Gesamtkunstwerk*,' she told him.

'A what?'

Isabel decided to overlook his abrupt manner. Nerves affected people in different ways. 'It means "total work of art"' she explained kindly. 'It's a kind of concept in concrete.'

'It looks like a multi-storey car park.'

'Are you applying here?' Isabel asked. Perhaps he was coming to visit someone.

He nodded gloomily. 'Wish I wasn't.'

'So why bother?' Isabel was tickled. He clearly had no idea she was a member of the academic staff. She decided to take this as a compliment.

As the boy pushed his hair back with long, pale fingers, Isabel glimpsed a silver skull ring, the skull pushed round to the inside of the hand. From the depths of his snowy cuff, a neon wristband flashed. 'Because,' he said in a tone of heavy resignation, 'my mother's obsessed with me coming to this university. She's pulling out all the stops. I've had a coach and everything.'

Isabel decided she liked this boy. There was something utterly disarming about his catastrophic lack of tact. Many of the sixth-formers she came across were coached and tutored up to the hilt, but this was the first one who'd ever admitted it.

'Poor you,' she said, meaning it. Parental pressure was a real burden. And not just on the children. The tiger mother syndrome was also the scourge of the Branston admissions department. Following the dispatch of rejection letters, angry mothers would ring up outraged that Bella or Guy's genius had gone unrecognised. Mothers of the successful ones could be even worse. Some over-protective parents accompanied their offspring to lectures. It was only a matter of time before they started sitting the exams.

'What's your name?' Isabel asked.

'Guy.' He gave an ironic roll of his eyes. 'Obviously. Everyone I know's called Guy.'

Isabel added 'ironic self-awareness' to the boy's list of virtues. 'Which Guy are you?'

'Guy Dorchester-Williams.'

'Well, good luck with it all, Guy. What subject are you being interviewed for, by the way?'

She imagined history. Languages, at a push. She was surprised to hear him say 'English', which was her subject. If he got a place, he would be in one of her study groups. She decided not to unmask herself. It might knock him off his stroke, such as it was. She hoped he would get in anyway. He would be fun to teach.

Guy gave an audible sigh. 'I'd better push off. Some old bag called Professor Green's waiting to torture me in there.'

Isabel snorted. Gillian Green was her boss and the formidable head of the English faculty. She tried to convert the snort to a sneeze.

CHAPTER 4

The same day

Victoria Dorchester-Williams swung her bottom over her head in accordance with the instructions on her *Total Pilates* DVD. How, she wondered, was Guy's university interview going? He had refused to let her accompany him to Branston and, rarely for her, she had agreed.

But now she regretted giving in. She was tortured by the thought of her son, her only child, seventeen though he may be, getting off at the wrong station. Or getting lost on the way to the college. Or losing his money. Or being abducted. Or having some unspecified horrible accident.

The DVD had moved on, she now saw. The lithe on-screen instructress was on her feet. 'Now roll down as far as you can go,' she beamed. 'Head forward, count the vertebrae . . .'

Victoria, scrambling up, could see herself in the mirror on the wall. The sun gleamed in the rich purplish highlights which, her stylist claimed, lifted the flatness of her natural dark brown.

Was her son managing to convince the interviewer that he had the capacity for deep thinking? Max Cramme, the coach she had hired at vast expense to train Guy for this encounter, said that was what the Branston tutors were looking for. Along with the ability to engage with new ideas at the highest level. Victoria's insides cramped as much in worry as from the exercises. Guy couldn't engage with the idea of getting out of bed most mornings, let alone picking anything up off the floor.

'Now we'll do a lovely double kneefold,' smiled the instructor.

Victoria strained from side to side as the obliques began. She would ring Guy just as soon as the DVD was over. She had put it on as a distraction, knowing otherwise she would just sit on the redial, phoning endlessly and driving herself mad when Guy didn't answer.

But it would all be worth it – more than worth it – if Guy got in to his first-choice university. Or, rather, his mother's first-choice university. Shame that the college had to be hideous Branston, though. Victoria would have preferred one of the pretty old ones like St Alwine's. But everyone knew that the old colleges were more competitive.

'Come back down slowly,' came the instruction from the screen. 'Replace each vertebra one by one and try to get the waist back on the mat before the hips. Now we'll do the single leg stretch . . . really give those tummy muscles a toning . . .'

If he got in – or when, more like – Guy would have to get out of Branston, Victoria was thinking. He would have to make friends in other, more prestigious colleges. James hadn't, of course. A Branston student himself thirty years ago, her husband seemed to have spent his entire three years inside it. In the bar, mostly– the Turd, Victoria shudderingly recollected – where he had hung around with those idiots he had been in that band with.

'Four-point kneeling, arch the spine then relax out long, keeping the tummy in . . .'

As always when the Mascara Snakes came to mind, Victoria

felt contemptuous. Years ago, when their relationship was in its infancy, she had dropped James off at the stag night of the former singer. She had found Spencer insufferably full of himself. And the others were obviously going nowhere fast. One muttered and had a monobrow while another – Mark, was it? – seemed permanently trapped in the lower echelons of the BBC. None of them fitted Victoria's idea of the going-places people her going-places husband should be going places with.

Her misgivings were more than justified when the stag night ended with James – James, of all people – in a police cell. From that point on Victoria had decided that these particular old ties must be well and truly cut. With a machete, preferably. Or a samurai sword.

'No tension in the face,' the instructor was saying. It was the winding down session, the end of the class, but she still had her legs in the air. Hurriedly, Victoria swung her bum down again. Then, still on her knees but with the speed of a striking cobra, she lunged for her smartphone to call Guy.

Her heart boomed in her chest as she waited for the other end to pick up. After many rings, it did.

'Guy? *Darling!* Were you brilliant?' Her tone was bright as steel.

There was a pause from the other end, then an uncertain 'Er . . . well, it was OK, I suppose.'

'Just OK?' Victoria pursued, desperately staving off her disappointment. 'Have they made you an offer?'

'Er, Mum, it's not quite like that,' Guy mumbled. 'They, like, send you a letter or whatever. Look, Mum,' he added, his tone brightening. 'I wanted to ask you. There's this festival, right? All the other Guys are going. It's a weekender, in July. Called Wild and Free—'

'Let me just stop you there,' Victoria cried, raising her hand to cut him off even though her son could not see it. 'You are *not* going to a festival.'

'*Mu-um!* Why not?'

Crossing to the mirror, Victoria rolled her eyes at her reflection. *Why not?*

There were at least a hundred reasons why her irresponsible teenage son was not going to a festival with his equally immature friends. Venting some of her frustration about the interview, she now proceeded to remind Guy of a recent incident involving a sleepover, wine and vomit. And the washing machine in which Guy and his friend had attempted to hide the evidence but had succeeded only in ruining cushion covers hand-made from some limited-edition ethical Italian damask. 'If there's trouble, you make straight for it,' she told him. 'You've got no common sense and you're very secretive.' The last was a dig at Guy's protracted failure to befriend her on Facebook.

Afterwards, Victoria called her husband. James was, as usual, at a meeting and so, as usual, she left a message with his secretary. Also as usual, because Tilly was far from the sharpest knife in the drawer, this took some time.

Victoria did her best to remain civil. Tilly's father was a friend. More than this, he was a newspaper executive who, at some time in the future, was expected to return the Tilly favour by giving Guy a job as a journalist. Victoria believed in thinking ahead.

Nor was Guy the only person on whose behalf she was thinking ahead. Things, she sensed, were not quite right with her husband. James hadn't said anything, but it was clear that something was wrong, and this was not good news. James was a senior partner in a private equity firm. He made an awful lot of money.

Victoria was no fool, however. She knew that her husband's

heart was not in the cut and thrust of usury. It never had been. He would have left it years ago had she not encouraged him to stay, and had he not found it so easy. Perhaps his very lack of interest was what made him so absurdly good at it. This was Victoria's theory, anyway. His detachment stopped him from over-identifying with the enduring City stereotype. You never saw James with his feet on his desk answering four phones at once and yelling 'Greed is good' into all of them.

But James wanted to leave it all now, even so. She could sense it. He was about to rebel, to throw in the towel. There had been a number of signs. Sorrowful looks out of taxi windows at beggars. Worrying remarks about wanting 'to make a difference'. Victoria had been preparing for some time for the moment when James turned wearily to her on the high-thread-count linen pillow and said he was thinking about a different direction but wasn't sure what.

Victoria was sure what. She had a suggestion. When James said he was ready to come off one track, she had another, all ready, to put him on to. He would become an MP.

Victoria had decided some years ago that being a government minister would suit her husband. It would suit her even more. She could see herself at Chequers, sparkling at state dinners, hobnobbing with the great and good.

To this end, she had been putting the word about whenever she could, which was, fortunately, fairly often. James being a senior banker, there were frequent social occasions where the financial world met the political one. It had been easy enough to drop hints in powerful ears. Sooner or later, something would come of it.

Now, after helping Tilly take down the details – 'yes, Victoria. V-I-C-T-O-R-I-A. As in the station,' – Victoria rose to her feet and looked about the sitting room which had doubled as her exercise studio. It was heavily influenced by the aesthetics of weekend lifestyle supplements and an interior designer called Buzzie Omelet. The 't' was soft. 'Rhymes with pay', James would remark.

Victoria had been impressed with Buzzie. She had that senior rock chick St Tropez glamour – all tanned lean limbs, acres of bracelets, eyeliner and arty, clinging layers – that the fuller-chested Victoria could never quite pull off. She'd have appreciated advice, but Buzzie styled houses, not people. Her 'signature' was the helicoid. Silver-coloured spiral objects of varying sizes but which all looked exactly like oversized screws were everywhere in the house. There was one on the newel post at the staircase bottom and another on the glass coffee table near where Victoria had just been swinging her legs.

Otherwise, Buzzie had brought what she called an 'urban-rustic vibe' to the house. In the basement kitchen, logs were stacked with artistic precision end-on beside the Prussian blue Aga. In the bedroom, the furniture was artfully mismatched, distress-painted and looked, James said, like the set for the servants' quarters in a film of *Pride And Prejudice*.

Victoria went down to the kitchen. The long, low room was dominated by an enormous scrubbed-pine table which Buzzie had sourced from a firm of upcyclers in Lichfield. She had declared it perfect for those great sprawling Sunday lunches that go on all day while the parents chat and the kids run about. Victoria had not liked to say that she never had lunches like that, or lunch at all, while James had wanted to know what an 'upcycler' was. It sounded, he said, like an Edwardian circus attraction. 'It's an upmarket recycler,' Victoria had snapped back.

On the upcycled table, beside the mugs left there by the cleaner and ironing lady – Victoria's brows drew together at this evidence that they had taken a break together – was a copy of her favourite mid-market tabloid. It was open at the page of her favourite columnist, Sarah Salmon, whose weekly diatribe always managed uncannily to echo Victoria's own thoughts.

'What's got Salmon smoking *this* week?' asked the strapline. Victoria made herself a cup of tea using the sink's special feature, a boiling water tap – 'my clients', Buzzie Omelet had said, 'are not the kind of people who wait for kettles to boil' – and settled down to find out.

The Salmon column was made up of paragraphs of varying sizes, all expressing a vehemently uncharitable viewpoint. It concluded, as usual, with a thunderous polemic about workshy spongers who made a career of fecklessness. Victoria read it carefully, nodding in agreement.

Suddenly her mobile lit up. It was James returning her call. He was being driven to a meeting at the Bank of England. 'Sounds like fun,' Victoria said.

She loved the idea of her husband at such august institutions.

'Not really,' James said wearily, staring through the tinted windows of his chauffeured car at the harassed passers-by. The women were picking their high-heeled way between the pavement cracks, the men shifting the backpacks that cut into the shoulders of their suits. Everyone had pods in their ears and was frowning into their phones or else squinting in the sun bouncing off the huge glass buildings. James's own office was at the top of one of those buildings. The height of it made him feel sick, but an important part of being successful in the City was not minding heights. Your success was measured by how many floors up you were and you could no more suffer from vertigo than a doctor could be squeamish about blood.

'How did it go with Guy?' James asked his wife. He had been doubtful about their son's chances of success. He had been even more doubtful about Max Cramme, an expensive waste of time in his view.

'Incredibly well,' Victoria assured him stridently.

'*Really?*' His wife's bulldozer-like approach to life awed James. What Victoria wanted, she invariably got. Take this Branston thing. He, James, may be the college alumnus but Victoria had been the force behind Guy's application.

'Yes, *really*. Guy's wildly keen and completely confident he's impressed them.'

Perhaps he'd got it all wrong, James was thinking. He saw far less of Guy than his wife did, after all. But he still felt that he knew his son better. His distinct impression was that Guy was less than enthusiastic about the prospect of university.

'Well – good,' he said doubtfully.

'More than good,' his wife determinedly corrected from the other end. 'Brilliant. All he has to do now is get four A stars.' It was not quite what Guy had said, but it would do.

'That all?'

Victoria either ignored or failed to pick up the irony. 'He's revising hard, so he's bound to get the grades.'

James did not reply. Whenever he put his head round his son's bedroom door Guy seemed to be downloading music. 'I wonder,' he said, thinking aloud, 'whether we should try and incentivise him a bit.'

'Incentivise him! He's getting the best education money can buy.'

James, who happened to be buying it, sidestepped this issue in order to concentrate on the main point. 'Is there anything he really wants?'

'Well, Wild and Free, I suppose,' Victoria said reluctantly, after a pause. She resented doing so, but the alternative was to admit that she didn't know what her son wanted.

'What is Wild and Free?'

'It's a festival.' Victoria bit out the words. 'He wants to go to it. His friends are all going, apparently.'

'A festival, eh?' His interested tone both surprised and annoyed her.

'Young people. Music. Hardly your kind of thing,' she returned crushingly.

Or yours, James thought, stung. Victoria's idea of a music festival was corporate entertainment at Glyndebourne. What made her think she knew what his kind of thing was, anyway? He had been young once, hadn't he? Interested in music? He'd actually been in a band, the Mascara Snakes. Amazing how easily the name came back. He hadn't thought about them for years. 'When is it?' he asked. 'This festival?'

'No idea,' Victoria said dismissively. 'He's not going, anyway.'

'Why not?'

He was arriving at his meeting, James saw. As the grey neoclassical bulk of the Old Lady of Threadneedle Street slid across the tinted windows, he felt his heart sink. 'We'll talk about this later,' he told Victoria.

No we won't, she thought, as the phone buzzed emptily in her ear. Her plans for her menfolk most certainly did not include festivals. What was James thinking of, claiming Wild & Free would 'incentivise' Guy? He'd been given everything money could buy; what more incentive to succeed did he need?

James's failure to fall into line and agree with her confirmed Victoria's growing fears, however. Just as well then that recently, and without consulting her husband, she had let it be known that an approach from party central would not be unwelcome. Her husband, she had explained, was too shy to ask himself. Victoria was an expert in the apparently offguard comment in

47

the right ear, the giggling sign-off to a conversation that carried the real message.

She was pretty sure that this message had got through. At the last fundraising dinner they had gone to she had sat next to a perfectly charming young man who had introduced himself as a 'party central pointyhead'. His head had not looked especially pointy to Victoria; it had looked round and bald. But he had listened, over the rubber chicken, to her deliberately artless account of how her husband was desperate to serve the cause, but was too modest to say so. Over the jam roly-poly and custard the pointyhead had told her, with an understanding press of her hand, that he would drop the right words in the right ears. Then there would be a phone call, a meeting with James at a London club, a by-election in a safe seat.

Of course, it was a gamble. James might object. But Victoria was certain she could talk him round, persuade him that this was the best way he could 'make a difference'.

And then she would step into the role that was made for her, that of a political wife. A lioness of the Westminster landscape, looking out for her husband! Making friends and influencing people! One of the fashionable new breed of political wives. Her diamonds would be eco-friendly and she would wear the sort of sustainably sourced couture obtainable only from tiny Chiswick boutiques run by the wives of film stars. They might even lend them to her for nothing. That, Victoria thought, with grim satisfaction, was about as wild and free as she was prepared to go.

CHAPTER 5

April

'Come on, mate,' Spencer wheedled on the other end of the line. 'You were brilliant in the band.'

Spencer might have changed tack lately, from insult to blandishment, but Mark still had no intention of giving in. The idea of reforming the Mascara Snakes was pathetic. And impossible, for any number of reasons. They had not played a gig for nigh on three decades. They had not seen each other for almost as long. Of all their various songs, Mark could not recall a note. Or how to play one even if he did; he had not picked up his guitar in years.

'It's a rubbish idea,' he told Spencer. 'I can't think why you want to do it.' He wanted to tell Spencer to stop calling him about it, especially at work, but had yet to summon the requisite rudeness.

'OK, I'll tell you. There's a festival. Wild and Free. It has a battle of the bands, which anyone can enter.'

Mark's initial urge to guffaw was replaced by incredulous horror. 'You're saying we should enter? The *Mascara Snakes*?'

'You got it, mate. The prize is a record deal.'

Mrs Garland had appeared at his office door. She was

pointing at her watch, reminding him he was due in the infants' classroom to observe Show and Tell. He decided to finish with Spencer fast.

He cleared his throat and summoned some headmasterly firmness. 'Look, Spence. I'm happy to meet for a drink in a bar or whatever for your birthday. But the other thing, it's a no, I'm afraid.' He was choosing his words carefully. Mrs Garland was still in the doorway.

'But *mate* . . .' Spencer objected.

'I'm sorry,' Mark said with brisk finality. 'But I've got to go.'

Sitting before her infants' class, nervously tucking her hair behind her ear, Ginnie Blossom was experiencing a powerful rush of embarrassment. She reminded herself that Mr Birch the headmaster was observing her Show and Tell session strictly for professional reasons and not because he had the remotest interest in her personally.

Ginnie forced herself to concentrate on her work. She clasped her plump white hands together and bent forward towards the semicircle of children sitting cross-legged on the floor in front of her.

'It's your turn now for Show and Tell, Alfie,' she smiled encouragingly at the bespectacled ginger boy who was smaller and thinner than all the others. 'Would you like to show us what you've brought?'

She hoped desperately that what Alfie Newwoman had brought would knock the socks off the rest of the class, but she knew the chances of that were as thin as Alfie himself.

With obvious reluctance Alfie got up. Ginnie, compassionate and alert, noticed that his skinny white legs were shaking as they unfolded and carried him to the side of the classroom. From here he carried a recyclable jute bag to the front, his knuckles white as he gripped the handles.

'Wonderful!' she said encouragingly. 'And what do you have in there, Alfie?'

He shot her an anguished look. His swallow was almost audible, a nervous clack from his throat. He inserted his skinny arm into the bag and pulled out a small book. It was A4 size and what Ginnie could see of the cover looked like a badly drawn child with something on its head.

'Have you written a story, Alfie?' she asked, surprised. She would not have credited him with such a bold move. Alfie's interests, such as they were, remained determinedly hidden within his shell, along with Alfie himself. But was this evidence that he was finally coming out of it?

She was gratified and interested enough to forget the fact – temporarily – that Mark was watching from the back. Sensing the drama, the headmaster bent forward.

As Alfie looked up, the overhead strip lights flashed in his bottle-bottom glasses. He said something that Ginnie could not hear. 'What was that?' she asked brightly. 'Your story, is it?'

A girl sitting in the front row raised her hand, smirking. Ginnie turned to her with trepidation. 'Yes, Alice?'

'He says it's not his story, it's his mum's.'

'His *mum's*?' repeated Ginnie, trying to disguise the instinctive horror she felt. If this was something to do with Lorna Newwoman it could not be good. The class had only just got over Alfie's ridiculous new surname. What fresh hell was this?

Alfie cleared his throat, raised his ball-shaped head on his skinny neck and stared with wild terror at the back wall of the classroom, which he now addressed. 'My mum's written a children's book. She wanted me to read it out, to sort of test it . . .' Alfie's courage now drained away with his words. He stopped.

Mark, at the back, experienced a pang of guilty alarm. The conversation with Lorna Newwoman came back to him. He could not remember the exact words, but Lorna had been raging about Roald Dahl being elitist, patronising and socially exclusive. He had suggested that, if she felt like that, she write some socially inclusive children's stories herself. He had only intended to get her off the phone but it seemed Lorna had taken him at his word. With the ghastly outcome that her poor son, once again the victim of her whims, had to read the no-doubt-dreadful result out to the entire class.

Mark could almost see Ginnie's generous heart swelling within that magnificent bosom. He could certainly see the bosom and was trying not to stare at it. He could guess her thoughts exactly. She had performed miracles with Alfie after the Newwoman business; protecting him from the worst of the teasing by facing up to the issue squarely and inventing a game where everyone in the class changed their surnames to the wildest they could think of. By the end, Alfie was almost an object of envy. Now all that good work was in danger of being reversed.

He gave her a wry, resigned smile, unwittingly sending butterflies skittering through Ginnie's insides.

She dragged her eyes away and tried to concentrate on Alfie. But the words 'Great, we're all dying to hear it, Alfie,' died on her lips as she saw the dumb appeal behind the thick spectacles.

Hurriedly, Ginnie changed tack. 'Would you like me to read it, Alfie?' she offered. Heroically, in Mark's view. Lorna Newwoman's story was certain to be terrible but Ginnie would far rather embarrass herself than her pupil. She was an angel, although she looked very much a woman with her richly healthy beauty, her generous curves, her low, soft laugh and her warm green eyes. Her softly blushing pink cheeks reminded him of a rose. She was also breathtakingly kind. No wonder the children adored her. For what it was worth – nothing, obviously; she would never be interested in him – he adored her himself. As, again, his glance caught hers, Mark looked hurriedly down.

Ginnie, unable to interpret his gaze, felt a vague excitement nonetheless. 'Give the story to me,' she urged the little ginger boy, empowered by a sudden, inexplicably happy energy. 'I'll read it for you.'

A brief flicker of relief illuminated Alfie's wan features. He nodded, thrust the booklet hurriedly at Ginnie and scarpered, stumbling over feet as he went.

Ginnie looked at the document in her hands. It was about a centimetre thick and stapled together, obviously home-produced. It was curled at the edges and smudged; Alfie had obviously been twisting it with worry. And with good reason. The cover, presumably by Lorna and extremely badly drawn, was of a cartoon figure wearing a crown, sitting on what looked like a toilet. The title was *The King Who Couldn't Wee*.

As Ginnie expected, this provoked an explosion of mirth among the children. Alfie, at the back, went purple with distress. Mark, behind him on the desk, felt his insides cramp in mortification.

Ginnie looked up, cleared her throat and set off at a brisk pace designed to get it over as soon as possible. 'There was once a king who couldn't wee,' she began.

Mark, watching and listening, felt his admiration for Ginnie increase by the second. She was trying so hard on Alfie's behalf, throwing her every dramatic gift at the pathetic tale to give it all possible credibility and conviction. His disgust with Lorna Newwoman increased exponentially. Was her definition of social inclusiveness, then, nothing more than scatology? Did she really consider anything above lavatory-level elitist?

At the front of the class, Ginnie ploughed on '. . . and all his servants came into the loo and saw him sitting there, and he STILL couldn't wee! And they turned the taps on in the basin *really hard* to make a gushing sound, and he STILL couldn't wee!'

The children were laughing, but not with her, Ginnie sensed. They kept turning to snigger at Alfie. Pausing for breath, she frowned at them and darted a nervous look at the back of the room. Seeing Mark still there, listening, she churned with embarrassment. What must he be thinking? How stupid did she look? She held the pages up, attempting to hide her burning face. Thankfully she was reaching the end now. End, certainly, seemed an appropriate word.

'. . . and everyone outside the toilet door, from the Lord High Chamberlain to the Royal Wiper Of His Majesty's Bottom, all listened really really hard until they heard the magic sound. PLOP. Then another PLOP. Then three in quick succession. PLOP. PLOP. PLOP.' Through gritted teeth Ginnie took in a final breath to deliver the punchline. 'He couldn't WEE, but he sure could POO.'

Amid the children's braying, unsympathetic laughter, Ginnie tried to collect together what remained of her dignity. She dared not even look at the back of the room.

How unutterably mortifying to have to read such rubbish before the man she was madly in love with. Swamped with a sudden, overpowering misery, Ginnie sensed, rather than saw, Mark get up and abruptly leave the room.

At breaktime, Ginnie reached distractedly for a chocolate digestive from the tin on the staffroom table. 'Unbelievable,' she told Brenda Garland, who was chewing on a custard cream. Ginnie had just finished recounting the horrors of *The King Who Couldn't Wee.*

'The only good thing about it,' she concluded, 'is that it was so awful and went down so badly with the children that surely it'll stop Lorna's career as a writer in its tracks.'

'I wouldn't be so sure,' said Brenda darkly, adding, 'What that woman needs is a man. That'll stop this nonsense, you mark my words.'

Ginnie didn't answer. Brenda was incorrigibly nosy, especially about people's personal relationships. While she stopped short of actually asking Ginnie why she was single, and refrained from specifically pointing out that the headmaster was single, her eyes as they rolled from one to the other said it all. Ginnie, unable to bear it, now fled whenever a situation loomed with the three of them together.

She forced these thoughts aside to consider what Brenda had just said about Lorna Newwoman. What man might conceivably be suitable for her made the mind boggle. He would have to combine blind, if not foolish, courage with impenetrably thick skin and impeccable political correctness. Presumably he would also be an admirer of puerile amateur writing. Ginnie had been about to add 'warmly paternal feelings towards Alfie' to the list but as Lorna conspicuously lacked maternal ones, they were perhaps not necessary. But even without them it was a tall order.

She looked out of the staffroom window at the playground, where she spotted a solitary figure sitting on the lonely bench. Alfie Newwoman looked intensely ill at ease. No one had come up and offered to play with him, which was the bench's entire point. Instead it was just serving to exacerbate and advertise Alfie's unpopularity.

Ginnie took another chocolate biscuit, feeling sad on Alfie's behalf. Several weeks had passed since the name-change; it was becoming forgotten. But *The King Who Couldn't Wee* had taken things right back to square one. Possibly beyond. What an unutterable monster his mother was.

Kay Green now came in, switched on the kettle for her breaktime fruit tea and ignored as she always did the transfat-stuffed biscuits. 'You're kidding yourself,' she said to Brenda, who was making a decaff cappuccino from a packet. 'Decaff gets blasted by loads of chemicals and the air miles involved are horrendous.'

'But surely there are air miles involved whatever sort of coffee you drink,' Ginnie pointed out, annoyed at Kay's sanctimoniousness. 'You can't grow it in Chestlock.'

'And this is for the headmaster anyway,' Brenda said, as if that settled the question. Bestowing a meaningful smile on Ginnie, she sailed out with the mug. The other two women looked after her; Kay ironically, and Ginnie longingly. How she would love to deliver Mark's hot drink herself.

'Do you think he's hiding from us?' Kay asked when Brenda had gone.

'No, he's still sitting there,' Ginnie said, looking at Alfie.

'Not that ginger kid,' Kay said scornfully. Her love for the planet did not extend to those who lived on it. Humans, in Kay's view, were greedy, destructive vandals to a man. 'Mark. *Mr Birch*,' she prompted, staring mockingly at Ginnie through her recycled-plastic glasses, then grinning knowingly as, despite herself, the Head of Infants flushed a bright, embarrassed red. 'He never comes in here, does he?'

'Maybe he's busy,' Ginnie said, willing the blush to go away.

Kay looked sceptical. 'Have you any idea what's in that?' she demanded now, gesturing at the third biscuit Ginnie had removed from the tin.

'Chocolate?'

'Crap.' Kay clumped out of the room in her vegetarian shoes.

Ginnie, left behind, defiantly munched her biscuit and wondered if the new headmaster really did think of them all as terminally unsophisticated. It was not impossible, and arguably justified. And yet she felt the reasons for his distance were more sad than they were snobbish. Something awful had happened to him, she was certain. Her full, creamy bosom, so recently swelled with sympathy for Alfie Newwoman, now heaved again on Mark Birch's account. How she would like to comfort him.

At night, his dark and haunted eyes floated before her and her body burned with desire. Ginnie longed to enfold him, possess him, surrender to him. But there was no possibility he was interested in her.

Long after everyone else had gone home, Mark sat in his office, returning a list of phone calls in Brenda's writing and also trying, in advance of a looming governors' meeting, to think up some wheeze to balance the school finances. St Stephen's was in dire monetary straits. Grants were down, costs were up and trouble was obviously on the horizon.

He looked at the next name and number on his list, took a deep breath and dialled. A minute later, he was being blasted with the views of the school's next-door neighbour about parents parking in front of his house during drop-off and pick-up time.

'It's just got ridiculous,' Mr Kettle expostulated. 'I never had this much trouble under Mrs Gilkes.'

Mark doubted this. One of the few insights the former head had passed on was that Kettle complained endlessly about parking.

'I have sent out several letters asking parents to park in the roads around the school, not right outside it,' Mark pointed out.

'Well, they haven't worked, have they?' Kettle snapped.

It was on the tip of Mark's tongue to say that they had in one case. Lorna Newwoman's scrupulousness about parking hundreds of yards from the school was something she reminded everyone else about every morning as she delivered Alfie. She did this mostly, Mark suspected, so she could tut and shake her head at the parents who dropped off outside the gate.

The real problem was not so much Kettle's grievance, which was genuine enough, but that he was such a hard man to sympathise with. He seemed the sort of person who enjoyed having something to complain about, which might be why he had bought the bungalow next to the school in the first place. The possibility that parents might use the road had been obvious, surely.

'Can't the council do anything about it?' Kettle bristled now.

Mark rubbed his eyes. He felt so tired these days. The fact that the Easter holidays were coming up was no comfort. He had arranged nothing. He lacked the energy, had no idea where to go, and besides, Claire had always handled holidays. He wondered where Ginnie Blossom was going to spend Easter. With her boyfriend, probably. Miserably he imagined them, hand in hand, wandering round some romantic, sunny European capital.

'Can't they put some signs up? Send a lollipop lady or something?' broke in the querulous voice at the other end. Kettle was really hitting his stride now. Or his strut, Mark corrected himself, having previously observed this crossing the playground. He roused himself to answer.

'I have,' he said wearily, 'rung the council and spoken to the Highways Department. They say that we can't have a lollipop lady – or safe crossing operative as they are known these days.'

'Political correctness gone mad,' interjected Mr Kettle, predictably.

'And a flashing sign reminding people to slow down would cost twenty-five thousand pounds.'

'Twenty-five thousand!' Kettle exploded.

'Apparently so, Mr Kettle. And being a small state-funded primary school, we don't have that kind of money, as I'm sure you can appreciate.'

'Well, you must have *some*.'

Mark fought a powerful wave of impatience. Did Kettle really believe the school was sitting on millions it could easily spend on traffic calming? He said nothing, however.

Kettle made a harrumphing noise. 'Sounds as if I might have to make a few phone calls myself. I still have friends in high places, you know.'

Mark tried to sound suitably awed as he ended the call. As he put the phone down he thought, not for the first time, how peculiarly appropriate the man's name was. Kettle was like a kettle, sitting there in his bungalow, boiling with rage.

He tried to return to the school accounts. But his mind was jumping about, rattled by Kettle and dogged, above all, by an increasing sense of hopelessness. He had not gone into teaching for this.

The phone rang. He looked at it apprehensively before picking it up and discovering that it wasn't Kettle on the end of it, but Spencer.

'Just calling to see if you'd changed your mind, mate,' he said breezily. 'About the Snakes and Wild and Free and all that.'

Mark opened his mouth to impress on Spencer once and for all that he hadn't and he never would. And more than that, to leave him alone. This was the second call today. It was practically harassment.

'Well, wait until you hear this before you say anything,' Spencer warned. 'Guess who else is up for it?'

'Jimmy?' Despite himself, Mark felt a sudden excitement. Of all the band, drummer Jimmy had been the one he was closest to and the one he most regretted losing touch with.

'Rob!' Spencer exclaimed triumphantly.

'Rob?' A much less attractive proposition. Rob, the bassist and fourth member, had been the band's man of few words. If Spencer had been the band's front man, Rob had definitely been its back. 'Why does Rob want to do it?'

'He's an accountant. I think he wants a bit of excitement.'

Rob had always wanted excitement, Mark thought. In the sense of lacking it. It was no surprise to hear he was an accountant.

'He's married to a chain of electrical shops,' Spencer went on. 'They've got some kids and Rob'll inherit the business when the old man's fuses go.'

Mark felt a sudden wave of sadness. He wouldn't have minded some kids himself, although Claire had never been keen. He had hoped some day to change her mind. But it was probably just as well, now, that he hadn't. A Fathers For Justice-type struggle for access, along with everything else, would have probably tipped him over the edge.

Nonetheless, it rankled. How had boring Rob managed a wife and children, while he himself had managed precisely nothing? He had always imagined himself as a family man, happy and loved, but he was as alone as when he had started university. Nothing had turned out as he had expected.

He wondered meanly if Rob's kids had a monobrow like their father. 'It's still a no,' he told Spencer.

CHAPTER 6

It was Olly's birthday and Isabel had arranged dinner out. The venue, towards which she was now walking, was the Blue Moon, their favourite Thai restaurant on the main road. It was determinedly old-school with its carved red and gold screens, statues, lanterns and cheesy indoor water feature at the entrance. There was jangly gamelan music on a loop and the chicken satay came garnished with turnips carved into roses, served by bowing waiters in embroidered silk jackets.

Isabel took the path along the river. She was thinking about the meeting she had just had with Gillian Green, professor and head of the Branston English Faculty. Gillian had briefed her on the new intake, students who now faced the necessity of getting the required A-level grades. While he had been given an offer, Guy Dorchester-Williams, the handsome, self-deprecating youth Isabel had met outside the gate, sounded unlikely to perform this feat. 'Didn't exactly set the world on fire,' was Gillian's brisk assessment. 'Also, he'd been tutored.'

'How did you know?' Isabel asked, aware that Gillian was absolutely right in her suspicions. And while she was glad that Gillian was giving Guy a chance, Isabel wondered why her boss, who was notoriously hard to please and very picky, had bothered considering Guy at all. Had it been his striking good looks? Gillian made an unlikely cougar, but you never knew.

'Because he told me straightaway.' The gimlet eyes behind the glasses gleamed briefly with amusement. 'Funnily enough, it saved him. Had he not admitted it, I'd have rejected him out of hand. But as it is he's got a stay of execution until the A-level results.'

Isabel smiled to herself as she walked along. It was a beautiful evening, and still light. The sun was lowering behind the lacy college buildings and there were punts out on the river. It was the Easter holidays, the official start of the season.

A father evidently new to the art of punting was attempting to pilot his family along. Rather faster than was ideal, he approached the bridge by the Boat pub, the realisation clearly dawning that he would never make it under the stone arch if standing upright. With an expression of horror he crouched down in the small craft, bending double and making the punt rock wildly. His family screamed.

An altogether smoother operation was the professional punter transporting upriver a cargo of tourists in matching yellow baseball caps.

'If you look ahead,' the chauffeur punter was telling them, 'you'll see New Bridge. Despite its name, it's the oldest bridge in town. You see those stone balls on top? In the Eighties a group of students made polystyrene balls to the exact same size and shoved them off on to a passing punt. Everyone bailed out, thinking they were about to be mashed by a ton of stone . . .'

Isabel smiled again, recognising an old story. She had no idea if it was true, but it had been told for so many years now it had acquired its own authority.

The yellow baseball caps had gone round the bend now and another chauffeur punter was gliding past. '. . . you see that low door in the wall by the river? It's where they flung the bodies . . .'

Actually, as Isabel knew, it was the door to that particular college's loos.

A third chauffeur punter had appeared. The river really was busy tonight.

'. . . home of a notorious society of cash-flashing, window-smashing toffs from hell . . .' he was announcing cheerfully to his captive audience.

Isabel took a deep breath. The punt was gliding past the river front of St Alwine's, and the passengers were being told about the ancient college's most celebrated association.

'. . . famous for parties with strippers and dwarves and initiation rites where people drank washing-up liquid and tore up money in front of the homeless . . .'

There was a chorus of shocked gasps from his captive audience.

'Is that really true?'

'I thought all that kinda thing was made up by the noospapers!'

The punter hastened to explain to the contrary.

'. . . banned a few years ago and the leading members all sent down.'

'Sent down where?' inquired one of the tourists, staring into the river as if that was what was meant.

'Expelled, in other words,' the chauffeur punter explained. 'The club's president actually went to prison.'

'You don't say!'

'Gee, that's serious.'

'There's a book about it all,' the punter told them. 'Called *Smashed Windows*. Written by an ex-student. It's won lots of awards.'

Isabel groaned and hurried on.

The phone in her bag now rang. It was still on silent as she had been in the library for part of the afternoon, but she could feel its insistent tremble through the leather. She fished it out; as ever it had slipped to some inaccessible corner necessitating the breaking and bending of nails. She hoped it wasn't Olly, delayed. His work was rather dominating things at the moment. The editor, his boss, was away and Olly was covering. They had had to make the birthday dinner early as it was so he could go in for seven the following morning.

It was not Olly, however, but the familiar, breezy tones of Isabel's close friend Diana. As usual, she got straight to the point. 'You don't fancy going to a festival, do you? One called Wild and Free? It's kind of literary and boho, but with bands. Very trendy.'

'I hadn't been thinking of it,' Isabel said. 'We've got a lot to do in the house still.'

Diana sighed. 'Shame. Rosie wants to go to it. And I feel so guilty saying no because I feel I owe her a treat. She's been so wonderful about everything for so long. The divorce, us moving here, me marrying Richard. She's been such a good girl.'

This was indisputably the case. Rosie was as angelic as her small sister Violet was naughty. This was the first recorded instance of her ever giving her mother a moment's trouble.

'And you don't want her to go to . . . Wild and Free?'

'No, and she's so cross with me,' Diana groaned. 'Really desperate to go. I feel so mean saying no. She's been pestering me to ask you, but I didn't think you'd want to. I can't see you in a tent somehow.'

Isabel shuddered as childhood summers – in name only – in Scotland flashed back to mind. Tents, clinging mist and clustering midges. 'Can't you go with her?'

Diana sounded incredulous. 'Are you joking? I've got Violet to look after and before you suggest it, taking her is just out of the question. You know what she's like.'

Isabel did not disagree. Diana's five-year-old could cause mayhem in a room on her own. The thought of her in a crowd was terrifying.

'Can't Rosie go with Shanna-Mae? She's pretty sensible,' Isabel pointed out. More sensible than most adults, in fact.

'Yes, but she's still only seventeen. Of course Shanna's going anyway. She's got a beauty bus.'

'A what?'

'Kind of a pop-up spa in a VW van. She's going to give treatments.'

'Oh I see,' said Isabel, as a penny dropped somewhere in her mind. 'That's what she wanted it for.'

'What who wanted what for? What are you talking about?' Diana asked agitatedly.

'Shanna asked me for a quote about beauty. She said she wanted it for some publicity, to run under her logo.'

'And what did you suggest? Something lovely from *Romeo and Juliet*?'

'No, something robust. Shanna wanted to make the point that there was nothing smart about looking a mess.'

'So what did you come up with?' Diana was intrigued.

'*Henry V*. "Self-love, my liege, is not so vile a sin as self-neglecting". That'll be brilliant on her bus,' Isabel said admiringly. 'Perfect for a literary-boho festival. Typical Shanna stroke of genius. She's amazing, that girl.'

'Yes, except I'm under pressure from her as well,' Diana groaned.

That was an uncomfortable place to be, Isabel thought. Shanna, for all her youth, was a woman of great force.

'She wants Rosie to help her run this Beauty Bus,' Diana continued. 'But I don't want Rosie to go with neither of them knowing anyone there to keep an eye on them. What if something goes wrong?'

'I'm sure it won't,' Isabel said firmly. 'Honestly, Di, I'd love to help but I'm completely allergic to camping and I'd earmarked the time to get Paradise Street finished. Finally get rid of those cardboard boxes everywhere. Can't you just let her go with Shanna-Mae?'

Diana sighed again. 'Can tell you're not a mother, Iz. You'll feel different when you are. Oh well,' she said, assuming her former bright tone. 'Enough about me and all my problems. How about you?'

'Everything's fine, thanks. It's Olly's birthday. I'm just going to meet him at the Blue Moon.'

'Oh, well, I won't keep you. Have fun, give him my love. Oh, and ask him if he wants to go to Wild and Free; it's quite literary, you know.'

Olly was late to the Blue Moon. And when he finally arrived he said he had something to tell her.

Isabel looked down fixedly at the bamboo-effect cutlery. She wished to hide her shining eyes. And the fact that for all she was a lifelong feminist, one of the English Faculty's rising stars and tipped to be a future professor, she was actually desperately hoping to be proposed to.

But why not? She and Olly had been together four years now. She loved him, both for his tall, broad, understated brand of handsomeness and for his kind heart and puppyish enthusiasm. Which was not to damn with faint praise; Olly was as brave, devoted and resourceful as any mediaeval knight and it was no overstatement to say that he had saved her during the ghastly St Alwine's episode. Their relationship had had a rocky start, certainly. But now it was characterised by absolute and obvious mutual devotion.

They also had a house together. Number 2 Paradise Street had been the last unrenovated dwelling in a gentrified terrace, which was why Isabel and Olly had been able to afford it. It had been damp and depressing with manky carpets and a colour scheme of cracked pumpkin-coloured paint.

Now, doors had been dipped, Victorian fireplaces exposed and a bathroom the colour of Germolene replaced with one of Homebase white. The rotting carpets had been removed to expose floorboards that Isabel had planed and polished for months. The rooms had resounded to grunts of effort and Radio 4. Even now the sight of certain knots in the wood brought back, with startling clarity, particular incidents in *The Archers*. There was still plenty to do, even so.

'Go on,' Isabel said, her voice high with the effort of holding her breath tightly within her.

Olly breathed in, as if to announce something of great importance. 'I've been invited to a festival! To talk about my novel!'

All Isabel's anticipation drained away. She had been expecting too much and felt stunned with disappointment.

A festival! She remembered the conversation with Diana. People seemed to be thinking about nothing else at the moment.

She remembered, too, Olly this morning, in a dark blue towelling bathrobe, hair wet from the shower and shining like an otter's. She had been going out as the post had come. He had waved goodbye absently as he examined an invitation card and some folded A4 sheets.

'Which festival?' Isabel asked, trying to dredge up the names of a few. 'Latitude? Port Eliot?' And what was that one Diana had mentioned?

'Wild and Free,' Olly's voice was squeaky and cracking as it did when he was genuinely thrilled.

That was it! Isabel's surprise flashed in her eyes and Olly saw it and mistook it for excitement. 'It's very hip' he assured her. 'It's quite an honour to be asked. There'll be loads of famous people there.'

'You'll enjoy that then,' Isabel said, unable to keep the stiffness out of her voice. On the other hand, it had at least the virtue of solving Diana's problem. Olly could keep an eye on Shanna and Rosie and get his guybrows done into the bargain.

'*I'll* enjoy it?' Olly's grey-blue eyes rounded with surprise. 'You mean . . . on my own?'

'You want *me* to come?' Isabel felt her insides shrinking. 'But why? You'll be networking and staying up all night. With all these famous people. I'd only cramp your style. Besides,' she added, 'I hate camping.'

His gaze remained on her, evidently hurt. 'Well, of course I want you to come.' He thumped the table, his bottom lip protruding in mock-petulance. 'I won't go without you, in fact. And it's in July, during the summer vac.'

Olly's exclamation was so loud that the neighbouring tables turned eagerly round. Both were occupied by couples who had hardly exchanged a word since coming in. Isabel flipped her auburn mane defiantly over both shoulders and lowered her voice, reluctant for this dramatic moment to be entertainment for someone else.

Hurriedly, she reminded him she always had work to do, even in the holidays. Some academic paper, some chapter of the thesis. He looked unconvinced. 'But you're my muse. You have to be there.'

Muse! Isabel wanted to scream. Oh God, why did Olly persist in believing her when she said it didn't bother her any more. It did. For all her best, most concerted efforts, it really did.

It really hurt that Olly would be telling an entire literary festival about what she had suffered at the hands of Amber Piggott and Jasper de Borchy and the drugs and the near-death and the discovery that Jasper was just using her.* The memory sent waves of misery and bitterness through her. That Olly clearly did not realise quite how powerfully all this still affected her made her feel more bitter and miserable still.

She pulled herself together and looked him in the eye. 'It's just a bit . . . close to the bone, I suppose.'

She saw irritation flare briefly in his eyes. Clearly he felt he had been through this many times before, as indeed he had.

'It's fiction, though,' Olly argued. 'You have to remember that.'

'Fiction. Absolutely.' She was trying valiantly not to sound sarcastic. But not succeeding, to judge from Olly's wide-with-concern grey-blue eyes.

He was falling over himself to reassure her. 'Elspeth's not *you*. She just, well, *experiences* some of the same things.'

To say the least, Isabel thought darkly. Elspeth, the student in the novel, was an innocent abroad. Easy prey for the calculating Topaz Bacon, a wealthy socialite, and Jupiter Garstly-Thugge, handsome president of a notoriously toffee-nosed student society. Disaster loomed until an intrepid local newspaper reporter called Billy exposed the criminal nature of both the society and its president, just in time to save the life of Topaz, who had taken an overdose, and rescue Elspeth, who Billy had long been in love with. Billy was, of course, a thinly veiled Olly.

Olly, his despair obvious in his face, now gave up on this line

* See *Gifted & Talented*

of persuasion. He reached over the table and took her hand. 'OK. Look, I don't have to go. If you want me to, I'll tell Wild and Free that I can't come.'

His pleading expression twisted her heart and she felt reassured. He was saying to her that she came first and was the most important thing in his life. Yes, he had toiled over his novel and been thrilled by its unexpected success. He would love to go to this literary festival. But he was prepared to throw that away, make the sacrifice. At the drop of a hat. If she wanted him to.

From the other side of the curry bubbling above its candle heater, Olly's brave resignation continued. 'Honestly, Isabel. Just say the word. I'll do anything for you, you know that.'

'That's really sweet of you,' Isabel had to admit.

This seemed to hearten him. 'I mean, I *had* actually thought you'd got over the whole business ages ago, and that it didn't matter. Didn't realise you were still festering about it.'

'Festering!' Isabel exclaimed. 'Someone nearly died, Olly.'

The starers at the next table whipped round in delight.

'Sure, sure.' Olly reached for his glass of lager and took a hurried swig. 'But they didn't, in the end. And the bad were punished and the good lived happily ever after. Didn't they?' His smile was charged with meaning.

She had to agree.

'And so that's that, I would have thought. But if you're still obsessing, so be it. I understand.' Olly took a deep breath before adding, in low tones, 'I *suppose*.'

Isabel frowned down at her red curry, angry and uncertain in equal measure. Perhaps she was being ridiculous. It *was* years ago. Was she merely being self-indulgent, and at Olly's expense? She bit her lip. 'Well, I had got over it . . .' she began, trying to convince herself.

He seized on this immediately. 'Well, I must say, I did think so. But if not, if you're still dwelling on it, fine. On the other hand, if you could see your way to letting this happen, it'd be a hell of a birthday present.' He cleared his throat.

Indignation now joined Isabel's hurt and annoyance. She had bought him a beautiful grey Scottish cashmere jumper which matched his eyes and which she had thought a hell of a birthday present too.

'Oh *Olly*!' she now burst out, exasperated. Again their neighbours turned round to enjoy the show. Isabel flicked them a hostile glance before continuing, in a lower voice.

'I'm not dwelling on it. I am over it. And . . .' she took a deep breath, aware that there was no going back on what came next. 'I don't mind if you go to this festival.'

'You *don't*?' Olly's face was a picture. Isabel felt a cautious gratification. She remembered she would be making Diana happy too, as well as Rosie and Shanna-Mae.

'Champagne!' Olly commanded a passing waiter, before Isabel could change her mind. Then, as Isabel looked at him, her face full of a sudden fear he would share Wild & Free and, worse, *Smashed Windows* with the whole restaurant, he turned to the adjoining tables and added, smiling sweetly, 'It's my birthday and we're celebrating.'

The waiter returned with the bottle and popped the cork with ostentatious loudness. As he poured the wine into glasses still warm from the dishwasher his colleague arrived with a chocolate slab cake in which a couple of sparklers had been thrust. The restaurant erupted into 'Happy Birthday To You'. In the spotlight of these benign ceremonials, Isabel tried to seem to be enjoying herself.

Olly's face, as he sipped the champagne, was wreathed in smiles. He was bubbling with excitement about the festival. He

had fished out his smartphone and had called up the Wild &
Free website which was, Isabel saw, a very sophisticated, slick
affair. The home page was dominated by an image of the Wylde
Estate, where the festival was being held. It was an enchanted
valley of rolling parkland with statues and formal gardens. The
house was a golden spread of mullioned Tudor stone.

'We'll be staying in the house,' Olly told Isabel, who had
been looking doubtfully at the village of tents on the website's
other pages. Even fluttering with pennants and bunting and
bathed in fuzzy golden evening light they looked unappealing.

Isabel glanced at him in surprise. 'How come?'

By way of reply, he showed her an e-mail from the festival
organiser, someone rejoicing in the name of Jezebel Pert-Minks.

'While most of our artists camp in the grounds,' Jezebel had
explained, 'a lucky handful get to stay amid the Tudor splendours
of Wylde Hall.' Was 'lucky', Isabel suddenly wondered, a
synonym for 'unpaid'?

If it was, it wouldn't stop Olly. 'We're going to have such a
great time. H.D. Grantchester's going to be there.'

That really was something, Isabel knew. H.D. Grantchester
was Olly's literary heroine. A much-feted author of historical
blockbusters, she had pulled off the rare trick of combining the
highbrow with the commercial. Olly, now pondering his next
writing project, longed to do the same. He was desperate to
meet the great woman and discover what her secret was.

Isabel had by now taken the phone and was scrolling down
Jezebel Pert-Minks' messages. There seemed to be a great many
of them, all dated that day. Whatever work Olly had managed
at the office must have been done in the odd five minutes not
spent corresponding with her.

'We like to mix things up at Wild & Free,' Jezebel told Olly
in one of them. 'Each of our authors features in two talks. One

where he or she is interviewed by a fellow author at the festival and another where he or she returns the favour and interviews the fellow author. In the interests of fairness, selection of authors is made by literary lottery . . .'

Olly was leaning over to see what she was reading, his shirt hovering dangerously near the bubbling dish of green curry. 'Sounds great, that, doesn't it?' he enthused. 'Sort of the FA Cup draw of writers.' His burning hope was that H.D. Grantchester would be the name pulled out of the literary lottery to interview him, and vice versa.

'Our lit-lot can have surprising and fun results,' the Pert-Minks e-missive went on. 'Imagine Richard Dawkins being interviewed by Harry Styles! Edmund de Waal interviewing E.L. James, and the Hairy Bikers getting the third degree from Mary Beard!' Jezebel stopped short, Isabel noticed, of claiming that any of this had actually happened.

Her most recent communication was an e-invitation to something called the 'Symposium', a party to be held in Wylde Hall on the Saturday night of the festival. As all those taking part were invited Isabel took this as evidence that Olly had agreed to appear at the festival even before he had asked her. The realisation was depressing, but not entirely a surprise.

She could not beat them, so she may as well join them. Accompanying Olly to his talk about *Smashed Windows* was, anyway, a way to help herself; to stop feeling insecure and show that the past really was in the past.

She dug back into her now-cold plateful. 'There's a catch.' She explained about Rosie and Shanna.

Olly looked delighted. 'But that's fantastic. Of course we'll keep an eye on her. Or vice versa. We could do with a grown-up to look after us.'

When they got home, Olly ushered her into the kitchen and

gestured at a small leather-covered box on the table. She caught her breath.

'Aren't you going to open it?' He was smiling and nodding. 'Go on.'

She reached for it with a shaking hand. Inside was a winking diamond, small but perfect.

Olly's voice: 'It isn't antique or my grandmother's or anything like that. It's a new one. But that means you're the first to have it. If you want it.' A scrape as the chair was pushed back. He loomed before her, then dipped to one knee.

The pulse of her heart swelled in Isabel's ears. But something was wrong. Olly's face had contorted in a wince.

'I'm kneeling on a piece of dried pasta.'

Through her snort of laughter, she heard him speak. 'Isabel, my darling. Will you be my wife?'

She was still rocking with laughter, but wanted to cry at the same time. 'You'd do anything to get me to go to this festival!'

He looked dismayed. 'It wasn't just that . . .'

'It's a yes,' she cut in. 'Yes, yes, yes.'

As he whooped and pulled her up from her chair, then whirled her round as best he could in the cramped space, she thought that now, at last, the awful past really was dead and buried.

CHAPTER 7

May

James Dorchester-Williams entered his City office building after yet another meeting at Number 11. He glanced at the contemporary sculpture dangling from the central atrium. A gigantic silver screw-shape, it was a much larger relative of the helicoid that sat at the foot of their Notting Hill stairs and was also by Buzzie Omelet. She had, James reflected, lost no time in converting the work she had done on his private house to an even more lucrative commission from his bank. Buzzie as she was, there were no flies on her.

There was something terribly appropriate about the shape, too. A screw was something you twisted, something that screwed things. From the time it had been installed it had seemed to James like a metaphor for what he did for a living. For money in general, perhaps.

Stepping out of the lift a few minutes later, he passed his secretary's desk. An idea suddenly occurred to him, a chance for a spot of research. Had Tilly, he asked, heard of Wild & Free?

Tilly lit up immediately. She tossed her glossy hair back over one shoulder, gave him a gap-toothed beam and unleashed her trademark plummy interrogative. 'Yahbsolootleh. It's, like, so cool? Loads of my friends go? You get really cool bands?'

'Thanks, Tilly. I'd love a coffee when you have a sec.'

'Sure,' said Tilly, tossing her hair back over the other shoulder.

James went into his large penthouse office, whose walls were entirely glass. The illusion was that you could just step out, into the light and air. James stood as near to the edge as he dared, his hands clenched in his pockets, and stared down at the carpet of tiny buildings. He noticed, as he always did, how the stone-white and gold in the City gave way to brick-red and concrete-brown in the areas beyond.

Seen from here, the Thames lay like a rumpled grey scarf dropped in the middle of a carpet of toy buildings. A toy Tower Bridge. A tiny St Paul's. Cranes swung. Red buses crawled. That none of the noise so obviously down there could be heard up here added to the sense of disorientation. The office was silent, apart from the faint hum of air conditioning. It would be nice, James thought, to be nearer the ground. See some grass, even. He couldn't see any grass from here. Not a blade. The only blade he could see was the Shard, sticking up like a giant glass knife.

It made him feel restless – as he so often did these days. The recurrent image of a field with tents kept coming to him at unexpected moments. Just now, in the middle of the meeting with the Chancellor, he had found his thoughts slipping to music festivals. His inattentiveness had made the rest of the meeting tricky; he seemed to have missed some central point. The Chancellor had kept grinning at him and said, 'Hear you want to join the ranks, old chap.' Some minor financial agreement, James guessed.

Guy going to Wild & Free was a good idea, whatever Victoria said. Compared to what James could recall of his own adolescence, Guy's life seemed very proscribed and regimented. A festival would do him good. It would do me good too, James was starting to think, when a crash and rattle interrupted his thoughts. Tilly was arriving with the coffee.

James turned as she came in, struggling to manage the tray in her high heels. Whatever her other limitations, Tilly certainly didn't share his vertigo. The white china shook convulsively as she carefully placed it on his vast glass desk. Laboriously she poured a coffee, then, frowning with concentration, tottered over with it.

'Thanks, Tilly.'

'No worries, Mr D-W.'

'By the way, Tilly. This festival we were talking about . . .'

'Wild and Free?'

'That's the one. Is it . . . well . . . what's the demographic?'

Tilly looked puzzled, then her face cleared and she smiled. 'Oh, it's very democratic. Like, lots of people go?'

James passed a hand over his mouth. '*Demographic*. Is it, well, family-friendly? Do you get—'

Tilly burst in. 'Oh right, I get it. You're asking whether you get old people there, people your age, am I right?'

James blinked. 'Er . . . well, yes, I suppose so.' He was all of forty-eight. Tilly was twenty-two. Did he think people of forty-eight were unbelievably ancient when he was her age? It was hard to remember. He was too ancient.

'Like, *loads* of old people go,' Tilly was assuring him enthusiastically. 'Like, parents and stuff? The Rolling Stones played Glastonbury a couple of years ago? And Mick Jagger's a great-grandad?'

'Er, thanks, Tilly.' She was trying to be helpful, he knew.

And while he didn't equate himself with Mick Jagger, he had, in the days when he'd drummed in the Mascara Snakes, fantasised about being Charlie Watts. The Mascara Snakes. The name – and the memory – was strangely cheering.

Tilly had had another thought. 'And Henrik and Maggie Oopvard went to Latitude with Immy last year.'

Oopvard was a colleague, a heavy-going Dutchman. James struggled to imagine the ponderous Henrik roughing it under canvas, let alone his ghastly social-climbing wife. But as it turned out, he hadn't. 'He and Maggie stayed in, like, a Winnebago?' Tilly went on. 'But Immy camped with her friends and apparently some awful people peed on her tent?'

James stared out of the window, fighting the urge to smile. Immy Oopvard was an objectionable brat. He would have peed on her tent himself. It made him warm even more to Wild & Free. It was centuries since he'd seen anyone play live. He'd like to catch up with what was going on musicwise, at least a bit. Guy was continually amazed at the bands he didn't know and laughed when James expressed his genuinely held view that good pop music had had its final flowering in the Eighties.

Wild & Free. A good name. Amusing and self-aware. God, it would be fun to go to a festival. Perhaps he would take Guy himself – why not? He deserved a holiday. He lifted up the phone and asked Tilly to find out the dates. The call came back after a preditably protracted period.

'The last weekend in July, Mr D-W.'

'Thanks, Tilly. Book a couple of tickets, would you?'

'Abslootly, Mr D-W,' Tilly said, sounding surprised. 'For the VIP area?'

'What's that?' asked James.

'Oh, you know, where the slebs go, and the BBC and the rich old people. It's more comfortable,' Tilly said with engaging lack of tact. 'There's glamping and yurts and gypsy caravans and whatnot. Hot showers, widescreen tellies, Japanese toilets.'

James had no idea what a Japanese toilet was, but nor did he care. 'It sounds like Marie Antoinette does Glastonbury,' he said.

'I'm not sure she's been.' Tilly sounded doubtful.

James smothered a chortle. 'Just a normal camping place with a tent would be fine.' Guy, he knew, would hate to be in a wealthy ghetto with dilettantes. He would want to be in a tent near his friends. As did James. He would like, he felt, to meet Guy's friends and also to prove to both himself and his son that he could still cut it under canvas.

Victoria would object, of course. Violently, without doubt. He would, James decided, choose his own moment to tell her.

Meanwhile, in the home James was working to maintain, his wife was reading the paper at leisure in the sitting room. Victoria could not concentrate, not even on her favourite interiors section. As she tried to follow a celebrity's column describing his new Japanese toilet, at the back of Victoria's mind was the worry that Buzzie Omelet had missed a trick by not installing one in Lonsdale Road.

The front of her mind was on her menfolk. Guy, at least, was on the right track. He'd got the offer from Branston, even if he doubted he could get the required grades and was still banging on about this wretched music festival. Well, there was no way he was going to that. He needed no distractions in these final vital weeks before the exams.

Victoria's glance kept straying to the baby grand piano in the corner, its black-lacquered surface covered in silver-framed photographs. In one of them, James was frowning manfully into the distance at the helm of a yacht, in another, flying through the sea on waterskis, his teeth as white as the spray, his wet, tanned biceps gleaming in the sunshine, tensed against the forces of wind and waves. Victoria happily imagined the pictures to come, of James with the Prime Minister, or *as* the Prime Minister, if all went according to plan. With the US President. With Colin Firth, even, if he ended up an arts minister and went to the BAFTAs or something.

Politics was so exciting. And quite simple, really, from what she had gathered from her many conversations with party fixers, all conducted while James was out at work. The main skill to being an MP, it seemed, was to keep out of trouble. The priority was to ensure that all media coverage about you was positive – and about the opposition, negative. It had been explained to her that, in order to qualify as a candidate, James must be certain that there was nothing in his past, pictures especially, that could embarrass himself or the party if they appeared in the paper. How Victoria had laughed. Compromising pictures! James's life had been all work and meetings for the last two decades at least. He had virtually slept in his suit.

No, the way was clear. And now the date was set. A meeting had been arranged for James to undergo the scrutiny of the party selectors and start the whole thing in motion in earnest.

He knew nothing about any of this – as yet. Victoria would carefully choose the moment to tell him.

CHAPTER 8

In the five months since he'd left prison, Jude had found freedom hard going. For a start, he was faced with what looked like an impossible task. Trying to put together a heist at a summer festival was more complicated than he had ever imagined.

He was, in addition, trying to do it alone. Having landed him with the merciless skill of a professional fisherman landing a salmon, only using a car and not a fly, Frankie had upped sticks to Capri where she was spending the summer with her new Mafioso boyfriend. She had, Jude discovered, never been interested in him. Too far below her pay grade, he supposed.

That much had become clear the moment Frankie first invited him into the mews house after she had picked him up from prison. She really had just wanted to talk about the job. She had never intended to invite him into her bed, or even let him sleep on her Knightsbridge sofa. He'd rented a shabby third-floor flat in Willesden for the duration. Jude had thought himself lucky to get it so cheap until it emerged that the person upstairs, a music student, had an organ in his bedroom and was subject to fits of middle-of-the-night inspiration. Otherwise,

Jude had dealt with his physical needs by looking up various old girlfriends. Venus in particular had proved more than pleased to see him.

Frankie had made it clear that she and Jude were business partners, nothing more. She was only seeing the festival job through because of a promise to Rich. The deal was that Jude would direct all operations while Frankie provided finance, though only up to a certain level. While undoubtedly promising, the festival robbery scene was as yet untested and the margins might be smaller than they thought. Hence the flat in Willesden.

The two challenges facing Jude were identifying the right festival and finding the right gang. Both were far trickier than he had thought. There were more bunting-draped boutique festivals with Winnebago-driving or yurt-hiring festival-goers than he had imagined. But which one was attracting the real high rollers?

After a while, Jude's careful monitoring of society gossip columns turned up the nugget he was waiting for. This was a relief, as wading daily through drivel about minor royals and celebrities he'd never heard of was almost as boring as being in prison.

A billionaire Russian called Badunov was going to a festival called Wild & Free, along with his latest wife, Daria, who, according to the column, 'never goes anywhere without a chestful of sparklers and changes her jewels several times throughout the day'. To make the point, there was a picture of Daria at an art exhibition wearing the tiniest denim shorts along with the biggest diamonds imaginable. Jude's expert eye estimated them to be worth ten million pounds at least.

He looked up the Wild & Free website and saw immediately that this festival had it all. Smallish and upmarket so not too heavy on security. And with a rich demographic: oligarchs aside, the festivalgoers ranged from rich kids and aristos through celebs and supermodels.

Jude had found his target. Now he needed the gang: accomplices to act as scouts, lookouts and getaway drivers. His initial idea was four, but he soon rounded this down to two. Even this had proved impossible, despite his setting about it with all the desperate determination that a Ferrari Monza 33 in the balance could command.

He'd begun in the obvious places, by looking up every old contact. But the original Diamond Geezers were either mostly incarcerated or, in the case of Rich, dead. And those who weren't had disappeared, the tatty East End flats they had lived in fallen to the onward march of contemporary artists' studios and edgy design ateliers. The London crime world, Jude realised, had moved on without him. Undaunted he had set about making contacts with its current masters, but without success. Of the few with whom he got so far as outlining the festival plan, none were interested.

Jude was starting to lose faith in the entire enterprise. The festival was getting nearer, mere weeks away now, but his intentions regarding it seemed a distant dream. For the Ferrari's sake alone he put off calling Frankie for as long as he could.

But just when it seemed he could put it off no longer, he had a great stroke of luck.

The call had come in the middle of the night. Jude, half-woken, had rolled over on the mattress on the floor of his bedroom and cursed. But as his mobile rang on next to his ear he realised that the cause of the disturbance was not, as he'd automatically assumed, his upstairs neighbour performing the Widor Toccata.

'Yeah?' Jude mumbled, flailing for the flashing screen.

The voice was low, Cockney and threatening. 'It's Big George. Remember me?'

Jude was awake instantly, his brain fizzing with agitation. Remember Big George? He still had nightmares about him.

He had first met Big George in the steam-filled, cabbage-reeking prison kitchen. They had both worked there; George had been his supervisor, despite not being able to tell the difference between an onion and an apple. He had a head the size and shape of a bear's, no neck that one could see, and his enormous, hairy hands were covered in scars and had fingers missing.

'How's it going, George?' Jude asked conversationally. That Big George was ringing at all, let alone at this hour, was as sinister as it was strange. Prison rules about phone calls were strict and he and George had not been especially close inside. That said, Jude had been scrupulously careful not to offend him. People who offended George lived to regret it, although some, it had to be said, did not.

'I'm out,' George growled bluntly.

Jude reared up on his mattress. 'Out?' he repeated. 'As in – released?'

It was unbelievable. George was doing twenty years for murder. And that was the murder he'd done in prison. Being let out early for good behaviour, or even parole, had not looked likely this side of the next millennium.

'As in escaped on day release,' George corrected him, and gave a throaty cackle.

'You what?' said Jude.

'They let us out in Guildford town centre. We scarpered.'

'We?'

'Thassright. I'm with Boz, ain't I?'

Jude's amazed shout of 'Boz?' elicited a bang on the ceiling from the upstairs neighbour. Jude ignored it. He could shove his Toccata where the sun didn't shine. Right now he had other concerns. Boz, for instance.

Boz was another Folgate inmate, a more recent arrival than George but doing the same stretch and, if anything, even more terrifying. He was enormously broad and tall, with very thick, arched black eyebrows and black hair shaved threateningly close to a strikingly small cranium. This was nonetheless attached to an inordinately large jaw which chewed food with great pressure and speed. His tattoos, which were numerous, portrayed scenes of what seemed, even to a convicted armed robber like Jude, frightening violence.

'*Boz* is with you?' Jude asked, wondering whether to trust his own hearing. It was difficult to hear now anyway as the upstairs neighbour was hitting back with 'Sheep May Safely Graze' with all the stops out.

'Yeah, and we need somewhere. We're on the bleedin' run.'

It was rare that Jude panicked, but he felt it rise now. He had enough to worry about without giving sanctuary to a pair of murderous criminals on the lam. He only had the one room; the kitchen and bathroom were shared with the organist. 'How did you know I was here?' he parried, playing for time.

'Venus told us.'

Thanks, Venus, Jude thought bitterly. She'd seemed so pleased to see him, too. Bloody women.

'So you going to let us in, mate?' George growled.

'*Let you in?*'

'We're downstairs. Outside the door.'

Jude closed his eyes and briefly lost himself in the red whirl behind his eyelids. That world seemed safer than the one with his eyes open. He could see it all; he'd be done for harbouring fugitives from the law, obstructing the course of justice or whatever. He'd be back in Folgate before you could say concrete boots, which would probably be his fate if he refused to help Boz and George.

He hurried downstairs in his Selfridges silk boxer shorts – while his full former sartorial splendour was unaffordable, he had nonetheless obtained some essentials. He was thankful only for the lateness of the hour. Given their distinctive shape and the menace of their appearance, getting Boz and George upstairs unnoticed had to be done under cover of night. But once they were there, how long would they stay? And what the hell was he supposed to do with them?

He had reached the downstairs hall before the answer struck him. It rose in his brain, a fully formed miracle. He had found his accomplices! Boz and George would not have been his first choice, but they knew all about robberies. And if – as was obviously the case – they needed somewhere to hide, where better than a festival?

A festival was the last place anyone would think of looking for them. They would fit in perfectly; as Jude knew from perusing endless websites, festivals were full of people who looked far weirder than Boz and George. A pair of escaped criminals would pass completely unnoticed.

Nonetheless, as he opened the door and saw George's meaty face and powerful shoulders and felt the barely controlled violent energy of Boz, Jude had to take a deep breath to calm his jangling nerves. He gritted his teeth. 'Hey! Great to see ya! Come in, guys.'

Boz shoved him out of the way and began stomping up the stairs in his vast black Dr Martens boots. George followed, with Jude scuttling in their rear. Halfway up the stairs, George turned.

'What the bleedin' 'ell's that then?' His huge head was cocked upwards, where 'Jesu Joy of Man's Desiring' was in full swing.

Jude felt his knees tremble, but made a stab at a nonchalant smile. 'It's my, er, neighbour. A bloody organist, would you believe.'

George was staring at him hard.

'I'll, um, go and ask him to pipe down. As it were.'

'Nah,' George growled. 'Me old dad was an organist. Got Grade eight piano meself, as a matter of fact. Like a bit of Bach, I do.'

CHAPTER 9

June

It was Friday and the end of the school day. Lorna Newwoman had failed to pick her son up. She had not called to say why. She had not called at all. Nor could the school get hold of her. The phone rang unanswered at the Newwoman residence and Lorna's mobile phone did the same.

'It's twenty minutes past the end of the school day now,' Brenda Garland reminded Ginnie. 'No one's turned up for him yet. Can you take him?'

Ginnie thought. Alfie was in her class and therefore her responsibility. If she took him home there was a good chance she would have to look after him all evening. All night too, perhaps. It being Friday, very possibly the whole weekend into the bargain. But this weekend she had a visitor; her old friend Jess, a barrister, was coming up from London.

Ginnie looked out of the staffroom window. There were still a few parents chattering in the playground. She could go and canvas them, find Alfie somewhere safe to go with one of his peers until his mother arrived.

Her initial efforts did not meet with much success.

'I'm not bloody getting involved,' Jane Buggins said, grasping

Brooklyn by the wrist and heading off at speed.

'I would take him, but I've got three children as it is,' whined Susie Savage, hurrying away with Amy, Emily and baby Baxter. Mandy Brinton, meanwhile, had rushed off with Harper and Tegan before the teacher could even get to her. Ginnie's mind, as she returned to the staffroom, was starting to tumble with depressing phrases like child protection officers and social services departments.

'I'd take him, but I've got a meeting of Vegans Against Wind Farms,' Kay said, less than helpfully. Then she smiled slyly. 'Why don't you ask Mark?'

On cue, Ginnie's face flamed red. She tried to shake her hair forward to hide it from Kay's amused stare. It had crossed her mind to ask Mark, but she had decided she did not dare. The headmaster had been looking particularly unapproachable today, his dark brows drawn in a preoccupied, unhappy fashion. Mr Kettle had been in to see him again, and that never exactly lightened the atmosphere.

'You couldn't have left him with any of the mums you were asking anyway,' Brenda pointed out sanctimoniously. 'None of them have valid CRB certificates.'

Ginnie did not say, as she wanted to, that they had their own children. Obviously that counted for nothing in the box-ticking world of education administration in general and that of 'safeguarding' in particular.

She stared hopelessly out of the classroom window and watched Kay in her vegetable-dyed skirt clumping out to her bicycle.

As it happened, Lorna was driving up at that very moment. The computer course she had been on with the aim of learning to self-promote her self-published work had overrun. That was the official excuse. In fact, she had had a coffee afterwards with Tenebris, the course leader.

Since school had ended twenty minutes earlier, none of the usual revving parents were blocking the road outside the gate, rolling back and forth on their clutches and honking. Lorna decided to cut herself some slack. She was rushed, she would be there for five seconds, she had never done it before and everyone else did it every day. So she would double-park outside the school. Just this once.

Leaping out, slamming the door and striding through the gate, she looked for Alfie in his usual position, drooping by the wall. He was not there. Lorna's brisk march quickened to a run. She stormed up to the entrance door at the same time a relieved Ginnie shot out of it.

'Ms, um, Newwoman!' Even after all this time Ginnie had trouble actually saying it.

Lorna raised her chin aggressively and looked Ginnie in the eye. Attack, after all, was the best line of defence. 'Miss Blossom. I'm running a few minutes behind time because I've been to a Self-Promoting Self-Publishing course.'

'I see,' said Ginnie, who didn't, not really. What was a Self-Promoting Self-Publishing course when it was at home?

'The course leader had some very interesting ideas on audience-building,' Lorna blathered on. 'Reaching out to readers in targeted places.'

The penny dropped with Ginnie. This was the dreadful *The King Who Couldn't Wee!* Lorna was late because she'd been learning how to thrust it on an unsuspecting public. Anger gripped the gentle teacher of infants. She could, she felt, have accepted such lateness in an emergency, but not if it was yet another of Lorna's idiotic vanity projects. She opened her mouth to deliver a politer version of this, but Lorna was still talking.

'He was very keen on festivals,' Lorna continued in her strident tones, her gaze, completely unapologetic and not even abashed, skewering Ginnie's through her wire-rimmed glasses. 'There's one called Wild and Free, apparently. It has a family area called the Hibbertygibberty Wood where there's a Story Jam. Writers read out their work to the children in a woodland theatre setting . . .'

Ginnie could bear no more. 'Ms Newwoman,' she began, voice high with indignation. It was ridiculous. Lorna hadn't so much as asked about Alfie. Who, as it happened, was sitting peacefully in the empty classroom, reading *Matilda* by Roald Dahl with unusual concentration.

Lorna held up a long, thin palm. 'Miss Blossom. I . . . I,' she repeated, for emphasis, 'was always taught that one should let the other person finish before speaking oneself.'

Ginnie stared. The cheek of it! Lorna Newwoman was notorious for her loud, rude interruptions.

From his office in the school building, his attention caught by raised voices, Mark Birch looked down on the playground. Seeing it was Lorna Newwoman and Ginnie his heart sank on the one account and shot into the stratosphere on the other.

He'd had to accept that his interest in the infants' teacher went way beyond the strictly professional. She haunted his dreams with her flowing chestnut hair, full curves and creamy flesh. Whenever her breasts brushed against him in one of the narrow school passages he felt that he might explode. He had tried to compensate by affecting a sterner persona than usual, but it was no longer possible to conceal the fact – to himself, at least – that he was very, very attracted to her.

Perhaps it was no longer possible to conceal it from anyone, Ginnie least of all. He was starting to wonder whether he should hint at it to her. Ask her out, even. He had seen no evidence of a boyfriend, yet surely she must have one. And her undoubted rejection of him would, Mark felt, come almost as a relief. He could then continue with his life and not blunder around in this heightened state of erotic preoccupation.

Below, Lorna self-righteously cleared her throat. Ginnie, meanwhile, was silent. Lorna looked at her angrily. 'You were saying, Miss Blossom?'

Miss Blossom raised finely drawn eyebrows. 'I was just waiting to make sure you had finished, Ms Newwoman. And if you have, I might just ask you to ensure that, in future, the courses you attend enable you to pick Alfie up on time.'

This was too much for Lorna. 'That's the problem with this school!' she raged. 'No community spirit! It takes a village to raise a child, or didn't you know?'

Ginnie felt that it actually took a mother, and a responsible and sensible one at that. She parted her lips to say so. But Lorna was now on the highest of horses, on the highest possible moral ground.

'No one makes an effort in this school!' she was ranting. 'There's not enough trying! Not enough aspiration! The children aren't encouraged to aim high enough!'

Ginnie's vision was going slightly hazy, and a feeling of unbounded fury possessed her. As this sharpened and defined itself into an overpowering urge to hit Lorna Newwoman, the Head of Infants realised she was in trouble. She had heard of red mist but never experienced it before.

At this moment, as her entire professional future hung in the balance, Ginnie was grateful and relieved in equal measure to feel, at her side, the reassuring presence of Mark Birch. One glance at Ginnie's face, bright red and spasming with anger, told the head teacher that his intervention was anything but a mistake.

'What seems to be the problem?' he asked Lorna Newwoman calmly as Ginnie leant against a nearby lamppost, relieved beyond measure to hand over responsibility to someone else. Mark had, she felt quite sure, saved her from an incident possibly fatal to her career. A second later, even, might have meant disaster. She gazed at him as he unhesitatingly tackled Lorna, feeling dizzy with love and gratitude.

The sound of someone else shouting now caught the attention of the three of them. An angry-looking man in a beige V-neck jumper was standing yelling at the gate.

'Oh no,' Ginnie groaned softly.

'What's he saying?' Lorna demanded.

'It's Mr Kettle from next door,' Ginnie explained. 'He goes wild if any of the parents double-park on the road.'

Quite right, Lorna was about to declare sententiously, when the shock of remembrance hit her. She looked in horror to where her ancient estate car stood guilty as charged, looking impossibly enormous and obstructive, hazards flashing to advertise its trangressions.

The colour – such as it was – drained out of Lorna's long, bony visage. For a few moments she was speechless with shock. Then, gradually, strangled sounds started to emerge from her windpipe.

'Is this your car?' yelled Mr Kettle from the gate, jabbing a thick finger in the direction of Lorna's vehicle.

Lorna swallowed. 'Yes. Sorry,' she called sheepishly.

'Well, move it!' shouted the old man. 'This is a public right of way, you know!'

'I'll get Alfie,' Ginnie said, her voice a mumble to hide a dangerously building guffaw.

Once Lorna had gone, Ginnie turned to Mark. 'Thank you so much. You came just in time.'

Mark stared down at the beloved face now restored to its usual calm, angelic state. His gaze plunged into the clear green eyes and traced every curve and point of the long feathery lashes. It swooped down her adorable nose with its delicate moulding, and traced the round of her cheek like a lover's exploring finger. Her warm perfume hovered round his nostrils and her rosy lips were parted; he could see her tongue. A pang of pure lust shuddered through him. He could no longer hold it back. 'You're welcome,' he said, strong feeling strangling his vowels.

It was now or never.

'I wonder,' Mark added in a rapid squawk, 'whether . . .'

'Whether what?' asked Ginnie, following his face intently with her eyes as she might one of her Reception class toddlers as they struggled to frame a sentence.

'Whether . . . whether . . .' Mark passed a hand through his hair and looked wildly at her. Why was it all coming out so wrong? He was a sentient being, a head teacher, not a tongue-tied teenager. 'I mean,' he added, in a frenzy of awkwardness, 'you obviously have a boyfriend, you might be doing something with him . . .'

He glared at the grey playground surface, urging it to swallow him up. Why – *why* – had he said that? It was all coming out like a stream of consciousness, he was speaking his thoughts.

'I don't have a boyfriend,' Ginnie calmly assured him. Her tones were placid, but a feeling of tremendous excitement was swelling her breast. Her fists clenched in ecstasy. Was he going to ask her what she thought he was going to ask her?

'Whether . . . whether . . .' Mark was ploughing bumpily on, 'you might like to come for a drink. I mean,' he added, with a grimacing effort at a smile, 'we probably both need one. After that,' he said, jerking his head over-emphatically in the direction Lorna had just driven off in. 'Now,' he added, all facility for language summarily deserting him in the face of her intent gaze. 'Drink. Now.'

Now it was all out at last, he was terrified of her reaction. He saw amazement flash through her face. She seemed to gasp, as if for breath, the bosom heaving wildly up and down. 'I can't,' Ginnie stuttered, a feeling equal in strength to his inhibiting her own speech so it came out, as was not intended, rather harshly.

That was enough for Mark. He had expected it. He turned on his heel, not feeling as relieved at the inevitable rejection as he had anticipated. He felt bitter, devastated, winded, as if she had physically hit him. And the effect of her nearness still raged like fire within him. He should go home and take a cold shower.

He tried to frame a polite 'goodbye' but the words would not come. He did not look at Ginnie again, but practically ran across the playground to the school entrance and the sanctuary of his office.

Ginnie looked after him in confusion and despair. It had come out all wrong, like a rude rejection. What should she do? Would it look crazy to sprint after him and explain that she would love to come, was desperate to in fact, but her old friend Jess was arriving and she had to pick her up from the station?

Yes, it would, Sensible Ginnie warned Impetuous and Romantic Ginnie. The moment had passed. She had missed her chance.

Had he really asked her out? It had happened so quickly, so unexpectedly, she could scarcely believe it. And yet he had shown no previous signs of being attracted to her. Perhaps, Ginnie thought, her euphoria dwindling, his reasons were merely pragmatic. He had asked her out from politeness. From professional concern and an acceptance that, as head, he had to motivate his staff.

Sobered, disappointed and embarrassed, she crept into the

school to collect her things. This necessitated going upstairs to the staffroom. The door of the headmaster's office was firmly and resolutely shut. Romantic Ginnie hesitated outside it, but Sensible Ginnie steered her firmly away.

CHAPTER 10

Later, with Jess in the small sitting room of her tiny Chestlock terrace, Ginnie had put the incident behind her. Certainly she had not mentioned it to her old university friend, to whom it would no doubt seem risible in its repression. 'Like something out of *Brief Encounter!*', Ginnie could imagine her exclaiming.

Jess herself was anything but repressed. She was voluble, exciting and glamorous, a willowy six-foot Nigerian beauty who had graduated top of her year at law school. She came, as Ginnie saw it, from a thrilling London world full of dastardly criminals, dashing barristers, wigs and gowns and polished shoes. A world where the best brains met the worst of humanity. How provincial and boring Chestlock must seem to her, Ginnie felt. And yet Jess had been more than keen to come.

They had been out for a curry – Jess the most dazzling thing the Bombay Palace had ever seen. Then last orders at Chestlock's one and only wine bar – Jess again the cynosure of all eyes in her tangerine shift dress. They were now back, lounging, one on each sofa with their feet propped up on the arms. Ginnie loved the fact it was the middle of the night. Being up this late made her feel wild and exciting; normally, it was *News at Ten* (or as much of it as she could bear) and bed.

They had drunk quite a lot and Ginnie had now switched to mint tea. Unlike Jess, who was still on the red wine, she had no head for alcohol. She was not the sort to recover with a big fried breakfast. If Ginnie had a hangover it lasted for days.

Jess was still filling her in on various mutual friends. The big news was that Rachel, a PA to the head of a glossy magazine publishers, was getting married. 'We've both got the call,' Jess said.

'Bridesmaids, you mean?' Ginnie's heart sank. It would be the fifth in recent years. Never the bride at this rate, although she knew better than to say so. Jess, single and proud of it, would castigate her for being unfeminist.

Jess grinned. 'I'm the chief bridesmaid, so you've got to do what I say. Which is what Rach says, essentially. Here are the dresses.' She fished out a tablet from a smart lilac suede holder and showed Ginnie photographs and sketches. Ginnie learnt that as a present to Rachel from her boss, the clothes would be made by some cutting-edge designer called Koo Chua. 'Koo's channelling a cool retro vibe, apparently,' Jess explained as Ginnie squinted to see in the limited light.

Ginnie stared at scribbly drawings of tightly fitting sheath dresses. 'Coffee satin' said more scribbles at the sides, with arrows pointing to the dresses. A shade more guaranteed to make her pale skin look like mud was hard to imagine. And the sheath style would make her look enormous. On Rachel's big day, Ginnie could see, she would be the biggest thing about it.

She adjusted her position on the sofa, conscious of her unflatteringly boxy black trousers and creased white linen shirt. The wide white fan of her unpainted toes spread out across the sofa arm. Would it help, she asked herself, if she cut down hard on the HobNobs from now on?

'Chippendales and a penis piñata,' Jess was saying. 'Binge-drinking and streaking in Barcelona.'

'What?' asked Ginnie.

'Just thinking about Rachel's hen night.' The other side of the dimly lit room, Jess's grin was a white flash in her dark face. 'It's my job as chief bridesmaid.'

Ginnie envied her breezy approach to the wedding. Jess wore being single so lightly. But then again, so had Ginnie herself, before Mark Birch had come on the scene. She felt heat rush through her body at the mere thought of him. The afternoon's incident came back to her in all its agonising detail. He had seemed so hurt, almost angry. The light had died in his eyes, his face had slammed shut. He had turned away without a word. Ginnie was already wondering about Monday. What could she say, where did they go from here?

'I've been wondering about festivals,' Jess was saying.

Ginnie blinked, trying to remember what they had just been talking about. 'For a hen night?'

'Well, Kate Moss did it,' Jess said, and Ginnie snorted. It was a standing joke between them that whatever Kate Moss did, Rachel wanted to do. 'She loaded two pink Hummers with thirty friends, a hundred and twenty bottles of rum and several magnums of champagne,' Jess went on. 'And they all went to the Isle of Wight Festival.'

Kate's alcohol list reminded Ginnie unpleasantly of her own recent over-consumption. 'I can't see Rachel at a festival,' she said. 'The wind might spoil her hair. And the rain would ruin her make-up.'

Jess cackled. 'I guess so. OK, maybe it isn't the right thing.'

Ginnie silently congratulated herself on having dodged this bullet. But Jess had not finished yet.

'Not for Rachel's hen do anyway,' she went on. 'But I'd love to go to a festival. Everyone else in the world has.'

Ginnie stared. Not in her world. She had never heard Brenda mention Glastonbury.

'Why don't we go to one?' Jess was sitting up on the sofa, eyes shining. 'Seriously, what do you think?'

Ginnie considered. The summer holidays were approaching and while festivals were not something she felt particularly drawn to, she had no other plans. On the other hand, leaving Chestlock meant leaving the magic circle where Mark was, where she might meet him or see him from a distance, at any time.

'I'm not sure,' she said slowly. 'Maybe.'

Jess flicked the iPad surface again. 'This one here, Wild and Free, looks good.'

She passed over the tablet.

'Quite a smart crowd,' Jess added. 'Kind of retro-eco-boho-aristo.'

'Kind of *what*?'

'Oh, shut up. They're got an image gallery on the site, a rolling one. Have a look.'

Ginnie looked and saw shabby-chic bunting rippling against a brilliantly blue sky with a mellow Tudor mansion in the background. The image gallery went from close-ups of cupcake-laden retro cakestands to adorable moppetty children with fairy wings and painted faces dancing in leafy groves. There were sensitive men with beards in Davos 2012 T-shirts and fawn-like women in floaty print Boden dresses. There were teenage girls in coloured wellies with hair down to the turn-ups of their tiny shorts. Even the trees were elegantly boho – hung with lanterns and chandeliers and candles in bottles – while the tables beneath were set with cloths, coloured glasses and mismatched vintage china. It was all whimsical, magical, fantastical, impromptu and alfresco.

And perhaps a little puzzling. 'What's a guerilla gardening workshop?' asked Ginnie.

Jess shrugged. 'Search me. But I like the sound of it. Guns, not butternut squashes.'

'Would you camp?' Ginnie asked cautiously.

'*We'd* glamp,' Jess said decisively. 'We'd either hire a pre-erected luxury yurt with proper beds or we'd get a Winnebago. Although there are Airstreams and gypsy bowtops as well.' She looked at Ginnie inquiringly.

Ginnie was lost. An Airstream sounded like a soda siphon while a gypsy bowtop might be a hairstyle. They were both types of fashionable caravan, she now gathered. 'I'm not sure,' she faltered, thinking of Mark again.

'Me neither,' Jess mused, again raising Ginnie's hopes of being let off the hook. Until, that was, she added, 'Gypsy bow-tops are a bit small. And for someone my height, legroom's quite important.'

Ginnie took a deep breath. Jess was unstoppable once she got going and she had that lawyer's trick of making you agree to something when you hadn't really. Unless they suited her to do otherwise, inferences, hints and other subtleties were things Jess ignored. If Ginnie wasn't to find herself knee-deep in mud waiting in a queue for portable loos she had better say so now, and in the plainest terms. 'I'm not sure I'm up for it, Jess,' she faltered, staring at the carpet rather than her friend's eyes. 'I think I might stay here this summer.'

Jess's face was a picture. '*Here?*' she repeated incredulously, eyes roving round the tiny room. 'In *Chestlock*? All summer?'

Ginnie nodded. 'It's been quite a term and,' she hesitated, dropping her gaze from Jess's disbelieving stare, 'I guess I'm a bit tired,' she finished hurriedly.

Jess said nothing for a moment. She poured herself another

glass of Merlot, crossed to Ginnie's side of the room and perched on one of the sofa arms.

'Come on,' she said, in a voice that warned nothing but the truth would do. 'Who is it?'

Not for the first time Ginnie cursed the fact that her closest friend was a top criminal barrister. As many a felon had discovered, lying to Jess was a pointless exercise. But she was going to have a bloody good go at it, nonetheless.

'I don't know what you mean,' she said, sipping her mint tea.

Jess threw back her head and laughed. 'You are *such* a hopeless liar, Ginnie!' She bent forward, her clever face tensed, her keen eyes fixed on Ginnie's face. 'Let me guess,' Jess mused. 'You've met someone. Someone round here.'

Ginnie stuck out her chin defiantly as she swung her head in a negative. She was not going to tell Jess. Her scorn, or amusement, would fall on the raw wounds like salt.

But Jess, a barrister used to fitting random facts together, now felt something mesh in her brain. 'It wouldn't be that headmaster, would it?'

Ginnie's arm jerked in shock; she spilled her tea. Her mind was rioting. *When* had she mentioned Mark to Jess? She might have said he had arrived at the school, but nothing more. Once again, the misery of the afternoon rushed back.

Her hand shook as she lowered the incriminatingly shaking mug to the floor. 'What headmaster?'

Jess spluttered. 'Oh come *on*, Gin. The one at your school. The one you fancy.'

Ginnie's face flamed vermilion. 'I don't fancy him.' It came out much more vehemently than she intended.

Jess nodded. 'You've answered my question. It *is* him that's bothering you, isn't it?'

Ginnie looked down, mortified. She had shown her hand.

'You're crazy about him,' Jess said softly.

Ginnie's head hung down further.

'You're in love,' Jess went on. 'Head over heels. Aren't you?'

Ginnie nodded. She raised her hot, pink face and looked at Jess in anguish. 'But it's hopeless. He asked me out today and I said no.'

'Why?' Jess shrieked. It was her turn to hang her head once Ginnie had explained. 'Oh God,' Jess groaned. 'It's all my fault!'

'No, it isn't,' Ginnie rushed to reassure her. 'It was just politeness. Due diligence as a boss and all that. He's not interested in me.'

'Of *course* he's interested in you,' Jess returned robustly. 'You're gorgeous, Ginnie. Absolutely beautiful.'

'Don't be stupid.' Ginnie's tone was almost angry. 'I'm . . . fat.' She swept a hand down her front in disgust.

'Gin!' Jess exclaimed. 'You're nothing of the sort. You're all woman. No man could resist you. Least of all a lonely headmaster looking for love.'

There was a pause. Ginnie stared, unseeing, at the wall beyond the foot of her sofa. Eventually she asked, in a low voice, 'How do you know he's a lonely headmaster looking for love?'

Jess shrugged. 'I don't. But he might be. You have to find out. It's your turn to ask him out now.'

Fear filled Ginnie. 'And how do I do that?'

'That's up to you,' Jess said bluntly. 'But you need to think of something. You'll miss your chance otherwise.'

Pricked by irritation, Ginnie twisted her head away. It was all very well for super-confident, beautiful, skinny, brainy Jess. While avowedly not interested in settling down yet, her success with men was legendary. She had been a magnet for them tonight, brushing them off like flies off a dress.

'Fortune favours the brave,' Jess added, reaching for the Merlot again.

Ginnie sighed. Jess was right, as usual. But could the prize really be hers, just for the asking? 'I just don't know how to do it,' she confessed. 'How to go about the whole thing. I mean . . .' she swallowed, looking nervously at her friend, 'how would *you* do it?'

Jess put the bottle down. 'OK, so we'll rehearse,' she said. 'I'll pretend to be the headmaster. What's his name again?'

'Mark.' Ginnie's face flamed.

Jess eyed her in awe. 'Blimey. You really have got it bad, haven't you? OK, so I'll coach you. Next time you see him you'll have him at your feet.'

'Thanks,' said Ginnie gratefully. Mark at her feet wasn't an easy scenario to imagine, but a wonderful one nonetheless, and she appreciated the general thrust.

Jess raised a finger. 'There is a but, though. A condition.'

Ginnie waited.

'You have to come to this festival with me,' Jess said. 'I actually need to go. I want to get away.'

'What's up?' Ginnie detected something uncharacteristically fierce in Jess's tone.

Jess sighed. 'It's silly really. Just a work thing. Someone I helped convict. He's escaped from jail.'

Ginnie's eyes widened. Jess was supremely self-contained. It was rare that she opened up, let alone admitted to being worried. She raised herself from the sofa slightly.

'I shouldn't worry about it,' Jess went on. 'I mean, I've sent lots of people down in my time. But there was just something about him.'

'What did he do?' Ginnie asked softly.

'He was one of that gang of jewel thieves called the Diamond Geezers. There was a lot about it in the papers.'

Ginnie vaguely remembered now. 'The ones who robbed all those hotels dressed as women. They sounded quite funny.'

'It wasn't actually all that funny,' Jess said sternly. 'Not if you saw the pictures of some of the victims. People got shot, you know.'

As Ginnie sank back, chastened, Jess reached down and picked her tablet off the floor. After tapping for a minute or two she handed it to Ginnie. 'Here's the guy I got convicted.'

Ginnie surveyed the police information site. A man with mad staring eyes and thick dark hair stared back at her from beneath powerful brows. 'He is rather . . . alarming,' she said.

'He's dangerous,' Jess said. 'I just hate to think of him being, you know, out. At large in the community. Whenever I come out of my office I imagine he's lurking in one of the passageways, or in some alcove.'

Beautiful and ancient as the Inns of Court were, they had, Ginnie remembered, lots of dark and poky corners. 'But do you seriously think he'd be after you?' she asked gently. Jess and paranoia was an odd combination. Yet she was clearly rattled.

'I was the prosecuting barrister.'

'Good for you,' Ginnie said stoutly.

'Well, it might not be,' Jess sighed. 'As he was being led down to the cells he looked up at me, fixed me with his crazed stare and shouted, "I'll get you if it's the last thing I do".'

'Oh dear.' Ginnie bit her lip. Then she raised her chin and added briskly, 'Well, you mustn't let that worry you.'

Jess raked her hair ruefully. 'It didn't, while he was inside. But him being on the run's a different matter. That's why I thought a festival might be a good idea. Get me out of chambers for a while.' She looked at Ginnie beseechingly. 'Do come. Please.'

CHAPTER 11

Thank God, Mark thought as he took his seat, this would be the last one until September. Meetings of the governing body were a necessary evil. The best one could hope for was that they would be over quickly.

This, admittedly, seemed a dim prospect given that the school's governing body, while small, contained several people whose enjoyment of the sound of their own voice was inversely proportionate to their intelligence. They liked meetings to last for hours, grinding through the most painfully boring and irrelevant minutiae. In vain had Mark pointed out in the past that even meetings of the Cabinet only lasted forty minutes. And they were running the country.

Chief offenders in this category were Leonard Purkiss and Sheila Wrench. Despite the fact that both had been nominated by the diocese, they had yet, in Mark's view, to manifest a shred of Christian charity. He dreaded especially the prospect of revealing to their untender mercies the parlous financial state that the school was in.

The meeting had now passed over the preliminaries; Leonard, standing in for the absent vicar, had said a pompous grace. Sheila, whose short, dry grey hair always reminded Mark of a dog's, continued to look scathingly round over her bifocals.

'Procedures of the last meeting of the Finance and Personnel Committee,' came the breathy voice of Brenda Garland in her capacity as Clerk of the Governors.

Mark took a deep breath and distributed clipped-together sets of accounts, one for each governor. Leonard frowned over his, turning the pages impatiently. Sheila, meanwhile, shook her head.

'Things could be better, financially,' Mark began wryly. He explained the position. 'It's to do with intake. We only get paid per child and the last year of leavers was quite a big one, while the incoming reception year was very small. Not our fault, just a birth pattern thing. There are many other schools in the same boat.'

Leonard Purkiss stared at him. 'I don't want to be rude, head teacher, but that sounds awfully like an excuse.'

Sheila, beside him, harrumphed in agreement.

Don't let them get to you, Mark told himself as he calmly set out the case for the defence. 'As you see, we've been making every saving possible. Brenda's even found a supplier who saves us two pence on every toilet roll. Haven't you, Brenda?'

He beamed manically at Brenda, wishing to give credit where it was due. 'One and a half pence,' she corrected.

There was an interruption – it sounded like a snarl – at the end of the table.

'What's the point of discussing it?' Leonard Purkiss demanded. 'It's obvious what we have to do.'

Mark gave him a calm smile. 'We're obliged to go through the options, Leonard, so we can make the right decision.'

'It's obvious what the right decision is,' Purkiss bristled. 'We need to get rid of one of the teachers. The most expensive one. Make them redundant and hire a cheaper one.'

Mark felt a bolt of pure terror. While the R word had hovered in the background for a couple of meetings now, it had not yet been aired. Hearing it said was like a slap. He glanced at Leonard, his thick body in its thin grey wool jumper, his flabby face webbed with purple veins, his grey, flat eyes with their curious metallic glint buried deep in folds of flesh. He felt a murderous loathing that he was aware sat ill with his position and responsibilities as head teacher of the school.

Even some of the other governors looked alarmed at this. 'It's a drastic decision, Leonard,' one of them pointed out. 'There may be steps we can take to avoid it.'

'Doesn't sound like it to me,' put in Sheila Wrench, folding her liver-spotted forearms and looking belligerent.

'Better to get it over with,' Leonard pronounced. 'You have to remember that you're talking to a former deputy director of the waste management department of the county council here . . .'

He worked in shit, Mark thought to himself, and he talks it, too. He tried to stop himself panicking. He had expected trouble from Wrench and Purkiss, but never this. On the turn of a sixpence, the meeting had become a nightmare.

'. . . so I know from my own experience,' Leonard continued, 'that it's kinder to get rid of people than keep them hanging on.'

'And Leonard's right that the most expensive teacher should go first,' sniped Sheila.

'Well, that's me,' Mark said loudly, aware that, after himself, Ginnie was the most senior. That she should go was out of the question. Utterly and completely. He forcibly steered his thoughts from even approaching the subject.

But he felt violently agitated, even so – as he had ever since her refusal of his date. This agitation had expressed itself through a greater than usual formality in his dealings with her; he had, he knew, been chill and curt at times, but he had been unable to help it. Anything less risked revealing how he felt, and that must forever now be hidden. She was obviously not interested.

As if to prove this point, she had been prickly and awkward. It had made for a difficult atmosphere between them these past few weeks. They had actively begun to avoid each other. Although he knew it meant not seeing her, which would be dreadful, Mark had almost been looking forward to the summer holidays. After the break, he reasoned, things might go back to normal and they could start again.

Leonard was tutting. 'Come, come, head teacher. We've only just appointed you. We'd hardly want you to go so soon. It would have to be someone else. So who?'

Ginnie was in very real danger, Mark now realised. While the school's financial straits were well known to him, he had never imagined for a second that it would come to this. Let alone this afternoon, and at such terrifying speed. Mark's face was burning and his chest felt tight. He wanted to shout and rant. He felt he might lose all control. But he had to do the opposite; he must put the brakes on things.

'Let's not be rash,' he began. 'What you're proposing is an extreme measure, and we need to consider all the options carefully.'

'Rubbish,' Sheila Wrench cut in with her customary rudeness. 'If a boil needs lancing, it needs lancing straightaway. Leaving it only makes things worse. We need to take immediate action and there's no time like the present.'

'Hear hear,' said Leonard, obviously, like Sheila, relishing the opportunity to wield power and see real blood on the carpet. His small metallic eyes were glinting with an almost sexual excitement.

Mark took a deep, ragged breath, wondering if his thundering heart could be heard in the quiet classroom. The meetings took place in the infants' room as it was the biggest one. But the fact they sat at child-sized tables on child-sized chairs never seemed to impress on people like Sheila and Leonard that they were dealing with essentially child-sized issues.

'Could I just say,' Mark put in, trying not to sound desperate and to stop his voice from shaking, 'that shedding a senior member of staff will have a potentially disastrous effect on the standard of teaching at the school. The programme of improvement I've introduced has just started to take effect, the results are just beginning to—'

'Blitz spirit!' cut in Sheila Wrench savagely.

Mark stared at her. He had absolutely no idea what she meant.

'Making the best of it,' Mrs Wrench snapped, glaring at Mark over her bifocals. 'You'll just have to make do and mend. You can't spend money where there is none.'

'Quite right,' put in Purkiss. 'If this school was a business it would go under.'

'It's not a business,' Mark wanted to scream, but heard himself saying quite politely and brightly. 'It's a school.' The memory of Ginnie protecting Alfie Newwoman in the Show and Tell floated agonisingly before him. 'We educate children here,' he said pleadingly to Wrench and Purkiss. 'We're doing incredibly well. Results are up and cutting the staff now would reverse everything we have achieved. It would be disastrous. Surely you can see—'

'You have to be professional about it,' Sheila Wrench interrupted acidly, mouth turned down in distaste. Her words seemed to sizzle in the air.

'If it was a business it would have absolutely no grounds for survival,' Purkiss ploughed pompously on from where he had left off before. 'Believe me, I know about business. As the former deputy director of the waste management . . .'

They were interrupted by the arrival of the vicar. He blinked mild eyes in a rabbity face. Papers were hastily shoved in his direction. 'School finances, vicar,' Brenda explained.

The vicar gave a humorous groan. 'God help us.'

Mark clung to the brief lightening of atmosphere like a drowning man clinging to a lifebelt. 'We estimate,' he appealed, smiling, 'that if we really cut hard on supplies we'll be able to make it through another year at our current staffing level.'

The vicar smiled glassily back at him.

There was a silence after this and Mark was almost beginning to breathe again when Purkiss piped up once more. 'Ah, but what about the next year?'

'And the year after that?' Sheila Wrench demanded. 'You can't go on knowing you're running up a deficit.'

'I don't see why not,' the vicar interrupted airily. 'The Government seems to positively encourage it when it comes to education. Look at tuition fees.' He twitched his nose and gave a bemused stare round.

As Purkiss cast a furious glance at Reverend Quaid, Mark found he wanted to laugh hysterically. Nerves, he knew. He cleared his throat and bent towards the floor, as if picking up a tissue.

'So who's the most senior teacher?' Sheila Wrench demanded in her acid voice.

'Ginnie Blossom,' said Brenda immediately.

Mark, crouching down, started so hard he banged his head on the underside of the table. He emerged, eyes dilated with shock, cranium throbbing, to find Leonard and Sheila staring at him coldly.

'Well, she'll have to go then,' Leonard pronounced. 'Vote?' He looked round, grey eyes glittering.

Mark pushed away the pain in his head. He had no time for that. He had no time for anything but saving Ginnie. He had counted on starting again with her after the holidays. Never had it occurred to him that this term would be the last one.

He stood up, legs shaking.

'The question is,' he gabbled, 'whether it is better for the children's education that we continue with current staffing levels for another year and work in the meantime to increase intake. Or vote now to make a teacher redundant with all that implies in reduced teaching hours, impact on results and so on . . .'

Sheila Wrench drew herself up. 'Ridiculous waste of money,' she pronounced through pursed lips. 'You've got to get someone cheaper.'

'Hear hear,' agreed Leonard.

The decision was put to the vote and it was decided, by one vote, that Ginnie's post should be made redundant and a new graduate brought in to replace her, with the support of an unpaid classroom assistant. Mark could hardly believe his eyes when both Brenda's and the vicar's hands were raised. His was the sole vote against. No one needed to vote on the fact that it would be Mark's job, as Ginnie's immediate superior, to tell her.

CHAPTER 12

'What is it?' Jess asked. In her legal black, she was hurrying between chambers and court.

Distracted as she was, she was concerned. It was rare for Ginnie to ring in the middle of the day, but from her upset tone of voice this was obviously an emergency.

'Mark Birch,' Ginnie replied vehemently, although whether in triumph or in tragedy, Jess could not tell.

'Have you asked him? At last?'

Ginnie had seemed to be putting the moment off endlessly. Her claims that the object of her affections had become suddenly very stand-offish and snappy sounded like excuses to Jess. Ginnie should, resolve stiffened and tactics honed under her own expert tuition, have asked Mark Birch out for a drink ages ago. She was wasting her opportunity.

Jess had repeatedly pointed out that Ginnie needed to strike while the iron was hot and it was getting colder all the time. Weeks had passed, now, since she was up in Chestlock. She had proffered strategic advice despite the fact that Ginnie's failure to commit to the festival trip had been a disappointment. Since returning to London Jess was keener than ever to go to Wild & Free; she was seeing men, possibly escaped criminals, with mad, staring eyes everywhere in the vicinity of her flat as well as the law courts.

'Didn't it go well?' she probed, as Ginnie seemed incapable of speech.

'Not exactly well, no,' Ginnie hiccupped. Her end was all snuffles and sobs; it sounded, Jess thought, as if she was crying.

'What happened? Did he say no, the idiot?' Jess had no great opinion of men in general. They had their uses, for which she picked them up and dropped them as she saw fit. But they were not creatures to be taken seriously, in her experience.

'He's sacked me,' Ginnie managed through gulping sobs, on the other end.

'*What?*'

'Made me redundant, rather.' Ginnie had held tightly on to her dignity throughout the meeting with Mark. But now she was sitting in her car around the corner from St Stephen's she was weeping freely. She felt she never wanted to set foot in the school building again.

'He can't do that!' Jess's professional as well as her private dander was up.

'It turns out that he can. It's redundancy; there's no money and I'm not being replaced. Not in any meaningful sense anyway. They're going to run the Infants with students and interns.' Ginnie blew her nose and then wept afresh at the pain of the double blow of losing her beloved job and knowing that her even more beloved department would suffer.

'I don't understand,' Jess said. 'It's so sudden.'

Ginnie took a deep breath and tried to control her hysteria. 'There was a governors' meeting last Friday. They had a vote. He voted against me, obviously.'

'But why would he do that? You're a wonderful teacher.'

'I don't know,' Ginnie wailed. 'Maybe because I turned him

down for that drink? He's been really strange with me ever since.'

'Don't be ridiculous,' Jess said immediately. 'He can't be that thin-skinned.'

'Well, what other reason is there?' Ginnie demanded. 'He would have voted for me otherwise.'

'Maybe he did, but the other votes were all against, so his wouldn't have made any difference,' Jess suggested.

Ginnie was indignant. 'Thanks, Jess. That's really helpful. Thanks a bloody million.' Her outrage gathered force from the fact that this had more or less been Mark's defence, but she had not believed for a second he had been unable to do anything about it. The fact that he owed his job to the governing body would, Ginnie felt, ensure the head teacher voted with the pack. And Mark's refusal – on the grounds of confidentiality – to divulge details of how the voting actually fell only strengthened her suspicions. She could not recall ever, in the whole of her life, feeling quite so angry.

'And anyway,' she added to Jess for good measure, 'Brenda – she's the school secretary – would never have voted for me to be sacked. Or the vicar, who likes me as well. So someone else must have been voting against, which was Mark, obviously.'

Jess did not reply to this. She had more experience than the comparatively innocent Ginnie of humankind's capacity for deceit. She had found vicars and school secretaries – their type, anyway – to be among the most two-faced of all.

'What did I ever see in him?' Ginnie was raging on the other end. 'I've been such a *fool*!' Mark Birch was a snake, a villain, a turncoat, a viper. That shy manner she had found so appealing had been no more than a mask hiding a vain and vengeful bully.

Jess, in Gray's Inn Gardens, stared at the swathes of green

grass before the elegant buildings. 'I don't know what to say,' she said. 'Apart from the fact that I'm so sorry.'

'There's nothing *to* say,' Ginnie answered with spirit, although she had said quite a lot to Mark Birch.

'Well, I'm not an employment lawyer, as you know,' Jess said. 'But I know plenty who are. Leave it with me, I'll have it looked into. We'll take him to the cleaners, and the school as well.'

She was surprised when Ginnie protested. 'No, no. They've got no money. The children are the ones who will suffer.' She thought of Alfie Newwoman and swallowed hard. Who would fight his battles for him now? 'I wasn't ringing to ask for legal advice anyway,' Ginnie added. 'It was something else.'

'Tell me,' Jess urged, glancing at her watch. She was due in court in five minutes. 'I'll do anything for you, you know that.'

'Thank you,' Ginnie said, welling up again at her friend's warmth and loyalty. To think that she had credited Mark Birch with such virtues!

'So what is it?' Jess pressed.

'Just to say that I'm completely on for going to this festival with you. I need a change of scene.'

Jess, in Gray's Inn Gardens, silently punched the air, much to the surprise of a passing senior counsel. 'Good,' she said cautiously, aware that it wouldn't do to sound as pleased as she felt. It had only happened because of Ginnie's catastrophe.

'No reason why not,' Ginnie said bleakly. 'It's not as if I've got anything to stay for here any more, is it? Not after the end of term, anyway. Frankly, the further I'm away from Mark Birch, the better.'

That evening, Mark sat alone in his rented cottage. The windows still did not open and the place felt fetid and unbearable He was staring at a TV talent show and thinking that it looked rather blurry. He must, he realised, need glasses and was uncomfortably reminded, once again, of what Spencer had said about him getting old.

Just now, he felt older than ever. He had drunk half a bottle of wine and the burden of what he had told Ginnie earlier was still unbearable. Actually, it felt worse. She had been dignified, but obviously devastated. She would not believe that he hadn't been to blame, and that confidentiality, as well as human decency, had forbidden him from telling her that her own colleagues had voted against her. Her eyes – those peerless eyes – had swum with angry tears. That incomparable bosom had heaved with emotion.

Afterwards, in the agonised, awkward silence that had ensued, she had raised her chin and swept out. Out past Brenda Garland, once again polishing the bookshelf outside his office. Out of his life, quite definitely, and perhaps permanently out of his school. He hadn't dared ask if she intended to come back the rest of the week, and to see out what remained of the term.

Triumphal music blared deafeningly out of the TV, celebrity mentors cried. A fat woman without make-up gave a lung-bursting rendition of 'The Wind Beneath My Wings'.

Mark wanted to cry too, give a lung-bursting rendition of another sort altogether. He wanted to howl with misery. This morning's interview with Ginnie had provoked an attack of the blackest depression. It was as if a dam had burst and everything he had been holding back, not just Ginnie being sacked but all the failure and disappointment of the past twelve months too, now poured through.

There was no longer any doubt about it. Coming to Chestlock had achieved nothing. Leaving London had seemed the answer to everything. But it had merely begged a new set of questions. What to do about Ginnie, most of all.

He was torn between a desperate need to convince her that it had not been his fault and the certain knowledge that she would never believe him. He remained in limbo between the two, in an unbridgeable, hopeless chasm. Not for the first, or even the hundredth time, did he curse Sheila Wrench and Leonard Purkiss, who had engineered the catastrophe.

The telephone's ringing joined the roaring from the television, making Mark jump. He decided to leave it for the answerphone. He did not feel like social interaction.

The machine clicked on. 'Mate . . .' the call began.

Oh God. Spencer. Not now. Not the festival again. It was the last thing he wanted to think about. Why couldn't Spencer bloody well leave him alone? Just take no for an answer?

He was only half-listening, but he heard Spencer mention Jimmy, the drummer, the band member he had been closest to. Mark felt a rush of nostalgia. Where had all those years gone? He wished desperately he could turn them back.

At the same time he was gripped with yearning to see Jimmy again. If he was on board, then the reunion would almost be worthwhile.

The idea caught fire suddenly and blazed like a new hope. Why the hell not, after all? What – specially after today – did he have to lose?

The thought of playing in a reformed, geriatric Mascara Snakes was still an awful one. But the alternative was a solitary summer in Hangman's Cottage with senility encroaching and Ginnie Blossom hating his guts nearby. There was no point trying to persuade her that what had happened was not his fault. She had made it clear this morning that she would never believe him. So being near her in Chestlock all summer would serve only to remind him of what had happened, and the fact that nothing could be done. In the unlikely event he met her she would only cut him dead.

Mark snatched up the phone. Spencer was still in mid-flow.

'OK,' he said. 'I'll come.'

'Knew you'd crack in the end, mate!' exulted Spencer. 'So now you can ring up Jimmy and ask him.'

'What?'

'Jimmy. The drummer, remember?'

'Of course I bloody well remember,' Mark snapped, realising he'd surrendered far too early. 'I thought you said just now you'd got him on board.'

'Nah, mate. Not exactly. Not as such. Was hoping you'd do the honours, in fact.'

'You mean . . . you haven't rung him at all?' The memory of how Spencer always made the rest of them do the work was returning with some force. Of how he would sit in the Turd surrounded by admiring females while the other three lugged amps and speakers about.

'No, mate. That scary wife of his always hated my guts. Especially after the stag night thing,' Spencer said in a determined but unsuccessful attempt to sound casual.

Mark had forgotten about Jimmy's scary wife. But now she too came back – on Jimmy's arm at the fatal stag night, the new girlfriend. She had an unnervingly direct gaze and had asked even more direct questions. Mark had the strong sense that they had not passed muster, and that was before the Leicester Square business.

After that, Victoria's fury had known no bounds. That none of them had been asked to James's wedding a few months later was perhaps to be expected.

'What makes you think *I* want to talk to his scary wife?' Mark demanded of Spencer now.

Spencer claimed, not very convincingly, that time might have healed. 'She'll be fine,' he said breezily. 'She'll have forgotten all about it.'

As Mark put the phone down he decided that there was no time like the present. Spencer would only nag him otherwise and it was clearly too late to turn back. Armed with the number he had been given, he took a deep breath and dialled.

In Lonsdale Road, Victoria lay on a sofa watching a box set of *House of Cards*. She was transfixed by Francis Urquhart's evil machinations and those of his equally evil wife. Were there really people like that at Westminster? James had better sharpen his elbows fast; so, Victoria supposed, should she.

The house was peaceful. James was working late, as was Guy, up in his room revising, a scenario unthinkable a month ago. Furious as she had been at first, Victoria had to give credit where it was due. Their son had been much more motivated since learning that his father would take him to the Wild & Free festival. And once she had got over her annoyance Victoria realised that the situation was rich in potential for her countermove. She would, she had said, give her blessing to the James and Guy festival trip only if James agreed to consider a parliamentary career.

He had been almost too surprised to resist. Guy's not-wholly-altruistic encouragement of his father had helped Victoria's cause too. Events had moved fast since. The all-important meeting with the central office selection person was scheduled. James was, in short, trussed up like a chicken for the parliamentary oven, whether he liked it or not.

When the phone rang, at a pivotal moment of the TV drama,

it made Victoria jump. She stared distrustfully at the lights rippling on the state-of-the-art instrument.

'Hello?'

At Victoria's crisp and urgent voice, Mark felt fear shoot through him. He mastered it, however. He was a head teacher, was he not? Pillar of the community. 'Can I speak to Jimmy?'

'Jimmy?' Victoria was disoriented. Relief that this was not, after all, her husband reporting that the meeting had gone badly combined with a new unease.

No one called her husband Jimmy except those losers he was at university with.

'James,' she stated, her iciness masking a growing fear, 'is not here. Who is this?'

A desperately polite Mark identified himself.

'Mark *Birch*?' Victoria clapped one hand over her mouth and the other, which held the phone, shook. A series of dread possibilities, and the threat they posed to her husband's new career, surged through her mind. There *had* been embarrassing incidents in the distant past – that stag night, for instance . . .

For a second, she could not speak, such was the convulsing of her throat.

'That's right. I knew Jimmy – *James*, sorry – a long time ago.' Feeling the chill blast from the other end Mark tried to inject some humour into his strained and apprehensive tone. 'We were in a band together at college . . .'

Silent but yammering panic was sweeping through Victoria. Oh God, that as well! That stupid band! Did photographs exist?

Her teeth chattered with mixed terror and fury. She felt as if all her plans were unravelling before her eyes. It was bad enough that James was taking Guy to the festival.

Her husband was on the brink of political greatness. There was no possibility, not the faintest shadow of a chance, that a pathetic university rock group was going to be allowed to wreck things. She would go through every box in the house just as soon as this call was over, destroy every document, picture, cassette tape, if need be.

'James is away,' she snarled. 'But I know for a fact that he has no wish *whatsoever* to revisit that aspect of his past. Do not call again.'

A hundred and fifty miles north, in Hangman's Cottage, Mark fought the urge to replace the receiver. Spencer could not have been more wrong. Far from having forgiven and forgotten, Victoria was more of an attack dog than ever. He steeled himself to try one more time.

'Please,' he said, desperately. 'Jimmy – *James* – needs to know about . . .'

'I'll be the judge of what he needs to know, thank you,' Victoria said freezingly and slammed down the phone.

CHAPTER 13

July

James had arrived for lunch with the party selection committee at the Parthenon Club, Mayfair. He was early. An efficient Baltic blonde in a fitted black suit showed him to the lounge.

For all the place's funereal calm, James had a sense of things spiralling beyond his control. What was he doing here? It had all happened so fast. The Parthenon Club meeting had been in his electronic diary before he even knew it. Only now did he reflect what an ominous sign that was. To get anything in that diary entailed instructing Tilly several times over. Ruthless determination was required.

He sat waiting and staring at the ceiling. It was typical of its kind, rectangular and coffered, rioting with gold plaster figures and blue grisaille panelling on which naked gods and goddesses frolicked. There were fluted columns and vast mirrors in gilded frames carved like palm branches. The sofa he sat on was long and upholstered in pale blue silk. These Mayfair gentlemen's clubs hid unimaginable splendour behind their demure brown facades.

The bewildered feeling was not going away, James realised. He was about to have a meeting about being an MP, but he was not sure what his political beliefs were. He knew he didn't want to work in the City any more, but was Parliament the change he was looking for?

At meetings where politicians were present he had always concentrated on the economics rather than the ideology. As for all the party dinners they had recently attended, he had thought he was going for Victoria's sake, so she could mix with the movers and shakers. It had been a surprise to discover they had been for his own benefit.

Victoria was uninterested in his doubts. 'I think you'll be perfect,' she had said firmly that morning.

The bank weren't helping either. Without him even asking, they had indicated their willingness to grant him a sabbatical if necessary. 'Always keen to help our chaps into the House,' his chairman had said. 'Always good to have someone there fighting our corner.'

As panic rose, James reminded himself that he was doing all this for his son. Coming here was the price for taking Guy to the festival. All James had to do was have a drink and a pleasant chat and hopefully part ways with the selection person with no obligations on either side. Honour would be satisfied. Everyone would be happy.

Thinking about the festival made him feel better. He was looking forward to it enormously. Guy, too, was thrilled about this unexpected granting of previously withheld permission and was, it had to be said, currently honouring his promise to 'swot his arse off'. He had not minded in the least that James was coming; had seemed to welcome it, in fact. Guy's main concern was escaping the constant surveillance of his mother. 'It's like being in, like, Guantanamo, Dad.'

The Baltic blonde reappeared with the Central Officer hurrying behind. James jumped to his feet to greet him. Central

Office was a neo-fogey with a damp handshake, a side parting and fishy eyes behind bakelite-effect specs. He wore a tweed suit, slightly creased, and looked and sounded like an announcer from the early days of the BBC. 'I'm Hodge,' he said. 'G and T?'

Over the first – stunningly strong – gin and tonic Hodge outlined the history of the Parthenon Club. 'You haven't been to the Parth before, really?'

The club's restaurant, visible from the lounge through a screen of columns, had panelling from a demolished château James heard. What glamour this conferred seemed belied by the current clientele: old men slurping soup while they read volumes propped on wooden bookstands. 'You see that table over there?' Hodge's voice dropped, despite the only others in the lounge being two more old men at the far end of the room.

James followed the stubby red finger stabbing at an alcove. 'That's where Burgess and MacLean had their last lunch. Before they defected to Moscow.'

He looked expectantly at James, who had heard the Burgess and MacLean story in connection with at least one other London club. It would obviously be deflating to say so, however.

'Can you imagine?' Hodge pressed excitedly.

James was certain that even if he had not heard the story, he would not have been remotely shocked at the idea of traitors in so Establishment a setting. Perhaps his *Tinker, Tailor* box set was to blame.

He sat as upright and alert on the sofa as was possible on such a slithery piece of furniture. He hoped the interview would be over soon. He had not yet been asked how long he had been a party supporter. Hodge seemed to take for granted that he had been born one.

The fishy eyes were consulting a piece of paper. It appeared to be some kind of report but the writing was too small for James to see what it said.

'You live in Notting Hill, I see,' Hodge remarked, his glasses flashing accusingly as he looked up.

James nodded guiltily. He felt he knew what was coming. Living in expensive West London was a political liability. It alienated voters. As it happened, Notting Hill was something he now had doubts about. He had recently begun to notice – really notice – how his enclave of the rich abutted those of the very poor. It amazed him that he had ignored for so long the poor people's housing above the shops selling pricey topiared bushes to put outside rich people's shining front doors.

He opened his mouth to say some of this but Hodge had moved on. His address did not seem to be a problem, after all.

'Got any performing experience?'

'What?'

'University drama? Those who've acted in the past find it very useful in the House.'

'I have done a bit of performing, actually,' James said thoughtfully. 'Might not count, though.'

'Go on.' Hodge looked wary, as if James was about to confess to being a strippergram.

'I was in a band at college. Sort of rock band.' James felt himself blush, aware how the term must sound coming from one as suited and senior as himself. But Hodge was hardly the personification of youth either, despite being actually young. 'Centuries ago, of course,' he added self-deprecatingly.

'But that's good,' was Hodge's unexpected rejoinder. 'Tony Blair was in a rock group. And he remains, whatever people say about him, the most successful politician of modern times.'

'Ugly Rumours,' James nodded.

'Actually, it's quite true.'

'Blair's, um, rock group. It was called Ugly Rumours.'

Hodge let this pass. 'And what was yours called?'

'The Mascara Snakes.'

Hodge raised his eyebrows, cleared his throat and started to discuss the role of the constituency office.

'. . . old bats with time on their hands. Swivel-eyed loons. Take care of the correspondence and phone calls . . .'

James tried to follow but was finding it hard to concentrate. He was reeling under the force of something like an epiphany. Just saying the band's name brought the memories rushing back. Mark, Rob and of course Spencer. Where were they now? Mark was still in the BBC most probably. Job for life if ever there was one.

'Devoted old birds, doesn't take much to keep them happy. Lunch once a year, doesn't have to be expensive, signed card from the PM, that sort of thing . . .'

And Spencer had gone into advertising. He'd be doing well there. Handsome, persuasive, *loud*, Spencer had been, of all of them, the Person Most Likely.

'Yes, you'll be a big hit in Wortley,' Hodge was saying. 'They love silver foxes like you.' He uncrossed his short legs.

James tuned back in. Wortley? Where was Wortley? Hodge was talking as if an actual seat was on offer.

Hodge's eyebrows rose above the bakelite frames. His small mouth twitched.

'For what it's worth – a not insignificant amount, I think you'll find – my view is that you'll make a very fine MP and we're pleased to have you in the House.'

'I'm not in the House yet.' James tried not to yelp. This was a shock.

'You will be.' Hodge gave him a conspiratorial smile. 'But keep shtum for the time being. The Member for Wortley-on-

Thames business hasn't hit the papers yet.'

James shot backwards into the cushions. 'Where on Thames? What business?'

'Wortley-on-Thames. It's near Windsor. And . . .' Hodge leant forward to explain the Member's business, which he communicated in a whisper.

'Oh my God,' James gasped. 'I didn't know that was physically possible.'

It was, but it had, thanks to a newspaper proprietor sympathetic to the cause, so far been kept out of the papers, Hodge explained happily. The MP had agreed to step down and a by-election was to take place the first Thursday in August. Canvassing would be the last weekend in July. 'All right?' he finished, with a satisfied beam.

Shock thundered round James's body. July? Something was happening in July. What was it?

'You're the man, no doubt about it.' Hodge leant forward and patted him on the knee. 'Just our kind of chap.'

'But . . .' said James. Panic had made his mind go blank. July. *July* . . .

'Something wrong?' From behind the bakelite frames, Hodge's gaze was piercing.

'But . . . is it that easy?' James stammered. 'Don't I have to meet the PM?'

'Oh yes,' said Hodge. 'But there's plenty of time for all that.'

James smacked his forehead. He had remembered. Wild & Free! The festival! 'Did you say the last weekend in July for canvassing?' he gabbled at Hodge in relief. 'I'm awfully sorry. I'm busy the last weekend. So I won't be able to fight a by-election.'

He sank back against the sofa's stiff back. Thank God for the festival. He flicked an apprehensive glance at Hodge, expecting him to puff out his chest indignantly and splutter that he'd jolly well better find a way not to be busy then.

Well, he could say that – he could say whatever he liked – but James would not be deterred. He was taking Guy. He had promised him.

Hodge looked quite unperturbed, however. 'I suppose you mean the music festival.' He was smiling.

This quite took the wind out of James's sails. 'You know about it?'

'Mmm. July the twenty-eighth until the thirty-first, am I right?'

'Yes. And I'd promised to take my son so you can see the problem.' James started to rise from the sofa. 'Awfully sorry and all that.'

'No problem,' breezed Hodge. 'And no need to be sorry. Took the precaution of checking your diary with your wife before we had this discussion. No point getting you all excited about it only to discover you were otherwise engaged.'

James stared at him apprehensively. The words 'diary' and 'wife' were an inauspicious combination. Nonetheless, the dates stood. He had nothing to fear.

Hodge had risen too. His small, badly kept teeth were bared in a smile. 'Your wife's very nobly offered to take your son to the festival instead.'

'What?' It came out almost like a shriek. '*Victoria's* going to go to Wild and Free? *Victoria*?'

'Wonderful, isn't it?' Hodge said ruminatively. 'She said she'd do it for the good of the party. We'd never get anywhere without our wives, we politicos. They really are marvellous, the girls.'

CHAPTER 14

Thursday night, 27 July

In the small house in Paradise Street, Isabel was lying awake. The night was still and warm. A moon like a car headlight peeped through the curtains. But this was not the reason why she could not sleep.

Months had passed since Olly's proposal; unusually busy months for both of them. Olly had been obliged to stand in as editor at the local paper, the *Post*, during his boss's brief illness; this had meant late nights and early mornings. Isabel, meanwhile, had had a steep increase in lectures, stepping into the battered Hush Puppies of recently retired David Stringer, a senior department don who had been her own supervisor in her first year at university. He and his wife Dotty, a former violin teacher, planned to spend what time remained to them 'seeking out new experiences'. Isabel was sad to see them go; Dotty, with her trademark auburn frizz, and David, with his trademark beard, had been a reassuring and friendly part of the college landscape ever since she had arrived.

The result of all this activity was that neither had had much time or energy to devote to planning a wedding. Only Diana, Isabel's friend and the college head gardener, was actively on the case, busily inventing schemes to soften Branston's egg-shaped concrete chapel using blooms alone.

In short, the arrangements had not moved forward of late. Was Olly deliberately dragging his feet? Or was it just the distraction of Wild & Free, now finally about to start? He had been fine-tuning his talk for weeks, as well as polishing his questions for H.D. Grantchester, whom he had now persuaded himself he would certainly be interviewing.

'But it's a literary lottery,' Isabel pointed out, in vain. 'You might get someone else.'

Olly obviously had no intention of countenancing this possibility. Fidgety with excitement, he had for weeks been monitoring the website, noting any additions to the line-up of literary, musical, art and media glitterati and lingering over the tabs about H.D. Grantchester and himself. Their lives, Isabel could see, were on hold until the wretched festival was over.

At least there was not long to go now. It started tomorrow and by Monday it would be finished. Normal service could then resume.

Isabel rolled on to her side in the hot bed. She also blamed the website for the fact that Olly had grown a beard. The images on it all gave the impression that no non-bearded male would be attending, and as a result bushy, prickly patches now sprouted all over her fiancé's previously manly, well-defined jawline.

It did not suit him. It made him look completely different. Scruffier, certainly, but also somehow less dependable. His newly long hair didn't suit him either. It was mouse-coloured and looked its best cut short. But now long, lank strands flopped over his eyes and ears. It might work on Brad Pitt – and it didn't work even on him all the time – but on Olly it just looked a mess.

'Oh, come on, Iz. Don't you want me to look like I belong

in the twenty-first century?' Olly had been hurt when she had objected. But Isabel did not believe these sartorial efforts were being made entirely for her sake.

Irrespective of the fact they should be saving for their wedding, Olly had also recently blown hundreds on checked shirts, grandad cardigans, T-shirts with ironic pseudo-intellectual slogans and shapeless jeans. He didn't look like Olly any more, he looked, Isabel thought, like someone from one of those fake-sincere bank ads accompanied by an annoying whistling soundtrack.

She yawned and stared at the slash of moonlight between the curtains. She felt exhausted; the long journey ahead, just a few hours from now, was a gloomy prospect. She would let Olly drive, overbrimming with energy as he was. But perhaps she would make him pin his new long fringe back first so he could see.

Such sourness was uncharacteristic of her, she knew. She hated feeling like this, especially as everyone else was happy. Shanna-Mae and Rosie, who would be driving down in the Beauty Bus, had been beside themselves for days. The plan was to meet at a service station en route to check how the girls were doing. Isabel's guess was that they would be doing a lot better than herself and Olly.

She wished that she was going in the wonderful, ingeniously refurbished Beauty Bus herself, rather than in Olly's small and battered car. It made her feel sick on long journeys and it wasn't as if they would even be alone. Tarquin Squint, proprietor of the Old Laundry Press and Olly's publisher, was coming with them.

Normally, Tarquin would have taken his own car. He had one, but alas not a licence. It had been rescinded after the Metropolitan Police stopped him driving the wrong way down a one-way street in Soho, when Tarquin had been several times over the limit. Nonetheless, Tarquin had seen no reason to be left out. He had never been to a festival before and had decided that this was the moment.

'We'll have to take him,' Olly said to Isabel. 'He started the whole *Smashed Windows* thing, after all.'

Their car was very small and Tarquin was very tall – well over six feet, in fact. He was also somewhat unreconstructed and washed less thoroughly than he might. It was, Isabel yawned, turning over again, going to be an awfully long drive to Somerset.

Meanwhile, in North London

Ginnie Blossom lay on a towel in the spare-room in Jess's flat. While sleeping on a towel was fine on a beach it felt different on a bed. Necessary, though, to protect the duvet.

Jess had insisted the spray tan would make all the difference. 'Come on, Gin! You have to look your best! You might meet the perfect man!'

'I don't want to meet the perfect man,' Ginnie had protested. 'I'm not interested in men any more.'

The thought of Mark Birch still hurt, all the same. They had spent the final couple of weeks of term at opposite ends of the building. He had made a short and intensely awkward speech before the school on her last day, after which Ginnie's class had presented her with flowers and cards and sung a specially composed song, the lyrics of which she had been presented with as well. 'We Luv Yo Mis Bloosom' made her well up whenever she thought about it. Alfie Newwoman had been especially affecting. He had shaken her hand solemnly and even managed a smile; he wished, she knew, to assure her that she was not to worry about him. His enormous bravery had brought her closer to tears than anything else.

Jess had also insisted on Ginnie buying new clothes for the festival. Gone were the unflattering trousers and boxy tops. Ginnie was now channelling 'gap year boho', whatever that was. Floaty and quite bright, on the whole, with wedged cork heels. She had to admit that it was flattering; the pretty dress brightened her up while the heels raised her and made her look thinner. But if, at any stage, she found herself wishing that she had adopted this look earlier so Mark Birch could have seen it, she quickly dismissed the thought. If she'd dated him – not to mention done any of the other things she had once so longed to – she would now not only be sacked, but dumped into the bargain. As it was she had her self-esteem, even if she lacked employment.

She had decided to leave the question of what to do with the rest of her life until after the holidays. The next step would be a big one – selling up and leaving the area, perhaps – and she did not feel, at the moment, sufficiently rational to consider it. Her focus was the festival; for all her initial doubts, she was now almost looking forward to it. Wild & Free would be a distraction, at least. As it would be for Jess; going, too, for reasons other than simple enjoyment. They were both escaping from something; she from the disaster with Mark Birch and her career and Jess from someone who actually had escaped. Although perhaps now he had been recaptured. Jess had said nothing further and Ginnie did not like to ask.

Jess was channelling the Seventies with a cheesecloth top, denim skirt and floppy hat. It sounded terrible in theory but looked sensational in practice – but then Jess would have looked good in the proverbial plastic bag.

She was driving them down tomorrow in her high-end

bachelor girl Mercedes convertible. Their yurt, rented from a company wittily titled Poles Apart, would be ready when they arrived. Ginnie's mind drifted once again, despite her efforts to stop it, to her erstwhile employer and what he would make of it. It was hardwired, this habit of endlessly thinking of him, more difficult to stop than she had thought.

Oh Mark! Mark! Ginnie thought, sleepless on a towel in Islington. How could he have behaved like that? She had adored him. She had been such a fool! But at least, now, she was a hundred and fifty miles away. There was no immediate risk of seeing him. With any luck, she never would again.

Mark was, in fact, a mere few miles away in a Paddington hotel. He and Rob, both coming from the provinces, had booked themselves into a cheap hotel near the station. They were meeting Spencer at Paddington in the morning and taking the train to Taunton, where a representative of the Vintage VW Split Screen Camper Van Company would be waiting for them. Spencer had insisted on hiring a camper van in the face of all objections: Mark's because it was such a festival cliché and Rob's on grounds of cost. But, as usual, Spencer had prevailed.

Over pints of lager in the hotel's crepuscular bar, Mark and Rob were catching up on three decades' worth of news.

Rob seemed to Mark hardly to have changed at all. He had the same bushy brown hair as thirty years ago, albeit now with sprinklings of grey. The same gangling frame, prominent Adam's apple and the same nearly-single eyebrow. Even his clothes looked the same: tight black jeans and a Nehru-collared grey shirt fastened with a diagonal zip up one side.

'They *are* the same,' Rob assured Mark when he said this. 'I never throw anything away. Hate to waste money.' He stretched out a long, thin leg. 'Vintage C&A, these.'

Mark looked at them. Claire had been a big vintage fan. He had gathered from her that it meant posh second-hand; labels like Chanel and Dior. He hadn't realised C&A came into that category.

'I've got most of my student wardrobe still,' Rob added proudly as he swilled his pint. 'Perfect for reunion gigs.' He was obviously looking forward to it.

Mark finished his drink and stared into the empty glass. He wondered how to tell Rob that, now the moment was almost upon them, the reunion gig mere days away, he was dreading it like he had dreaded few other things in his whole life. What on earth had possessed him to agree?

Then Ginnie Blossom's eyes, at that ghastly last interview, came into his mind and he remembered.

He listened as Rob pondered on the prospective playlist. He did not recognise a single song title.

'You haven't listened to *any* of the old stuff?' Beneath his monobrow, Rob looked disbelieving.

Mark did not want to admit that one reason – although by no means the only one – was because the old stuff remained, in cassette form, at the bottom of a box in some cupboard in Claire's London flat. The flat he had walked out of, never to return. Least of all to return to pick up a tape of the Mascara Snakes.

He had been rattled, too, by Victoria Dorchester-Williams' savage repulsion. The woman had been hysterical at the mere mention of his name. It hurt to think that, as Victoria had assured him, Jimmy shared her views. He had never even got close to mentioning the festival, but it was obvious what the response would have been.

Spencer had been characteristically breezy about Jimmy, saying they could get round his absence with 'clever guitar work'. But this seemed unlikely to Mark. They'd never had any clever guitar work in the first place.

Rob was reminiscing about student gigs.

'That one in Newark, where there was just one guy and he was there by mistake anyway. Then the one near Peterborough – can't remember the name of the place – where they were still booing the last act when we came on . . .'

'Tell me about your family,' Mark said, abruptly changing the subject.

Rob struggled in his C&A trousers for his smartphone and was soon showing Mark pictures of his nearest and dearest. There was a plump, sleek wife and a pair of blank-faced daughters, followed by a large new stone house amid rolling, close-cropped lawns.

'Mandy's dad built it for us as a wedding present,' Rob told him. 'You married?' he added. 'Claire, wasn't it? You met at the BBC.'

'Sort of didn't work out,' Mark said hastily. 'The BBC didn't, either. I retrained. Became a headmaster, of all things.'

He plunged into what was meant to be a light-hearted description of St Stephen's Primary. And whilst he tried not to mention Ginnie more than anyone else he found himself wondering longingly how she was and what she was doing. Not going to Wild & Free, that was for sure.

He finished and noticed that Rob was regarding him meaningfully. 'Sure you don't fancy her?' he remarked mildly.

'Who?'

'That Miss Blossom?'

'*Course* not.' He had over-emphasised, Mark realised. Beneath his monobrow, Rob was looking sceptical.

'Not pretty?'

'*Very* pretty, actually.'

138

'Married?'

'No.' He said this more forcefully than he meant to. Rob now looked amused.

'Boyfriend?'

'Probably. I don't know.'

'I bet you do.'

'I bloody don't. Look, Rob—'

'You do fancy her!' Rob crowed. 'You're getting all indignant!'

'No, I'm bloody well not.'

'How old?'

'Mid-twenties.'

'What's wrong with that? You're hardly Methuselah.'

'And it wouldn't be very, well, professional.'

Rob surveyed him. 'Why not?'

'Because, well, I'm the head teacher and she's, well, an infants teacher and . . .' Mark took a deep and steadying breath. 'Look, Rob. In the unlikely event that she was ever interested in me, I've just had to make her redundant, OK? She's hardly my biggest fan. To be honest, I think she hates me.'

'Oh,' said Rob, surprised.

'Yes. *Oh*. Look,' Mark was standing up, 'I'm off to the bar again. Another pint?'

Technically, it was Rob's turn, but Mark had noticed that technicalities like this seemed to pass Rob by. He had always been the tight-fisted one.

Mark went to bed soon after that. The window would not open. He lay on top of the bed, breathing in the stuffy air. He realised he was more accustomed to the country than he had imagined. When he had lived in the city he had rarely slept with the window open. Now he wanted to knock a hole through the wall.

Drowsy as he was, his mind raced indignantly. Damn Rob

and all those questions about Ginnie Blossom. Damn Sheila Wrench and Leonard Purkiss. Damn himself, most of all.

He waved the chunky black remote control at the TV mounted in the corner. It was huge, heavy and old-fashioned and would certainly kill anyone whose head it happened to fall on. If it fell on him during the night, Mark found himself thinking, it would save him a lot of trouble.

The news was on, and Mark was startled to see a familiar face flash on to the screen along with JAMES DORCHESTER-WILLIAMS, WORTLEY-ON-THAMES BY-ELECTION on the rolling-news red ribbon beneath.

All sleepiness suddenly gone, Mark sat bolt upright against the headboard, eyes fixed on the screen. No wonder Victoria had cut him off at the pass when he had called about the festival. Jimmy clearly had completely different plans for the summer.

His old friend looked remarkably well for one who had been married to Victoria for nigh-on twenty years. He had always been good-looking in a tall, fair, open-faced sort of way but had acquired the additional burnish of prosperity since: his still-abundant hair, while grey, was well cut; his tie and shirt positively screamed Jermyn Street and his skin had a cared-for glow. Jimmy, in short, was a fully-fledged silver fox. Well, good luck to him in Parliament, Mark thought. He looked the part, and as if he knew what he was doing. They'd miss him at Wild & Free, but Jimmy was obviously on another track altogether these days.

CHAPTER 15

Friday, 28 July

As the early morning sky turned rose-pink over Willesden, a door opened in the centre of a tired Victorian terrace. Three men nipped swiftly down the stairs, one slender, one short and thickset and the last strikingly tall, catching the dustbin with his enormous booted feet. The ensuing metallic racket prompted the willowy figure leading the way to turn round and gesture frantically for quiet. 'Fuck off,' responded the bin-kicker.

'LangWIDGE!' growled his thickset companion.

Jude, striding to the rented people carrier, tried to control his fury. Boz was so bloody ungrateful. Had not Jude sheltered him and George in his flat for several weeks now? And it had been hell, frankly. Worse than hell.

He knew from HMP Folgate that George was frightening and Boz was terrifying. But at least there Jude had been in a separate cell and not forced into their constant society. Being cooped up with the two of them had not only brought terrible memories of imprisonment back, but posed Jude practical problems such as how and when to feed Boz and Big George without anyone else in the house seeing.

Thanks to nightly bulletins on the television news, the entire nation knew that his guests were wanted men. But the faces in the police mugshots, coldly hostile though they were, were a good deal less frightening than their living counterparts, Jude felt.

For their part, Boz and George were indignant about the TV coverage.

'They're calling me an escaped murderer,' George complained. Jude looked at him. 'Well you are, aren't you?'

'It was an accident,' George protested. 'Someone got in the way of my gun.'

Had the upstairs neighbour kept regular hours, the kitchen and bathroom needs of his impromptu guests would have been relatively simple for Jude to meet. They could have bathed and eaten at night even if Jude had to prop his eyes open with matchsticks as he cooked for them. But the organist was a fitful insomniac whose routines corresponded to nothing that could be remotely described as normal. Day or night, meals, baths and trips to the loo had to be grabbed guerrilla fashion.

Nor was this Jude's only challenge. He had been hoping to conceal his visitors until the time came to leave for the festival, but George's habit of singing loudly along to any hymns the organist played – the first Jude had heard about his staunch Methodist upbringing – constantly compromised and threatened his plans.

While Boz admittedly did not roar along to 'The Old Rugged Cross', he was in other ways the more difficult of the two. Being, once again, effectively imprisoned did not improve his already violent temper and it was to help contain his constantly simmering rage that Jude had set up a punch bag.

But after Boz split the entire thing at the first blow, this had had to be abandoned, Jude more disturbed than he cared to show about the raw brute force displayed. Being at close quarters with a partially exploded human bomb meant that being murdered in his sleep seemed a nightly possibility.

Apart from being a psychopathic thug, Boz stank like a polecat, a condition that could not be alleviated even by opening a window as the curtains had to remain drawn at all times. Jude was taking no chances.

Fortunately George's nose – either from cocaine or fights or maybe both – had long since lost any olfactory faculty. He was unable to smell Boz and had therefore shared Jude's mattress with him. Jude, meanwhile, had had to huddle on the floor on piles of unwashed clothes.

It had been difficult, in this state of smelly, crepuscular, sleepless and psychologically torturous incarceration, to plan a jewel heist. Especially as the festival setting lacked any of the familiar signposts such as luxury hotel foyers, jewels in glass display cases and fast getaways on motorbikes. Adding to his difficulties, neither George nor Boz were keen on the festival idea; unsurprisingly, neither had been to one.

'There's a lot of potential there,' Jude argued, showing them the Wild & Free website on his tablet. George and Boz had wrested it from him and stabbed through the various tabs. He had watched their faces darken as they read – slowly, and with moving lips – about the various whimsical attractions on offer.

'What the bleedin' 'ell are Eton Mess cocktails?' George demanded in puzzled disgust.

'Revolting Peasants – ex-Royal College musicians playing the theme from *Star Wars* on authentic early instruments,' spelt out Boz, after a great deal of difficulty.

The fact that a disco for dogs had also just been added to the line-up did not, Jude felt, make his task easier.

Actually, Jude thought afterwards, if there had been a Dunkirk moment in his campaign, the disco for dogs was it. He had been on the point of throwing in the Wild & Free towel, of abandoning the whole enterprise, walking away and shopping Boz and George to the police. Only the thought of the Ferrari stopped him; along with the consideration that as he had taken the escaped criminals in, he would be as accountable to the law as they were.

He had painted himself into a corner; he had no choice. Because he had wasted both time and money in the fruitless exercise of trying to put a gang together, and then taken in a pair of criminals, Wild & Free was now his only hope.

So Jude had gritted his teeth and shown the others the picture of Daria Badunova in her diamond parure and tiny shorts. Minds – or what passed for them in George and Boz's case – had soon been concentrated after that.

'Very well cut,' growled George, approvingly.

'Magnificent stones,' Jude agreed, relieved that some aspect of the venture had passed muster.

George stared at him with his small, cold, devil-dog eyes. 'I'm talking about the shorts.'

Jude suppressed a sigh and once again his faith in the enterprise wavered. So much about it was uncertain. What if Daria Badunova decided not to come; oligarchs, Jude had gathered from the social pages, were capricious creatures. And was it really possible for Big George and Boz to be at Wild & Free without being recognised? Now they were being advertised nightly on the news?

Hastily, Jude pulled himself together. While he could do nothing to influence Daria, he could take action over Boz and George. He forced himself to think tactically. It seemed to him that a disguise was necessary. Better still, Boz and Big George should have a role. Be an act, even. Wild & Free was a festival, acts were its lifeblood and purpose. Some of those on the website had looked very strange indeed. Boz and George would fit right in. They had dressed up before after all, in the famous Handbags and Gladrags raid on Monaco. They could do drag, no problem.

Jude felt, for all the onerous circumstances, almost excited. This was the answer! If Boz and George had a routine worked out and were able to perform it, even if they walked around in women's clothes in between times, no one would ever suspect them of being escaped criminals. In the context of eccentrically-garbed festival-goers, a pair of enormous armed robbers in drag amounted to camouflage and would not merit a second glance. It was genius, just like the Monaco raid, which had worked for the exact same reason.

The judge at the trial had expressed amazement that anyone, let alone the security guard of a top Riviera jeweller, would let in someone so risible-looking as Boz 'disguised' in huge stilettos, his hairy, bandy legs in a tight skirt. But as Jude had remarked, to much mirth in the courtroom, the location had made it possible. People in Monaco routinely looked so strange there was nothing remotely unusual about Boz's appearance. The judge had not been amused, unfortunately.

'Brilliant, no?' Jude now beamed at Boz and Big George after laying the plan before them. He was indefatigable in his urge to motivate. Someone had to, and that someone obviously would not be George. Still less Boz, whose idea of motivating someone was to put his enormous, hairy hands round their neck and press down hard on their thorax.

His enthusiasm was uncontagious. While Boz had smouldered dangerously, George bitterly complained. 'We'll be a bloody laughing stock if this gets out.'

'Precisely,' Jude put in smoothly, as another brilliant idea struck him. 'You should do something funny. A funny act.'

He had the bit between his teeth now, and the courage of his convictions. Eventually they agreed; as George observed to Boz, their options were pretty limited. Boz had cast a glance of cold fury at Jude, implying that there was always the option of annihilation. Thus it was that the Rogues and Vagabonds Theatre Company was born.

'Bit of a giveaway, that name, innit?' Big George had growled. But Jude pointed out that it was the perfect double bluff, very festival, and would only increase their inconspicuousness.

Jude did the research and soon established that the best opportunity for amateur comic acts was in the Family Area, the Hibbertygibberty Wood. They had something called a Story Jam, where all comers were welcome to compete with each other for the Hibbertygibberty Cup.

The potential this offered was considerable, especially after Jude discovered, on consulting the festival map, that the Hibbertygibberty Wood was practically next door to the yurt, tepee and Winnebago VIP area. The area of Wild & Free, in other words, with the highest potential volume of valuable jewellery per square inch. And – always supposing she turned up – where Daria Badunova and her chestful of sparklers was almost certain to be.

All that was needed now was something to perform. Jude set himself to compose a children's entertainment and, rather to his surprise, completed it in one afternoon. It reflected the conditions and especially the odour in which he had recently been living. It was called *The Storyteller's Stinky Underpants* and was to be narrated by Boz, reading very slowly from a very large-print script with no words over two syllables. George was to sing and supply fart noises by pumping his arm over his hand.

Rehearsals, timed to coincide with the organist going hammer and tongs on the floor above, had proved a welcome opportunity to release tension. They had even managed an *esprit de corps* sufficient to produce a piece of scenery between them, a giant cardboard cut-out of a toilet, viewed from the side. Jude, on the few quick trips out he dared risk – always tightly timed as the possibility that George and Boz would kill each other or otherwise reveal themselves was always high – had put together the costumes, scouring the local charity shops. It had taken much patient rummaging to turn up dresses and shoes of an appropriately enormous size, as well as hats and, crucially, gloves. There were more copies of his, George and Boz's fingerprints in circulation than was either comfortable or convenient.

Now, as he hurried the Rogues and Vagabonds Theatre Company, plus tents, into the Mojo people carrier he had hired for the festival's duration, Jude breathed a mighty sigh of relief. The stars, finally, seemed aligned in his favour. It was all coming together. At last.

CHAPTER 16

Paddington Station

It was 7.50 a.m. and Spencer had not shown up. Mark and Rob waited on the platform with their rucksacks and guitars – two guitars in Rob's case, acoustic as well as bass. He was, Mark thought, self-identifying with the band revival to an alarming degree.

Meanwhile, the train to Taunton prepared to depart without them.

'I don't bloody believe it,' Mark fumed. Propelling his annoyance was panic. He didn't want to go to the festival but he wanted even less to return to Chestlock and run into Ginnie Blossom.

He remembered James and his election campaign on the TV last night and reflected that he had had a lucky escape. He had told Rob about it over breakfast. Rob had raised a monobrow and expressed his intention to lobby his old bandmate over lowering the tax thresholds.

Now, at five minutes to blast-off, Spencer rolled into view. 'Hi guys.'

Mark stared, as arrested by Spencer's appearance as by his nonchalant lateness. His outfit was a strange combination of totalitarian politics and Seventies children's TV. A white shirt printed with small red hammers and sickles flapped open over a vintage T-shirt featuring Peter Purves. To complement this Spencer wore tight-legged mustard jeans and a pair of Converses whose laces were a different colour on each foot. On the back of his head was a straw pork-pie hat.

'Love the look,' Mark said ironically.

'Likewise,' riposted Spencer. A dig, Mark knew, at his clumpy hair, department-store jeans and trainers with no style subtext whatsoever. He didn't care. At least, unlike Spencer's get-up, it was age-appropriate. Spencer's hat was just embarrassing.

Once upon a time, even so, he had dressed similarly himself. Claire, who was very fashion-minded, had presented him with a steady stream of modish leisurewear. He too had worn pod-shaped shoes and classic duffel coats with a twist. He too had observed Movember.

But he had left the bulk of his old wardrobe behind when he left, and you couldn't buy clothes like that where he lived now. The nearest fashion outlet to Hangman's Cottage was the local branch of Sainsbury's. You occasionally saw trendy types in the town, but the only locals habitually dressed in the head-to-foot retro that would have earned applause in Shoreditch were pensioners whose fashion references were unintentional.

On the train Spencer unzipped his bag. His wrists were decorated with neon rubber wristbands and plaited leather bracelets which, Mark noticed, contrasted with the obvious vast expense of a watch the size of a dinner plate with the complexity of an aeroplane flight deck. Rich funky dude, seemed to be the message.

'Guys. Present for you,' Spencer said, tossing over the table some slithering cellophane-wrapped packets to Rob and Mark.

'Got a couple of the guys in the promos department to do 'em,' he beamed.

Mark stared at his T-shirt. It was large and white. Printed in black capitals all over the front were the words: 'The Guys. The Group. The Live Reunion Gig. Wild & Free Festival 2014.'

'We're a band,' Spencer was telling the man sitting next to them, turning the garment round to reveal the Mascara Snakes logo which, Mark remembered, they had designed in five minutes on the back of a beer mat one night in the college bar.

Their neighbour looked unimpressed. 'Never heard of you,' he said rudely.

'You will,' Spencer said smoothly. 'We're headlining at Wild and Free. You know, the festival?'

Mark wanted to sink through the bottom of the carriage to the clinkered track below.

They arrived at Taunton to find no sign of the expected representative from the Vintage VW Van Company on the platform. Finally, after a couple of phone calls from Spencer, a white Rasta with lime-green dreadlocks and a jaunty walk materialised. 'So, I'm Piers, guys. And you're the guys from the Wholesale Homestore corporate away day, yeah?'

Mark stared, offended. Was that what they looked like?

Fortunately, Spencer chose to see the funny side. He was waving his guitar around in its case. 'Nah, mate. We're in a band,' he told Piers, gesturing to his personalised T-shirt.

Piers yawned. 'Sure, we get a lot of guys in bands hiring our vans.'

He lurched off in the direction of the car park. They were evidently meant to follow.

'It's called Miss Scarlett,' the Rasta revealed after they had dutifully admired their allotted van's shining red exterior. 'Like, in Cluedo? That game for oldies?'

Spencer was too busy exclaiming to hear the last bit. 'You don't say, mate!' he exploded. 'I used to play Cluedo when I was a kid. Colonel Mustard, in the library, with the lead piping and all that.' He chuckled reminiscently.

Mark stuck his head round the door of Miss Scarlett. Arranged on the bed at the back was a row of cushions printed with iconic album covers. *Let It Bleed* was there, as was *Never Mind the Bollocks* and the Velvet Underground's *Andy Warhol*. On the cutting edge of rock one minute, Mark thought, and a middle-youth lifestyle accessory the next. *Sic transit gloria mundi*.

He felt a nudge in his back and heard Spencer saying, 'Mate! Mate!' in an urgent tone of voice. Piers was looking at him in a way that seemed significant.

'Mate, you won't believe it,' Spencer was saying, his persuasive teeth flashing in the sun. 'But I still can't find my credit card.'

Piers confirmed this with a steely smile. 'Perhaps you could step into the breach, mate.'

Rob was nowhere to be seen. 'Gone to the bog, mate,' Spencer said, smilingly guessing his thoughts.

Eventually, they were on their way, Bowie on the Shuffle.

Spencer was singing along the loudest, hands spread wide on the VW's large steering wheel, the open road before him. From time to time he looked round at the others and beamed. 'Guys, isn't this *great*?'

Bristol

A mass of glittering car bonnets stood unmoving under a blazing sun on the Bristol Channel flyover. Halfway across, at the point the arch was at its highest, Lorna Newwoman sat gazing furiously out from the passenger seat of an ancient camper van. After driving from Chestlock for six hours solid she'd hoped to be nearer to Wild & Free than this.

She turned to glare at the driver. Tenebris had obviously gone the wrong way. He might know all about self-promoting self-publishing on the internet, but he clearly hadn't the first idea about how to get to Somerset.

Lorna was beginning to wonder if Tenebris was the man for her after all.

He had seemed full of potential on the 'Self-Promote Your Self-Publishing' course she had taken at the Chestlock library. They had gone for coffees, which had graduated to drinks. Over a pint of Old Belter in Chestlock's only wine bar Lorna had discovered that Tenebris, too, was a divorcee. His ex-wife worked for a charity and as she was away in Africa all summer saving the children it was up to Tenebris to save their own children and give them something to do. When Lorna – clocking the fact that Tenebris had a camper van – had suggested the Hasps come to Wild & Free with herself and Alfie he had bitten her hand off.

Lorna had been equally keen. She had always been drawn to skinny, submissive men with wispy hair. And this one, with his technical expertise, could help her conquer the world of children's books.

Or so she had thought. But it now turned out he couldn't even get her to Somerset. Especially not in this horrible van which lacked not only a satnav, but every other innovation of the last four decades. Rusty, brown, dented and sun-faded, its design was boxily 1970s, and what remained of its shattered bumpers was angular black plastic. All that could be said for it was that it moved – for the moment, anyway.

Tenebris, for his part, was looking miserably down the bridge-sides at the baking mudflats where the water would be if the tide was in. The actual Bristol Channel was far away, a glittering line on the horizon. Its name stirred something in his memory. A poem, something his mother used to read to him. Something in the poem had lost something here, in the Bristol Channel. Then, in a sudden rush, it came back, and Tenebris slapped the steering wheel in excitement. 'The Pobble Who Has No Toes!'

'What?' Lorna asked, irritated. It wasn't just Tenebris; she was pre-irritated with Buster and Django, his two small sons. Just now she had been engaged in the literally thankless task of reading to them as they lounged with ill grace on the split and battered banquette seat behind. Lorna's initial encouraging tone had soon slipped its moorings and was now careering around like a tent in a gale at the high and hysterical end of the vocal register.

Tenebris knew the feeling. Django and Buster never listened to him, either. They never listened to anyone apart from their own inner voices urging them to wilful, violent and destructive acts in flagrant disobedience of parental instructions.

'The Pobble Who Has No Toes,' Tenebris repeated.

'What's that?' Lorna snapped, giving vent to some of her frustrated fury.

'A poem. By Edward Lear.' Tenebris looked at her in surprise. She was a children's author, wasn't she? 'Have you really not heard of it? My mother used to read it to me.'

He realised immediately he had said something wrong. While Lorna was obviously hot – they all were; the van pre-dated air conditioning – her expression was distinctly frosty.

'Imperial-colonial-racist-and-sexist Victorian claptrap,' Lorna fumed. Through metal-rimmed glasses a pair of cold green eyeballs bored into Tenebris.

He suppressed a sigh. He had initially thought Lorna an admirable person. In stark contrast to almost everyone else who signed up for his local-authority-sponsored desktop-publishing classes, she had been interested, hard-working and motivated. Most of his so-called students were the local unemployed who, lacking online access at home, tended to use his course as a cover for going on Facebook, eBay or the Argos website, or exchanging e-mails with unsuitable-looking men who were no doubt grooming them for sex. But Lorna had given him a purpose, and while her books weren't quite his thing he had been flattered to feel that he could help her. He also had a history of finding assertive women attractive.

But this elitism thing bothered him. Tenebris wasn't sure that, as Lorna claimed, there were no socially inclusive stories for children any more. And if there weren't, did it matter? Did children worry about that sort of thing? His own, certainly, were unbelievably selfish and lazy and had no sense of responsibility of any sort. Lorna's son Alfie – Tenebris now turned his head to see the ginger head on the back row staring hopelessly out of the window – was not quite as aggressive, admittedly. But his habitually catatonic state did not suggest great altruism either. It was difficult to say what it did suggest, apart from fear of his mother. Which Tenebris could fully identify with.

He was relieved when, after a few more seconds of glaring, Lorna took up where she had left off, midway through *The King Who Couldn't Wee*. On whose royally inhibited behalf he had created a website, a Twitter account and a hashtag. Much to Lorna's indignation, however, it was not trending yet. Nor, to her still greater frustration, had the Wild & Free website picked it up and promoted it on its own pages as they had some of the other attractions such as the appearance of H.D. Grantchester.

'But she's won the Tesco Book Prize three times,' Tenebris had pointed out, immediately wishing he hadn't as Lorna proceeded to denounce the *Nasty, Brutish and Short* trilogy as elitist on the grounds that anyone lacking a thorough grasp of English mediaeval history wouldn't know what it was on about. And while Tenebris accepted the last part of her argument, what troubled him was the accompanying implication that knowing anything about anything was elitist. The logical conclusion of this was that everyone should exist on the same *tabula rasa* of ignorance.

When he attempted, admittedly hesitatingly, to point this out to Lorna, she just slapped him down. 'You can't stand things being accessible, that's all,' she accused. adding for good measure that he was an old fart.

'Fart! Fart!' his sons gleefully chimed in.

There was also the fact that Lorna, for all her egalitarianism, had been distinctly princessy about his beloved Westfalia camper van.

All in all, Tenebris was now regretting the moment of beer-fuelled madness mixed with paternal desperation in which he had spotted a way to cope with his sons that summer. It had been the work of a second to offer the Westfalia and suggest the Hasps accompany the Newwomans – or was that Newwomen? – to the Wild & Free festival where, Tenebris understood, Lorna planned to take something called the Story Jam by storm.

He also understood now – too late, alas – that, for Lorna, the festival wasn't mere recreation with a spot of book promotion on the side. The promotion was the be-all and end-all. The facile nature of *The King Who Couldn't Wee* – something surely no one could take seriously – had blinded Tenebris to its author's terrifying determination.

Now he realised that Lorna was set on launching herself as a children's author, and for her Wild & Free was the first crampon in the cliff face from which she would haul herself upward to the very summit of the storytelling world. That was insane enough. Even worse was the knowledge that he had been whipped in to give her lift-off.

Sweating away behind the Westfalia's wheel, Tenebris tried to look on the bright side. He had once – centuries ago, it now seemed – lived in South London, where festivals like Wild & Free were established summer favourites among urban hipsters. From the website he knew it to be cool, arty and rocky, a bookfest combined with music and very family-friendly. The boys, at least, should have a good time.

'It's moving!' Lorna said sharply, breaking off from *The King Who Couldn't Wee*. At least, Tenebris hoped she was.

Meanwhile, further back on the M4

The traffic was slowing; there was clearly some obstruction ahead. Jude, revving impatiently at the wheel of the hired Mojo, stared out in despair.

Behind him, safely concealed behind the people carrier's tinted windows, Boz and Big George were getting restive. Jude could feel Boz's growing, violent frustration; smell it, too. Thanks to the confined space and the heat the odour was near-unbearable. Not for the first time he found himself wondering if some of Boz's antecedents might have been skunks. It seemed unlikely at any rate that he came from an unbroken line of humans.

The air-con had long since given up; the Mojo, Jude was finding, was less reliable than he had hoped. He closed his eyes briefly and forced himself, yet again, to picture that far superior car, the vehicle of his dreams and his ultimate reward, Rich's Ferrari.

The magical car had a magical effect. The car in front began to roll forward, but just then the Mojo's engine stalled. Jude turned the key urgently. Nothing.

He wrenched the key round, hard. Still no answer from the engine. He tried again. Still nothing. Again, he tried, and again. The sweat beading his brow had nothing to do with the blazing temperature. 'Oh fuck,' said Jude.

'LangWIDGE!' admonished George immediately.

'Whazzup?' spat Boz.

'I think the engine's overheated,' Jude said nervously as the vehicles around them began to hoot.

Boz exploded into a stream of obscenities, while George, turning a blind ear to them for once, turned his huge bear's head to Jude and glared. 'Well, you'd better bleedin' well unheat it then.'

'We'll have to phone the AA,' Jude started to say before remembering that he was not a member and furthermore his passengers were fugitives from the law. Sweat trickled down his forehead as the cars, vans and lorries started to flow past them. Some hooted. Boz, in reply, smashed a vast fist against the rear window.

'Steady,' warned Big George, sounding nervous himself now. He glared at Jude. 'So come on, Einstein,' he growled. 'What do we do now?'

'I'm not sure,' faltered Jude. His mind had gone blank. Like the car, he felt unable to function.

He looked bleakly out of the window. The traffic had eased

now and carful after carful of fortunate-looking people glided past. Laughing families, en route to seaside holidays. Smiling van drivers with tanned arms resting on the rolled-down window. Jude watched miserably as a VW camper van came up behind him. It was beautiful, reconditioned vintage. Its glass headlights shone appealingly, its split screen glittered, its burnished chrome bumpers glowed and the angles of its lovingly polished claret-red body were all rounded and friendly. 'Miss Scarlet', it said in Forties lettering above the round VW logo on the front. The three men in it, all cool and relaxed-looking, seemed to be singing.

Jude felt a wave of violent envy. It was all he could do not to open his own driver door, flag them down and beg them to take him with them.

A painful nudge interrupted his train of thought. He met Big George's mean little eye, in which the light was fading. George's expression had become cold; on his monumental brow, the creases had deepened. His huge face was so close to Jude's the latter could smell his meaty breath. 'I asked,' George growled, 'what we do now.'

Jude swallowed. 'I'll think of something.'

A gust of meaty breath again. 'Make sure you do, eh?' Something brightly metallic flashed and Jude felt a sharp edge pressed against his cheekbone. 'Or you won't look so pretty when I've done with you.'

Now came more bright flashes, but in his driving mirror this time. Someone close to his rear bumper was honking their horn. As they swept past making obscene hand gestures, Jude saw that his aggressors were a couple in their eighties.

His humiliation was complete. Jewel robbery was not meant to be like this. It never had been in the high days of the past, the Handbags and Gladrags raid, for instance.

Of course!

The answer hit him like an avalanche. He remembered the women's clothes in the back. Boz and George just needed to put them on, that was all. Just a little bit earlier than planned. Then they would be safe and he could call the AA. A breakdown service man, occupied with the vehicle, was unlikely to question the fact they were a drag act bound for a festival. Jude's confidence rushed back.

He turned, smiling brightly, to George, whose face remained set and hostile. Jude did not feel brave enough yet to look at Boz.

'OK,' he said. 'Here's what we do . . .'

CHAPTER 17

Wortley-on-Thames, near Windsor

James was standing, as instructed, by the statue in the town centre of Wortley-on-Thames waiting to meet his Party handler. It was the first day of by-election campaigning. As he loitered self-consciously he studied the statue, a modern affair in dull grey metal which stood in a beige-coloured circle of plasticky fake gravel, on a circular plinth of ersatz small red bricks. Whilst recognisably a human figure, it was carefully unspecific. It looked vaguely industrial, he thought. But what industry it practised was anyone's guess.

He felt nervous, although he knew he was well prepared. The party advisers had drilled him on every detail, especially language. Always use two words where one would do. Denials were never just denials, they were categorical denials. Clarifications were always absolutely clear, not just clear. Was that absolutely clear?

Nor, James discovered, did he ever want to prove something. He desperately wanted to prove something. As well as bearing all this in mind he must appear spontaneous and unscripted while never putting a foot – or word – wrong.

'How can people do it?' James had gasped to his constituency agent, a somewhat curt blonde called Rebecca de Sendyng who went shooting at weekends and whose father, Conn, was an old friend of the party leader.

James wasn't entirely sure Rebecca was on side. His side, that was; her political affiliations were abundantly clear. Her ankle bore a small but discreet tattoo of the Party logo. But she seemed to rather look down her nose at him.

'They can't do it,' Rebecca sniffed. 'That's why you're here.'

'I'm not sure I can do it either, though.'

If he was hoping for reassurance, he had been disappointed.

James shifted from foot to foot and wondered miserably what Guy and Victoria were doing now. How he wished he was going to the festival instead of his wife!

Last night, he had gone up to say goodbye to Guy. They might not be going to Wild & Free together any more, but James felt even closer to his son these days. After all, they were both under pressure. He had to get a seat in Parliament – at the absolute least – and Guy had to get enough stars in the A-level A grade firmament to meet the conditional offer at Branston. Guy claimed the exams had gone well, but there was a narrowing at the corners of his eyes when he said this, and a strained note in his voice, that made James somehow doubt it.

Guy was hunched, as usual, in front of his laptop. At James's salutation he turned round, the movement revealing the screen in its entirety.

'You're on Facebook,' James said. 'I thought you couldn't connect to it.'

Guy's handsome face assumed a cagey expression. 'Er,' he said.

James sympathised with his son. He wouldn't want to let

Victoria in to his social media circles either. While her surveillance no doubt sprang from the best intentions, surveillance it
remained.

'Looking forward to the festival?' he asked.

Guy rolled his eyes. 'As much as I can with Mum going.
Wish you were coming instead.'

'Me too. But high office calls.' James was trying to sound
wry; he was not quite succeeding. 'I'm sure,' he added, 'that
your mother will relax once she gets there.'

Guy's expression was incredulous. 'You reckon?'

James changed the subject. 'Well – I'll be gone before you
get up. So – have a good time. Go forth and rock.'

Guy snorted. 'That's funny. Is that from Spinal Tap?'

'It's what my band used to say to each other before gigs.
Then we'd do this.' James demonstrated an ironic fist-pump.

Guy was eyeing him uncertainly. James knew that his son
didn't entirely believe him about the Mascara Snakes. It wasn't
that Guy thought he was lying, more that it was some sort of
fantasising senior moment.

James had scoured the house to find evidence of his band. A
tape, a battered photocopied poster, a single drumstick even.
The Mascara Snakes predated the internet, so nothing had made
it on there, but surely there was something?

Unfortunately he had been unable to find anything to show
the Mascara Snakes had ever existed. And he had wanted to,
badly. Even if Guy laughed – which he very probably would –
he would at least realise that his father hadn't always been a
breadhead in a suit. That he had been young once. Interesting,
even.

James had started to wonder himself if he had imagined
it all. But once he had thought to ask Victoria, the mystery
was solved.

Of course, she told him briskly, there weren't any pictures. They had been obvious hostages to fortune. On the advice of his own Whips' office she had, in his own interests, destroyed anything that was potentially embarrassing or that could be used against him as a candidate.

His rock and roll past, James found, had been airbrushed out like a disgraced member of Stalin's Presidium. Thinking about it now he felt angry all over again.

'Gosh, you look cross!'

A woman had bowled up to him.

'Oh,' said James, surprised and abashed and suddenly not wanting to look cross at all in front of this woman, who had spinning curls of brown hair, wide and distracted eyes and a broad mouth quivering with amusement.

'Just what is that, anyway?' She was looking at the statue now.

'Search me.'

They studied the statue together. After careful consideration James said he thought it was a man in an old-fashioned worker's cap striding jauntily along, his coat flying out behind him.

'Awful, though, isn't it?' the woman said. 'A meaningless, meanly rendered piece of municipal modernism standing in a cheaply built shopping centre, ignored by all. People deserve better. Don't you think?'

James felt dazzled both by this display of eloquence and by the sudden beam she then turned on him. 'Ignore me,' she added. 'I used to study art history, a million years ago. Are you my polling agent, by the way?'

He realised instantly she was the candidate for the other main party. 'Hardly, I'm the opposition,' he said, unsure whether to make a joke of it or be embarrassed. Just what was the form here?

She had no doubt at any rate. She guffawed; a deep, warm, throaty chuckle. 'I'm Nadia Ramage. How-do-you-do.' She stuck out a strong, warm hand.

James stared at her. She was unimaginably different from the 'harridan with the droopy trouser crotch' the party pointyheads had warned him of. The thought of this woman's crotch made his face start to warm.

'Oh God! What a way to meet you!' Nadia was still laughing and it made him want to laugh as well. 'James, isn't it?'

'James Dorchester-Williams.' It sounded incredibly pompous. Perhaps she thought so too because this just set her off again.

She was wiping streaming eyes. Her mascara was streaked now but somehow it didn't detract from her appearance at all. There was something terribly attractive about her and her spontaneous, windblown look. As Nadia peeled a length of wavy brown hair out of her eyes and grinned at him, he found himself staring back, bewitched. Never, since he had met Victoria, had he as much as thought about another woman. But now he felt as if the very tips of his ears were on fire.

It was absolutely the last thing he had expected to happen to him in Wortley-on-Thames.

'That's just hilarious,' Nadia was shaking her head. 'You're up against me. As it were.'

James continued to stare at his highly polished shoes. His gaze strayed the few inches to Nadia's toe tips: a pair of scuffed and battered boots.

'Your first time, is it?' Nadia asked, then laughed again. 'Oh God, I'm sorry,' she said, dabbing at her nose with a scrunched-up tissue. 'I seem to be channelling the Two Ronnies this morning. Nerves, I suppose.'

'Are you nervous?' James asked. She did not seem it.

'Not really. It's not as if I'm going to win.' Her smile had faded, but only a bit. 'I wish I could, though. There's such a lot of work to do round here and I know I'm the woman to do it.' Her eyes sparkled with resolve and it was obvious she meant it. James felt a rush of admiration. He was a male adrift and here was his direct opposite, a woman with a purpose.

'You might win,' he hastened to assure her, while knowing otherwise. As seats went, Wortley could not be safer if a thousand lavatory blocks were attached to its rim.

'I doubt it,' Nadia said. 'I'm only doing it out of sheer masochism. Hoping against hope.'

James was still searching for a reply when Nadia waved at someone behind him. James turned to see, speeding towards them, a young man on a bicycle. His T-shirt bore the legend 'Ramage for Wortley'.

'Don't you just love that slogan?' Nadia snorted. 'There's something ever so slightly rude about it.'

'Is that your agent?'

She nodded. 'Hugo's very sweet and terribly efficient. But also very partisan, so I'd better stop fraternising with the enemy. Good luck anyway, it's been lovely meeting you.'

'And you.' He stared after her. He felt, somehow, rather winded.

He tried to collect himself as Rebecca clicked across the brick path towards him, her Party tattoo twinkling in and out as she walked. She was tapping her agitprop ballpoint impatiently against her teeth. 'OK, so let me run through this morning. First it's a local eco-initiative where kids collect egg boxes. Load of green crap, obviously, but we have to be seen to support it . . .'

'Actually,' James cleared his throat. 'I'm not against eco-initiatives.'

Rebecca ignored him. 'Then it's coffee with the swivel-eyed loons – the Women's Association. Then a primary school. Head's not exactly on-side, I'm afraid, but you'll just have to steamroller him.'

'Steamroller him?'

'He's probably going to bang on at you about budget cuts to schools, which he claims destroy social mobility.' Rebecca paused and swivelled her protuberant glassy eyes. 'And he's not pleased the library's shutting either. They haven't got one at the school so the town one's the only one.'

'Well,' James said brightly. 'That all sounds like a *lot* of fun.'

As Rebecca glared at him, he felt his heart sink yet further. Oh God. Why was he here and not at Wild & Free? It was ridiculous that Victoria was there instead. She should be in Wortley; she was much better suited to the cut and thrust of electioneering. She would make a much better MP.

And he should be at the festival, with his son.

CHAPTER 18

Rob's iPod was now playing what he described as 'The Mascara Snakes Greatest Hits'. It seemed he routinely spent entire weekends rescuing, remastering and uploading ancient student recordings from battered cassette tapes.

'Guys! Isn't it *amazing* how they stand the test of time,' Spencer, at the wheel, was enthusing.

Mark could not disagree more. The prospect of their old songs had been bad enough in theory, but the reality now blasting from the VW's surround-sound speakers exceeded his worst nightmares. Spencer's singing over his and Rob's guitar playing was like someone yelping along to a garden strimmer. The entire session appeared to have taken place at the bottom of a well.

Drink might have helped him cope, but they had already exhausted Piers' 'welcome pack' of beer: three small bottles of some boutique brew called Sad Bastard which it had been hard not to take personally.

As befitted a student band from the highly politicised 1980s, the Mascara Snakes had written songs about the burning issues of the day. Listening to 'Jonathan Livingston Scargill' and 'Poll Tax Blues', Mark felt a combination of surprise at the fervour of his past political commitment and certainty that songs about Margaret Thatcher, F.W. de Klerk and the DHSS would not cut it with a contemporary audience.

Rob, self-appointed official archivist, or perhaps archaeologist given the age of the exhibits, had brought along a box of the original cassettes.

The covers all featured photocopied black-and-white photographs of the four of them in dark coats with their collars turned up, standing against industrial backgrounds and staring in different directions whilst sucking their cheeks in and pouting. Looking at the cover of *Exile to Siberia*, their third 'album', Mark had been annoyed to find himself pouting still.

The Greatest Hits wore relentlessly on.

'You know what, mate,' Spencer threw at Mark from the wheel. 'You're the Lennon to my McCartney, you really are.'

'No. I. Am. Bloody. Not.'

Spencer stared. 'Mate?'

Mark decided not to beat about the bush. He was being cruel to be kind. 'It's not just that the songs are outdated,' he began. 'They're, well, they're crap. Whoa there,' he added as Spencer, driving Miss Scarlet round a bend, almost crashed into a hedge.

'*Crap*?!' exploded Spencer, once he had swerved to avoid disaster.

'*Crap*?!' echoed Rob from the rear, sheer outrage sending his normal monotone several octaves higher.

'Crap,' Mark reaffirmed. 'And I can say that because I wrote them.'

'I wrote *some* of them,' Spencer put in sulkily, clearly reluctant to abandon the Lennon/McCartney comparison.

'And I did the chorus on "Findus Crispy Pancakes, Vesta Curry and an Arctic Roll",' Rob threw in, irritating Mark further.

He had forgotten how carpet-bitingly boring Rob could be.

He had spent the early part of the journey droning on about his guitar, musing whether to remove his lower E string to create an open G tuning. He could remember the catalogue numbers of every picture disc he had ever bought, even the Spanish ones.

'Well, I wrote most of them,' Mark insisted. 'And they're rubbish.'

'"Brezhnev A GoGo" is one of our best songs,' Rob put in sulkily, as the aforesaid ditty now came on.

'It's crap,' Mark maintained steadfastly through the muddy blare of guitar. 'We'll be a laughing stock if we enter this competition. The other bands will be young and hip and so will the crowd – if there is one. Songs about Derek Hatton and Greenham Common just aren't going to do it for them.'

From the driver's seat, Spencer turned a pair of wounded dog's eyes on Mark, who stared resolutely back. Spencer's eyes were the first to drop.

'OK then, mate,' he said. 'You win.'

'Good.' But Mark was privately surprised that Spencer had given in so easily. He had not expected to carry his point without a battle. The next battle now loomed, to make Spencer drop the whole band idea so they could just enjoy the festival for its own sake.

With the necessity of performing taken out of the equation, it might actually be fun. He'd seen the website and there was plenty going on: lots of literary things – talks and readings – and some food and drink. Some of it, admittedly, looked pretty silly. The dog disco, for example. But better, even so, than being back at Hangman's Cottage alone.

Mark's glance dropped to 'Miss Scarlett' painted on the dashboard in Forties curvy lettering. The board game character depicted here was much sexier than he remembered. She had a ready smile, rippling hair and a fabulously curvaceous figure.

She reminded him irresistibly of Ginnie Blossom. Oh Ginnie, thought Mark, longingly. He wanted to see her so much, explain everything. But what could he say?

Spencer cut into his thoughts. 'So, OK, guys, we *won't* sing those old songs.'

'We won't?' Rob, in the back, sounded miffed. 'But I've been rehearsing all the bass lines.'

Mark felt scornful. Their invariably two-note bass lines hardly required much rehearsal.

'No, we won't,' said Spencer, looking meaningfully at Mark. 'Because you're gonna write us some new ones, aren't you, mate?'

Mark was about to reply angrily in the negative when something so utterly unexpected happened it distracted him completely.

A shining blue Mercedes convertible zoomed past them on the outside. It was driven by a glamorous black woman, and the woman next to her in the passenger seat looked amazingly like Ginnie Blossom. Mark stared after it, heart pounding, his mouth open.

Just as quickly he shut it again and gathered himself. Ginnie? Impossible. She would be miles away in Chestlock. He was thinking about her so much he was now starting to actually see her.

Perhaps he was simply going mad.

Meanwhile, further back on the M4

Buster and Django had been desperate for the loo ever since the first service station signs came into sight. Both were officially dyslexic but it was amazing what they could read when they wanted to.

'Can't you pee in a bottle?' Tenebris pleaded, aware that the sweets counter of W.H. Smith and the inevitable toy-dispensing machines at a service station might be central to the rear seat's calculations.

Unhesitatingly, the children played their trump card. 'It's a POO, Daddy!' shouted Buster. 'And we're HUNGRY!' added Django.

Lorna tugged at the bulging rucksack at her Birkenstocked feet and produced a Tupperware boxful of hummus sandwiches. The children had no option but to take one each, but Tenebris had no doubt that when they arrived at the festival and got out – *if* they arrived at the festival and got out – soggy triangles of wholemeal bread smeared with Lorna's home-made hummus would be discovered squashed and uneaten in the rear. He could smell the garlic now, rising in the heat.

The Westfalia was now chugging painfully towards the half-mile-to-the-service-station sign which his sons effortlessly recognised as the last chance saloon. 'I'm TOUCHING CLOTH, Daddy!' Buster screamed.

The astonishing vulgarity of this phrase almost caused Tenebris to veer off the motorway. He was unable to imagine where Buster had got it from. Then he remembered that it featured heavily in the sequel to *The King Who Couldn't Wee*, *The Princess Who Couldn't Poo*.

Persecuted by his offspring – Alfie, throughout, had remained unnervingly silent in the rear – Tenebris took the line of least resistance and the service station exit. He wasn't a caffeine drinker normally but it would get him away from the garlic smell for a bit.

'I'll take them to the loo,' he assured Lorna as they rattled into the car park of the services just south of Bristol. This was no small matter, as Buster was still in nappies despite being five. Tenebris's ex-wife insisted that he needed to make his own decisions about toilet training.

His relief to at least get out of the van lasted precisely as long as it took Buster to spot, in the service station foyer, *House Of Death 4*, a video game featuring murderous zombies and with frighteningly life-like machine guns attached to the display unit. 'Dad! You've got to let me have a go! It's AWESOME.'

'But I thought you were touching . . . thought you needed the loo,' Tenebris hurriedly corrected himself.

'Oh yeah. In a minute, Daddy.' Buster's attention was still on the zombies. 'Look, it's only ten pounds for two minutes.'

Meanwhile, Django had started up. 'Can we go to McDonald's, Daddy? Can we? Can we?'

'Er . . .' said Tenebris, knowing that his ex, who disapproved of multinational corporations, would never have agreed in a million years. He knew that his sons knew this too, and that they knew he knew.

'I've never had a Happy Meal,' Django said beseechingly.

Alfie, skulking in the rear, said nothing. His mother had the same view of McDonald's as Tenebris's ex-wife, but he had no intention of revealing this. He had never had a Happy Meal either. A happy anything, really.

Meanwhile, Lorna sat on in the Westfalia's passenger seat. Her insides were a tight curl of tension on account of their not being at the festival yet. She should have been there by now to stake her claim to the top spot in the Story Jam running order. To go last, in other words, so she remained at the forefront of the judges' minds. At this rate she'd actually arrive last and have to go first, which was no good at all.

She glared as a VW camper van pulled up beside her. It was

painted a shining cream and had silly eyelashes over the head-lights. 'The Beauty Bus', it said on the side in very neat black capitals, adding, underneath, 'Pop-Up Festival Beauty Salon And Spray Tan'.

Lorna regarded it scornfully. Pop-up beauty salon indeed! How surrendered and unfeminist was that? Pandering to men by keeping women under their yoke! Disempowering women by encouraging them to obsess over their appearance! If this unprincipled, unemancipated, ideologically retrograde outfit was heading for Wild & Free, she for one would be giving it a wide berth.

She folded her arms over her black T-shirted front and turned her hard green stare on the other arrivals and departures. An enormous, shiny grey four-wheel-drive was parking next to her on the other side, blocking out all her light, which was outrageous. Light was a human right.

A woman got out, a yummy mummy type, Lorna saw with disgust. Her fingers blazed with diamond rings. She looked at the Beauty Bus with interest before heading off to the service station building.

She had left someone asleep in the back, Lorna saw. A boy, one of those god-like teenagers that were all super-affluent background and expensive orthodontistry. He had thick black hair and full lips. Elitist bastard.

CHAPTER 19

Victoria Dorchester-Williams, owner of the enormous, shiny grey thing, was unaware of transgressing international moral law and only too pleased to be mother of an elitist bastard. She had just joined the end of the queue for Costa Coffee.

Looking across to the vast lines at McDonald's, she noticed a wimpy-looking man with wispy hair, an anxious, thin face and battered combat trousers trying to restrain two large, very scruffy-looking boys. A third, very different-looking boy, very skinny with bright ginger hair, loitered in the rear, his expression inscrutable through thick-lensed spectacles. They were, a disgusted Victoria deduced, all the wimpy man's children from different mothers.

Broken Britain encapsulated, she thought to herself. Obviously the wimp was a multiple-divorcee and the children were passed endlessly back and forth between warring parents. Service stations were notoriously the places where such passing took place. Probably he had just been handed them for the weekend.

It was exactly like Sarah Salmon said, Victoria thought, glancing back to the column she had been reading as she queued. Its target this week was feckless, work-shy part-time fathers who fed their children fast food when it was their turn to look after them.

The Broken Britain man and boys were at the front of the queue now. They were all being handed small plastic trays with Happy Meals on them. Victoria dug out her mobile to see if James had messaged her from the campaign trail recently. He had not.

Guy, meanwhile, was crashed out in the back of the car. One minute she had looked in her mirror to see him tapping away on his smartphone; the next he had fallen asleep with both his iPod earplugs stuck in his ears and turned up so high she could hear them from the driving seat.

Perhaps it was the exams, Victoria thought. Guy claimed to have worked very hard and she was desperate to believe him. Hopefully the results in August would bear out this faith – they had better.

Guy had also, she suspected, been up all night. Getting up for the loo in the early hours, she had seen that his light was still on. She had put her head round his door and heard the frantic clicking that indicated an incriminating on-screen page being exchanged for a more innocent one.

'Oh, you're back on line,' Victoria had observed dryly. 'So how about friending me on Facebook before it crashes again?'

Queuing for her coffee, Victoria shook back her shining hair – who knew when she'd be able to wash it again. She would normally be impatient but was in no hurry now. Not to get to Wild & Free.

That James had booked an ordinary camping pitch, not a yurt or a tepee, had been an unwelcome discovery. Victoria had never camped before. She had never had the least desire to.

And while the prospect seemed, at first, unimaginable, she had girded her loins and reminded herself that it was all in the family's best interests. The promise to Guy must be honoured so James could further his political career.

But if Victoria was to camp she was doing it her way. If a tent had to be pitched, that tent would be the most high-end tent imaginable. The super-luxurious one she had eventually settled on was from a famous designer's limited-edition 'Festival' range, acquired from a smart Kensington lifestyle emporium. It featured pink flower sprigs on a white background, contrast pink guy ropes and pink pockets around the edge inside to slip champagne glasses into; they would, Victoria thought, also be a good, safe place to put her rings in at night.

According to the salesgirl, the tent obligingly put itself up as well. 'You, like, just open the bag and it jumps out? Oh, wow, you're taking it to Wild and Free? That's so cool!'

'Is it?' Victoria had asked, amazed.

The salesgirl's round eyes grew rounder. 'Like, totally. Totally cool. Really fashionable.'

Victoria was cautiously gratified. But one swallow did not make a summer and as the acid test of fashionability was what the yummy mummies in her Pilates class thought, she would put it to conclave there. The smoke was white. They were wildly impressed. And now Victoria turned the page of her newspaper to find, to her enormous gratification, a big feature about Wild & Free.

'Belgravia In The Country' was the headline. 'The Ultimate Smart Outdoor Party'. Among the bright young socialites expected, Victoria read, were Lady Tamara Wilderbeest and Bliss Slutt, daughter of legendary rocker Brian Slutt.

Victoria's forehead wrinkled in thought. She was sure Guy knew Tamara Wilderbeest – and if he didn't he should; they'd been on the same party circuit all summer. Yet if pressed, he always denied any such acquaintance.

Looking, unseeing, at the baristas busy in the distance, Victoria's troubled brow smoothed and she managed the beginning of a smile. Yes. If Guy could link up with the likes of Lady Tamara Wilderbeest at Wild & Free, going to the festival would be more than worthwhile.

Out in the car park, Guy had only been pretending to sleep. It was another tactic – along with the sustained Facebook non-friending – that he had developed to avoid his mother. Having no wish to trail after her into the service station, as if he was ten years old, he had let Victoria go on her own.

God only knew how he'd get away from her at the festival. He was supposed to be meeting up with the Guys from school – they really were all called Guy – and a few girls they all knew from the eighteenth birthday circuit – Tamara Wilderbeest, Bliss Slutt and Ottilie McMerkin.

He wasn't entirely sure he wanted to see Tamara, although he knew she wanted to see him. She had been texting him constantly to say so. They had met a few weeks ago at a Babylon Beach Party – he had forgotten whose. Or where. Just that they had been dancing on the roof as Lady Muck spun the decks.

He had drunk far too many Pink Oiks and things had gone a bit Monet, all blurry. He'd come round to find Tamara doing unmentionable things to him against a wall in the garden room while, outside, fully dressed guests were being pushed into the pool.

He'd slightly hoped not to see her again but London was party central at the moment, what with everyone turning eighteen. There had been that James Bondage one where she had come as Pussy Galore and he'd got totally hammered and . . . oh God.

And now he'd see her at the festival and she might expect

more of the same. Tamara was sexy but completely vacuous. Her interests in life were shopping, parties, sex and drugs. And while the sex was fair enough, he hated shopping, was getting bored of the parties, and drugs had never been his thing.

Drugs were certainly Bliss's thing, though. Her supplies seemed unlimited. Rock and roll, Guy supposed. The Slutt heritage. While the others, for obvious reasons, all hung on her every word, he personally thought Bliss incredibly boring, always banging on about Iggy Pop coming for Sunday brunch, Brian Jones setting fire to his farts or Queen writing their albums in her playroom.

Guy had been careful not to mention Tamara's presence at the festival to his mother. He hated talking about anyone he knew who was titled or well connected because his mother was obsessed with such people. This had been the deciding factor in her choice of his school. The academic side was merely incidental, although not, Guy knew, when it came to the upcoming exam results. That they would not be four A stars was certain, which meant the end of Branston College.

Guy groaned, pushed his hands back through his hair and stared at the car's padded ceiling. Results day was going to be one massively heavy scene. He could see it now: a distraught Victoria screaming, 'Thirty thousand a year! For five years! And this is what I get!' But he'd never asked to have a hundred and fifty grand spent on his education!

And he'd certainly never wanted to go to Branston College. That fearsome old professor woman grilling him about Shakespeare . . . and the place was a concrete nightmare. The girl he had met at the gate was all right, but that had been it.

But what did he want to do instead? It was hard to say – impossible, in fact. All his life he had been pointed at university, and beyond that, at some acceptable profession: barrister or consultant or the City like his father.

None of these appealed to Guy. He enjoyed working with his hands, building things, fiddling with gadgets. But if he ever even suggested doing anything more practical, even manual, something that didn't involve years of exams, his mother was down on him in an instant. Practical jobs, she said, were for thickos.

It wasn't fair. None of the other Guys' parents seemed to expect anything of them – let alone follow them to festivals to keep an eye on them. They did not seem to notice what their offspring got up to, or care. They asked no questions, just handed out more money.

The other Guys were already at Wild & Free. He'd been getting texts and selfies of various Guys in policemen's helmets and neon bandanas posing with plastic pint glasses of cider and enormous spliffs. Tamara was there too, in a bikini, CND sunglasses and a totally embarrassing Red Indian feather headdress. He'd had a selfie from her too, a rather intimate one.

Oh well. He'd go into the service station, get a burger or a milkshake or something. Stretch his legs, at any rate. Guy was six foot three and his legs were very long.

CHAPTER 20

'I could murder a McDonald's,' Shanna Mae said to Rosie as they crossed the service station car park. 'With fries and a milkshake and the lot.'

Rosie nodded in agreement. She was attracting a few stares as she loped, gazelle-like, in her hi-viz dungarees, string vest and the shoulder bag she had made out of a purple leather jacket from a charity shop. The look, topped off with a party-shop tiara glittering brilliantly in the sunshine, should not have worked. But as ever, on Rosie, it did.

Shanna, beside her, was attracting equal if not even more interest. To match the Beauty Bus she wore a long, flowing cream dress caught in at the waist with a wide black belt. Her make-up was intricate and theatrical; she had on so much foundation she looked airbrushed. But the main event was her hair, glossy, thick, treacle-coloured and swept up in a loose topknot.

'Wonder where Olly and Isabel are,' Shanna added, looking round. 'We're late getting here but they're later.'

'They're miles back, probably,' said Rosie. The traffic around Bristol had been terrible.

* * *

Guy was walking across the car park when he saw Shanna-Mae and felt something explode within him. He had been half asleep, but now he felt wide awake. Never before in his life, in fact, had he ever felt quite so wide awake.

Jesus, she was beautiful. This girl had a real body, full and curvy and solid, not skinny and brittle and insubstantial like Tamara Wilderbeest's. She wore a long, floaty white dress with lots of folds and drapes, which made her look like a goddess. Her plump brown arms glittered with gold bracelets and she wore gold gladiator sandals – straight from Olympus. Aphrodite in the very generous flesh. Guy was so flustered that he dropped his phone; it clattered loudly on the tarmac.

Shanna-Mae saw the instrument slither to a halt at her feet. She picked it up, noting it was the latest, most expensive model. 'You don't want to break that,' she remarked. 'Cost a fortune, they do.'

She looked him up and down as she handed it over. Incredibly tall, *check*, too much hair, *check*, embarrassing mirror shades, *check*, that sleepy look, *check*, that slouchy walk, *check*. A public schoolboy, without doubt. Her local university was full of them. No doubt this guy was there too, or going after his gap yah.

Shanna had nothing against posh types, but they didn't attract her. They lived in a different world to her, a less interesting one. A world where you stumbled round the cobbled town centre waving champagne bottles with shrieking girls in tarty dresses. It all looked pretty boring, although Olly, admittedly, had sent it up brilliantly in *Smashed Windows*.

Guy, still in turmoil, looked down at his phone. He'd never really thought about the cost of it. Nor had anyone else he knew. At one party, they'd played ducks and drakes with their Smartphones, skimming them through whoever's ancestral lake it was. It had seemed hilarious at the time, but not so amusing the morning after when none of the phones had worked.

'You're welcome,' said Shanna-Mae.

As she walked away, Rosie nudged her. 'Shan! He's really staring at you!'

'So what?' Shanna-Mae shrugged. Of course he was staring at her; everyone did, and she welcomed it. She was going to be head of a global beauty empire one day; attracting attention was her business.

All the same, she was surprised to see the phone boy gangling around in front of her. He'd sped past her and now faced her again, apparently trying to attract her attention. Boys like this weren't usually interested; they went for the posh skinny ones with the badly applied make-up.

'Hi,' he said, in a slightly breathless drawl.

Shanna looked him up and down suspiciously. 'And you are?' she said imperiously.

'Guy. Obviously.'

Shanna-Mae was amused, but did not show it. As Guys went, he was indeed central casting. She liked that he could make a joke about it. 'Hi, *Guy.*'

Was that a spark of amusement in her thickly lashed eye? Guy was not sure, and uncertainty drained away his usual ease of manner. Glad of the sunglasses which disguised his pathetic eagerness to please, he waited for her to tell him her name. When she did not, this didn't seem to him a good sign.

'Er . . . going on holiday?' he hazarded next.

'Not exactly.'

There was an impatient note in her voice, as if she wanted to get away. This was, to Guy, quite irresistible. His curiosity was piqued, as well as his vanity. Normally he was the one keen to leave. He summoned his courage. 'So where are you going?'

Shanna folded plump brown arms on which, Guy noticed,

there was not a single tattoo. Most of the girls he knew had at least one. Tamara had several, including her family crest complete with Latin motto. 'I'm going to the Wild and Free Festival, if you must know.'

'Me too!' It burst out, just like that. He sounded, he knew, ridiculously over-eager, but he could not help it.

She raised her eyebrows but made no remark. These tall, good-looking rich sorts expected the world to fall at their feet. Shanna intended to demonstrate that she was not the world.

Guy slapped his pockets for his cigarettes, dragged out a crushed packet and lit one up. Girls normally liked the fact you smoked.

Shanna-Mae's reaction was to screw up her powdered nose and bat away the fumes with a pale and perfectly manicured hand. 'Ugh. I hate people who smoke.'

Guy dropped the cigarette and ground it to powder with a few twists of his shoe. He noticed as he did so how dirty they were.

'Nice shoes,' said Shanna-Mae. She didn't mean to encourage him but she could never resist really good footwear. She could tell at a glance that these were the very best. Could do with a polish but the nobility of line was unmistakeable.

Guy glowed. It was only his shoes, but it was a start. 'I've just finished my A-levels,' he gabbled into the silence that ensued. 'It's a sort of celebration, going to the festival. Same for you too, I guess?' She was the same age as him, he estimated, and everyone his age had just done A-levels.

Between the thick – false? – lashes her incredibly beautiful brown eyes looked dismissively at him. 'I didn't do A-levels actually. I'm doing vocational training.'

Guy guessed it was the kind of training his mother didn't approve of, the sort that taught you practical things. He was filled with a sudden desperation to go on such a course. You learnt interesting, useful things and met girls like this.

'What in?' he asked.

In reply Shanna gestured at the Beauty Bus.

'That's yours?' Guy regarded it in awe.

She was a business, and she was so young! She was awesomely together. Much more together than he was, or anyone else he knew. She made him feel pathetically inadequate.

Rosie had been watching the drama unfold. Observing Shanna-Mae have her usual devastating effect on a boy was always enormously entertaining.

None of them could resist her, for all her size. *Because* of her size, Rosie thought. Shanna-Mae was proud of her extra poundage and carried it well. She was supremely self-confident and that was irresistible.

She had known that this boy had no chance from the start. But he was very good-looking, Rosie thought, even if his hat was silly and his shades just embarrassing.

'Are you going on your own to the festival?' she asked Guy curiously.

Guy stared as if looking at Rosie for the first time, which in fact he was. He simply hadn't registered there was anyone else there, let alone a gangly girl in hi-viz dungarees and a tiara. He tried to cobble together an answer.

What could he say? Admitting he was going with his mother would completely shatter his efforts to look cool. Thank God she was still in the service station.

He shook his head. 'No. I'm with an, er, friend.'

In the Costa Coffee queue Victoria Dorchester-Williams was awaiting her flat white and reading the newspaper piece about Wild & Free. The final few paragraphs concerned the festival's aristocratic host. Sir Ralph de Gawkrodger, 11th baronet and denizen of Wylde Hall sounded most eccentric. Apparently he had been married six times and liked riding motorbikes round the house. He had also painted a rather rude mural all over the Great Hall. He sounded slightly alarming, but marvellously English somehow, Victoria thought.

Her patriotic musings were interrupted by a loud and violent noise. A mad person seemed to be in her midst. A woman in glasses, holding the small ginger boy by the scruff of the neck, was screaming at the Broken Britain father.

'HOW DARE YOU TAKE ALFIE TO MCDONALD'S!!'

Tired of waiting in the Westfalia, Lorna had entered the service station. After searching the loos and the playground she had passed McDonald's. Over four trays of upturned Happy Meal boxes and half-eaten burger bun she had met the doglike, guilty gaze of Tenebris.

With the coffee the barista had just handed her, Victoria strode past the raging Lorna with a superior air. Unlike the Broken Britain father, she had some control over her family. Guy may be asleep in the car just now but when he was awake and at the festival, she would make sure he'd be meeting only glamorous well-connected types like Lady Tamara Wilderbeest.

It was, therefore, a rude shock to emerge into the car park and find Guy not only awake but outside the car and talking. To the plumpest, most over-made-up, commonest-looking creature Victoria had ever seen.

Worse, he was actually leaning towards this girl with an expression that could only be described as smitten. While *she* was playing hard to get, leaning back, plump arms crossed against her massive bosom and looking sceptical.

Utter panic blazed through Victoria. She began to run. 'GUY!' she yelled. 'GUY!!'

Shanna-Mae turned to Guy. 'Who's that?' She had clocked in a second Victoria's well-cut hair and the large emerald blazing on her finger. And that her lipstick was the wrong colour.

Guy was staring hard at his dirty shoes. His face was so hot with embarrassment he felt it might blow off. 'My mum,' he muttered.

'GUY!' shrieked Victoria again.

Rosie watched the handsome youth leap like a scalded cat and, with one helpless, apologetic glance at Shanna-Mae, dive into the car. His sunglasses, flying off in the action, crashed on the tarmac. He snatched them up even as the four-wheel drive backed violently out of the parking space and screeched away.

'Just missed my bumper,' exclaimed Shanna, tapping its shining aluminium with a perfect oval nail.

'Bad luck, Shan,' Rosie said.

'S'all right. There's no damage.'

'Not the van. The boy. He was hot,' Rosie grinned.

She was gratified to see her friend blush beneath her foundation. Her only reply was a shrug, however.

'*And* you didn't get his mobile,' Rosie went on teasingly.

'Why would I want that?' demanded Shanna-Mae. But Rosie was not fooled. There was something in Shanna's expression which might almost have been regret.

CHAPTER 21

It was lunchtime in Wortley-on-Thames and prospective MP James Dorchester-Williams, unaware of his family's dramas in the service station, was having adventures of his own.

He was sitting on a chunky plastic sofa mere inches from his bitter political rival in the by-election. It was lunchtime, the middle of the campaigning day, and they were snatching a sandwich together in the bar of the local Stayhotel. It felt delightfully naughty.

Nadia Ramage fascinated him. She seemed to take the whole electioneering business so lightly, yet did it all so supremely well. The advisers had told him to smile more, but he could never smile like Nadia did. Unlike his, hers was genuine; it was actually bewitching, a flash of pure delight across her face. It made everything else look false and brittle and James found himself thinking more than once of Victoria and what her smile was like.

It had struck him that, likewise, Nadia's chaotic, scraped-back, spontaneous appearance seemed the essence of sincerity, besides which his wife's glossy, groomed perfection seemed the opposite. He had tried to bury these thoughts. They were ridiculous, disloyal and inappropriate. Not only was Nadia his political opponent, he had known her a mere twenty-four hours. And Victoria had been a loyal wife for twenty-five years.

This lunchtime, both he and Nadia had managed to temporarily shake off their handlers. Both Hugo and Rebecca were now busy self-actualising with their mobiles in the hotel lobby.

'They're far more important than we are,' Nadia chuckled between bites of a ham and cheese toastie, watching Hugo striding up and down in his jeans and suit jacket skewered with an oversized Ramage rosette. His angry voice came floating towards them. 'Well, you can just tell the editor of bloody *Any Questions* from me . . .'

James could see the sharply-cut suit of his own party helper through the glass doors. Frowning and smoking furiously as she talked on her mobile, Rebecca looked as if she were trying to solve the Cuban missile crisis rather than organise a Q&A session at a local nursery, which was what she had gone out to do.

Nadia was looking up at the bar TV. It was showing footage of the 'other' by-election candidates; the Monster Raving Loony representative was making his pitch. He was a smiley, cheerful, plump-faced man in a grey topper festooned with yellow and black rosettes. 'Hard not to like him, especially as he wants to make Wortley a more fun place,' Nadia remarked.

The Local Party representative was on now, with his neatly trimmed grey mullet. 'I know Wortley, and Wortley knows me. I understand Wortley, and Wortley understands me.'

'It's like Gershwin,' James mused. 'I've got plenty of nothing, and nothing's plenty for me.' Nadia guffawed and he felt his heart do a little skip.

A group called the Wortley Regionalists were represented by a man with a big heraldic flag. He claimed to be standing for a new type of government 'bottom up, instead of top down'.

They both snorted at that.

'And I rather love this Peace Party man,' Nadia said, squinting up at the screen. 'He's such a darling, with his sweet grey ponytail, saying he believes in peace and respect and tolerance.' She sighed. 'I mean, seriously, can I really offer more than that? Can anyone?'

After two sessions on doorsteps, James knew what she meant. In particular he recalled the bright little girl in one of the town's poorer areas. Her mummy wasn't very well, she had told him, and could not come to the door. But could he tell her what he wanted to say so she could tell Mummy about it later?

An anguished James had gone through his manifesto, veering away from the council budget cuts which would close the local library. The little girl had told him she liked reading and got a lot of books from there. He had walked away feeling an utter worm.

'It's difficult, isn't it?' Nadia's warm gaze held his.

'Bloody difficult,' he agreed. Under her sympathetic look he felt himself wanting to confide. They were all so new, so unsuspected, these real-life worries on these real-life doorsteps. None of the party advisers had prepared him for such things. Their emphasis had been on look, on language, on the message. But these people he met, they weren't interested in the message. They expected him to understand their problems. Worse, they seemed to think he could actually do something.

'Sometimes I just don't know what to say,' he found himself confessing. Why hadn't he expected politics to involve real people with real problems? He had felt like someone from another planet, listening to some of it.

'Oooh. You're on.' Nadia was smiling up at the screen. 'Don't you look smart?'

James disagreed. He felt that, against the background of droopy willows, he looked like a sad dog. He watched himself, giant 'Dorchester-Williams For Wortley' rosette in his Savile Row lapel, answering his interviewer. 'All I'm doing is going out there, speaking to the people, getting my, um, ideas across . . .'

The BBC man had been one of those arm-swinging, skinny and excitable types in a long dark blue coat with a red cashmere muffler. James had found him alarming, and he felt this now showed in his face.

'Fantastic!' said Nadia, rocking back and forth in excitement, her bitten-nailed fingers clamped round her solid knees. 'The interviewer's hanging on your every word.'

But James, watching himself, felt he was just gabbling. 'Er, I want, I *desperately* want, to prove I can . . . People are really concerned, *desperately* concerned, about, er, jobs, you know, filling their car up with petrol. I'm talking to them about the good news story we've got on that.'

Good news story. Another Party-approved phrase. It had made him feel like an evangelical minister. 'I give a straight answer because that's what I do,' he saw himself saying, in blatant contradiction of the facts.

'Jupiter' now swelled stirringly around James with a fruity actorly voice declaiming over it, John of Gaunt's famous speech from *Richard II*. 'This royal throne of kings, this sceptered isle . . .'

'Very affecting,' Nadia remarked. 'But how come your lot get the monopoly on Shakespeare? I'm stuck with "Walking on Sunshine" by Katrina and the Waves and a quote from *Only Fools and Horses*.'

'Why?'

'We're the inclusive party.' She rolled her eyes.

'Yes but – "Walking on Sunshine"?' James gave a disbelieving shake of his head. 'It's the worst song in the world.'

'According to the strategy wonks it puts people in an upbeat mood. But it has the opposite effect on me.'

James snorted. 'That song was everywhere when I was a student. I used to be . . .'

He stopped and blushed. She would think he was pathetic.

'Used to be what?' urged Nadia.

'In a band,' James muttered, feeling his face heat up.

'A band!'

'Believe it or not, I wasn't born in a suit with a rosette attached.'

'I didn't think for a minute you were.'

'Well, the point is, we did a sort of cover version of "Walking on Sunshine". Called "Walking on . . ."' He stopped just before the incriminating word. What had seemed funny at eighteen when you were blasted on college lager just seemed puerile now.

'Walking on *what*?' Nadia pressed.

'Nothing,' James said hurriedly. But the first verse was now playing in his head loudly. *There's something bad stuck to my trainers . . .*

He looked fixedly at the bar's flat-screen telly again. The actor was still going. '. . . this blessed plot, this earth, this realm, this England . . .'

James chewed his bottom lip. He wasn't sure how blessed a plot it was for the girl whose mummy wasn't very well and who was about to lose her library. All very well for you, of course, he said silently to his own suave figure on the screen.

The arm-swinging BBC man was now introducing Nadia.

'Oh my God, look at my hair!' she shrieked. 'I must have forgotten to brush it!'

James shot her an admiring glance. Victoria would as soon forget her head as go out without perfect hair.

Nadia's mobile went off. She glanced at it and her eyebrows rose in surprise. 'The Dear Leader,' she said and hurried off to answer it in private.

As the pie chart showing the percentage of the vote now appeared, James was embarrassed to see that his chunk was twice the size of Nadia's. He was on course to win, most definitely. According to Rebecca and the rest of the party pointyheads, it was all going like clockwork. There was no way he was going to lose. On his last day of campaigning, he was to be joined by a whole wave of ministers – or whatever the collective noun for ministers was. A persuasion? A backstab?

But did he want to win? Should he? Did he really have what it took to be one of the lawmakers?

Nadia was being interviewed now, her warm smile and unwavering good humour very much to the fore. She seemed both braver and more committed than him. She was also promising to keep the little girl's library open. It was the centrepiece of her manifesto.

'You OK?' Nadia asked, returning from her call and plopping back down on the sofa. 'You look a bit sad.'

'I'm fine.' James snapped out of it immediately. 'How was the Dear Leader?'

'Quite bouncy. For him.'

Their eyes met and they shared a complicit grin, then something over his shoulder caught her eye. 'Oh look. They're back.'

James turned. Marching towards them across the foyer, grim-faced, were the disapproving minders.

As he was escorted by Rebecca to his shiny campaign bus, James spotted Nadia's rather more battered vehicle pulling out of the hotel car park. 'Walking On Sunshine' was pumping out of the loudspeakers fixed to its roof. He gave her a thumbs-up.

CHAPTER 22

Victoria and Guy had arrived at Wild & Free. They had erected her limited-edition designer floral tent – a more difficult process than the shop made it sound, not least because of Guy's horror at its appearance – and she had sent him off to find his friends.

He was under strict instructions to return in an hour, and also to find Tamara Wilderbeest. Thanks to forensic questioning in the car following their hasty exit from the service station, Victoria had now established what Guy had been trying to hide: that he knew her, and quite well.

Inside the tent, Victoria spread out the Cath Kidston sleeping bags. Hers featured cabbage roses while Guy's had a cute little repeat cowboy motif.

She set up her fragrance diffuser and decided she much preferred the rose-sprigged, pink-shaded safety of the interior to the open-air world outside.

She had been expecting alternative, but not actual *weird*. And there was a lot of weird at this festival. She had known instantly – from the moment the jaunty young man at the entrance had banged the side of the car and said 'Have a good one!' – that it wasn't her sort of place. However fashionable the Pilates yummy mummies thought it was.

What had looked shabby-chic but essentially orderly on

the website was much more anarchic in reality. For a start, free-range children, a particular pet hate of Victoria's, were everywhere. They had names like Buzz and Mermaid, and she had heard a Wolfie, a Dynamo and an Inigo as well. Ridiculous.

The Portakabin loos were even worse than she had feared, and in the queue had been a man in a seersucker suit with a big plastic Canada goose on his head. At least, she had hoped it was plastic.

Everyone seemed so alien, so very different. Victoria yearned to find Someone Like Her. Someone who wasn't wearing a mankini and a fright wig. None of the celebrities the papers claimed were coming seemed to be about, although they were probably all in the VIP area. On the other hand, a deadringer for Evan Davis had come past a few minutes ago and admired her little pink mallet.

Going back out to set up the folding chairs, Victoria saw, strolling towards her, a group wearing tights, jerkins and pointy felt hats and playing strange wind instruments that looked like table-legs. The tune she vaguely recognised – *Star Wars*, was it? In the wake of the group came a troupe of female morris dancers with wild black hair, black leather corsets, mirror shades and tattoos of Celtic crosses on their exposed and considerable biceps.

Victoria stared. Why anyone would want to dress and behave like that was completely beyond her. She longed to go home, to her peaceful white Buzzie Omelet bedroom, but knew she couldn't because she was fulfilling an obligation to both husband and son. She hoped, in both their cases, that her sacrifice would be worth it.

Guy, for his part, had finally hooked up with the rest of the Guys. He had been in no hurry. His first priority had been to find the girl from the car park again, and to that end he had roamed far and wide. He had no name to go on, but the Beauty Bus should be easy enough to spot.

As he searched, he felt scared and excited in equal measure. He longed to see the girl again, although it was surely impossible that she felt the same. He'd hardly been impressing her even before his mother had picked the worst imaginable moment to come out of the service station.

Driving away at speed, Victoria had been vociferous in her denunciation of 'that frightful fat girl'. Resentful and angry though he had been, Guy had resisted hitting back by telling his mother that the Beauty Bus was coming to Wild & Free – but only because she would have unhesitatingly turned round and driven straight back to London.

Now, after searching in vain, Guy suspected the girl herself had been the one to turn around. Perhaps, he thought miserably, she was giving the festival a miss, because of him and the rudeness of his mother. He could hardly blame her.

By the time he reached this depressing conclusion he had been in the food section, going round in circles because he was unable to see for the smoke.

'Try a dawn-gathered-nettle sausage!' invited a jaunty man from a stand called The Luxury Foraging Company. Next to it, a stall called Dreadful Trade offered samphire-flavoured chocolate. 'Just cleaned my teeth, thanks,' Guy had muttered, hurrying away. Straight into, as it happened, the Pop-Up Nordic Food Lab. Here a man with a beard and rimless glasses had seized him and taken him through the world-famous insect menu of what Guy gathered was a fashionable Bergen bistro. He had escaped only once the beard went off to get his signature flambéed scorpion.

Thereafter Guy had blundered, disoriented, through a blur

of pop-up this and fusion that. Someone from a rapper's website had been demonstrating North Korean patisserie. A Tongan butter specialist had joined forces with a biodynamic smallholding in Herefordshire. There were clams from the Coast of Death and Siberian vegetables fertilised by rhino dung. There was a pig farmer on first-name terms with his porkers. He had been the word-of-mouth hit at the Sundance Film Festival and had formerly run a multinational but, he told Guy, it just hadn't worked out life-work balancewise.

After all this, Guy had been vastly relieved to spot, in the distance, the policemen's helmets and neon bandanas of the other Guys. He was less relieved when he got closer and saw that they were with Bliss, Ottilie and Tamara. Moreover, they were all bombed out of their heads and stumbling around to the music – if, Guy thought, you could call it that – of some nose-ringed crusties banging oil drums with baseball bats.

The knowledge that this was what he had originally come here to do himself was embarrassing. But now he no longer felt like it.

Tamara lurched up to him in her Red Indian headdress. 'Come on, Guysie.' She wound her long thin arms around his neck and breathed a lungful of cannabis smoke into his face. 'Camberwell carrot?' She proffered the huge spliff between forefingers glittering with jewels.

'No thanks.'

'Uh?' She blinked, surprised.

'I don't feel like it, OK?'

His head spun and he felt nauseous. But he knew it was more than the weed he didn't feel like all of a sudden. He didn't feel like his friends either. Felt, too, that he was seeing them in a new light. Possibly through the eyes of the girl he had met in the car park.

Meanwhile, at The Vintage VW Split Screen Camper Van Company, Taunton

'We've come because we need to hire a van to get to a festival,' Jude explained to the green-haired white Rasta with the jaunty walk. 'We're a drag act, you see,' he added, gesturing at Boz and George looming behind him. George cut a striking figure in a long ginger wig and pleated frock of sequinned purple nylon, while Boz just looked bizarre in a picture hat designed to cast the maximum shadow over his mad staring eyes and a pink print dress whose hem fell just north of his enormous, hairy knees.

Piers rolled a red-rimmed pale blue eye over them and sucked his teeth. A horrible certainty that he would recognise them gripped Jude.

Apparently he hadn't, but what he said was almost as bad. 'Man, you're so out of luck? We just hired our last van.'

'I don't believe it.' Jude closed his eyes briefly in despair before casting a look at Boz and Big George which warned them against any furious eruption.

Jude had had it up to here with the two of them. It had required every remaining drop of his rapidly dwindling patience to contain them in the Mojo as they waited for the breakdown service.

A wait of over an hour in the heat had been made infinitely worse by George's constant demands that he ring the AA and ask where they were and, when he did so, Boz grabbing Jude's mobile to shout expletives into it in the apparent belief that this would speed up the breakdown man and encourage him to provide the best possible service.

To add insult to injury, when the Knight of the Road had finally shown up, Boz had wrenched the Customer Satisfaction form on its clipboard out of Jude's hand and circled the 'Unhappy' emoticon with terrifying force. It had made for an uncomfortable journey into Taunton, especially as the breakdown man obviously harboured deep-seated doubts about Boz and Big George. He kept glancing narrowly at them in the driving mirror in a way that squeezed Jude's heart each time.

'Not bein' funny, and it's a free country like,' he murmured to Jude as they drew up in the forecourt of the Vintage VW Split Screen Camper Van Company, 'but if God had meant men to dress as women he'd have given them smaller feet.' Jude had nodded hurriedly and got out as fast as possible. They were here, this was the van hire company closest to the motorway, and with any luck they'd soon be back on the road again.

In a VW camper van, too. So not a Ferrari, but classic styling all the same, and with that distinctive full roar of the engine. Hopefully a nice colour as well. At the prospect of driving one Jude felt positively cheerful. He realised that, since Boz and George had come on the scene, he had almost forgotten what cheerful felt like.

But now it seemed his optimism had been misplaced. All the vans had gone. 'Like, soz, guys, yeah?' yawned Piers.

'So you don't have anything left at all?' Jude's voice was sharp with alarm as he pictured himself and the two cross-dressing escaped criminals wandering willy-nilly round Taunton. It hadn't looked like a big place and the risks of being spotted and all of them ending up back in HMP Folgate seemed to be growing by the second.

'Nope,' confirmed Piers, who seemed rather to be enjoying

being the bearer of bad news.

Jude's normally-agile brain felt like the redundant engine of the people-carrier. There was no movement, no ideas, no solution. Was this, after all his efforts, finally and in all senses the end of the road?

But as he stared at Piers in despair, Boz took the initiative. From behind them came a seething liquid bubble, as of lava churning in the base of a mighty throat. This developed into a roar and a great fist shot out and grabbed Piers by the matted green rat's tails of his hair.

Boz's huge face, dark and violently distorted, now pressed itself against Piers' sunburnt cheeks. 'Get us a fucking van, OK?'

George glared at Boz. 'No need to swear.'

Boz ignored him. He released Piers with a suddenness that sent him staggering across the forecourt.

Jude had not thought things could get any worse. He now saw that he had been wrong. This was it. Their cover was conclusively blown. He looked resignedly at Piers, who probably even now was speed-dialling the police on the mobile in his pocket.

Actually, Piers was making pacifying gestures and saying 'Now look, guys. Just keep it cool, OK. I might have something.'

'You'd better,' Big George snarled.

'Or I'll kill you, ' Boz added, helpfully.

'Anything with wheels would do,' Jude offered politely, pouring oil on troubled waters.

As Piers scuttled away, Jude rounded on his accomplices. 'You fucking idiots.'

'*Oi!*' said George.

Jude gritted his teeth and pressed on. 'He'll have gone to phone the local nick. We'll have to make a break for it.'

'In these?' George looked down at his enormous feet in their even more enormous silver pointed stilettos. Willesden, Jude had concluded after finding several similarly sized pairs, had a thriving transvestite community. The shoes had a label in them: 'Chaussures Ernest, 50 Avenue de Clichy, Paris 18e'.

'Just take them off and hold them,' Jude snapped back.

Piers was loping slowly back across the forecourt. Had he been told to keep them talking until help arrived?

'OK, guys. Walk this way. You're in luck.'

Jude decided that they may as well. They couldn't escape anyway. And there was the tiniest possibility that Piers actually meant it. Following the loping figure with the green hair, Jude fanned this possibility into a bright hope, the only one they had.

After him clacked Boz and George, bow-legged, cursing and staggering on their heels. Piers led them into a large garage. After the bright sunlight, it was initially difficult to see in the gloom. But after a few seconds the gleam of metal could be discerned in a far corner.

'It's not quite what you wanted,' Piers said, 'but we had a hen party cancelled and so . . .'

'I'm sure it's fine,' Jude put in hurriedly. Anything with a bloody engine would do. They had to get out of here, especially after Boz's explosion. He might do it again any minute. Or something even worse.

'You're joking, aren'tcha?' Big George had clomped ahead and was now looking at the vehicle. 'You've gotta be bleedin' joking.'

Jude swallowed. It was too cruel. He, who of all people appreciated a beautiful car, was reduced to driving . . . this?

The car was bright pink and looked, in the dim light, infinitely long. It had silver bumpers and a great silver grille. It was half-tank, half-limo and entirely ridiculous. It was a stretch Hummer.

Piers opened the back. It was like a very small nightclub.

There were lots of hard, shiny metallic or mirrored surfaces. The cciling was illuminated, as was the floor, in bright blue.

An L-shaped padded pink and silver sofa ran underneath the blacked out windows on one side of the car and turned right to run along the back of the driver. There was a flat-screen television and a cocktail bar packed with a surprisingly large number of glittering cut-crystal glasses into which hot-pink paper napkins were stuffed.

Built in to the pink surface of the cocktail bar was a sunken ice-bucket from which an open bottle of champagne protruded. Elsewhere was a blazingly blue-lit stereo system. 'We throw the retro disco CDs in for free,' Piers explained.

'I'm not fucking going in that,' Boz spat.

'You mean,' George corrected immediately, 'that you aren't going in that.'

'Take it or leave it,' said Piers, hurrying away.

Jude gave him a few beats to get out of earshot, then turned furiously on Boz. He had, he decided, had enough. No more Mr Nice Guy.

'You fucking . . . you effing are going in that, Boz,' he began with an icy authority which surprised even himself. 'Because you have no effing choice. First because there are no vans and this is all there is. And secondly,' he added, after glancing round and lowering his voice, 'because the alternative for both you and George is rearrest and a return to HMP Folgate with an extension on your sentence. Whereas your reward for the jewel job is enough rocks to set you up for life.'

And mine, he added silently, *is a five-million-quid vintage Ferrari*.

'Yeah, but in *that* bleedin' thing?' George waved an objecting, meaty red hand at the gleaming pink flanks. 'We'll stick out a bleedin' mile.'

'In which case we'll just have to make a virtue of necessity,' Jude snapped.

The two criminals stared at him.

'Eh?' said Boz.

'You what?' echoed George.

Jude explained rapidly. 'Double bluff, see? Same idea as you dressing up. In fact,' he added, as the idea took hold, 'it strengthens the disguise. It's true we're going to stick out a mile, and that's a good thing. No one's going to expect a couple of escaped robbers to cross-dress and drive around in the most noticeable car at the whole festival. Bloody genius,' Jude beamed, now almost convinced. 'Besides,' he finished, 'it's got blacked out windows.'

This argument, which was indeed a compelling one, took the day.

As soon as Piers, who worked infuriatingly slowly, had crawled to the end of the hiring paperwork, they were on their way. Jude tried to ignore both the rude gestures from other drivers on the motorway and the nausea induced by the winding roads off it. Most of all he tried to ignore the fact that Boz and George, in the back, were behaving like the hen party that in the end hadn't hired the vehicle. They were drinking champagne and singing along lustily to Eighties pop hits.

'You're indestructiburlllll . . .' they bawled waving their champagne glasses about.

Jude muttered crossly to himself as he wrenched the long car round another hairpin bend in the country road. These roads – lanes, really – had been designed more for ponies and traps, not Hummers, let alone ludicrously extended ones. And the shaggy hedges bordering them, Jude had already discovered from one near miss, were not as soft as they looked. Immediately below the flowers and leaves were great hunks of stone.

The only good thing was that the journey was almost over. According to the satnav, Wild & Free was a mere few hundred yards away. They should see the entrance just round this bend.

Jude twisted the steering wheel as he exited the bend. But not quite in time; there was a distant bang from the front end and an awful metallic scraping noise audible even over Spandau Ballet. Jude rammed into reverse, but only grinding, both of engine and car against stone, was the result. He then jerked his heel down on the accelerator, but this just seemed to wedge the car even further into the wall.

'After the second bend, turn left through the gates', repeated the satnav woman in her robot vibrato. Jude slapped her off violently.

He could hardly believe it. They were stuck – stuck, moreover, at an angle across the road blocking traffic in both directions. Practically outside the gates of Wild & Free.

Despair was by no means an unfamiliar sensation to Jude, particularly since teaming up with Boz and George. But never had he felt it quite so crushingly as he did now. The heat, his ever-present exhaustion, their immobility, the pounding of Spandau Ballet and all the difficulties of the recent past pressed heavily, hopelessly down on him.

There were shouts of 'Oi' and 'Why've we bloody stopped?' from the back.

Jude lowered the dividing screen, twisted round and stared into the back. It was carnage. The champagne buckets had upturned and the ice in them melted in the heat of the underlit floor. Peanut islands and archipelagoes of pink napkins and soggy crisps now floated in a sea of ghostly blue.

'I'm getting out,' he muttered, lunging at the door and wrenching it open.

Summer air drifted sweetly into the fetid interior. Jude found himself looking out on a scene of beguiling beauty. In the distance, a graceful red mansion reclined on lush green tree-shaded lawns. Before it in the sunshine stretched a mass of colourful tents, some fluttering with little flags. A helter-skelter rose from the centre, gaily painted in the Victorian way. A line of white awnings bordered a lake which flashed in the sunlight. So near, Jude thought longingly, and yet so far.

He heard a car approaching and shut the door hurriedly. A van drew up, and its driver and passenger got out. They stared at the enormous pink car. 'Is it Beyoncé?' asked a pale-faced woman in a Pussy Riot baseball cap with sunglasses that flicked up at the sides like Dame Edna Everage's.

'Nah,' said her companion, whose T-shirt said 'Unexplained Item In Bagging Area'. 'Not headlining. It's Petronella And The Fridge this year.'

Other cars were drawing up behind them, Jude saw in alarm. A serious jam was forming. Only motorbikes could get past him, thrumming impatiently, gesturing obscenely, chrome fittings blazing in the sunshine and laden with tents and panniers. A few wiry types in clinging black nylon shorts also pushed their bikes through, looking like red and sweating aliens in their lurid plastic cycle helmets.

He switched the engine back on and tried once more to execute a multiple-point turn, but again without success – the enormous chrome front just mashed further into the wall. The vehicle was going nowhere.

More people were gathering and peering at the blackened windows which concealed, did they but know it – and there was a chance that they might find out any second – a pair of danger-ous wanted men. Fortunately – in as far as anything in the situation was fortunate – Boz and George had so far had the sense to keep quiet. But how long that might last was anyone's guess.

'It's Sienna Miller.' A henna-haired woman in a Fifties print dress and biker boots was now bending and staring into Jude's window, the only one you could see into. He felt like a fish in a bowl and glared back at her.

'As if!' scoffed the champion of Beyoncé. 'Sienna Miller would never go in something that uncool.' She gestured with contempt at the stuck vehicle's gleaming strawberry-ice-cream sides.

'It's ironic,' said the Sienna Miller woman, ironically.

Jude hammered at the steering wheel in sheer frustration. How much more of this could he take? Desperately, he revved the car one last time.

'Oh my God!' shrieked the woman in biker boots. 'It's lifting off the ground!'

With a horrible scraping sound, the car jolted violently backwards. Boz and George roared in fury as they were thrown to one side. Then the other, as it jolted forward again. Jude, screaming in delight, twisted the wheel wildly and revved for all he was worth. Miraculously, the car veered round, regained the right direction and screeched away.

CHAPTER 23

'Here it is guys!' Spencer announced excitedly as they reached the top of a hill. 'The Wild and Free Festival! Yay!'

Mark looked down on the scene below. It looked more or less as it had on the website. A thick scatter of tents before a red-brick Tudor mansion. A tasteful period helter-skelter. Some big, striped marquees, one of which, presumably, being the theatre of humiliation which would witness the reunion of the Mascara Snakes.

Spencer was drumming the wheel with excitement. 'Woohoo! Let's get down there!'

The procession of vehicles moved steadily into the park. Just inside a pair of imposing gates topped with stone pineapples were two open-fronted tents, each rippling with bunting and displaying a prominent 'Welcome To Utopia' sign in whimsical curly lettering. A large black plastic dustbin outside each tent bore an additional sign in the same lettering: 'Cares. Woes. Hassle. Real Life. Work Shit. Please Dump In Here Before Entering The Festival'.

Mark eyed it. Was there enough room in there for all the work shit he had? Not to mention hassles, cares and woes. But at the same time he hated the bins for their glibness. His problems weren't solved that easily.

A young man in sunglasses, shorts and hiking boots, his torso brown and naked under the bright yellow neon of his safety gilet, was poking a beard of Victorian proportions expectantly through Miss Scarlett's driver window. He wore a badge which said 'Checkpoint Charlie'.

'Hey there! How are you guys doing?'

'Great, thanks,' returned Spencer cheerily. Mark waited for him to produce the necessary documents.

'You booked online?' prompted Checkpoint Charlie.

'No. We're performing.' As Spencer pointed proudly to his T-shirt, Mark felt the familiar squirm of extreme embarrassment.

'At the Battle of the Bands, yeah? Still means you have to pay to go in, guys.'

Mark looked at Spencer. 'You did book this?'

He himself had paid for both Miss Scarlett's hire and – as Spencer had been unable to find his credit card at the crucial moment – Spencer's train ticket as well. He had done so on the assumption that Spencer had bought the festival tickets and reserved a place to camp on the site. The possibility that Spencer had not done either of these things now dawned on Mark.

Checkpoint Charlie drummed jauntily on the doorframe. 'OK, guys, so three people, one van, that'll be . . .' he said, naming a sum so vast they could, Mark imagined, have spent the weekend in Claridge's for less.

'You're joking,' he said.

'You pay a premium if you buy your ticket on the day,' returned Checkpoint Charlie brightly.

Spencer turned to Mark. 'Couldn't get your credit card out again, mate, could you?'

He bloody well could not, Mark decided. He was a provincial schoolteacher, while Rob, yet to stump up for anything, was heir to an electrics empire. He looked meaningfully into the back.

'Bird of prey up there, look,' said Rob, leaning violently to his left and squinting up through his window. 'I might just get out to have a look.' Before Mark could object, Rob's door was open and he was haring away across the grass.

As there was clearly nothing else for it, Mark leant over and, under Spencer's approving gaze, shoved his card rather harder than strictly necessary into the portable chip and pin machine.

'Bear the online option in mind next time, yeah?' counselled Checkpoint Charlie, handing over the receipt print-out from the machine along with a bundle of flyers, tickets and festival wristbands. 'There's still some room in the pagan field,' he advised. 'Head for that, yeah?'

'Pagan field?' Images of a burning Edward Woodward and goatish old men dancing about naked with their bits flying everywhere crowded unpleasantly into Mark's mind.

'Come off the track over there and drive on the field, yeah? You can offroad in this, yeah?'

'Yeah,' said Spencer, before Mark, not sharing his certainty, could demur and think about the insurance premium.

Rob returned. Mark looked at him accusingly but Rob innocently returned his gaze. 'Two shags,' he said triumphantly.

'Fast work, mate,' chortled Spencer, predictably.

Mark stared out at the car now drawing up at the tent on the other side. It was small and very crowded. Someone very tall was sleeping in the back, propped up by a pile of bags. He wore a tweed jacket and had his mouth open. A beautiful redhead sat in the front and what looked like her boyfriend at the wheel. Despite some ill-advised facial hair, he seemed very pleased indeed with life. As well he might, Mark thought enviously, with a girlfriend like that.

He felt a pang of pure misery. Always, in the centre of him, there was a dark space. A black hole getting ever bigger. Soon he would be hollowed out and there would be nothing inside at all.

He sighed as Spencer bumped, whooping, across the grass. 'Guys, guys, how good is this! Pagan field, here we come!'

Five minutes later

'"Cares. Woes. Hassle. Real Life. Work Shit,"' read Olly. '"Please Dump In Here Before Entering The Park". ' He mimed flinging something into the large black plastic bin. He turned to Isabel, beaming. 'How about you, Iz?'

Isabel could only manage a tight smile. She thought the bins were stupid but saying so would obviously hurt his feelings. She felt out of sorts and tired. They had set off early and Olly's publisher, currently sprawled and snoring in the back, had indulged in easily as much garlic as he had wine the night before. Isabel was not usually afflicted with travel-sickness but the smell had been unbearable.

A figure in shorts with a jester's cap and bells now appeared beside the car. After executing some sort of little welcome jig, he hunkered down beside the driver window to below their eye level. Pinned to the hi-viz gilet he wore over his naked chest was a badge saying 'Checkpoint Jake'. His arms writhed with serpent tattoos.

Checkpoint Jake bounced on his hunkers and gave them a huge, white, expensive smile. 'Welcome to Wild and Free, guys. Sixty-four million dollar question coming up. Got your tickets?'

'I'm Oliver Brown,' Olly said proudly. 'I'm an author.

Giving a talk?' He smiled inquiringly at Checkpoint Jake. 'We're staying in the house.'

Checkpoint Jake put up a hand. His smile had dimmed somewhat. 'Wooah. *Wooaahh.* Can I just stop you there, guys? This is complicated. OK, let's take it from the top. You haven't got tickets, right?'

'Er, no, because . . .' Olly repeated himself.

Eventually he made himself understood. Checkpoint Jake crossly shoved a pile of mixed flyers, wristbands and booklets at him. Olly released the handbrake. The car set off across the bumpy grass.

'We're in!' Olly crowed.

In front of them, a sweep of parkland with stands of graceful trees stretched as far as the eye could see. In the distance, an encampment of tents looked like a mediaeval illustration, all graceful peaks and fluttering pennants. Beyond, in the distance, Wylde Hall held out red-brick Tudor wings in welcome. Three rows of wide mullioned windows winked in the sun. It was all very pretty, Isabel had to admit.

Tarquin, in the back, cleared his throat noisily. 'This earth of majesty, this seat of whatsit, This thingy . . .'

'This other Eden, demi-paradise,' prompted Isabel.

Tarquin took no notice. 'This thingy. This whatsit, this precious stone set in the silver sea . . .'

They were soon in the midst of it all. Isabel could see a man in a silly hat and even sillier glasses trying to cycle through the grass on a bicycle attached to a large cart painted with 'Indian Street Food' in decorative letters. At a dressing-up stall called the Ambassador of Curioso, a sweating figure in a Dick Turpin mask was encouraging punters to try on battered boaters and mildewed morning coats. A signboard outside a marquee announced that former Congolese child soldiers were performing in a circus mounted by The Ethical Entertainment Company.

'I've got to go check in with the organiser,' Olly said. 'OK if you look round the festival by yourself for a bit, Iz?'

'Great,' said Isabel, trying to look as if she meant it.

Tarquin, in the back, was looking around excitedly, rubbing his mouth as he did so. On what had seemed at times an endless journey, Isabel had learnt to connect this gesture with Tarquin's need for alcoholic stimulation. 'I say,' he suddenly exclaimed, pointing at a stand where teenage boys in black suits and straw hats wreathed with flowers were serving drinks. 'Look at that! Eton Mess cocktails!'

There was a scrabbling, a gust of breeze, a slam and Tarquin was out.

'Fancy a cocktail Iz?' asked Olly.

Isabel shook her head. The thought of cream and meringue mushing around with champagne made her feel worse than ever. 'I'll go and find Shanna-Mae and Rosie. They're here somewhere, they texted me.'

Elsewhere at the festival

That Poles Apart had done a good job was something even Ginnie had to admit. The yurt they had supplied, 'Genghis', was sparklingly clean, with its own wooden floor and little camp beds spread with clean white duvets and ethnic striped blankets.

Wall hangings in purple and red embroidered with small mirrors, tassels and bells hung above the heads of each bed. Cushions were scattered artistically about the floor along with rugs and big lanterns of Eastern design with sides of coloured glass. Smaller lanterns dangled from various points of the ceiling.

There was a strong scent of joss sticks.

Despite its somewhat bloody name, Genghis was inescapably romantic, and this tugged on Ginnie's heart. It was all too easy to imagine being here with someone you loved, as she had loved Mark Birch, rather than someone who was just a friend, like Jess. The red drapes, the shadowy intimacy, the drowsy perfume, the exoticism – it was all so sensual, so obviously made for love. Ginnie felt a wave of overwhelming misery. She had to get out. She went to the door of Genghis and looked out. All was hot, bright and busy.

She turned to Jess, lying face-down on her bed, long dark legs gleaming amid the sequinned rose of the covers. 'Shall we go and explore?' Ginnie suggested.

Jess was tapping at her laptop; reading the online news, Ginnie suspected. 'Maybe later,' Jess said vaguely.

'Can't you forget the news for a minute?' Ginnie groaned.

Jess smiled, but it was a strained smile, not her usual great white flash.

'What's up?' Ginnie perched on the edge of Jess's bed.

Jess rolled over on to her back, sighed and stared at the roof of Genghis. 'I know it's silly, but it's that guy. The one we were talking about. The . . . murderer? With the mad staring eyes?'

Ginnie looked briefly confused, then nodded. 'The Diamond Geezer? The one who pointed at you in court and said, "I'll get you if it's the last thing I do"?'

Jess swallowed. 'Er, thanks for that. But yes. That's the one. He's still on the run.'

'But . . .' Ginnie interjected, brimming with good sense and reassurance.

'Oh, I know it shouldn't bother me.' Jess raised her voice defensively. 'But for some reason it does.'

Ginnie threw herself immediately into reassuring her friend. It was rare for Jess to be anything but upbeat; she must be very worried.

'You're just tired, that's all. All that driving,' Ginnie persuaded.

Jess's face was turned to the magenta fabric wall embroidered with tiny mirrors. Could she see herself? Ginnie wondered.

'It's more than that,' Jess muttered. 'I completely see how silly it is. After all, I work for the criminal justice system. I should have more faith in it.' She rolled back over and looked hopelessly at Ginnie. 'But somehow it's the knowing that makes me so worried. I know what can go wrong.'

Ginnie tried again. 'But he's hardly going to be *here*, of all places, is he? That's why we've come, remember? You don't get jewel-robbing homicidal maniacs at summer festivals!'

'Or love-rat headmasters,' Jess said, turning over and managing a grin.

CHAPTER 24

Victoria was sitting in her flowered chair outside her tent. She was feeling more at home now she'd prised the lid off her Heston Blumenthal coolbox and poured herself some rosé. The glass, beaded with condensation, glowed invitingly in the afternoon sun.

Merely looking at the bottle label gave Victoria a pleasant sense of status reinforcement. The wine, Château Nobby, had come from an estate near their holiday home in Provence. It was owned by an Englishman, hence the name. Victoria had always found Nobby himself – or, as he was really called, the Honourable Edward Stagge-Hunter – strong meat and a bit of a bottom-pincher. But his wine was unquestionably delicious.

Soon she was happily sipping. Her glance swept across the sunny green park with its yurts and tepees to where the diamond-pane windows of the Tudor mansion flashed in the sunshine. It really was a lovely setting.

The wine had greatly improved her ability to cope with the numerous festival weirdoes. Such as the man now passing in an opera cloak and a monocle roaring out something Victoria thought she recognised – 'Che Gelida Manina', was it? He was followed by a woman on stilts doing big foam jazz hands. Two more men now passed. 'Fancy the instagram masterclass?,' the one whose T-shirt said 'Midfield General' asked his companion, whose T-shirt was going to 'End Child Poverty By 2020'.

Victoria chuckled and refilled her wine glass.

A monstrously long pink car now bumped slowly by over the grass. Victoria assumed it was full of chavs. Had she but known it, it was full of armed robbers looking keenly at her rings.

'Look at them bleedin' rocks over there!' Boz exclaimed. His mad staring eyes had turned out to be keen as a hawk's and could spot an emerald from miles away. But this one was much closer than that.

'Mark it down,' Jude instructed George, who was drawing up a site map in which X marked the spot of any jewellery.

Having finally, in the face of all odds and obstacles, arrived, they were driving slowly round doing a recce. Of their ultimate quarry, Daria Badunova, there was as yet no sign. But plenty of potential elsewhere, like this woman and her rings. Nor were hers the only ones they'd spotted.

Jude was beginning to feel that things were going his way after all. Finally.

Oblivious to the danger her possessions were in, Victoria reached for a caviar-flavoured crisp made from hand-reared specialist potatoes. She had found them on one of the food stands, next to the superfood frittata. There were some good stalls, many of which she knew from London. Both the Hackney Sourdough Company and La Petite Croissanterie de Bermondsey were represented, as was the Camden Honey Man in his high-button waistcoat, plus fours and hobnailed boots. He looked, Victoria thought, like Alan Bates in *Far From The Madding Crowd*, only with bees and a beard. They had got chatting and he turned out to be the former CEO of an internet search engine.

She was checking her phone for messages from Wortley when a shadow fell across her. Guy, she assumed, back from meeting Tamara and the Guys. 'Hello, darling,' she said to the dark figure before her, impossible to make out in the bright light.

The figure stepped slightly to the side, enabling Victoria to see that it was not her son after all. She additionally identified a super-good haircut with expensive blond highlights that almost (but not quite) distracted the eye from a rather red, puffy face. The print dress this woman wore over white leggings was on the front of the new Toast catalogue. Victoria had almost bought it herself.

'I wondered if I could ask you a few questions,' the woman said in a loud and commanding voice. 'I'm Sarah Salmon and I'm here to write a feature article about this festival—'

'Sarah Salmon?' Victoria interrupted excitedly. 'The *columnist*?'

She was so excited she rose to her feet. A fellow human being! A Person Like Her! At last!

'For my sins,' the woman gurgled in a self-congratulatory sort of way.

'I *love* your column!'

Sarah Salmon, who had rather counted on this response, continued edging herself towards Guy's empty cowboy-print seat. She had been at the festival an hour and was bored already. No one seemed to recognise her, and her gypsy bowtop caravan, while it was provided free by the St Mellion press office, was tiny and cramped and made her feel like Mr Toad. No bloody wifi connection either. 'But we can get you a crystal ball if you like,' the press office smartarse had suggested.

The gypsy bowtop was also very near a block of unsalubrious lavatories. Nor was there a drinks fridge. If she wanted a drink

– one that she did not have to pay for – she would have to wait until the weekend's inaugural party, the Gymnasium or whatever it was called.

Disgusted and thirsty, Sarah had gone outside. Which was when she had spotted Victoria. Her spirits had lifted immediately. Her absolute central casting reader, armed with a bottle of rosé! A bottle which, for the moment, remained obdurately in the silly woman's hand.

'That looks good.' Sarah stared meaningfully at the wine.

Victoria was all a-fluster. 'Oh, do sit down, have a glass. I can't tell you how glad I am to see you!'

Sarah was gratified. She wielded power, certainly, but had never been especially popular. Her line of journalism was not conducive to close friendship.

'So you're writing about the festival?' Victoria probed.

'That's right.' Sarah watched twitchily as the glass was filled up. She seized it and downed half of it on the spot. 'Colour piece, as we call it in the trade. Picking out the interesting bits.'

'What fun!' Seeing her guest's glass already empty, Victoria hastily reached again for the Château Nobby. She was entertaining media royalty, after all.

This wine was good, Sarah thought. Listening to Victoria explain its origin, her mind started to spin. Second home in Provence, eh? That meant a free holiday if she played her cards right.

This woman's hands were positively bristling with diamonds, too. That was a serious emerald. But where did all the money come from? Interested, Sarah started to question Victoria about her husband. A hedgie, she had no doubt.

But no. 'An *MP*?' Sarah repeated, intrigued. He was very rich, for an MP.

Victoria raised her glass and stared happily at the campsite through its pink lens. 'Not an MP quite yet,' she said complacently. 'But we've been assured it's a *very* safe seat.'

'Have you now,' Sarah said softly. Quickly and with practised ease, she gathered the details, some of which had already crossed the newsdesk. So that dishy silver fox James Dorchester-Williams, candidate for Wortley, was her new friend's husband! Some people had all the bloody luck.

She drained her glass in a manner Victoria could not fail to notice. Out came the Château Nobby again.

Sarah slurped and racked her brains. There had to be an angle here, but what? She needed a good story. A really hot piece of gossip. 'Sarah Salmon Goes Wild & Free' had seemed a brilliant idea in the editor's conference. A special report, from the festival.

'Just as long as you don't mention that moron Tamara Wilderbeest,' the editor had warned. 'I'm sick of the sight of her. I'm not running another item about her, ever.'

That had been a blow. Sarah had good contacts with Tamara Wilderbeest. Most journalists had. Tamara could be accused of many things, but underselling herself was not one of them.

In addition, Sarah had to promise to send through only the most sensational stories. The editor had not troubled to disguise the fact that there would be hell to pay if she didn't. Her entire column, possibly. Sarah had known for some time that younger, keener, better connected people were circling round it. She needed to consolidate her position.

Sarah swigged back more Nobby to keep the doubts at bay. While it was interesting to find herself pitched next door to the wife of an MP fighting a by-election, it was still hardly front-page stuff.

The perfect scenario would be that James Dorchester-Williams, thinking-woman-voter's crumpet and obviously dripping with money, would be tempted to stray whilst out on the stump. But that was pretty unlikely, especially if the only available totty was the opposition candidate Nadia Ramage. She always looked like a bombsite.

All the same, Sarah decided, it would be worth keeping this woman – Vanessa, was it? on side. Not least because she had a lot of good rosé. She leant forward, holding out her empty-again glass. 'I wonder,' she said, as Victoria eagerly filled it, 'if you might want to come to a party with me, Vanessa. It's in the big house on Saturday.'

Victoria was too excited to care about the misnomer. Come to a party in the big house? What else would she be doing? The family coracle workshop?

'I'd love to.' She reached for her tablet and began to send a text. 'And you must meet my son if you're interested in young people.' Sarah Salmon would be a good contact for Guy, especially after he got his work placement on Tilly's father's paper. 'He's here with friends,' Victoria paused importantly. 'Actually, you might be interested in one of them. She's very newsworthy. Lady Tamara Wilderbeest?'

Meanwhile, elsewhere at the festival

Guy and his friends had moved on from the crusty drummers and were now lying down to watch some street performer who repeatedly hit himself in the face to produce a percussive effect.

'Isn't he, like, awesome?' drawled one of the Guys. 'I've read about him. He's called Machiavelli's Lawnmower.'

The Guy who had spoken had Ottilie McMerkin's head in his groin. She was lying there, attempting – with long, thin fingers displaying even more diamonds than Tamara's – to fashion a small chair from the cage of a champagne bottle. 'Do you think I could sell these?' she yawned. 'I could do doll's house furniture with them. Maybe Moët et Chandon would hire me for, like, an ad campaign?'

'They should, definitely,' the Guy she was sprawled on concurred. 'You're, like, seriously talented, Ott.'

'Ott stuff,' remarked one of the other Guys, which provoked hysterical laughter.

Guy turned away. He could hardly believe he had been here just a few hours. It seemed like days already. Machiavelli's Lawnmower had just thwacked himself on the nose, he saw. It was bleeding. Rather a lot.

There was some stoned-sounded whooping from the other Guys; they were being joined, Guy learnt, by Clemmie van Walthamstow. She was a friend of a friend of someone. She wore a big floppy hat and had a wide, blank, chemically assisted gaze behind her horn-rimmed spectacles. The look was completed by a black crochet bikini and wellies. 'Like, let's go see something else?' she drawled. Some St John Ambulance people were leading away Machiavelli's Lawnmower.

Somone produced a festival programme. 'What about the On Hold Collective? They did that album of what gets played when they put you on hold on the phone?'

'Awesome,' said Clemmie.

She was lying on the ground as well now. Only Guy himself maintained a sitting position, his arms wrapped round his knees. Inside he was awash with despair.

'What do you think, Guy?' cooed Tamara, draping herself around him again. 'You like the Ambridge Slags, don't you?'

Guy shrugged. The Ambridge Slags were young men in tight black jeans with pointy shoes and floppy fringes who bombed about the stage in vague imitation of the Arctic Monkeys. He had liked them once, but now he felt indifferent.

'There's a totally sad Battle of the Bands competition on Sunday night for *amateurs*,' remarked Bliss. 'Like, how lame is that?'

A jolt of annoyance woke Guy. He resented her sneering tone. What the hell had Bliss Slutt ever done apart from be a professional pop princess? 'Why is it sad?' he heard himself demanding. 'You've got to start somewhere. It's good that people get a chance to try.'

Everyone stared in amazement. The idea of trying at anything, still less starting from nothing, was so far from the experience of anyone present that it was some time before the surprised silence was broken. And when it was, a sense of ranks being broken, of betrayal, lingered like a whiff of cordite. Guy realised that no one was meeting his eye.

An uncomfortable silence ensued.

'I've got another idea,' slurred another of the Guys. 'Why don't we go and see Doghead? He was at my prep school and he's quite a cool guy.'

Guy disagreed, although silently. So far as he was concerned, Doghead was just another hairy falsetto type channelling James Blunt.

What was the matter with him? He'd been looking forward to the music side of the festival, especially Petronella And The Fridge. But her trademark St Trinian's stockings and Edwardian high collars no longer seemed the exciting prospect they had.

Bliss was droning on about some vintage thrash metal band. 'We could go backstage. Their lead singer knows my dad. They used to come by for brunch when we lived in the Upper East Side . . .'

Guy shifted restlessly in the drumming heat. His insides ached with boredom.

Ottilie semi-roused herself from the groin of her swain. 'Let's go and check out the Battle of the Bands thing anyway?'

Her interrogative tone was driving Guy round the bend. As if, he thought, you would ask Ottilie anything. She was more vacant than a row of empty loos. Not that you saw many of those round here.

'We could enter ourselves,' one of the Guys suggested.

An unwonted sense of purpose now rippled through the group.

'I could sing "Happy Birthday" in Chinese, it's my party piece,' said Clemmie.

'And I can play "Livin' on a Prayer" on the spoons,' offered one of the Guys.

'My dad knows Jon Bon Jovi *really* well,' Bliss instantly put in. 'When we lived in Richmond, he was always coming over to swim in our pool.'

Guy stared at the grass. He felt, quite suddenly, like flinging himself down and biting it. Or perhaps biting Bliss.

He knew this was because of Shanna-Mae. He wished he could find her, although no doubt she would laugh in his face. Or cold shoulder him. Or maybe both. But even that seemed preferable to hanging out with this lot.

CHAPTER 25

'Right,' Spencer said, as, finally, they pulled up in the Pagan Field. It had taken a lot of finding. The site was difficult to get around, what with tents and people blocking the view and what seemed like hundreds of feral kids running right in front of the wheels almost. 'Let's hit the ground running,' Spencer urged the other two. 'Get the axes out and have a jam. Let's start with Jonathan Livingston Scargill.'

'I can't remember the chords,' Mark said quickly, playing for time.

'OK then,' Spencer said equably. 'How about this one.' He began to sing the first verse. '*There's something bad stuck to my trainers . . .*'

'Oh God, not that,' Mark interrupted loudly. 'It's horrible. No one wants to hear songs about dogshit.'

'Actually, I used to think it was quite funny.' Spencer sounded injured.

'Anything's funny when you're eighteen and out of your tree on lager,' Mark rejoined. It struck him, after he had said it, as strangely profound.

'Who's that?' asked Rob. A woman dressed like Guinevere and with startlingly red hair streaming over her shoulders was flowing towards them.

She looked with interest at their chests. 'I see you're the guys, the group and the live reunion gig.'

Mark rolled his eyes. Spencer's bloody T-shirts were so compromising. You could hardly find anything else ridiculous, not even a full-on hippy like this, when you were wearing one of them.

'You got it,' Spencer beamed. 'And you are?'

'Rowan.' She spoke in a low, husky voice.

'Hi, Rowan.' Spencer was clearly much impressed. The bodice of Rowan's gown stretched tightly over generous breasts. It remained tight to hip level where the skirt flowed out to accentuate her curves. 'You look totally *Game Of Thrones*,' Spencer told her.

'I'll take that as a compliment,' Rowan replied, without batting an eyelid. 'Come over. We're having merrymoot.'

'Is that a cider?' Spencer asked.

Rowan giggled. 'It's a pagan gathering.'

Mark felt a pull of anxiety. 'We're not actually pagans ourselves, not as such.'

Rowan looked surprised. 'But this is the pagan field. It's reserved for bards, ovates and druids.'

'What's an ovate?' Spencer asked. 'It sounds like a sheep.'

Rowan, it turned out, had a proselytising side. 'It's really easy to become a pagan,' she said encouragingly, her small white teeth flashing in the sunlight. 'All you have to believe is that each of us has the right to follow their own path as long as it hurts no one else. And that the higher power of nature exists and that nature should be venerated.'

'Well, that sounds fair enough,' said Spencer. He looked brightly at Mark and Rob. 'Guys? Fancy some mead and some, like, mooting?'

'No thanks,' said Mark quickly. He had a job as headmaster

of a Church of England primary school to hold down. The vicar of the local church was an understanding sort but no doubt there were limits. And what the likes of Lorna Newwoman would say did not bear thinking about. Thankfully she was hundreds of miles away and he need not see her until September.

Mark could see what were presumably Rowan's pagan colleagues sitting in a rough circle under a tree. Confusingly, there was a man dressed actually *as* a tree, along with a witch in a velvet robe and a woman pretending to be a raven with a long black beak. Another old man had ivy leaves on his head and a dark purple robe tied with a silk cord girdle.

'That's Chris,' Rowan said. 'He's our leader.'

'Is he a full-time, um, bard sort of guy?' Spencer asked.

Rowan shook her shining hair. 'None of us are. I'm a headhunter for public sector recruitment. Dave – he's the one dressed as a tree – is a retired university professor. And that's his wife Dotty, next to him.'

She looked pretty dotty, Mark thought. She was the one with the beak.

'Dotty's a music teacher,' Rowan said. 'She plays the harp too. Our rituals are much better now, musically speaking. Perhaps,' she added, smiling at them all brightly, 'you might be interested in taking part in one of our rituals?'

'These rituals,' Spencer said, his eyes on Rowan's cleavage. 'They're all about sex, is that right?'

Rowan was obviously not easily shocked. She shook her hair back and gave him an indulgent smile. 'Everyone thinks that.'

'And is everyone wrong?'

'There is a sexual energy,' Rowan allowed. 'And the sexual union happens within every ritual.'

Spencer's eyes lit up. 'Really?'

'Usually symbolically,' Rowan warned. She tucked a long

white hand under Spencer's bicep and beckoned to Rob, whose eyes were boggling.

Mark found himself, reluctantly, trailing over after them. The woman called Dotty pushed up her beak and smiled at him. She had short reddish-purple hair and a lot of eyeliner. 'Are you all right, dear? Only I can sense even from over here that your aura's not everything it could be.'

'My aura's fine, thank you very much,' Mark replied stiffly.

'Come on,' Rowan was urging. 'Have some mead with us.'

She exchanged glances with Spencer, then wafted away to the other side of the van. Spencer sidled up to Mark. 'Relax,' he grinned. 'Why be so uptight? What harm can it do?'

A sudden, mighty wave of exasperation crashed over Mark. His good nature had been pushed too far. He had had enough. The reasons that had originally persuaded him to come here seemed somehow to melt away and he was left only with the fact that he was, and no longer wanted to be.

How had it happened? Spencer had tricked him about Jimmy, who was never going to take part in some embarrassing reunion of a long-defunct band. A band that had, artistically speaking at any rate, been defunct even when they were still going. Spencer had, additionally, tricked him into paying for everything. And now Spencer wanted him to drink mead with people dressed as trees. Well, Mark decided, he bloody well wasn't going to. He'd had enough. And if that was uptight, then too bad.

Over the other side of Miss Scarlett, Rowan and the pagans were starting to chant. It was a repetitive ditty whose only words seemed to be 'merrymoot'.

'MerryMOOT, merryMOOT,' sang the pagans. Mark could hear a faint metallic rippling, which might be Dotty's harp.

'Come on, mate,' Spencer urged. 'Some mead might help you relax. Get into the spirit.'

Mark felt he understood as never before the foot-stamping infants in his school. Only with difficulty did he stop his own trainer angrily pounding the grass. 'I don't,' he said through gritted teeth, '*want* to drink mead. I *hate* mead. And I don't want to get into the sodding spirit. I want to go home.'

Another voice had started up, a high, unsteady female one. Perhaps it was Rowan. 'You can't stop,' it sang, 'you can't stop the spirit of the dragon.' There was a chorus of agreement. Then Rowan reprised the theme. 'You can't STOP. You can't STOP the SPIRIT of the DRA-A-GON.'

'Oh God,' said Mark, in pure despair.

Spencer held up an admonishing finger. 'Not sure that's the guy they have in mind, mate!'

Mark glared at him.

'Oh universal force that flows through the world, flow through us,' a male voice was imploring.

'FLOW THROUGH US! FLOW THROUGH US!'

The sun chose this moment to slip behind a big grey cloud. The day, formerly so positive, now took on a stormy aspect. Mark groaned. He could not imagine how he could get through the next three days.

Spencer's hands were extended in a gesture of appeal. 'Look, mate—'

'Stop calling me *mate*!'

'OK, OK,' Spencer said hurriedly. 'Look, I can see this isn't your idea of fun—'

'Too right it bloody isn't. You talked me into it, you bastard.'

'And I can understand why you're fed up. But if I could just, you know, explain a bit.'

Mark hesitated. 'Explain what?' He was suspicious. Spencer's golden tongue had been famous in its day. He could talk his way out of anything, and into anything too, which was presumably why he had had such a successful career in advertising.

Spencer leant back against the van. His head was tipped up; he addressed the clouds. 'I just wanted to go back, mate. You know? To the glory days. Branston.'

'*Glory* days?' Mark echoed. He thought of the Turd and the Incinerator. Of the egg-shaped chapel.

Spencer nodded. 'We had a good time at college, the four of us. Sometimes it seems like nothing's been that good since.'

Mark wanted to say something cutting, but didn't. He waited for Spencer to speak again.

'I just feel it's kind of gone downhill,' Spencer said. 'Life, you know?'

Mark did not answer. He had no intention of admitting that he knew, all too well.

Spencer went on. 'I'm sick of power lunches and cocaine and going to Soho bloody House. I'm fed up of hanging out in the Groucho with all the other old saddoes. And now my fiftieth birthday's coming at me like a freight train . . .' He hesitated, cocked his head, flashed his teeth in the old way. 'Hey. *That* might make a good song. Whaddya think?'

He slapped his thighs in rhythm and began to croon in mock-blues style. 'Woke up this moww-ning, mah fiftieth birthday comin' at me like a freight train. A freight train, wooh yeah, a freight train, wooh, wooh, that old fiftieth birthday freight train . . .'

Mark now found his voice. 'Just shut the fuck up, Spencer.' He had the feeling – not a new one – that Spencer was laughing at him, somehow. That he was not serious, even now.

Spencer stopped crooning, cleared his throat and stared down at the grass. 'Look, mate. I can't blame you for being pissed off. I drag you here when I've been out of touch for twenty years without so much as a Christmas card.'

Mark did not reply

'But you know,' Spencer said, returning to his theme, 'the further away we get from Branston, the more I realise that they were the best years of my life. College. The Snakes. You, me, Jimmy and Rob.'

'It's just nostalgia,' Mark was about to snap, then he saw that Spencer's eyes were glistening. He stared, surprised. Was Spencer capable of sincerity after all?

'So when I saw the Battle of the Band competition, I thought, why not?'

Mark could think of many reasons, but aired none of them.

'Last roll of the dice,' Spencer went on with a wistful smile.

He had had enough, Mark decided. 'Oh come on, Spencer. Get a grip. Just how much of a midlife crisis cliché are you?'

'Yeah, yeah. I know. Saddo or what?' Spencer gave a self-deprecating shake of his head and pushed at the grass with a Conversed toe. Then the chin came up and a glance of surprising power was turned on Mark. 'But what about you?' Spencer said.

'Me?'

'Yeah, you, mate. OK, I admit it, I put pressure on you. But, really, what the hell else were you doing, up there in nowheres-ville? Your life's as crap as mine, isn't it? Probably worse. Admit it. Nothing's worked out for you either, has it?'

Mark was gripped by an icy fury, all the more as it was the absolute truth. 'That's crap,' he growled nonetheless. 'Things are fine with me. They're great.'

On the other side of the van, the pagans cheered.

Spencer cocked his head sceptically. 'Oh yeah? That's not what I heard.'

'So?' Mark's heart was hammering. 'What did you hear?' He hoped it wasn't a mistake to call Spencer's bluff.

'Well, you told me yourself that you split with Claire,' Spencer said, looking him in the eye.

'So what? That's all in the past now.'

'But that teacher you fancy isn't,' Spencer shot back. 'Is she? The one at your school. The one you've just had to sack.'

Mark's nostrils flared. His fist burned with the urge to bury itself right in those persuasive teeth. 'Who told you that?' he roared.

'Rob.'

'*Rob?*' Mark screamed.

'Yeah, and you should do something about it, mate. Time's passing. Don't miss your chance.'

Mark was temporarily lost for words. Spencer's effrontery was legendary, but this was remarkable even by his standards. 'I don't have to listen to this,' he muttered eventually. 'I don't have to be here at all.'

He was going home, whether he bumped into Ginnie or not. In fact, Mark decided, he *wanted* to bump into her. Avoiding her was pointless; she haunted him night and day as it was. He wanted to seek her out, to face her down, to tell her, for what it was worth, what had really happened. He had been too honourable by far about that meeting, had kept other people's confidences to his own detriment, and where had it got him? Only into trouble.

Well, he needed her to know the truth. That he alone had stood up for her. She would never believe him, but he no longer cared. The sting of her scorn, the humiliation of her shouting at him in a public street even, would be better than this. Grinding his heel furiously in the grass, he stomped away.

CHAPTER 26

Only by pointing out that it was the only place she could smoke had Ginnie succeeded in getting Jess outside. Now they were looking for a coffee stall. One called Has Bean was doing a brisk trade, but the queue before it was almost as enormous as the one for mobile phone recharging next door. So much for getting away from it all and leaving real life and work shit at the entrance, Ginnie thought.

'How about here,' she suggested, gesturing at a set of leather armchairs set out on the grass along with items including a wind-up gramophone, a birdcage, a carpet-beater and a standard lamp.

Jess consulted a driftwood sign hanging round the neck of a large plaster goddess. '"Wild and Free's Only Pop-Up Gastropub." But does it do coffee?'

The landlord was a lanky, irascible, Richard E. Grant type. He was complaining to a skinny blonde with piled-up hair who was writing on a menu board. 'It's *not* wild pig!' the man was shouting. 'You're writing wild pig!'

'But that's what it said on your note, Merlin. Wild pig muffins.'

'Wild *fig*!' screamed Merlin. '*Wild fig*!'

Jess and Ginnie hurried on. 'What about here?' Jess asked, after a few minutes.

Before them was a red, green and yellow vehicle shaking with the force of loud reggae music. 'Ital Freedom Fighters' Surf Shack' was the hand-painted legend on its side. Two gangling white crusties were skanking behind a serving counter. In front of it stood a man in green wellies and a boater.

'Can I order something?' the man was shouting. 'Are you a café or not?'

One of the freedom fighters reluctantly stopped dancing and dragged himself to the counter. 'So what can I get for yu, whitey?'

'You're white yourself,' Green Wellies responded bluntly.

'Only on the surface, man.'

Jess nudged Ginnie. 'Forget it. Come on.'

They wove through the stalls. They seemed to have hit the homeware section. Behind a bunting-draped signboard reading 'The Pop-Up Buzzie Omelet' was a display of leather chesterfields sprayed purple, chaise longues upholstered in frayed denim and vast wooden screws covered in decoupage flowers. At a portable inferno, a brawny blacksmith wearing a 'Forge Ahead' T-shirt offered Vegetarian Weathervanes.

'What are vegetarian weathervanes?' Jess stopped, intrigued.

'They don't have cockerels on them,' replied the blacksmith, who was very well-spoken and turned out to be an ex-commodities trader.

The girls hurried on. The terrain changed to large white tents with notices outside, listing events. 'Ooh,' Jess said, pausing by one of them. 'This is where all the writers are speaking.'

'There's an H.D. Grantchester talk,' Ginnie said, reading the list. She had loved the whole of *Nasty, Brutish* and *Short*, although *Brutish* had probably been her favourite.

'And I'd quite like to see Oliver Brown's event,' said Jess. 'Who?'

Jess looked at her in surprise. 'You must have heard of him. As in *Smashed Windows*? As in the book every north London reading group is talking about? Actually,' she added, looking into the tent through the open flaps, 'I think that's him over there.'

At her voice, two people inside the tent looked over. One was a young man whose open, handsome face was obscured by a beard and long mousy hair. He was with an attractive, if hard-faced, blonde in skinny jeans and a strappy top. She wore a headset and so many lanyards she looked like a maypole.

They were bent over a table, the blonde tapping into a smartphone while simultaneously explaining something procedural to the man, who was looking alarmed.

Jess put her head further in.

'Hello. You're Oliver Brown, aren't you?'

Before he could respond the blonde stopped tapping, looked up and said, in a proprietorial manner, 'Yes, he is.'

'And you are his spokeswoman?' Jess asked, with deceptive sweetness.

The blonde scowled. 'I'm Jezebel Pert-Minks? Festival organiser?' One of her mobiles rang and, eyes coldly on Jess, she answered it.

'I'm looking forward to your talk,' Jess took the opportunity to tell Oliver. 'I really enjoyed your book.'

Olly was delighted and was about to say so when Jezebel Pert-Minks drew her phone away from her ear to appropriate the conversation.

'So do you mind not breathing your fumes in here?' she instructed Jess. 'All festival interiors are non-smoking?' She returned to her phone call.

Olly, dismayed at such rudeness, wanted to apologise. But Jezebel would only pile in again.

One phone had buzzed and the other trilled throughout the entire ten minutes they had been together. In addition, she was continuously reading and typing texts and e-mails. As was presumably the purpose, Olly was now conscious of his relative lack of importance in the scheme of things and Jezebel's much greater significance.

'Sorry,' Jess said to Jezebel, shooting another nostril-full of cigarette fumes into the interior. As she winked at Olly and withdrew her head, Olly looked down to hide a smile.

Then he turned back to Jezebel. The brief spike of happiness that Jess had provided was now replaced by the deflation and agitation he had felt prior to her arrival. Jezebel had, between calls, just broken the news that the lit-lot had just been drawn by Sir Ralph de Gawkrodger. And Olly had not, as he had hoped, got H.D. Grantchester. He was to be paired with a chick-lit author of whom he had never heard. Her name was Sparkle D'Vyne and her debut novel was called . . .

'*Vixens of Knightsbridge?*' Olly had spluttered, incredulous.

'That's right,' Jezebel said briskly. 'She's quite well known, I gather. At least, if you read the newspaper gossip pages.'

'Which I don't,' Olly put in swiftly.

Jezebel was frowning at her e-mail again. 'Socialite, friend of the royals, full-time partygoer. The book's chick lit, but sort of autobiographical as well, or so I gather.'

'You haven't read it?' Olly demanded.

Jezebel looked up, astonished. 'I book the authors,' she replied loftily. 'I can't be expected to read their stuff as well.'

Olly stared at the ground. He, a serious author, was paired with his polar artistic opposite. Sparkle D'Vyne, socialite and friend of the royals. It was a bitter disappointment. And a situation he was now, desperately, trying to get reversed.

Jezebel's phone buzzed. She thrust the palm of her hand at him as she answered it. It was a long phone call concerned with the location of some cardboard boxes.

When Jezebel was finally off the phone again Olly took a deep breath. 'Look . . . about *Vixens of Knightsbridge* . . .'

Jezebel was looking at her e-mails again. The trilling phone went off.

'I can't interview someone who's written a book called *Vixens of Knightsbridge*,' Olly bleated as Jezebel now began a conversation about balloons.

'Can't do what?' Jezebel was off the trilling phone now but answering the buzzing one. She paced around some distance away, tossing her hair, her passes slithering in agitation around her torso. It all looked very urgent but from what Olly could hear it was about staplers.

When, finally, she came marching back he pleaded desperately. 'I don't know anything about chick lit.'

'So now's the time to find out?' Jezebel suggested absently. She pressed a button, tossed back her blond hair and stuck a phone to her ear. 'So tell him to look in the fridge? There's a half-pint of semi-skimmed. I put it there myself.'

Realising, once she had sorted out this burning issue, that he had a window of a few seconds, Olly seized his chance. 'I'm a serious author.'

Jezebel's reaction was to look glacial. 'So Wild and Free is all about mixing it? Highbrow with lowbrow? Serious with chick lit? So it's a fun, free-wheeling rock-and-roll cultural mash-up?'

Olly wished he had a free wheel to rock and roll over Jezebel. 'No one's going to come and see me talk to someone called Sparkle D'Vyne!' he burst out petulantly, even as Jezebel's phone rang yet again and she began theatrically to untangle someone's printer-ink issues.

'I'm not even being *paid*,' he wailed when this was resolved.

'So you're staying in Wylde Hall in lieu of a fee?'

But so what, Olly thought. He hadn't even seen his room yet. And as he'd driven through the festival he'd thought that the tents looked carefree and colourful. Would offering to camp swing him a lit-lot redraw?

On the other hand, he had promised Isabel a stately home, and they had not brought a tent anyway. Unless they spent the night in Shanna's van, but she was going to need that herself. Frankly, the Hall was all he had left to impress her.

Jezebel, rummaging in a cardboard box under the table, straightened and handed him a fat pink paperback on whose cover two women in skimpy underwear writhed suggestively. Above this was proclaimed, in loopy pink writing, *Vixens of Knightsbridge*.

'Isn't there anyone else I can interview?' Olly begged. 'I'll do anyone. Sven-Göran Eriksson, Papa Smurf, I'm not proud.'

'Papa Smurf,' snapped Jezebel, 'is not appearing at the Wild and Free festival.'

'You know what I mean,' Olly appealed. 'Anyone but Sparkle D'Vyne and *Vixens of Knightsbridge*.'

Jezebel ignored this and handed him a schedule. 'So you're in the main marquee for ten for your talk on *Smashed Doors*?'

'Windows, actually. And – ten?'

'Bright and early,' Jezebel said, a steely glint in her eye.

'But that's the graveyard slot,' Olly said miserably. Who was up at ten in the morning at a festival?

'If you'd rather not, there are plenty of others who will.'

Olly sighed. 'Fine. I'll do it.'

Jezebel was tapping her phone again. Her nails rattled

agitatedly against the plastic. 'I have to go.' She turned on her heel.

'Er – so that room we just talked about?' Olly exclaimed, stumbling after her. 'How do I find it?'

Jezebel turned in mid-stride, both phones clamped to her ear. 'So you need to tweet my assistant Squiz? Twitter – @FestivalFairy? She's got the accommodation brief.'

CHAPTER 27

'Come on, mate!' Spencer had yelled after Mark as he stormed off from the pagan field. 'We may as well do the gig, now we're here?'

Spencer could, Mark thought, stuff the gig where the sun didn't shine. He was going, and that was that. Home – in so far as Hangman's Cottage could ever be thus described – to Chestlock. Most of all, to Ginnie Blossom. Better to be near her even if she hated him rather than hundreds of miles away.

He hurried along wildly and without direction. Through bush, through briar, like Puck. Over camping stove, over guy rope and through middle-class family hunched over festival programme. 'You bloody oaf!' one irate red-trousered father roared after him, threateningly waving some pâté on toast.

'For God's sake!' exclaimed a red-faced blonde sitting with another woman before a flowered tent and grabbing the neck of a rosé bottle just in time.

Mark had reached the lakeside. It was wide and silver and beautiful and was the sort from which, in another mood, he might have expected to see a slender arm clad in white samite appear holding a legendary sword. As it was, there was a boat with a flag fluttering from it that said 'Floating Hairdresser'.

Mark was trying to work out how one took advantage of this service when a sudden and very disturbing vision of Ginnie rising from the glittering waters drove everything else from his mind. She stood before him as if real, completely naked, her pearly flesh on triumphant display and staring at him with blatant suggestion. As the vision faded, leaving him surging with frustrated desire, Mark felt he was going mad.

He now realised he was not alone. A very trim and excessively tanned man in skimpy shorts was hanging about, shooting him encouraging looks. He had smooth dark hair and a gold medallion glinted from his pectorals. 'You going to try it?' he asked, showing ultra-white teeth in a suggestive smile.

'I don't think so, thanks.' He was obviously being picked up, and while this was flattering and absolutely fine, Mark was not on the bi-curious market.

'It's very liberating,' the man with the tan assured him earnestly.

'Yes, I'm sure it is, but—'

'All about communing with nature,' continued his new friend. 'There's something actually quite bestial about it.'

For the second time in the past hour Mark felt the time had come to be completely, if awkwardly, frank. 'I'm heterosexual,' he blurted, reddening.

'What's that got to do with it?' The man was looking at him strangely. He gestured at a notice on the tree: 'Wild Swim Here'. 'What did you think I was suggesting?'

Purple-faced, Mark muttered his apologies and stumbled away. The entire festival had become, not just farce, but humiliation. The sooner he found Miss Scarlett the camper van, got his bags and guitar and went, the better.

'Look' Jess was saying. 'You can get a facial. Manicure, pedicure, massage. Even a spray tan.

They had come across the Beauty Bus. A very pretty, plump

girl in a long white dress was sitting outside under a cream awning. She looked up as they approached.

'Spray tan, did you say?' she said, rolling an appraising eye over Ginnie. 'You look as if you could do with a top-up.'

Jess explained, laughing, that Ginnie's tan was the work of an expensive West End salon.

Shanna-Mae was unimpressed. 'Well, they've made a right mess of it. It's all patchy, look here.' She poked Ginnie's elbow. 'That tidemark!'

Shanna gestured towards the tall black tent. 'Walk this way,' she instructed Ginnie. 'I could do your make-up while I'm about it. You've a really pretty face, you should make more of it. Your hair, too.'

Jess was amused at her assurance. 'Is this your business? Young, aren't you?'

Shanna tossed her strawberry-blond updo. 'I wouldn't say so. Just know what I'm doing, that's all.'

A younger girl appeared and both Ginnie and Jess stared at her outfit. A tiara shouldn't work with dungarees, still less a plate of chips. And yet it did somehow. 'Shanna-Mae's going to have her own shop one day,' Rosie told Ginnie and Jess proudly.

'Empire,' Shanna corrected with a grin.

Jess regarded her steadily. 'I wouldn't be at all surprised.'

Ginnie looked down at her arms. 'You really think they're that bad?'

'Terrible,' said Shanna-Mae.

Ginnie looked at Jess who said, 'Come on, Gin. Let Shanna-Mae make you beautiful.'

Why bother, Ginnie wanted to demand. She was inhibited from saying it by Shanna-Mae's intent appraisal of her features. But really, what was the point of looking beautiful – in the unlikely event that it was possible in her case? She didn't want to impress a man. She'd tried, so far as she could, and it had been a devastating humiliation. Instead she said challengingly to Jess, 'Why don't you get your make-up done?'

Ginnie had intended to pass the *maquillage* buck but realised she had been misunderstood, or more likely sidestepped. Jess grinned. 'Good idea, I'll do it too.'

Shanna-Mae leapt in to seal the deal. 'I'll do two for the price of one,' she offered generously.

'What are we waiting for?' Jess drew Ginnie's attention to the quote running in black italics beneath the Beauty Bus logo: *Self-love, my liege, is not so vile a sin as self-neglecting. Henry V.* 'How many beauticians quote Shakespeare?'

Ushering the two women in, Rosie and Shanna-Mae exchanged a glance of triumph.

Just at that moment, Mark, hurrying past and trying to find the Pagan Field so he could get his things from Miss Scarlett, stopped dead in his tracks. The woman climbing inside that cream camper van with 'Beauty Bus' written on the side looked exactly like Ginnie Blossom! He could see her only from the rear, but he would know that rear anywhere. It was incomparable, generous, divine in shape and he had gazed at it longingly on so many occasions. Now, as then, it made his heart skip.

But just as soon as the idea formed itself, Mark dismissed it. It could not possibly be her. What would Ginnie Blossom be doing at Wild & Free? Especially in a bright and clinging dress swirling with neon orange and pink. That simply wasn't her style. Nor were beauty parlours, especially pop-up ones in vans. The fact that Ginnie Blossom's full-bodied, creamy beauty was entirely natural and she didn't so much as pluck her eyebrows was one of the very many things Mark admired about her. Adored about her.

Even mistaking someone else for Ginnie brought all his longing rushing back, followed by a slipstream of regret and frustration. Because if it had been her, away from conventional Chestlock, in such an extravagant, improbable setting, unlikely things such as her believing he hadn't conspired to sack her might have been possible.

On the other hand, Ginnie's being here would have unfortunate consequences, such as her knowing about his embarrassing old college band. Perhaps it was just as well it wasn't her.

He decided that he needed to eat something, all the same. Clearly he was starting to hallucinate. Perhaps it was the sun, perhaps the fact that he hadn't eaten properly since the train buffet trolley had rattled past.

He was, Mark saw, now entering the festival's food section. You could tell because of the thick pall of smoke hanging over the entire area. People were coming out of it coughing but holding plastic boxes with salads in them.

He did not want a salad, Mark decided. What he wanted was a burger. Served quickly and without comment by someone who recognised he was just hungry and not necessarily looking to be browbeaten about beef quality.

He dived into the food-scented fog and immediately found Absolute Balls.

Absolute Balls weren't burgers exactly, but they were mince. They made bespoke meatballs from heritage herds using a reconditioned Edwardian butcher's mincer. They believed in letting the meat speak for itself, although Mark's server, whose neon orange T-shirt aimed to 'Close Guantanamo Now', spoke for it at some length and had especially firm views on seasoning. Eventually Mark was handed what seemed, for the money, an absurdly small pot of spaghetti and meatballs. He took it gratefully even so.

Shoving the food in hungrily, Mark recommenced his search

for the pagan field. But the festival site was deceptively large, bewilderingly various and generally confusing to get around. He kept losing his bearings and now found himself near the striped Big Top that formed Wild & Free's ceremonial epicentre. And the setting, on Sunday, of the Battle of the Bands, an event with which, thank God, he no longer need concern himself.

A whiteboard stood outside advertising events in the Big Top over the weekend. Tonight's main draw was a Shagpile Retro Disco with DJ Belle Bottoms. Tomorrow's attractions included a Graffiti Masterclass in the morning, Strictly Come Dad Dancing at lunchtime and, in the afternoon, Beatbox 'Messiah' with the Stoke Newington Mothers' Collective. Sunday's main event was of course Battle of the Bands. Win a Record Contract. Amateurs Only. Sign up Now.

Mark stared at the board, finishing his meatballs and savouring a pleasant sense of danger avoided. Perhaps, even so, he would have a peek inside.

The entrance flap was open. He passed into the muggy interior. It was surprisingly large. He looked up into the striped apex of the roof and straightaway imagined loud cheers. He could almost see the beam of spotlights splitting through smoky gloom, hear the echo and thrash of guitars. A powerful thrill, the like of which he had not felt for three decades, now shot through him like an electric charge, leaving in its wake a piercing sensation in his nose and a pricking in his eyeballs.

He blinked hard and began to turn away to the exit. But his glance snagged on something. At the far end of the tent was a largish stage on which microphones were set up. It looked, Mark had to admit, quite professional. At the opposite end was a mixing desk. A very big one, unexpectedly big. And quite smart. Some sort of calypso music was coming from the speakers, which sounded fun and jolly. It made you want to hang around, and plenty of people were. The usual roadie types, with long, stringy grey hair and beer bellies under black T-shirts. Noting the gaffer tape still protruding from the bulky back pockets of their jeans, Mark felt a violent rush of nostalgia.

He wanted to leave the marquee, yet he couldn't. The empty stage seemed to be speaking to him. The urge to go on it, to feel it hard and gritty beneath his feet, was almost irresistible. It looked so wonderfully familiar and reassuring, as if he'd performed on one only yesterday. And yet it had been years since he had seen a stage like that, up close, snaking with wires and covered with plugs and amps. Years since he had stood before a mike, adjusted it and said to the mixing desk, 'Testing. One, two, three. Mary had a little lamb.'

Despite the heat in the tent, Mark felt a chill of pure excitement move down his spine as far as his knees. At the same time a lump pressed in his throat and the hairs rose on the back of his neck. Spencer's words sprang suddenly to mind. *Last roll of the dice.*

He blinked hard, swallowed and braced himself against the memories now rearing above him like a tidal wave. But he could not, he was undone; the years were rolling back. He remembered everything all at once: the knot of fear before a gig, the going on stage, the performance and afterwards the relief, yet regret it was over. The applause, the sound of one hand clapping. Two, sometimes . . .

He looked at the speakers. They were enormous. It was quite likely, Mark thought, that even the Mascara Snakes might sound reasonable coming out of those.

Then he shook himself. Was he mad? What was the matter with him? There was no way – no way on God's earth – that he was performing in the Battle of the Bands. Staying at this festival, even. He was about to leave, and leave he would.

'You entering, then?' asked one of the gaffers as Mark headed for the exit.

'Me?' Mark attempted a hollow laugh. 'Bit old for that. Bit past it.'

'You reckon?' The gaffer looked him up and down. 'You'd be surprised. Plenty older than you have put their names down.' He gestured towards a large blackboard by the stage. 'There's one lot, the Upward Mobility Scooters. They're all over eighty.'

'Well . . . good for them,' said Mark.

The gaffer seemed inclined to chat. 'And you ever heard of chap hop? We've got some of them entering too.'

'What's that?'

He grinned, showing gap teeth. 'Like hip hop, but posh blokes in monocles and spats. Lord Edgware and the Bull-Nosed Morrises, they're called.'

Exiting, Mark held the flap open for a group of youths and girls. The boys were tall and slouchy and the girls wore very little. One was in hornrims and a black crochet bikini while another wore an enormous feathered Red Indian headdress. 'I've got it!' she was exclaiming. 'Let's call ourselves Winnie Bago and the Glampers.'

Once outside, it seemed to Mark that everything looked different. Some sort of spell had been cast on him in the Big Top. It was making him want to stay, to perform, even. Which was madness, obviously. He tried to resist the enchantment by thinking of how infuriating Spencer was. But somehow his friend didn't seem quite so annoying now. Even the thought of the new songs Spencer had high-handedly commissioned failed to elicit its former jab of outrage.

Not after he had seen that stage. He must find his things and go, Mark realised, as soon as possible.

CHAPTER 28

Half an hour later, Ginnie and Jess came out of the Beauty Bus. Despite Shanna and Jess's assurances, Ginnie felt wildly overdone. Her tan was deeper than ever, although possibly a better colour, and her make-up the most extreme of her life. She had trusted Shanna-Mae to do a good job; there was something about her confidence and sheer force of personality that made you repose absolute faith in her. But was it all a bit too much?

'You look *fabulous*,' Shanna-Mae assured her. 'Your skin is *gorgeous*. Just look at the way I've brought out your cheekbones.'

She held up a mirror and Ginnie stared. She still looked like herself, just a much better version. With clever use of brushes and shadow, Shanna had brought shape to her cheeks and highlighted her eyes with colour, liner and fake lashes so they now looked huge and dominated her face.

Ginnie's brows had been expertly plucked by Shanna to a graceful arch. A bright, clear gloss that matched one of the bright shades in her dress had been slicked across her lips. Her hair had been teased up into a glamorous, shining pile beneath which her face, which looked to her as big and pale as the moon sometimes, now appeared small and delicately boned. She was beautiful, Ginnie saw, amazed. Really beautiful. She had not realised, never even suspected, that she could ever look like this.

The wonder of it filled her, followed by a sense of utter waste. Because what was the use now? She tried not to let the thought surface, but up it irresistibly came: if only Mark Birch could see her now. She felt she hated him, but wanted to see him one more time. Just so he could realise what he had missed.

Jess, who had allowed Shanna the most exuberantly free of reins and now looked like one of the Supremes, paid up for the treatments and the various Beauty Bus brand lotions Shanna had recommended. Dangling from her fingers now as she cheerfully rejoined Ginnie were the twisted black silk cords of two Beauty Bus cardboard carrier bags. They were the work of a commercial graphics student who also admired Shanna.

'Come on,' urged Jess. 'Let's go and break some hearts!'

As soon as she said it, she wished it back. Ginnie's enormous green eyes had filled with tears. She bit her brightly glossed lip, shook her shining updo and stared at the swimming, blurry grass below.

Mark, still in fruitless search of the pagan field, was passing the front of a big white tent now. The sign over its entrance proclaiming 'Special School' featured a badly drawn crest on which a pair of crossed canes and some large spectacles could be made out. The motto below read: *Reductio ad absurdam*. According to the curriculum posted outside, the syllabus included insults in Latin, rubber-band-pinging contests, food-fight tactics and apple-pie bed masterclasses.

Mark paused. It was all pretty silly, but he couldn't help being interested from a professional point of view. A flush-faced young man in a gown and mortar board was bending a cane in both hands. The blackboard propped against a guy rope revealed him to be Dr Flogg, the school's headmaster, giving

'Six of the Best: a talk on caning, with demonstration. Audience participation is sought.'

A giggling crowd was gathering around him. 'Six of the best!' Dr Flogg roared at his audience. 'A half dozen of our very finest English thwacks. Now do I have any volunteers? Step up quickly now, please. Or . . .' he leant forward, his lip curled in pantomime malevolence, 'do I have to flog the lot of you?'

Squeals of excitement greeted this. And then, from the midst of them, came a dissenting voice. 'Down with educational elitism!'

There was something horribly familiar about it. Mark looked in its direction and experienced a violent shock.

Those lozenge-shaped glasses through which the eyes bored like hard green marbles . . . Familiar marbles. Marbles that had on many occasions bored into Mark. It was Lorna Newwoman, all right. And Alfie, looking more diffident than ever.

Mark's first urge was to escape. If Lorna Newwoman found out about the Mascara Snakes and the Battle of the Bands he would never hear the end of it. And yet, for the moment, he could not move. The crowd was still and silent, waiting to see what Dr Flogg would make of the Newwoman intervention. Any effort to escape might draw the Newwoman attention.

Heads turned. There were a few nervous titters. Dr Flogg took a step forward. 'My dear lady.'

'I'm not your dear lady!' roared back Lorna Newwoman. 'You patriarchal, socially divisive, schismist running dog!'

'It's possible you might be taking it a tad seriously,' Dr Flogg suggested. He looked nervous and Mark sympathised. He was possibly the only other person in the crowd who knew what it was like, as a headmaster, to face Lorna Newwoman bellowing for all she was worth.

'. . . irrelevant and non-inclusive agenda promoting the

repressive reinforcement of plutocratic values . . .' she raged.

This was too much for Dr Flogg. He ran back inside the tent. Mark now prepared to move on, but it was too late. There was a movement at his side and he found himself staring into a pair of familiar narrow glasses.

'Mr Birch! Didn't expect to see you here.'

'Or I you, Ms Newwoman,' Mark replied as pleasantly as he could manage. 'Alfie too, I see.' He smiled encouragingly at the small boy. Alfie returned it with an apprehensive one of his own. 'And are these your friends, Alfie?' The two small thugs sniggering behind him didn't look particularly friendly, though, Mark thought. And who was the cowed-looking man with the haunted expression? He looked at Lorna for introductions, but none were forthcoming.

'I'm here in a professional capacity,' Lorna informed him. 'I am performing in the Hibbertygibberty Wood.' As usual, she spoke as if everyone knew exactly what she was referring to.

'The what?' Mark felt he had stumbled round most areas of the festival now, but the one just named had eluded him.

'The Family Area?' Lorna threw him an irritated glare. 'Then again, you probably haven't been there. You haven't got a family, have you, Mr Birch?'

Sensitive as ever, Mark thought, maintaining a steady answering smile. 'And what exactly are you doing in the Hibbertygibberty Wood, Ms Newwoman?'

'It's the world premiere of my children's story *The King Who Couldn't Wee*.'

Memories of this masterpiece being read by Ginnie came flooding back to Mark. What a hero she had been. These were followed by memories of the phone call with Lorna, months ago, in which he had suggested she write her own stories. It was he, ultimately, who had unleashed this bilge on the world.

Lorna was looking him up and down with her hard green-marble eyes. 'Why are you wearing a T-shirt saying "The Guys, The Group, The Live Reunion Gig"?'

'It's for charity,' Mark said quickly, before looking at his watch. 'Gosh, is that the time?' He hurried away.

'It's on Sunday!' Lorna roared after him. 'Three thirty, but come early to get a front-row seat!'

But Mark had disappeared into the crowds.

'Typical,' snorted Lorna, turning in bitter satisfaction to Tenebris. 'Isn't that teachers all over? Never support parents in any way if they can help it.'

'I don't believe it,' said Ginnie. They had just arrived at the marquee. 'It's Lorna Newwoman.'

'Who?'

'And there's Alfie,' Ginnie added, spotting the familiar wilting ginger figure. He seemed to be with two other boys who looked a good deal more robust.

But now she had been spotted herself. 'Miss Blossom!' Lorna's tones rang out like a klaxon. A pair of beady glasses were bearing down on her.

Ginnie beamed, determined to face Lorna down. Now, of all times, with her devastating new look, that was possible, surely.

Lorna went straight for the jugular. 'Really, Miss Blossom, what can you think you look like in all that make-up? You gave Alfie quite a shock. And Mr Birch! Well, you certainly kept this quiet,' Lorna harrumphed.

'I'm sorry?' Ginnie said, feeling the world shift slightly on its axis.

'Mr Birch,' repeated Lorna irritably. 'He was here just now. You're together, I assume. Well, none of us parents ever suspected. Never had the faintest idea, I must say . . .'

'Mr Birch is here?' Ginnie repeated, stunned. '*Here*, at the festival?' She reached out a hand for Jess. She felt, especially in the heels, that she might fall over.

'Oh, come, Miss Blossom,' returned Lorna scornfully. 'Spare us the subterfuge. Yes, he *was* here, as surely you must know. Wearing a very peculiar T-shirt.'

Ginnie's glazed glance slipped to Lorna's own T-shirt. Clinging closely to her skinny body was an approximate facsimile of the already-rough *King Who Couldn't Wee* cover. Under Lorna's hectoring guidance, Tenebris had done it with fabric pens the night before departure. Around his own, even skinnier body he was wearing an even less successful version himself.

Ginnie was too shocked to say anything further. She could not even think. She turned confused eyes to Jess, who steered her away.

Lorna looked after them unsympathetically. 'I don't know who she thinks she's fooling. They've been bonking in the staffroom all term, I bet.'

This was greeted by appreciative guffaws from Buster and Django.

'Willies!' said Django.

'Boobies!' added Buster.

Lorna regarded them fondly. 'So uninhibited!' she said appreciatively. She had been impressed with the interest Tenebris's boys had taken in the festival's Sex Education tent with its informative attractions. Only Alfie had shown a marked reluctance to take part in the 'Great Sperm Race'. Forced nonetheless to line up at the start with everyone else, he had been the first to be waylaid and knocked off course by volunteers in inflatable suits pretending to be STDs.

A thin, small voice now spoke. Lorna turned angrily on the tiny ginger boy.

'What was that, Alfie? Do speak up.'

Alfie's eyes were large and scared behind his glasses. Having long ago recognised the dangers of doing so, it was rare he made any value judgment. But something, now, was spurring him on.

Lorna was bending over him, eyes flashing with irritation. 'You think what, Alfie?'

'I think . . .' Alfie said, terrified but bravely ploughing on, 'it's nice that Miss Blossom likes Mr Birch. And that Mr Birch likes Miss Blossom.'

His mother looked at him in disgust. 'He's totally bought the sexist-conservative-patriarchical relationships model,' was her withering conclusion.

Tenebris said nothing. He was thinking that it all sounded depressingly familiar. His ex-partner the charity worker had placed great stress on the importance of not pressurising their sons to choose any one interpersonal sexual template over another. The result of all this sex talk, while doing little to enlighten them, had made Django and Buster obsessed with reproductive functions.

'Boobies!' Django was now shouting at his brother.

'Willies!' Buster yelped in excited reply.

'Fannies!'

'Sex!'

'Bums!'

Alfie was looking appealingly at his mother. He couldn't bear Django and Buster. As well as being loud and frightening, they kicked and punched him when no one was looking. And sometimes when they were as well. Please, Alfie begged her silently, take me away from them.

But Lorna was scanning a crumpled festival map she had just produced from her pocket and now announced her intention to recce the Hibbertygibberty Wood in advance of the competition.

'Can I come too?' Alfie implored, seizing this heaven-sent opportunity with both skinny little hands.

His mother's hard green eyes bored into him through her glasses. 'No. I'll need to be alone. To concentrate. Visualise.'

Tears of desperation filled Alfie's eyes. 'I won't be any trouble.'

Lorna turned on him impatiently. 'For Goddess's sake, Alfie. I'm trying to launch myself as a children's storyteller. I can't be entertaining you. Go with Tenebris and the boys.'

CHAPTER 29

Shanna's Beauty Bus was incredible, Isabel thought. It was ingenious, inspired, a triumph. She especially loved its elegant little drawers filled with make-up, Shanna's own patent Beauty Bus lotions and all the tools for facials, pedicures, manicures and the rest.

But most of all she had loved being with the girls. Their excitement about being here had buoyed Isabel up too. She had been able, in the light and heat of their happiness, as well as the blazingly good weather, to put her own doubts and cavils aside. She had enjoyed, in loco parentis, calling Diana and reporting their safe arrival at the festival.

Her friend had listened avidly to Isabel's account of how Rosie was beside herself with fashion-related excitement. Since arriving, she had practically lived in the festival's Great Big Dress-up Marquee where festival-goers created their own look with the help of various fashion-industry professionals.

'I hadn't heard of any of them either,' Isabel admitted, having reeled off what she could remember of the cutting-edge milliners, stylists and fashion writers on hand in the tent. 'But they all knew Rosie. Did you know she writes a fashion blog? Quite a famous one, apparently.'

Diana didn't. 'I don't know where her fashion gene comes

from,' she sighed. 'It's definitely passed me by.'

Now reunited with Olly, Isabel's spirits had deflated again. He had given her a determinedly upbeat version of the interview with the festival organiser, but it was obvious, to the ever-acute Isabel at least, what had really happened. She felt sorry for Olly, so obviously struggling to match his astronomic expectations to the offhand reality. But expressing this sympathy was difficult; Olly was thin-skinned and, especially when under pressure, prone to taking offence.

They had just met up with someone called Squiz who, Olly had explained, was to show them their room in the Big House. He was obviously expecting something amazing and had promised her as much. But Isabel was not holding her breath.

Squiz was short, plump, strutty and busty, and it was hard to imagine her being – as she apparently was – in her third year of circus studies at Bristol. You would, Isabel thought, have to have a strong trapeze.

Olly was on edge too. He sensed his fiancée's impatience. She was saying nothing, but he knew she was taking everything in. He suspected that she was not impressed, even that she thought the festival was silly. It made him feel defensive. He had, he thought petulantly, credited her with more of a sense of humour. But perhaps he had been wrong.

Her imagined disapproval had punctured his fragile self-esteem as a pinprick pierces the thin skin of a balloon. Despite his efforts to think positively, he could not avoid, now, seeing negatives. Sparkle D'Vyne had been a bad start; Isabel, when he told her about it, had confined her comments to a sigh. If she had spoken, Olly felt, she would have said, 'I told you so.'

Still, Olly the ever-optimistic reminded himself, here they were with Squiz, who was about to show them to their room in Wylde Hall. Olly imagined, indeed, confidently expected somewhere splendid. The Hall's magnificent carved front door and enormous entrance hall suggested floors of beautiful Tudor bedrooms with leaded lights and four-posters. Exactly the sort of thing that would come in very handy just now. It would delight Isabel the Shakespeare scholar, whose favourite architectural period it was. And it would reassure Olly himself that the festival really did value his appearace and contribution, and that Sparkle D'Vyne was just one of those things.

But it was hard to escape the impression that Squiz at least did not seem to value him. First, she had taken a humiliatingly long time to find him on the accommodation list – 'How exactly are you spelling Brown?' Then, before taking them anywhere, she had decided to update the festival's Twitter feed and Facebook status.

Isabel's expression had been that rare thing for her – scornful. Now Squiz had stalked off at a pace surprising for someone with such short legs. As he and Isabel hurried along the spacious corridors after her, Olly's hopes were rising all the time of a great four-postered suite with adjoining bathroom complete with polished copper piping and claw-footed bath.

'Wow,' he said to Squiz. 'This place is magnificent.'

'Hashtag seriously*DowntonAbbey*?' Squiz agreed in her plummy voice.

'Different period though,' Isabel muttered. Olly shot her a look. She was so pedantic sometimes.

His irritation turned to triumph as they reached a red-carpeted bedroom corridor lined with wide white double doors whose little gold frames bore cards with names. Olly had slowed down and stared expectantly before each door.

'"Dame Hermione Grantchester",' he read, and '"The Hon Sparkle D'Vyne",' before doing a double-take. *Sparkle D'Vyne?* Utterly obscure author of *Vixens Of Knightsbridge*? If she had been given one of these rooms, surely to God he had too and his name would be next. It was not, however. The final door bore the legend 'Mr and Mrs Boris Badunov'.

Olly stared. 'Not the oligarch guy? What's *he* doing here?'

Squiz looked at him. 'Wild and Free's a very hip, happening, high-profile social event? Hashtag beautifulpeoplemagnet?'

'I thought,' Isabel put in rebelliously, 'that it was a rock and roll cultural mash-up.' Olly gave her another annoyed glance. Whose side was she on?

'Daria – Mrs Badunova –' Squiz corrected herself, 'is a patron of the arts. She's very cultured. As well as very beautiful and stylish. Changes her jewellery five times a day. Hashtag breakfast lunchanddinneratTiffany's.'

'That's a lot of jewellery,' said Olly. He frowned, working it out. 'If she's here for the four days, that's twenty different sets.'

'Something like that,' Squiz casually confirmed. 'We've been asked to give her the room with the best security and the biggest safe. Which is this one.' She waved a hand at the door they were standing outside. 'The safe's hidden behind the picture over the fireplace. Hashtag FortKnox! Except the lock's supposed to be a bit dodgy.'

'Should you be telling us this?' Isabel queried. 'And shouldn't Mrs Badunova know? If security's an issue, I mean?'

Squiz tossed her head. 'Like, who's going to rob her here? This is a festival, right?'

They now left the grand corridor. Squiz had turned right and disappeared up a staircase. Olly and Isabel's footsteps thumped on the bare, dusty wooden treads as they hurried after her. Just like that, they had entered another world.

The narrow stairs led to a cramped and narrow corridor with a low ceiling. It was silent and dingy and its brown paint was shabby. That this had been the servants' quarters was obvious.

Possibly that of the servants' servants. Olly's last hope, that Squiz was using this as a short cut to more magnificent apartments, now fizzled out as she stopped before a narrow door and opened it.

The miserable little doorway revealed a cold, gloomy room almost entirely filled by two narrow iron bedsteads. One small, dusty window looked out over a moribund stable-yard smothered in moss and dankest shade. It didn't look as if the sun had ever shone there.

Isabel said nothing, just looked at the dusty floorboards. Olly looked at Squiz. 'Is this it? Is this where we're staying?'

'Hashtag loveyouandleaveyou,' Squiz said, checking a text and promptly disappearing.

Olly could not bear to look at Isabel. He went in and sat down on one of the beds. *Vixens of Knightsbridge*, in his rear jeans pocket, pressed uncomfortably against his buttock. But he dared not drag it out. He had no wish to remind Isabel of what had been the first of a series of let-downs.

Isabel, meanwhile, sat down on the opposite bed. The thin and presumably ancient mattress did nothing to pad the springs creaking ominously beneath. The atmosphere was a miserable one, not only between her and Olly, but because of all the sad ghosts she could sense here. Barely teenage girls, leaving home for the first time, condemned to a life slaving for those born to better and luckier circumstances. She clenched her knuckles, full of a sudden violent anger.

Things, Guy felt, were going from pretty bad to unimaginably worse. He was now part of a band called Winnie Bago and the Glampers and they were entering Sunday's Battle of the Bands contest.

Bliss had been swift to appoint herself Winnie Bago the lead singer. He, Ottilie, Tamara, Clemmie and the other Guys were the Glampers. Their ranks were swelled by another friend of Clemmie's called Bastian. Bastian was a weak-looking youth in shiny green Aladdin pants, a bowler hat and giant glasses; Clemmie had spotted him as he wandered past carrying a red bassoon. Only after being recruited to the Glampers did it emerge that he couldn't play it. 'Oh well,' Clemmie said philosophically. 'It looks good.'

It looked stupid, Guy thought. Or rather, Bastian did. Why carry around a huge, primary-coloured wind instrument you couldn't get a note out of? On enquiry Bastian had just blinked, smiled pacifically and said, 'Why not?'

As a consensus on a possible set-list had yet to be reached, they had been roving about in a state of musical indecision for some time and were now nearing a red, green and yellow-striped food outlet covered in unsteadily painted black cannabis leaves. It boomed with reggae music and had 'Ital Freedom Fighters' Surf Shack' painted all over the front and sides.

Ottilie paused. 'Hey, gottanidea. Let's do a reggae set.'

This was well received by the Guys, who started singing 'Stop That Train' before petering out after a few lines, uncertain of how the words went.

'Let's ask these guys to join the band,' suggested Tamara, grooving and grinding in her Indian headdress to the thundering bass currently shaking the caravan. 'They might have some ideas.'

Guy doubted this. The guys in question were two lanky, spectacularly vacant-looking young men in Rasta hats gyrating behind the counter. They were staring appreciatively at Tamara, nudging each other and pointedly ignoring the fact that in front of the Surf Shack was a customer.

A witch – a real witch – in a pointy hat and velvet robe was peering, apparently unimpressed, into the contents of a poly-styrene cup. 'This coffee's cold,' she told the freedom fighters, who were now waving at Tamara and performing, apparently for her benefit, a comic Ancient Egyptian-influenced skank in the space behind the counter.

'THE COFFEE'S COLD!' the witch shouted.

The freedom fighters hardly paused in their skanking. 'Yeah, everyone's been saying that.'

'Classic!' chortled the Guys approvingly.

From over her crushed-velvet shoulder, the witch shot Winnie Bago and the Glampers an irritated look. 'But if every-one's been saying it,' she said, turning back to the counter in exasperation, 'shouldn't you do something about it?'

The freedom fighters looked blank. 'It's the boiler, right?'

As the Guys howled with amusement, Guy wondered why people doing a bad job was funny. Yet he knew that once, and not very long ago, he would have found it funny too.

The witch walked off in disgust and the Guys and the girls crowded up to the counter. After a very few minutes it was established they had people in common. 'You know Tash and Phoebs? Get outta here!'

The freedom fighters were called Freddie and Caspar. Soon an enormous spliff, concealed beneath curled fingers, was doing the rounds.

'No thanks,' Guy muttered when it reached him.

'So, like, how did you end up here?' one of the Guys asked Freddie.

Freddie adjusted his knitted Rasta hat. 'Um, well, deciding what to do on your gap year is pretty challenging?'

There was loud agreement.

'We tried to train as lifeguards,' Casper put in, 'but we couldn't even save our own lives let alone anyone else's . . .'

Braying laughter.

'So we decided we'd better stick to flipping burgers? And so, like, a mate of ours owns this shack . . . ?'

Guy edged away. He could easily imagine what Shanna-Mae would make of all this. And yet until recently Freddie and Casper's attitudes had exactly reflected his own.

Shanna-Mae. Where was she? Throughout their recent wanderings he had kept a constant lookout. But the festival was a confusing place to get around and it was easy to lose your bearings. Of the Beauty Bus and its incumbents he had detected as yet no sign.

CHAPTER 30

Hundreds of miles away, in the Stayhotel in Wortley-on-Thames, James Dorchester-Williams was getting a dressing-down from his constituency agent. The day out canvassing had been long and hot and hard. Now they were debriefing amid rattly white tea things in the bar, although it was fast approaching six and James's thoughts were drifting helplessly towards alcohol.

'Clear blue water!' Rebecca de Sendyng was hissing and thumping the table so hard that the 'Vote Dorchester-Williams' rosette quivered with her agitated bosom. 'You've got to put clear blue water between the opposition's policies and ours. Between you and Nadia Ramage.'

'So you're saying I'm too friendly to Nadia?' James folded his arms and stared stubbornly down at the trousers of his Savile Row suit. 'But I like her. Why shouldn't I wave at her if I see her out canvassing?'

Rebecca's tights rasped angrily as she crossed her legs the other way. 'Nadia. Ramage. Is. The. Opposition,' she said with savage deliberateness.

'Yes, but she's also a human being.'

He watched Rebecca's blue-painted nails drive into her pink

palms. He sensed her battle to keep her temper and he marvelled that she should care so much. She was only a party worker, after all. It was he who was the prospective MP. 'It's politics!' she exploded. 'It's a dog eat dog world. No one is a human being, as you put it.'

'Well, I am, I'm afraid,' James said mildly.

Rebecca turned a pair of exasperated exophthalmic Conservative-blue eyes on him. She would clearly have preferred someone else, anyone, rather than him as a candidate. But she was stuck with him and her task was to get him elected. A process which, from her point of view, he was doing everything in his power to scupper.

'Look,' she said. 'The point is, even though this is a safe seat, we can't let anything go wrong. Give the papers any damaging gossip, say.' The eyes bored into his.

'I only waved at her,' said James stubbornly. 'You'd have to work quite hard to make trouble out of that.'

'They do work hard, believe me,' Rebecca said ominously as she clicked her laptop together, slipped it in her bag and heaved herself up. She looked down at him doubtfully. 'I'll see you tomorrow.' It was obvious from her tone that she did not relish the prospect.

James watched her go, then ordered a stiff gin and tonic to celebrate. He downed it and ordered another, relishing the agreeable stiffening feeling spreading through his body.

The hotel bar, with its rectangular maroon chairs and curved white plastic bar front, was filling up. Fat, trotty women in their twenties were heaving themselves on white plastic bar stools, cackling and ordering from the list of humorously named cocktails.

'I'll have the Simon Cowell! Tall, rich, dark and in a high-waisted glass.'

'Ooh, and I'll have the Stephen Fry! Smooth, sophisticated and with a witty curaçao twist!'

James knew he should ring Victoria, who, he guessed, would be finding the festival a trial. There had been several missed calls from her and he feared the worst. But he didn't want to call his wife, he decided, with a rare sense of rebellion. What he really wanted, James realised, was for Nadia to come into the bar. He could hardly believe it when, in a flurry of papers, wide eyes and tendrils of hair, she burst through the entrance, saw him and hurried over.

'Isn't that Gina Lasagne?' Victoria shrieked as she put her phone away. It was evening now, her first-ever on a campsite, and she was fuelled by a delicious sense of daring, as well as a great deal of wine. All doubt and inhibition had long since been drowned in Château Nobby and the excitement of her glamorous new friend.

It was such an adventure, sitting here with Sarah, watching the world go by. Delighting in the passing show. And now, thrillingly, she had spotted a real, undisputed celebrity; the familiar bosomy form of a well-known TV cook. 'Fancy her being here! You'd think after that court case she'd be lying low.'

Over her umpteenth glass of Château Nobby, Sarah regarded Victoria pityingly. 'That's not how the media works. The only thing worse than being talked about is not being talked about. Was that,' she added carefully, 'your husband on the phone?'

'He's not answering,' Victoria said absently, her attention on the departing domestic goddess and scanning the passing crowd hopefully for further luminaries.

Sarah wanted to strangle her. She was boiling with frustration, as well as what, even now evening was falling, remained considerable heat. Talk about an uphill struggle. She'd invested hours in this bloody woman and had nothing to show for it. Not even a hint of political gossip, let alone sexy stories from the stump. From what she had established so far, Victoria and James Dorchester-Williams were as interesting as Barbie and Ken. If it carried on like this she might have to go and find Tamara Wilderbeest after all. Whatever the editor said.

'Ooh!' Victoria exclaimed, spotting a heartthrob celebrity gardener shaking his tousled locks. 'It's Lorcan Peaseblossom!'

Sarah's eyes flashed with malevolent interest. 'Now I am surprised to see him. We're about to splash on what he's been getting up to.'

'What has he been getting up to?' Victoria was agog. She held her breath as Sarah put her mouth to her ear. 'No!'

A mean smile was pulling Sarah's thin mouth. 'Absolutely. Left, right and centre. With anything with a pulse. As it were.'

Victoria looked doubtful for a second. Then, getting the joke, she spluttered with messy laughter. 'Oh yes. With a *pulse*.'

Sarah Salmon watched scornfully as Victoria's hysterics subsided. She steeled herself for yet another attempt. 'James must be missing you,' she cooed through gritted teeth. 'Poor ickle wamb. Home alone after a hard day on the stump. Why don't you try him again?'

'Oh God,' said James, in the Stayhotel bar. 'My wife's ringing again.' He cursed himself for even looking at his phone. But he had left it on ring for some reason and could hardly ignore it. The tune was so embarrassing – a tinny Nimrod put on by the image people, who claimed no detail was too small to make a political point.

'Why oh God?' queried Nadia, eyebrow raised. 'Bit disloyal, surely? Shouldn't you be saying how wonderful, it's my helpmeet and supporter without whom I would not be able to fight this campaign?'

James met her glance. Was it teasing or admonishing? Ironic or not? Deciding it was unsafe to comment further, he got up and walked past the gang of screaming, tipsy women now hanging off the bar stools having partaken of more Stephen Frys and Simon Cowells than was good for them.

Victoria returned to the tent. She was drunk, but not sufficiently to forget official Party advice never to make calls to her husband in the presence of someone else. Sarah watched her sourly as she sat heavily back in her seat and began once again looking happily around.

'Everything all right?' she asked, hoping desperately that it wasn't. 'Missing ickle wifeykins, is he?'

Victoria beamed at her. Sarah was so sympathetic, so friendly, so wonderfully concerned. 'Oh no,' she said gaily. 'He's not missing me at all. He's enjoying himself, I think. When I spoke to him just now he was having a drink with Nadia whatsername. He seems to rather like her.'

Sarah's eyes widened, but she looked down to disguise it. Was this the scent of a story? Hers was a mind paid to think the worst of everyone. Was there a lucrative worst to think here?

'I've just got to nip off and call the newsdesk . . . I mean, go to the loo,' she said, counting on the noise of the passing crowd and Victoria's general distraction to cover her slip.

CHAPTER 31

Having left a distraught Ginnie in Genghis, Jess was out walking round the festival. Given her reasons for coming to Wild & Free in the first place, she felt exposed and alone, but she needed, she felt, some time apart from her hysterical friend. Ginnie, for her part, needed to calm down and accept that leaving Wild & Free straightaway, as she claimed to want, was both impractical and a waste of money.

And, Jess felt, unnecessary. Surely it was far too much of a coincidence for Mark Birch, or whatever he was called, to be here at the festival? Besides, from what Ginnie had said about him, he hardly seemed the Wild & Free type. That crazy Newwoman woman must have imagined it. Poor Gin, having to put up with parents like that. *Who would be a teacher?*, thought Jess.

A passing conversation caught her ear. 'Shakespeare was totally rock and roll,' a woman in a Union Jack onesie was saying to a man in a bustier.

'Totally,' agreed the man. 'Hamlet was so badass? He so had his thumbs in his belt loops?'

Jess hurried away in the direction of Wylde Hall. She had read in the festival brochure that the house was open at various times throughout the weekend. Festival-goers could go in and look around. It occurred to Jess, ever-vigilant for a certain pair of mad, staring eyes, that being in the house might make her feel safer. Being outside in this teeming, unpredictable, eccentric mass of people was bringing on agoraphobic tendencies.

As she approached the house, she admired the projecting bays of soft Tudor brick set with stone mullions. Behind the gabled roofline, terracotta twisted chimneys twirled up into a deep blue sky. In the rich evening light, diamond-paned windows rippled and glittered. Soft pink roses lolled on the walls

Crossing the small knot garden before the house, Jess breathed in the scent of sun-warmed rosemary and lavender. The great front door was closed, but she went up to it anyway. On trying the latch, she found it moved easily upwards. The door swung slowly inward, revealing a big cool hall which looked very inviting compared to the heat and light outside. Catching a honeyed whiff of beeswax, Jess hovered longingly on the worn stone threshold. Should she go in? There was no obvious barrier to doing so, no sign or rope.

Jess stepped over the threshold. Her sandals made no sound on the chequerboard marble floor. She looked up; the ceiling seemed alive with plasterwork animals. The walls shone with polished oak and at one end was a minstrels' gallery. Beneath, a couple of suits of armour stood attentively, as if still listening to the long-departed troubadours. It was all very calm and still.

Mellow sunlight fell through a long mullioned window set with glowing coats of arms in stained glass. Opposite, over an elaborate carved fireplace large enough for someone to stand inside, extended an enormous painting. Jess gazed at the proud Tudor gentleman with the spade-shaped beard who sat on the left of the picture. On the right was an equally-satisfied-looking woman in a white cap and between them a line of children stretched like railings between two posts. Five boys and five girls, Jess counted. If these were former owners, they were prodigious breeders.

Had the present owner followed this magnificent example? He was certainly a prodigious bridegroom. Jess, who rarely forgot anything she had read, now recalled in crisp detail the festival web page devoted to Sir Ralph de Gawkrodger, who had got through six wives. He was a painter, apparently; there was a picture of some huge mural he had done in one of the rooms. It had looked horrible, Jess thought. And the photograph of Sir Ralph had looked positively bizarre, with curtains of hair, a patterned cape and platform boots. Jess hoped that he would not spring out now from the shadows.

She turned on her heel, half-intending to go outside again. But the beautiful interior called to her, urged her to linger. Hesitating, Jess felt her heart suddenly lift and a warm sense of welcome wash through her. For the first time since arriving at the festival, she felt relaxed. Let scary Sir Ralph appear. She could cope.

Or could she? As a noise from behind set her heart racing horribly, Jess whipped round to see two men coming in through the open front door. Was one of them the formidable owner? It appeared not. Neither had capes or platform boots.

One was fair, strikingly handsome and dressed with Cary Grant-ish simplicity in a crisp white short-sleeved shirt and loose grey trousers. His companion, who was missing several fingers and whose nose seemed mashed into his face, was dressed as a woman. Jess tried not to stare. It took all sorts to make a world. And this was a boho festival.

She was about to say something – a friendly greeting – but the men hurried off. Jess watched as they crossed the hall, passed between the suits of armour and disappeared under the minstrels' gallery.

'Who the fuck was that?' Jude growled.

'Langwidge!' warned Big George.

Jude glared at his co-conspirator. He was seriously rattled. Wylde Hall was supposed to be closed at this time of day. And had been – he had just unlocked the door himself. He and George had come to case the joint, but then Jess had appeared in the garden and they had shot behind a bush to hide. He had thought Jess had gone away. But she had bloody well gone in.

It was, Jude reflected, the first ripple in what was so far a smooth procedural pool. Hall security had been lax beyond his wildest dreams and it had been an easy job, on an earlier recce, to spot the front-door key on a hook and slip it into his pocket. Perhaps slip was not quite the word; the key was massive and of black cast-iron, but luckily his trousers were big enough. He had just looked spectacularly well-hung.

Jezebel Pert-Minks had been a simple matter too. It had taken Jude, the practised charmer, less than half an hour of trowelling flattery to find out which room the oligarch's wife was staying in and during what events she was likely to be out of it. Now he needed to work out an escape route for himself, the Geezers and the gems. Which was why he and George were here now.

The final piece of the puzzle was the exact location in the Badunovs' room of the safe in which twenty different changes of jewellery would be left to look after themselves. But he was meeting Jezebel later and would find that out then. She clearly intended to take him to bed, and he was more than up for that. Strictly speaking she wasn't really his type, but if she was the type who could point him towards millions' worth of precious stones she suited him just fine. And she was clearly smitten; she'd tell him anything he asked. Which, so far, had been quite a lot.

'Charlie!' she drawled, caressing his cheekbone with her

finger. 'You are so interested in me, Charlie! But I don't know anything about you!'

'There's nothing to know,' he had told her. Especially not his real name.

He wished the heist was tonight. He would prefer to strike while the iron was hot, or before the place got hot, in terms of people starting to notice them. A classic smash and grab, wham bam, surgical strike, out on the instant, would be perfect.

But according to Jezebel, the oligarch and his wife were not arriving until the following evening. There was to be a big party which would, Jude calculated, provide their first opportunity for the theft. Until then, they had to wait.

To look on the bright side, a day in hand would give the Diamond Geezers the necessary time to find the answer to a pressing problem, which was what to do with the haul once they'd hauled it. The rocks needed to be hidden, but the likely size of the Badunova hoard meant that the method Jude had initially imagined using – stuffing jewellery in their clothes and George and Boz's capacious underwear, even under George's wig and Boz's hat – would now be insufficient. Stuffing anything in the car was equally out of the question, but for a different reason; it could never be a getaway vehicle. The double-bluff it represented would only stretch so far, certainly not to the extent of them escaping in a pink stretch limo.

Another lingering fear of Jude's was that the ever-volcanic Boz would blow his stack in some act of terrifying destruction. His constant smouldering presence was horribly wearing on the nerves, and it was to grant himself some temporary respite that Jude had dispatched Boz earlier to make contact with the organiser of the Story Jam in the Hibbertygibberty Wood. While it was a risky strategy letting all that walking manic violence loose on its own, the risk was a contained one; the children's story festival organiser would surely be some submissive type unlikely to bring down Boz's considerable wrath.

Now he wondered whether dispatching Boz into the unknown hadn't been rash for a different reason. The woman in the hall had looked at them with disturbing keenness. Had seemed suspicious, even. Had Boz been around, he could have dispatched her before she knew, quite literally, what had hit her. In the Diamond Geezers, it had been his speciality.

Now, in the passage outside the great hall, Jude hesitated. Should he and George still go upstairs and plot their escape route? Or should he try and work it out tonight when he was with Jezebel? He decided on the latter course. And to go and see how Boz was getting on.

Unaware of the concern she had occasioned, Jess had now penetrated to what seemed to be the main reception room. She presumed that the murky, messy painting now extending round all four sides was Sir Ralph's mural, as featured on the website. It looked worse in the flesh than it had on screen. It was supposed to feature Sixties celebrities, but she recognised no one in it.

Jess went up close to a cavorting couple and tried, unsuccessfully, to make them out.

A soft, clipped voice now spoke in her ear. 'Margot Fonteyn and Lord Lucan. Look ghastly, don't they? And that's Peter Sellers and Princess Margaret next to them. Not that you'd know it.'

Jess looked round in surprise. Her interlocutor was a tall gentleman in late middle age. He had side-parted silver hair and his deep-set eyes were the piercing bright blue of the summer sky outside. His skin was clear and fair and his expression gentle, and somewhat wistful.

'Artist drank like a fish,' continued her informant. 'Painted like one too.'

A house guide, Jess decided. One remarkably free with his opinions. Especially considering he was talking about the house's owner.

She looked at him curiously. 'Sir Ralph de Gawkrodger, do you mean?'

'No, that's me.'

'*You?*'

'That's right,' the man mildly confirmed. 'I'm Sir Ralph de Gawkrodger.'

Jess stared, trying to reconcile this unthreatening creature with the crazed rake in the cape and platforms.

'Nothing to do with me, this,' Sir Ralph de Gawkrodger was waving dismissively at the mural. 'Wanted to make sure you knew that. Saw you looking at it and just thought I'd say.'

'But I read that you'd done it,' faltered Jess. 'It says so on the website.'

'All part of the myth,' Sir Ralph sighed. 'As is that ghastly old picture of me they insist on using. With all that frightful long dark hair.' He ruffled his silver thatch. 'I've been prematurely grey since 1979.'

'What myth?' asked Jess. What was he talking about?

Ralph gave her a weary smile. 'Apparently people coming to boutique festivals expect an eccentric aristocrat. That's what the organisers say. And I've never liked to argue with them; they might go somewhere else. There's a woman called Jezebel Pert-Minks . . .' He paused and pulled a face. 'She's terrifying.'

'Can't you just run it yourself?' Jess suggested. 'Then you could just be you.'

Ralph looked fearful. 'I couldn't run it. I'd be hopeless. I know nothing about music and I never read.'

'Never *read?*'

He smiled. 'My dear, the hand of formal education has scarcely touched me. At least, never for very long, and rarely in the same place.' He gave a sudden smile like a flash of sunshine. 'Heigh ho, it makes no difference to me. They pay, which is all I care about. Keeps the old place standing. For a bit longer, at any rate.'

Jess was fascinated. 'So is it *all* a myth? It's not true that you had six wives, either?'

He seemed too nice to be called, as the website had had it, 'the Henry VIII of festivals'.

'No, that's quite true. They call me the Henry VIII of festivals.'

There was a pause. 'Six marriages,' Jess mused. 'It's, well, quite a tally.'

'I've no one to blame but myself.' Ralph mournfully shook his thick silver hair. 'I'm catnip to women who like titles and stately homes and I'm far too stupid to see through them. I always believe they love me for myself alone. I fall for it every time.'

A grin twitched Jess's lips. His candour was as irresistible as it was unexpected.

'I'm actually a hopeless romantic,' Ralph went on. 'You don't need to know this, but I met my last wife at an American trauma resolution clinic.'

'Oh dear.'

'Yes, the trauma I was resolving was being left by the wife before that.'

'Oh *dear*.'

A rather brooding silence followed, during which Ralph looked uncomfortable. She suspected he felt he had said too much.

'Well it's a very successful festival,' Jess remarked brightly. 'You must be pleased about that at least.'

She was surprised to see his face fall again. 'Too successful. We've got an oligarch arriving tomorrow. A Mr Bad something. The name didn't fill me with confidence.'

Jess stared. 'Not Badunov?'

'That's the one. You know him?'

Jess raised her eyebrows. 'I know *of* him. Someone in my chambers handled his last divorce. Or maybe the one before, I can't remember. He leaves his wives so often one rather loses count.' She had completed the sentence before remembering this might not be terribly diplomatic. Ralph did not appear to take offence, however.

'He seems to be much better at divorcing than me,' he observed ruefully. 'All mine took me to the cleaners. Whereas, from what I understand, Mr Badunov buys bigger yachts all the time.'

Jess nodded. 'And houses. And sinks an endless sequence of ballrooms and gyms beneath said houses. One of my other colleagues has been instructed to contest one of the latest planning applications. Why on earth is he here, though? I didn't really see him as a country festival kind of guy.'

Ralph pushed a long hand through his white sheaf of hair. His signet ring flashed a dull gold. She could not quite make out the device. 'Well, now he owns everything else he wants to own a festival. And the mansion it comes with. He's been heard to say it will be good for storing his third-best art collection.'

Jess was astonished. 'He wants to *buy* Wild and Free?'

Ralph shrugged. 'I don't pretend to know how these people's minds work. But the usual pattern seems to be that if something is fashionable, they're not content to merely attend it, they have to own it.'

'That would figure,' Jess agreed.

'The organisers are very keen,' Ralph sighed. 'Ms Pert-Minks is probably thinking of tripling her fee. Badunov's been put up in the best guest bedroom.'

'But would you sell?'

Ralph gave her a troubled look. 'Wylde has been in the family for ten generations. I don't want to be the generation that gives it away. The problem is there's no one for me to hand it on to.'

'You had no children?' Jess was surprised. After six wives! How disappointed the Tudor ancestors would be.

'No, and after six wives too. You can imagine how embarrassing that is. People don't just see me as a serially rubbish husband, they think I must be terrible in bed as well.'

He sounded so aggrieved, Jess burst out laughing. Ralph looked gratified.

'You're very easy to talk to, I must say,' he remarked. 'But I expect you're spoken for. I only hope your boyfriend knows what a good thing he's on to.'

'Actually,' Jess said, 'I'm not spoken for. As you put it.'

Ralph's bright blue eyes widened below his craggy brow. 'That,' he pronounced with asperity, 'tells you everything you need to know about the young men of today.'

'Thank you.' Jess felt abashed at the compliment.

'I say,' Ralph said hopefully, 'you're not busy tomorrow night, are you? They're having a party here and I'm allowed to bring a guest. Just the one.' He rolled his eyes.

Jess thought. It would mean leaving Ginnie on her own for the evening. On the other hand, Ginnie was a grown-up. She could cope.

And I, Jess decided, deserve a little fun. If a very sweet, courteous, funny old-fashioned man asks me to a party in his ancestral home, why say no? She smiled at Ralph. 'I'd love to.'

CHAPTER 32

Lorna Newwoman was in the Hibbertygibberty Wood. She was observing the scene with the intention of giving herself an advantage in the Story Jam competition the next day. Her plan had been to find the stage and then assess its various exits and entrances to decide which one had the maximum dramatic impact. Walking the stage, as the professionals called it. Lorna had been reading up on stagecraft.

So far, however, she was frustrated in her quest. She could not find the stage, let alone its exits and entrances. The Hibbertygibberty Wood was an impenetrable thicket comprised mostly of a huge, gloomy, out-of-control rhododendron with big slippery leaves. Once you entered its darkly gleaming depths, nothing else could be seen at all. The only clue that it was part of a wider, if invisible, festival was a few balloons bobbing about and strings of fairy lights draped in a hurried manner suggesting the draper wished to get back into the daylight as quickly as possible.

No festival official had been around when Lorna first got there. Never at a loss for long, she had immediately rung the number on her wristband.

The Wild & Free Festival might promote itself as hand-made, boho, spontaneous and a welcome holiday from the call centres and materialism of the rest of life, but all of its operators were busy nonetheless. After being put on hold and entertained by the Clash at full volume for more than five minutes, Lorna had to content herself with leaving an angry message.

She resumed her search for the stage. As she explored, she made the discovery that the area was not as empty of life as first it looked. It was in fact home to a large and hungry species of mosquito and she was repeatedly obliged to slap her arms and forehead.

While she hadn't expected the Regent's Park Open Air Theatre exactly, Lorna had imagined something more developed than the rough clearing she eventually found. There were no exits and entrances to 'walk', just gaps in the encroaching bushes. A few boards had been laid down and what looked like pieces of scenery shoved into the bushes.

Lorna inspected them: a large and crudely painted piece of wood shaped like the side view of a lavatory and a big piece of pink rubber. She stared at them, outraged. The Story Jam was a competition for amateur storytellers! It wasn't about performing a piece of theatre!

A drawling Goth called Pixie drifted into view talking into four mobiles at once. 'So I'm your contact here?' she told Lorna, breaking off briefly from one of them.

Lorna lost no time in sharing her furious views about the inadequate stage and the evidence of theatrical intent.

Pixie, now back on one of her four phones, merely held up a pale, child-sized hand covered in silver skull rings.

Lorna waited, burning with impatience. When, finally, Pixie was free, she jumped in. 'It's a story jam!' she exploded. 'Theatre groups aren't eligible to compete!'

Lorna in full bullying mode was a formidable force and she

had expected Pixie, who could not weigh more than six stone and stood about four feet five, to be a pushover. It was a surprise when she proved unexpectedly obdurate about the amateur theatre group.

And then the amateur theatre group itself appeared in person.

'So I'll leave you all to get to know each other?' Pixie exclaimed brightly and was gone in an instant.

Lorna turned belligerently to face the amateur theatre group, all her arguments ready on the tip of her tongue. She was not sure what she had expected; not what happened now, certainly.

A very tall, broad-shouldered woman with piercing eyes, huge feet and dressed in a huge floppy hat and a baggy pink dress now stepped forward and hit Lorna very hard in the face.

The crashing blow rang in her ears and made red fireworks explode behind her eyes. The world swam around her. She teetered backwards, grabbing handfuls of slippery rhododendron leaves.

The woman looked ruefully at her vast fist. 'Blimey,' she grunted in growling, rather masculine tones. 'Don't know my own bleedin' strength.'

So shocking had been the assault on her person, Lorna was temporarily deprived of the power of speech. 'Whhhhgg?' she spluttered. 'Ffffgggg?'

'There was a massive mozzie on your forehead,' her aggressor now explained.

Lorna felt her head gingerly just to make sure it was still all there. Her ears continued to ring. She had never been hit so hard in her life. Normally she would have reared up in fury, demanding compensation and threatening to sue. But instead she just replied 'thanks'.

Her strikingly clad assailant now introduced herself as Boz, of the Rogues and Vagabonds Theatre Company.

'Boz?' Strange name for a woman, Lorna thought. But she decided against saying so. She wasn't sure, for one thing, that she could remember any actual words.

'We see ourselves very much in the outlaws and thieves tradition of acting,' Boz growled, flashing alarmingly big teeth in what Lorna hoped was a smile. Any idea this was her normal expression was terrifying.

Beneath an enormous floppy hat which had obviously seen better days were very thick, arched black eyebrows and a glimpse of close-shaved black hair. Her knees were enormous, Lorna noticed. And her tattoos, which were numerous, looked absolutely terrifying. She had not expected to be competing against people like this.

Lorna now understood why the Rogues and Vagabonds were being allowed to do a theatrical piece. She understood, too, why Pixie had run away. This did not make it right. But did she dare object?

What she really wanted to do was sneak away too, but Boz seemed to want to talk. 'You in this jam thing as well?' Lorna was asked.

'I'm doing,' Lorna said meekly, '*The King Who Couldn't Wee.*'

She watched helplessly as a look of annoyance darkened Boz's already-dark face. She now discovered that her own scatological masterpiece was to face off in the Story Jam with the Rogues and Vagabonds' *The Storyteller's Stinky Underpants*. How could she refuse when a run-through was offered?

Hence the giant cut-out toilet bowl she had seen lying in the shrubbery. And the large piece of pink rubber – blown up with a mere two mighty exhalations from Boz's colossal lungs – turned out to be an enormous inflatable bottom.

The run-through got under way very quickly. In a matter of

seconds, Boz, in the improbable hat, was jerking wildly around the makeshift stage. His knees, to the terrified Lorna, looked huger than ever and the enormous shoes even vaster. Worse, now that Boz was acting – after a fashion – and had a licence to behave extremely, Lorna sensed a raising of already terrifying levels of only-just-suppressed violence.

'What a honk! What a hum!' Boz roared in a deafening voice, holding up the rubber bottom.

It was at this point that Jude and Big George appeared on the scene. And only just in time, Jude saw. He had not credited Boz with the ability to remember even these lines, but he seemed to be making an unexpectedly decent fist of what passed for the script. He watched Boz thunder past the terrified-looking woman in glasses who pressed herself backwards into the rhododendron leaves. Lorna could feel that she was being bitten all over by insects, but she didn't dare even scratch herself in case Boz hit her again.

'Good, isn't it?' Boz yelled at her, rolling his disturbingly bright, large black eyes. 'You get it, yeah? I'm the Stinky Underpants!'

Lorna felt she was about to scream with fear. She was vastly relieved when someone else appeared from the bushes, a very handsome blond man in a white shirt.

'Think we might stop it there,' Jude said to Boz, who was completely out of control and thundering, screaming, about the stage. He shot Lorna a conspiratorial smile. 'He's very Method, you see. Gets carried away.'

'He?' faltered Lorna fearfully, realising she'd had her suspicions from the start.

George joined in helpfully, but soon got out of his depth. 'Boz is very educated,' he confided. 'He was doing a literature degree before . . . before . . .' His voice lowered to nothing.

'Let's not go into that now,' said Jude brightly.

Boz shot past again. 'Yurkkhhh! What a stink!'

A man! Lorna thought. She could completely see it now, especially since his hat had fallen off and revealed his close-shaven, brutish little head. Out of his dark, stubbly face, Boz's alarmingly excited eyes bored into her. As he walked about in his sinister dress Lorna noticed his slightly stiff and rolling walk, as if he had been kicked very hard in the balls. But who, she wondered, would dare kick Boz in the balls? Someone even more frightening, presumably. She wanted to get out. Never in her life had she been so frightened. She edged away, backwards, through the bushes.

'Bleedin' ell,' said George, watching her go. 'Come on, Boz, mate. Let's get you back to the tent.'

'Yes, come on,' Jude said, noticing that, like George, he spoke in the persuasive, soothing tones one might use to a dangerous mental patient. There was a reason for that, of course.

They headed back to the tent, which they had pitched as far away from everyone else as possible. Neither Jude nor Boz had had the first idea how to put up a tent, but George's Methodist boyhood, the church camps in particular, had come in useful at last.

Jude hurried the three of them through the festival, heads down. He needed to get Boz away from human view as soon as and for as long as possible. He felt jittery, for all his outward calmness. Could they contain Boz until the robbery? It was like trying to hold with buttery fingers a bomb with a lit fuse.

CHAPTER 33

To Mark's relief, Spencer had not been in the vicinity of Miss Scarlett when, eventually, he came back. Rob was, though, sitting outside the van in the evening sun on one of two deck-chairs whose seats advertised retro ice-cream brands. He was tuning his guitar in the pedantic manner Mark remembered: plectrum in his mouth, looking up and down the strings with narrowed eyes and frowning as he turned the pegs. As Mark approached, he flicked him a look from under his monobrow.

'You're back,' he remarked.

'Yeah.' Mark's tone was defensive. Whatever he said risked looking like a climb-down. And what could he say anyway? He was not going to admit that a chance glance of someone who might have been a work colleague was the reason he had stayed. Still less did he plan to describe his near-epiphany in the music tent. There was no way he was playing with the Mascara Snakes.

But Rob did not seem to require an explanation. He merely said 'Good' and carried on twisting his tuning pegs.

After hesitating for some seconds Mark sat gingerly down on the deckchair beside him. After a few seconds more, he stretched out his legs.

It was comfortable here in the sunshine. He felt tired after what had been a long and extraordinary day. He accepted with surprise as Rob passed him a bottle from a small cooler bag at his side. It was the first drink Rob had ever stood him in living memory.

'It was under the van seat,' Rob explained. 'Two four-packs of lager, as chilled as you like. Other stuff too. Cheese and pickle, that sort of thing.'

Mark took a swig from the bottle and put his hands behind his head. 'Where's Spencer?' he asked.

Rob shot him a look. 'With that hippy woman. They went off to do some sundown ritual.'

'Is that what he's calling it?' Mark met Rob's eye and they both snorted. For Mark, it felt like the first time he had laughed all day. All week, all month, probably.

He had his eyes closed and now felt something big and light land on his stomach. Rob had passed over his guitar. Mark looked at it. He had his own in the back of the van, of course. But it was battered by years and use, as well as neglect and disuse, and by no means as posh as this. Rob would never have been able to afford one like this in his student days. Mark would never be able to afford one like this now. He let his hand fall over the strings; the notes sang out under his fingers. He felt something tighten round his heart.

Rob was smiling at him; or perhaps just squinting in the rich evening sun.

'Go on. Play something.'

Mark looked down at the gleaming lacquered front of the instrument. His fingertips tingled with the urge to use it. Even so, the thought of 'Brezhnev A Gogo' or any other terrible Mascara Snakes ditty made his blood run cold. He looked up. 'I can't, I'm sorry. I really hate all that old stuff.'

He had expected Rob to react angrily, but he just shrugged.

'And I can't write anything new either,' Mark added, before Rob could suggest it. 'I haven't written a song for years.'

Rob raised his eyebrow. 'Well, if you can't, you can't.'

Mark had been expecting admonishment, but Rob's tone held only disappointment. It made him feel yet more defensive. In the unlikely event that he wanted to, just what could he write a brand-new song about?

Ginnie Blossom had been the obvious candidate. But now she hated him. And even if she didn't he was out of practice – always assuming he had ever been in it – with love ballads. With everything musical. He had not written a song since Margaret Thatcher was Prime Minister.

Mark looked around. A harrassed father in a Ramones T-shirt and red Hunter wellies had somehow strayed into the pagan field. He now clearly wanted to get out of it. He was cursing as he struggled to get his high-end Bugaboo baby carriage through the long grass.

Mark started to tap on the guitar side with his fingers and sing softly.

> 'Oh Mr Bugaboo-Hunter
> It must be such fun ter
> Stay with you in your yurt . . .'

Rob cackled. 'See. The old magic's still there.'

'Hardly magic,' Mark said, about to hand the instrument back. But then he felt something almost physical stop him. Some strange force was keeping one of his hands on the instrument's gleaming neck while the other toyed with the strings. Something was stirring in his mind, a song he had thought about for years. He relaxed his wrist and strummed the opening chords.

'Aha,' said Rob instantly. '"Life is a Chocolate Factory Somewhere in the Milky Way of my Mind".'

Mark, crooning softly, only nodded. He had written it as a joke acid-funk-hippy song. But it had come out far better than he expected and he had always liked it the best, though it had rarely made it on to set lists because it wasn't political enough.

It was amazing how it all came back, words, pauses, rhythm, everything. It was as if he had last sung it only yesterday. The tune now seemed somehow to thicken and deepen in his ear and Mark realised that Rob had started to join in with the harmonies. He sounded better than Mark remembered.

Mark sang on, letting himself slip away on the gentle melody and the wistful whimsy of the words. It made him feel lighter, as if all his recent troubles were slipping away from him. Not just Ginnie, but everything else: Leonard Purkiss and Sheila Wrench. Hangman's Cottage. Even Claire. Mark closed his eyes and felt as if he were in a boat on a river flowing all the way back to his youth.

In Genghis, Ginnie Blossom was waiting for Jess. She still fully intended to leave the festival but she could hardly do so without saying goodbye. Her quarrel was not with Jess anyway; moreover, Ginnie needed her friend to drive her to the nearest bus stop or station. Walking was out of the question given her bags, not to mention the wedge heels.

The broiling heat outside had made Genghis uncomfortably stuffy. It was, Ginnie was finding, difficult to maintain an icy high dudgeon in such temperatures, especially those infused with the powerful, heavy scent of joss sticks. The smell and heat was fogging her mind and making her tired; her resolve was starting to slip. One question kept returning to her again and again; the only question. Was Mark Birch *really* here?

Jess, for one, doubted it and had said so. She had challenged whether the testimony of Lorna Newwoman, whose unsoundness of mind was well known to Ginnie, was either trustworthy or sufficient to justify the drastic action of leaving. But Jess, Ginnie reminded herself, would say that. Jess had her own reasons for wanting her to stay.

And can I go, Ginnie was also starting to ask herself, when Jess is still worried about the man with the mad staring eyes? The thought, accompanied by a stab of terror, now occurred to her that perhaps Jess had fallen into his clutches, and that was why she was not yet back.

Ginnie rolled off the bed where she had been wallowing and decided to go outside. The fresh air would help her focus and the exercise would do her good. In addition, a spot of comfort eating always helped in a crisis and Genghis was very handily placed for the food area.

Outside it was fresher but still very hot. Crowds were milling everywhere Ginnie looked and the air was full of snatches of music, of scent, of talk. She had found the layout of the festival confusing from the start; it was amazingly easy to get lost. It was almost as if landmarks shifted about and reappeared elsewhere; when you thought you knew where you were you were some-where else altogether. Was the food area in front of Wylde Hall? Or over there by the striped helter skelter? Ginnie plumped for the latter and had walked for some time before realising she had gone in completely the wrong direction.

Far from heading, as she had supposed, towards the hand-made burger emporia and esoteric cocktail bars, Ginnie was, she now discovered, walking in the exact opposite direction.

A pretty direction, nonetheless. Mature trees were casting long shadows over wildflower-studded grass of a brilliant green. Beneath the trees, Ginnie now saw, a strange gathering of people was performing something that looked like the hokey-cokey.

Her eye was drawn to a woman with auburn hair and a flowing crushed-velvet dress. She looked, Ginnie thought, ethereally pre-Raphaelite with the evening light clinging palely to the curves of her face. She was throwing her magnificent hair about and making huge circular wheels with her arms, alternately raising them to the dying sun as if in worship, then swooping them down to touch the ground. A druid priestess, Ginnie assumed, rather awestruck.

The woman's companions, while just as strange, were not quite so romantic. There was someone wearing a bird beak and twanging a golden harp; someone else was dressed as a tree. An elderly man in a purple toga was banging a Celtic drum, clapped along to by a woman whose cleavage rose like twin suns out of a leather corset and whose bottom half seemed mostly foliage.

These creatures formed a circle; dancing in the middle of it was a man with flowers in his thick, short dark hair. Apart from his ecstatic expression, he looked the most conventionally dressed of all of them. Sort of middle-aged trendy, Ginny thought, with tight-legged tan trousers hanging off his bottom. His Converse trainers had neon laces. Perhaps he was some sort of initiate.

The circle dance finished and the man in the purple toga now led a conga line of the celebrants. They were joined by some people with antlers on their heads who now appeared from behind the trees. Transfixed, Ginnie realised too late that the woman in the red dress had spotted her. As she stood, rooted with fear as well as a strange excitement, the priestess glided over the grass towards her, long red skirts swishing.

'Come,' she said to Ginnie in a low, euphonious voice. 'Come and join us.'

Ginnie swallowed. She looked into the woman's big, dreamy

eyes and felt the thrilling tones pulling her in. The sun chose that moment to slip behind the clouds, plunging the scene into deep shadow. The trees loomed, branches raised, like phantoms of nature. It was all, Ginnie felt, a bit spooky.

'No thanks,' she gasped, twisting herself away with an effort and stumbling over the grass.

She felt relieved now to enter an area where vehicles were parked and tents erected. Civilisation. The most striking of the vehicles, set slightly apart from the rest, was a shining red VW camper van. Ginnie made her way past the front of it; its inhabitants, she saw out of the corner of her eye, were sitting in deckchairs to the side, playing guitars.

Glancing up, Mark saw to his surprise that he and Rob had attracted a small crowd. People were swaying gently from side to side in time to the music; others had raised their arms in post-ironic joke hippy fashion. They were young, mostly, teenagers, some of them – the age he had been when he had written this song. He didn't care if they laughed at him. Wait until they were nearly fifty. It wouldn't be long. Not as long as they thought, anyway. Who was it that had said the tragedy of old age wasn't feeling old, it was feeling young?

He softened his voice for the wistful bit and found that he wanted, suddenly, to weep. The song was coming out so perfectly, he couldn't remember performing it better, ever. He had written it in one of those white-hot moments of middle-of-the-night inspiration exclusive to the very young. It had taken less than an hour, both words and music. He would never reach such heights again, no more than he would ever be young, and so there was a poignancy to singing it now that hadn't been there before.

Most of all, it was a love song and Mark found he could put into it all the despair and tenderness he felt about Ginnie, who, like the lost years, would never come back either. From time to time, as he sang, he looked up at the people gathered around; they were smiling at him, nodding encouragingly, and with quite unexpected suddenness Mark felt a lump rise in his throat and the tears blur his eyes. He swallowed and blinked, looking down to disguise how very moved he was.

Ginnie found herself slowing down. The song the men were singing was a lovely one. She did not recognise it but it was beautiful; sad and romantic. Listening hard, she could make out references to chocolate – always a subject close to her heart – and flowers. It seemed to be funny as well because the men were laughing at some of the lines, and beating time on their guitar sides.

Watching the crowd enjoying the music, watching the friends perform, Ginnie felt a pang of longing, a sense of parallel lives which would never meet. Perhaps, in other circumstances, she might have got to know these easy, untroubled companions who you could tell went back years together, singing a funny, sad song in a field as the sun went down at the end of a lovely day.

She felt a sudden sense of great sadness. Her throat hardened, she felt a piercing sensation in her nose. She sniffed and blinked hard. The grass was blurry with tears.

Oh, it was such a waste that she who so longed for love should be denied it, destined to an endless sequence of romantic disasters! And there was something in the cadences of that singing voice – raw with feeling at times – that spoke directly to her disappointment, frustration and fear. Ginnie sensed that the singer knew all about her despair, that he had felt it too. Like her he had wondered whether he would ever be really, properly loved.

Irresistibly drawn by this fellow suffering soul, Ginnie crept closer. One of the men was dressed in very tight black clothes. The other wore jeans and a white T-shirt. There was something about him that drew the eye and Ginnie watched as he tucked a hank of hair that had been hanging over his face behind his ear. As it exposed part of his face she felt something explode within her. He cleared his throat, and it exploded again. As the song finished Mark kept his head bent. He stared at the grass, tight with emotion. Then, as the applause began, and the whoops and the cheers, he looked up and smiled.

An almost physical shock hit Ginnie. It really was him. This carefree and boyish figure currently holding a crowd enraptured was the same stern and unsmiling headmaster who had made her redundant and made the last few weeks of term such a misery.

But what on earth was he doing here?

And what if he saw her?

She could not, even so, tear herself away. Mark was talking to the crowd and, impelled by the urge to hear what he was saying, Ginnie crouched forward on her wedge heels, kept her head low and crept up. She was behind a knot of people; he would not be able to see her from here.

'I won't be playing live, no, I'm not here to perform,' Mark was protesting to some questioner in the crowd. 'I'm here because of a mate's midlife crisis. He wanted to get our old college band together.'

He was half-expecting laughter but instead there was a smattering of applause and a few whoops of 'Aw-right!' and 'Cool!'

Mark felt gratified. Amazed, too, at just how good it felt to play and sing again. Therapeutic didn't even come close. It had been fantastic. Perhaps, he was beginning to think, he should go on stage with the boys. He owed them one. He remembered the stage in the Big Top. The Proustian moment before the microphone. Steady on, he told himself. Whoa there.

'I'd like to see you play with your band,' a woman urged him from the crowd. Ginnie, from the other side, glanced at her, taking in the doe eyes, the rippling hair, the slender figure, the pretty dress. The sudden bolt of jealousy she felt almost knocked her over.

'No, you wouldn't,' Mark said with feeling.

But the woman protested and others in the crowd were agreeing with her. So far as he could make out, their admiration was perfectly genuine.

'Great song you just sang,' said a man with a shaven head whose T-shirt advised 'If It Swells, Ride It'. 'Dylan, is it?'

Mark felt his face flame. 'Actually, I wrote it myself.'

Ginnie, hidden, gasped softly. He had written that lovely music, those dreamy words? Mark Birch, that closed, cold, cruel betrayer of devoted teachers of infants?

'You've got to play,' a teenager was telling Mark. She had a blunt pink fringe topped with a red tartan tam'o shanter. 'I'd love to see your gig.'

Others joined in.

'Me too.'

'Are you on tonight?'

Mark stared at them, lost for words.

Rob cleared his throat and raised a hand. 'He is performing, actually.'

Cheers greeted this. Mark glared at Rob, but he merely winked in return and stood up. 'We're called the Mascara Snakes,' he announced in his thin voice, 'and we're in the Battle of the Bands on Sunday evening. So come along and support us.'

'You got it!'

'Woo!'

'Yay!'

'Hang on a minute . . .' Mark muttered to Rob. He had the by-no-means unfamiliar sensation, especially where Wild & Free was concerned, of events running away with him. 'But—'

'But nothing,' Rob muttered back. 'What more encouragement do you want? You'll be there by popular demand.'

Mark opened his mouth to argue, then closed it again. Reasons not to rejoin Rob and Spencer and take part in the Battle of the Bands seemed harder to pinpoint now.

'So?' Rob was urging from beside him.

Mark sighed. 'S'pose so.' He couldn't beat them; he may as well join them.

'Great. Wait until we give Spencer the good news.'

The crowd was dispersing but Ginnie, her eyes still fixed on Mark, remained crouched and unable to move. She now felt a hand on her shoulder. She jumped again. The ripple-haired woman was looking down at her, doe eyes full of sympathy. 'Are you all right?' she asked. 'Is it your back? Only I'm a Wiccan physiotherapist . . .'

Ginnie straightened hurriedly.

The movement caught Mark's attention. His body recognised her before his brain, struggling against the possibility, would admit it. But there was no mistaking the cause of the sharp animal thrill that pierced him. He knew by the pounding of his heart, the trembling of his knees, the giddy, tight feeling in his stomach – with every fibre of his red-blooded, passionate male being, in fact –, that he had glimpsed Ginnie Blossom. It really had been her, climbing in to the beauty bus. It was her here, right now. Although not any more. She had gone.

It had been a split second only, and she had looked very different. He had seen smoky eyeshadow, big hair, thick lashes, a tan. But he had also seen the upward swing of that unmistakeably magnificent bosom. As much as he was certain of anything in this strange and spinning world, he was certain that it was *her*.

He sprang to his feet. The whys and hows of it did not interest him. This improbable, incredible coincidence had one meaning alone; it was an incredible, improbable second chance. He must seize it. Eagerly, he pushed through what remained of his small audience. But Ginnie had gone.

CHAPTER 34

Lady Tamara Wilderbeest, Clemmie van Walthamstow, Ottilie, Bliss Slutt and the Guys were digesting their first major artistic disappointment. Casper and Freddie from the Surf Shack were unavailable to join Winnie Bago and the Glampers because some guy was coming to mend their boiler. There was outrage among the group at such lack of commitment.

Guy Dorchester-Williams didn't care. He was lying on the ground with the rest of the group, chewing a straw of grass and thinking about Shanna-Mae. It was late evening now and while the midsummer sky above was still blue, the ground was deep in shadow and the festival itself a mass of lights.

Ropes of coloured bulbs and strings of fairy lights shone from the stalls; candles in jars and bottles hung from the trees; and from the outer circles where the tents were, torches bobbed up and down and flames flickered from barbecues and braziers.

Guy was now thinking, with a sickening clutch to the stomach, that Shanna-Mae had not come at all. Perhaps she had just been winding him up in the service station. It would be no more than he deserved.

He could hear, behind him, Tamara and Ottilie engaged in

a desultory discussion. Between crippling bouts of spliff-induced lassitude they continued the theme of whether or not their tans needed topping up. They had earlier spotted an on-site spray facility, but were doubtful about the beautician. 'She was really fat.'

'Massive,' Ottilie agreed with relish, stretching out a skeletal forearm from which her elastic festival wristband dangled.

There was a whooshing sensation in Guy's ears. He felt tight around the chest. 'Where is this place?' he asked, trying and failing to sound casual.

The girls looked at him in surprise. 'The other side of the helter skelter somewhere,' said Ottilie. 'Why you asking, Guysie?'

'Just interested.'

Tamara whooped with laughter. 'Going to get your back, sack and crack done?'

Guy gave her a smile, the first he had managed since getting here. Then he got up.

'Hey!' Tamara shouted. 'Where are you going?'

Guy did not stop to explain himself. Finally, he had the information he wanted. As he hurried away from the group, he wondered how Shanna would receive him.

The best scenario, though admittedly the least likely, was Shanna seeing him approaching across the light-twinkling festival field and rushing towards him, eyes alight with love, as Tchaikovsky's *Romeo and Juliet* overture swelled climactically around them.

More likely, although still optimistic, was her greeting him in characteristic cryptic fashion whilst intimating that his overtures were not unwelcome and she actually quite fancied him. The one eventuality he could hardly bear to contemplate was her refusing, after his mother's rudeness, to have anything to do with him at all.

It was to the middle possibility that Guy was clinging as he threaded his way through the hordes wandering around in the dark, the occasional stall-lights glowing on their faces and limbs like a Caravaggio.

Guy passed the red and white striped marquee in which the Battle of the Bands was to be held. Where Winnie Bago and the Glampers would be making their debut, in the unlikely event they got their shit together. It was not shit he was planning on being part of.

The tent was lit inside, pumping with music and crowded with people. The entrance flap was open and a bright orange triangle of light revealed a disco in full swing, not to mention strut and jive; the punters looked quite senior, Guy thought, squirming on their behalf. As old as his mother, some of them. The music was retro – Seventies funk at the moment – and there was some really embarrassing dad dancing going on. People in their fifties moving like Jagger; on the other hand, Jagger was over seventy so perhaps that was age-appropriate.

Guy passed on. In front of a giant movie screen on which a man and woman in Forties dress were clasped in a black-and-white clinch, steam rose from a group of crowded Jacuzzis. 'The Original Hot Tub Cinema' proclaimed the sign at the entrance.

Guy's hopes soared as he realised he had finally come across the body beautiful area of the festival. Incorporating, presumably, the camper-van spa section.

Surely the Beauty Bus could not be far away?

And then suddenly, just like that, he saw what he was looking for. The van loomed at him out of the dark, like a vision. A shiny, cream vision with comedy eyelashes over the headlamps. Heart in his mouth, Guy walked up to it. He felt each footstep, suddenly convinced this was one of the momentous journeys of his life.

Admittedly the bus seemed a bit quiet, as well as a bit dark, but the possibility that Shanna and her assistant had packed up for the day and gone out to explore was not one, at that stage, he had been prepared to entertain. Now he had no choice. He was right up against the vehicle, looking in. There was no one there and nothing going on. The rays from some distant arc-light irradiated rows of bottles, boxes and neatly folded towels in the front, and a sleeping area arranged at the back. Through his bitter disappointment Guy noticed that even the duvet had the 'Beauty Bus' livery on it and was the same cream as the van.

'*Self-love, my liege, is not so vile a sin as self-neglecting*', he read, as he trailed disconsolately away. He would be back tomorrow, obviously. But oh, what years stretched between now and then!

His mother shouldered her characteristically determined way through Guy's gloomy mind. There was nothing for it now but to return to their tent and see what awaited him there. No doubt Victoria would be furious with him; admittedly he probably deserved it. He had not, as arranged, kept in close touch with her. But given that he was trying to find the girl she had so publicly scorned, that wasn't surprising. And his mother had had her own distractions anyway. 'Just having a drink with a journalist friend', one of her – unexpectedly infrequent – texts had read.

All the same, he was expecting to have to face some pretty loud and angry music on his return. And, no doubt, more forensic questioning about Tamara Wilderbeest, with whom his mother had seemed obsessed.

But to his relief and surprise, Victoria was snuggled down in her rose-patterned sleeping bag and snoring when he arrived back. The air was heavy with her scent diffuser and her face shone with night cream. Guy stared down at her, struck by how content she looked. The annoyed creases on her face that he had seen so much of lately seemed to have melted away. She looked young; happy, even.

Guy felt a sudden great wave of affection for her. She might have set back by several light years his cause with Shanna-Mae, but there was always tomorrow. Now he knew the whereabouts of the Beauty Bus he was going back first thing. His mother would not approve, but she did not, for the moment at least, need to know.

She had distractions of her own, anyway. That journalist friend she had run into, for one thing. Guy hadn't realised his mother had any journalist friends, but if this one provided entertainment for her, so much the better. They'd had quite a few drinks, if the wine bottle empties stacked neatly in the designer recycling bag out the front were anything to go by. No wonder his mother was so happily snoring. As he slipped into his own sleeping bag, Guy wondered how his father was doing.

It was eleven p.m. and in the bar of the Stayhotel, Nadia and James were still chatting about their day on the stump.

'I meet a lot of people who rant on about foreigners,' Nadia was musing, 'but it's just a front. It's always something else they're really upset about. It all comes out over a cup of tea.' She reached for her wine, tucking a strand of messy hair behind her ear. 'Usually it's personal debt, payday loans, all that.'

James's insides squeezed guiltily. Money had been his business, after all, his trade. It might still be if he didn't get the seat. He felt cold at the thought of not getting it, but even colder at the prospect of success.

Nadia seized her glass of house red and raised it. 'To you.'

'Why me?'

'Well, you're obviously going to win. Which is fine.' Nadia paused for some wine. 'Apart from anything else,' she resumed cheerfully, 'do I really want to be sitting on a Tuesday afternoon debating the remaining stages of the Groceries Code Adjudicator Bill?'

But did *he*, James asked himself. And *should* he? Because someone had to do it. Parliament was where the law was made. But should he be one of the lawmakers?

The conversation drifted from the political to the personal. 'What was your band called?' Nadia asked. 'The one you told me about this morning, the university one.'

'The Mascara Snakes,' James admitted sheepishly.

'The Mascara *Snakes*?'

'Awful name, I know.'

'I quite like it,' Nadia said consideringly.

'It wasn't meant to last,' James said defensively. 'Which it hasn't. I haven't seen the others for about thirty years.'

Even as he said it he felt surprised. Had it really been that long?

'Pity,' Nadia remarked. 'It sounds like you enjoyed it.'

'I did,' he said quietly, and more longingly than he meant to.

But longing, suddenly, was what he felt. A great wave of nostalgia now broke over him.

He hadn't thought about the band for ages. About Spencer. Or Mark. And the other bloke who played the bass, the one who was always last to the bar. What had his name been?

Nadia asked, out of the blue, 'Why did you want to become an MP?'

James marshalled the various official reasons, then caught her sceptical eye and hesitated. 'I don't really know,' he confessed helplessly.

He half-expected her to laugh at this but she said nothing, just continued to regard him with large brown eyes. Then she glanced at her watch. 'Well, I'm off to bed.'

Outside the hotel, at that moment, Dave Bishop, newspaper photographer, was screeching into the car park on his motorbike. It had been a crap evening. Boiling hot, the traffic bloody awful and he'd been diverted by the picture desk en route on a tip that Prince Harry would be at a certain Indian takeaway at a certain time sporting a new girlfriend.

Neither Prince nor girlfriend had showed, so that had been a waste of time. Now he was here on an even more unpromising tip-off, one from Sarah Salmon at Wild & Free. While there was no love lost between Dave and the paper's most notorious columnist, it would at least be a change of scene to go to a festival. There'd be a few bands there. Decent beer. It had been disappointing, to say the least, that the tip-off didn't concern a couple of titled brats behaving badly, but a couple of would-be MPs. And they weren't even at the festival, but at that concrete dump Dave knew of old, the Wortley-on-Thames Stayhotel.

He dragged his hot black helmet off and scowled at the prefabricated grey front with the shabby purple company flags waving above. It didn't look like front page stuff to him. And he could do with a front page. Could he ever.

Resentfully, Dave thumbed the details of this so-called job up on the greasy screen of his smartphone. Nadia Ramage and James Dorchester-Williams. He'd never bloody heard of either of them. Give me strength, thought Dave. MPs in general were a drag; these ones hadn't even been elected.

He cast a professional eye over the ID supplied by the picture desk so he could recognise his quarry. Hardly the femme fatale, the woman. The guy, though, a different story. Good-looking silver fox, groomed and obviously filthy rich. He didn't look her type, and she didn't look his. You developed an eye for this sort of thing in his job. Nah, thought Dave. *Never*.

CHAPTER 35

Saturday morning

Jezebel Pert-Minks had enjoyed another night of *droit de seigneur*. As head honcho of Festivals First: Outdoor Events Solutions, she had the pick of the hot guys at Wild & Free. It was a perk, in every sense of the word.

On Thursday night, as the festival set up for its Friday start, it had been Danny, lead singer of folk-mash-indie band Maison Trois Garçons. She had been surprised by the tattoo of Mrs Pankhurst on his left buttock.

But last night, Friday, had been an entirely different kind of surprise.

Normally Jezebel kept a lofty distance from the amateur acts in the Hibbertygibberty Wood. Family entertainers, especially the desperate, untalented and unpaid ones appearing in the Story Jam, were not only horrendously unsexy but also occupied the lowest possible point in the festival pecking order.

She had already absolutely refused to get involved with some madwoman called Lorna Newwoman. She had been intending to mete out the same lofty treatment to the manager of a Hibberty-gibberty Wood-bound act called the Rogues and Vagabonds. But that was before she had seen the man calling himself Charlie Croker.

It was a funny sort of name, and one Jezebel felt she might have heard somewhere before. And she'd seen poorer imitations of Charlie smouldering from magazine fashion pages in ads for aftershave and the like. But Charlie himself was unlike anything she had ever seen in the flesh before: the best-looking man she had ever seen in her life.

The attraction had been instant, like a lightning bolt. And mutual. He seemed absolutely fascinated by her, asked her endless questions and had proved unslakable in bed. 'Honestly,' Jezebel had exclaimed merrily at one point. 'It's like you've been locked up for years and only just got out!'

Having awoken, Jezebel cast a satisfied glance round the enormous panelled bedchamber. A plum room in the house was another of her perks as festival organiser. As, now, all her BlackBerries suddenly started ringing, one after the other, she remembered its downsides.

Beside her, enmeshed in sheeting, Jude stirred. 'Whatha-fuckzat?'

Jezebel went round the entire room twice, hunting for communications devices of various sizes, shapes and sorts. No sooner had she found one than it stopped ringing and another started. 'I'm sorry, Charlie,' she said, turning submissive eyes towards him. 'I'll turn them all off.'

'No, don't do that,' Jude said hurriedly. If she did that it meant that he would again be the focus of her uninterrupted attention and last night had been exhausting. The woman was unstoppable and he was, for obvious reasons, out of practice. As a result, he'd had hardly any sleep and needed space to collect his thoughts.

It had been a reasonably successful night, nonetheless. The joint had been thoroughly cased. Jezebel had shown him the oligarch's room now, and the location of the safe.

Jude had thought his excuse ingenious: that he wanted to make love in every empty bedroom. But after Jezebel told him there were up to fifty in Wylde Hall, and some complete wrecks, Jude was even keener to get the robbery over with as soon as possible.

So much remained to be organised, though. He had never before done a job as messy as this, with so many variables. It made him nervous.

Timing was only one unresolved issue. While the where and the how were fairly obvious, the when was not. The Geezers could do the robbery tonight, but Boris and Daria Badunov would be in their room. That could be dangerous. Oligarchs were not usually pussycats and often had bodyguards as well. They could do the heist during the evening drinks party, at which, Jezebel had told him, the Badunovs were guests of honour. But then Jezebel had mentioned the Badunovs' reputation for unreliability. They could arrive at any time, or – and Jude's blood had run cold at this – they might not arrive at all.

He had pushed this hideous prospect from his mind and turned it instead to another pressing question: how to hide the haul once they had hauled it. Obviously the Geezers had their own disguises worked out; the *Stinky Underpants* costumes had worked far better than Jude had ever imagined given the hurried, chaotic way he had assembled them. Boz and George, thus far at least, had passed through the festival without attracting a second glance. This was, Jude felt, partly because of the eccentricity of the event but also because most festival-goers were too self-absorbed to notice anyone else. Even the most solipsistic coxcomb, however, could not fail to notice two large men in drag carrying a jewel chest.

As he worried away at all this, Jude kept half an ear on what

Jezebel was saying. She was sitting on the chair before the dressing table; it had a rattan seat which must be pressing uncomfortably into her naked bottom. Her uncovered bosom was heaving. She was throwing her hair about and seemed considerably agitated. The conversation appeared to be about dogs.

'What about "Hound Dog"?' she was exclaiming. 'Oh, you've thought of that. Hang on, I'll ask.' She turned. 'Charlie?'

Jude's head had half twisted to look behind him when he remembered that he was Charlie. 'What?' he repeated when she had finished. 'What pop music is good for dogs to dance to?' He snorted. 'This is a joke, right?'

But Jezebel, at the dressing table, did not smile. Every atom of her unclothed form transmitted the fact that she was in deadly earnest. 'We have,' she snapped, 'a dog disco disaster situation.'

'A dog disco disaster situation?' Jude incredulously repeated.

Jezebel eyed him impatiently. 'The DJ's stuck in New York and we need to come up with our own canine-appropriate music.' She rapped her fingernails on the dressing table's oaken surface. 'Come on!' she demanded hysterically. 'Think of something!'

Jude flopped back on the bed and stared at the distant cracked ceiling. 'Don't be bloody ridiculous.'

Jezebel stood up. 'You don't get it, do you?' she demanded. 'I've just had a message. The Badunovs are coming today . . .'

'They are?' Jude interrupted. That was a relief. One nightmare scenario could be crossed off. 'But isn't that good news?'

'No!' Jezebel shrieked. She looked so unhinged it reminded Jude unpleasantly of Boz. 'It's a bloody disaster as things stand. Daria's desperate for her dog to go to the disco. His name is Alexandr and he loves dubstep. So we've got to make it happen!'

Jude reared up under the sheets, no longer in any doubt about the urgency of the issue. Alexandr must have his dubstep and Daria must see him having it – during which interlude there might be an opportunity to rob her. Jude furrowed his brow, his every cognitive power bent on the burning question of canine-specific dance music.

'"Dog Eat Dog" by Adam and the Ants?' he suggested eventually.

Jess pounced on this and scribbled it down. 'More!' she demanded. 'Come on! This is an emergency!'

'"Puppy Love" by the Osmonds? "Lipstick on Your Collar?"' Jude was trying not to dwell on how ridiculous all this was. He dwelt instead on Rich's vintage Ferrari.

The Beauty Bus was open for business, Guy saw with relief. Shanna-Mae had obviously been up with the larks and had put up her logoed cream awning in the front, as well as the tall black erection which had 'Beauty Bus Spray Tan Booth' stencilled on the side. Under the awning was a table draped in a contrasting black, with ruler-neat rows of cream-coloured jars and bottles spread out along it. Their labels also sported the black and cream Beauty Bus logo. The only other colour was yellow, from two carefully arranged small piles of lemons placed each end of the counter.

Guy hurried towards it, full of excitement. Shanna herself was not there but her friend, the girl he'd previously seen wearing a tiara and dungarees, was behind the counter wearing a cream Beauty Bus T-shirt. On her bottom half was what looked like a pair of lederhosen, finished with some red satin ballet shoes. She was in the act of completing a sale and slipping some of the cream pots into a Beauty Bus paper carrier.

Guy seized his moment and galloped up to the counter. 'Er . . .' he said. But he was unable, now he was actually here, to get the words out.

Rosie grinned at him. She recognised him, Guy realised, gratified. 'On your own then?' she asked.

All the wind disappeared instantly from Guy's sails. At this obvious reference to his mother, and the excruciating scene in the service station car park, he felt awash with shame, as well as dread that his worst fears were realised. Was his mother's behaviour definitive, so far as these girls were concerned? He looked down at his shoes, the shoes Shanna had admired yesterday. Wearing them had meant wearing his jeans again, when it was already boiling hot and obviously going to get hotter. It had seemed worth it when, ten minutes or so ago, he was breathlessly shining them and lacing them up; he was less sure now.

'Is, um . . .' he began.

'Is Shanna here?' Rosie completed his sentence. 'She is, but she's a bit busy. We've got a bit of a technical hitch.'

Guy felt a leap of hope. If it was something practical that needed fixing, he was the man. Perhaps a shelf had fallen somewhere, or a seat broken. He loved to mend and build things, although rarely got the chance. If he could help, perhaps Shanna would forgive him for what his mother had said. 'What's wrong?' he asked.

Rosie shrugged. 'It's the spray-tan machine. Shan thinks it might have overheated or something yesterday. We were at it all day, the queues were all round here.' She made a snaking movement with her hand intended to suggest an untold volume of humanity. 'If we get the same today,' Rosie added, 'we could be in trouble. Demand is unbelievable.'

Guy pushed his fringe back over his brow. There was a problem here to solve, if only he could solve it. He had no idea what a spray-tan machine looked like, but presumably it had a motor of some sort. He was quite good with motors, with electricity. 'Is there a generator?' he asked.

Rosie shrugged. 'I'm not sure. Shanna said something about batteries.'

'I might be able to help,' Guy said hesitantly.

As Rosie shrugged again, apparently unimpressed, Guy told himself that she wasn't meaning to be rude and off-putting. It was just that teenagers were like that; they lacked social graces. He had been like that himself. Until about yesterday, in fact.

'Can I see the, um, spray thing?' he asked humbly. Rosie shambled off through the grass in her ballet shoes to the tanning tent. Watching her open the flap and lean in, Guy caught a glimpse of cream pleated dress inside and felt a surge in his heart even as his head warned him to prepare for the distinct possibility that Shanna might come out, glare at him and tell him to go away. Back to Winnie Bago and the Glampers. Guy felt he could not bear it if she did.

The conversation now going on in the tanning tent – none of which he could hear – involved lots of gestures from Rosie. It seemed she was attempting – with increasing exasperation – to persuade her friend about something. Guy guessed miserably that Shanna wanted nothing to do with him.

His expression must have been desolate because when Rosie finally reappeared looking flustered, she gave him what was definitely a sympathetic smile. 'Shanna's just coming,' she said.

Unexpected joy swooped through Guy's every nerve. From being a potential vale of tears, the world was a bright and beautiful place.

Shanna-Mae emerged from the tanning tent. He gasped softly at the sight of her. She looked more magnificent than he even remembered, curvy and capable in her Beauty Bus T-shirt. The long cream pleated skirt beneath it had a queenly flow to it. As yesterday, her hair shimmered in a magnificent pile on her head and her make-up was perfect, although Shanna's expression lacked the mocking triumph of the day before. The word, Guy had to accept, was reluctant. Very reluctant. The full lips were pouting in frustration, the wide, well-marked brows creasing the forehead in an expression of beautiful pique.

More than he had ever wanted anything, Guy wanted now to help and be the hero of the hour. 'You have a problem with your spray machine,' he said, through a suddenly dry throat. 'I can help,' he added rashly.

As Shanna-Mae now properly looked at him, Guy could see that he was not forgiven. Her maple-syrup eyes swung on him, burningly clear between the curled-up lashes. It was a glance of magnificent disdain. She drew herself up. 'You?' she said.

'Yes, me,' Guy said doggedly. 'I'm good at fixing things.'

Shanna-Mae put her well-kept hands on her generous hips and stared at him doubtfully. 'Well, you won't be able to fix this. The battery's gone on my machine.'

'You haven't got any spare batteries?'

'Would I be standing here if I had?' As Shanna gave an indignant toss of her hair, a lock flopped out of the glossy pile and bounced deliciously down, tracing the strong line of her cheekbone and just touching the corner of her mouth. Olly stared at it for a second, transfixed.

'And before you ask,' Shanna added witheringly, 'no, I haven't managed to track down any spares. I've been ringing round the festival organisers for hours and they don't have any either. *Useless*,' she said vehemently. 'And apparently the nearest shop's twenty miles away.'

As she turned away and began muttering to Rosie again, Guy realised his presence was not welcome. He couldn't be of any help.

Or could he? Somewhere in his memory stirred the shadow of an idea. In a remote corner of his brain, something now started to fire. A physics lesson, learnt at school, later replicated at home. Battery circuits. You could make them yourself, with coins, wires and acid. He had lit up his Action Man fort and powered a device for reading comics after light out . . .

Excitedly, Guy felt in his pockets and drew out a pile of small change. So far so good. Glancing assessingly at Shanna's stall, he saw that garden wire had been used to lash down some of the material. All he needed now was acid. He looked at the bottles, then dismissed the idea. They were unlikely to contain vinegar. Then his eye caught the fruit. A picture sprang to mind, himself as a small child, crouched on the floor of his playroom, two ends of wires plunged into the upturned face of half a lemon, secured with crocodile clips. He could use hairpins. She was sure to have those.

'Hang on a minute,' he called out to Shanna as she walked slowly back to the tanning tent. 'I can help. It won't last for long, but you'll be able to make a start and in the meantime I'll fetch you some batteries.' One of the Guys had a car, he knew. Although he might be able to think of something else. The engine battery, maybe . . .

Shanna turned. All the scorn had gone from her face. It was not quite radiant with gratitude, but it looked a lot more friendly. 'Thanks,' she said, her tone low and surprised. 'Thanks a lot.'

'What's he doing with those lemons?' Tamara hissed to Clemmie.

They had been coming back from an all-night drinking session when they had spotted Guy. Clemmie had had too many gold-leaf cocktails to be able to see much beyond a blur; she had, in addition, lost both her contact lenses. But Tamara had a harder head; a keener eye, too. They followed Guy at a distance and now lurked out of sight but within view of the Beauty Bus, in the shadow of a gourmet ice-cream stall called Cold Comfort Farm.

'Seems to be cutting them in half,' Tamara mused.

'Maybe he's making some lemonade?' Clemmie suggested brightly.

From behind the round black sunglasses on which the CND symbol was set in diamonds, Tamara glared at her. 'In that case,' she snapped, 'why is he sticking wires in them?'

Clemmie had no answer to this. But she was no longer all that interested. The Cold Comfort Farm stall was opening for business and the owner was explaining some of his flavours to an interested passer-by. One flavour was aril, which Clemmie had never heard of but which was the papery white stuff you peeled off pomegranates, apparently. Another was made of special crocus bulbs you only found in Turkey. Clemmie was impressed. She had not realised crocus bulbs came from turkeys.

Tamara, meanwhile, continued her angry surveillance of Guy and the fat girl. They were doing something on the counter, something very fast which involved lemons and various other bizarre and apparently random items whose significance Tamara could not imagine even if she cared to, which she didn't. She was far more interested in what was going on between the fat girl and Guy.

They were working together, apparently in perfect harmony. There was a happy urgency to their actions, a natural partnership, that made Tamara feel like an outsider, a jealous one at that. How dare the fat girl look at Guy in that teasing way? Or he gaze back at her in helpless worship?

You'd have thought they were a couple, Tamara silently fulminated. But that was impossible, because she and Guy were the couple.

Impossible, too, because surely no one could possibly prefer this *colossal* creature to the famously gorgeous, titled and emaciated Tamara, scion of the ancient Wilderbeest line.

Tamara's agitated heart now sped up yet further and her hollow temples throbbed. Because just then, *right as she watched*, and so quickly she was hardly sure it had really happened, the fat girl flung her arms round Guy. And kissed him full on the lips! At the same time, or possibly just before, a faint roar started up, some sort of tinny machine on the beauty spa stall.

Tamara blinked hard, just to make sure she was seeing straight. It was late – or rather early – her veins were probably one hundred per cent proof and she had not eaten for days, not that that was unusual. But Guy and Fat Girl were still there; she had now finished thanking him, though, and was hurrying back to the spray tan tent, her huge rear wobbling beneath her skirt. Guy, for his part, was turning away and walking straight towards Tamara, although he had obviously not seen her. Tamara was semi-concealed in any case and Guy was looking absolutely dazzled. His eyes were starry and his expression soft with wonder. It dawned on Tamara that Guy had never looked at her like that.

Fury gripped her. Hurt and shock, exacerbated by heat and narcotics, now passed through the crucible of fury to produce a hard and twisted urge for vengeance. Tamara's thin hands curled murderously at the ends of her skinny arms. She turned on her pink Croc-ed heel and stomped off, Clemmie scuttling behind. 'Hey Tam! Wait for me, yeah?'

It was hot, even though it was early. But the heat in her head was more than that; it was, Tamara felt, as if her brain was actually burning in her skull. What should she do? How could she punish him?

No one treated a Wilderbeest like this. She came from one of the first and finest families in the country. She was going to do something.

Exactly what, she was not sure. Something that he would not easily forget, anyway. Or the fat girl. Yes, Fat Girl most especially. She would learn the hard way, Tamara resolved, what happened to people who annoyed the Wilderbeests. Not for nothing was the family motto Strength Through Fortitude. Or was it Fortitude Through Strength? Whatever, Tamara thought.

CHAPTER 36

'Here we are,' Jess said, entering the tent. 'This is the Oliver Brown talk.'

Ginnie, following her in, was hardly aware of where she was or what she was doing. Automatically, obediently, she sidled after Jess along one of the battered wooden benches that had been set out on the grass inside. She had an impression of a stage area with microphones, lots of other people, and of the fact it was hot and muggy. But her thoughts were, in the main, focused entirely inwards, on the happenings of last night.

She had slept badly, merely dozing, falling into dreams about Mark Birch from which she awoke with alarming suddenness. The scene outside the camper van replayed itself endlessly in her head; she recalled snatches of the song he had been singing. These romantic pictures and the wistful feelings they evoked made it very difficult for Ginnie to summon any of her old fury concerning her former boss. They seemed to suggest it was entirely possible that what Jess had said, and what Mark himself had tried to assure her of, was true. Whoever had voted for her sacking, it had not been him.

Ginnie had struggled against this conclusion even so. The alternative was a much neater explanation. Otherwise, what could she think about him? What should she do?

'Quite crowded, isn't it?' Jess, next to her, remarked conversationally. 'But then, *Smashed Windows* did pretty well, I think. And he's sharing this talk with someone else, Sparkle D'Vyne.'

When Ginnie failed to reply, Jess rolled her eyes. Her friend seemed very distracted this morning and looked utterly blank and preoccupied. All the more so since all yesterday's theatrical make-up had been removed and Ginnie was back to her old scrubbed, peachy-skinned self.

Jess decided to give up any effort at conversation. She, too, had a lot on her mind; she too had spent half the night awake.

Was she being ridiculous? She had known him hardly any time, and it was against all expectation and logic, but she was drawn, Jess knew. She was definitely drawn to Ralph de Gawkrodger.

Of course, the two of them were wildly unsuited. She could still – just – be described as young, while he was definitely ascending the higher rungs of late middle age. He had had six wives while she was single. Ideologically they were miles apart too; a socialist by inclination, she had never previously warmed to the landed gentry. But then, Jess thought, she had never met an example of it quite like Ralph.

And she would be seeing him again this evening; he had invited her to the author party. Jess felt an almost childish excitement at the prospect. She was looking forward to it more than she could ever recall looking forward to anything. She had not yet broached that subject with the uninvited Ginnie – or indeed any other given her current distracted state. But would she have wanted to talk about Ralph anyway? Jess was not a shy person, but she felt shy now.

Why, she was not sure. She was not sure about any of it, it

was all new territory. But she felt, at the same time, a strange happiness. It filled her thoughts and distracted her, finally, from those manic black eyes always burning in her mind.

Isabel, sitting close to the stage area, felt tired and apprehensive. She had spent an uncomfortable night on the narrow bed in the maids' room; one largely alone with her book as well. Olly had been at some event at which, he claimed much later when he stumbled in drunk and merry, he had made lots of important new contacts. To add insult to injury he had fallen into bed and gone straight to sleep, while Isabel had lain awake wondering if she should have gone to the party after all. Her excuse had been tiredness, but it was not just that. Isabel was a respected academic, a rising star in her own field. It was an unpleasant sensation, at Wild & Free, to feel like a mere appendage to Olly.

And she was tired, too, of wandering endlessly round the festival on her own. Shanna-Mae and Rosie, the only other people she knew, were always busy, or planning to see something that did not interest Isabel. Such as the Big Fashion Swap yesterday evening, at which everyone attending was expected to exchange clothes.

And once it got dark, Isabel was still less inclined to wander. The festival was large, larger than it first seemed, and confusingly laid out. She'd got lost once or twice already. It was like *A Midsummer Night's Dream*, only without the fairy king and queen. There was an ass, though. Isabel looked at Olly as he appeared bleary-eyed with Jezebel Pert-Minks. He had woken with a hangover and now looked positively green as he dumped himself on a chair and clung to the seat as if to hang on.

Olly cleared his throat, looked round, saw her and managed a wink. Isabel stared stonily back at him. It wasn't just Olly leaving her alone the previous evening that annoyed her. Or her status as a literary WAG. Not even his lack of interest in the wedding, or his new beard and clothes. Isabel had spent a long night waiting for the dawn to come and in that tired and weakened state her defences had been down.

She had been forced to admit, to herself if nobody else, that the basis of the insistent, increasing discontent she felt was the fact that Olly was here to promote a book based on some of the worst months of her life. More than this, he seemed oblivious to the fact that this might upset her. It made Isabel feel resentful. Olly may be a writer, but he conspicuously lacked imagination.

And now the moment had come. He was about to speak. Isabel stared down at her hand and saw how the muted light inside the tent glowed inside her engagement ring. The diamond winked at her comfortingly and reminded her that there was a life beyond all this. Once the festival was over things would get back to normal and the wedding preparations get underway.

Olly, seated on one of two fold-down wooden chairs behind the microphone, was nursing his throbbing head and cursing himself for overdoing it the night before. He was in no condition to address a literary gathering at all, let alone in the witty, thought-provoking fashion he had intended. He had planned a dazzling performance, but now, thanks to the fog and pain in his head, he could hardly remember anything he had meant to say.

Earlier that morning he had been unable even to recall the title of his own book. But that, fortunately, would not be a problem now because piles of *Smashed Windows* were arranged at the rear of the tent on a trestle table, ready to be sold and signed afterwards. Twin pink towers at an adjoining trestle signalled the accompanying presence of Sparkle D'Vyne's deathless prose.

Olly was glad that he had, despite Isabel's criticisms, persisted with growing his hair and beard. It gave him something to hide behind now. He peered through the lank locks flopping over his eyes and saw Isabel in the audience. She looked cross, Olly realised gloomily. Still cross. She'd been cross ever since she got here. He was beginning to regret persuading her to come at all, but it was too late for that now.

Hopefully he could redeem things by putting in a great performance at this talk. Just as well, though, that he only had Sparkle D'Vyne to contend with. His initial disappointment at not having drawn H.D. Grantchester in the lit-lot was now replaced with relief; he was in no condition to do justice to someone of such towering intellect. A chick-lit-writing socialite was about his level at the moment.

He would, in any case, meet H.D. at the party later on; he intended to take full advantage of that encounter and hopefully forge valuable and longstanding literary links. But for now, this morning, Olly thought, he'd simply try to control his nausea and coast through the Sparkle D'Vyne encounter. He hadn't read her book, but that was not a problem. He would simply employ the old trick of asking her to describe what *Vixens of Knightsbridge* was all about.

And that would be pretty funny, Olly thought, brightening, because it was almost certain to be ghostwritten and Sparkle would be keen to conceal the fact. He could ask her for plot details and then throw in questions such as whether, for instance, *Vixens of Knightsbridge* contained any particular moral, metaphysical or social themes she wished to point up. As the satirical possibilities gathered momentum, Olly's lips twitched. Yes, there was a deal of highbrow fun to be had at Sparkle's expense!

The no-doubt literary audience, after all, were hardly likely to be here to listen to some airhead friend of the royals. They had assembled to hear him talk about his own award-winning work. Well, thought Olly gleefully. Here was the perfect way to entertain his fans as well as make Jezebel Pert-Minks think twice before she paired a ditzy bonkbuster writer with an author of his calibre again.

He shook back his shaggy fringe and peered at the crowd through bloodshot eyes. He had been wrong about the graveyard slot; this was a biggish one given the early hour, only just past ten. Quite a lot of people would witness his lightly humorous skewering of worthless commercial fiction. His spirits were rising all the time. The session, Olly reflected, might make his name yet.

There was still no sign of Sparkle D'Vyne, but that was only to be expected. Writers like her could hardly be described as professionals, or serious in any way. Nonetheless, Olly was conscious of a new impatience. He had been dreading meeting Sparkle; the association, he had thought, could only be toxic. Now, glimpsing an opportunity to benefit from their contrasting artistic status, he was impatient for her to appear.

Nonetheless, she didn't. Olly continued to sit, head throbbing, on the hard chair as the buzz of conversation around him grew and the heat, despite the early hour, began to gather force. An old man in the front row fell asleep. Behind him, lounging against a tent pole, Jezebel Pert-Minks fielded various emergencies on a battery of phones.

Suddenly there was a stir at the tent entrance, a giggly exclamation and someone half-fell in. There were, Olly thought, taking in long blond hair, skin-tight metallic silver dress and towering wedge heels, no prizes for guessing who this was.

Jezebel Pert-Minks now hurriedly finished her call and strode forward to seize the microphone. It had been made clear to Olly that Jezebel was the only one permitted to use it. It detached from the stand and could roam about the audience; Jezebel would be in charge of fielding audience questions.

'Guys!' Jezebel addressed the audience. Her trademark throaty, cracked tones were hugely amplified by the microphone. 'I hope you're as excited as I am! I'm just dying for this D'Vyne–Brown literary mash-up to get started.'

'Divine Brown?' Olly saw the dozing old man in the front row wake up with a start and whisper loudly to his equally elderly neighbour. 'Wasn't that the woman . . . Hugh Grant . . . goodness, didn't realise *she'd* be here.' With obvious effort he twisted round and watched Sparkle wobbling in her high heels down the central grassy aisle between the benches.

The round of applause that accompanied Sparkle to the microphone area sounded, to Olly's ears, ironic. He stood and, rolling a knowing eye to the audience, shook Sparkle's thin hand with its long red nails. The very obvious glamour of her appearance was offset, he now saw, by a pair of black, round glasses with very thick rims.

'Great, aren't they, my specs?' Sparkle giggled in tones almost as polished as her toenails. 'They don't have lenses in. They're to make me look literary. Like you!' She beamed at Olly.

There was a ripple of laughter from the crowd at this. As he and Sparkle now both sat down, she arranging her long, brown legs to maximum effect, Olly shot the audience another knowing look. This, he thought, was going to be easy. Candy from a baby territory. If he could have rubbed his hands together, he would have.

Sparkle now turned to Olly and patted his knee. 'Go on then! Ask me a question!'

Olly did not hesitate. 'So,' he began, adopting a magisterial drawl to excite the envy of H.D. Grantchester herself. 'Tell us what your book is about, Ms D'Vyne.'

Sparkle stared back at him. 'Haven't you read it?' she challenged.

Checkmated on the first move, Olly realised. He had not expected this. Her eyes were holding his; his were the first to drop. 'I've not quite finished it,' he sidestepped, to titters from the audience.

'What?' he asked, missing whatever Sparkle had just said.

'I said that makes two of us.'

'What makes two of us?'

'You not having read my book.'

'Well, I didn't quite say *that*,' Olly riposted before remembering he was in a hole and had better stop digging.

'Don't worry.' Sparkle waved a nonchalant, diamond-braceletted hand. 'I haven't read it either.'

'But . . .' Olly frowned, 'you wrote it, didn't you?' Perhaps she meant she composed in a creative firestorm and never read the work back afterwards. Some people wrote like that; not him, however. He started each day's work by rewriting what he had done the day before. And then rewriting that the day after. Moving on could be a problem sometimes.

Sparkle was laughing; an unaffected sixth-form chortle. 'Course not. Someone wrote it for me. A ghoul. No, ghost.' She laughed again.

Louder laughter from the audience at this. Olly gave them an incredulous smile before turning back to Sparkle. She had bowled him a lifeline but was obviously too dim to see it. He felt more in control now. This was going to be good, after all.

He went immediately on attack. 'So you haven't even read it?' His tone was triumphant. 'You didn't write your own book and you haven't read it?' He shook his head incredulously at the crowd in the tent. This was even easier than he'd thought.

He had expected Sparkle to look crushed; to look angry and

defensive even. But instead she shook out her shining hair, seemingly utterly relaxed. 'I don't have to read it, darling, I've lived it! But I have read yours and I enjoyed it very much. A searing polemic against the corrosive effect of too much privilege, I felt.'

The audience laughed again, but the tone of the laughter was warm. They were definitely leaning to Sparkle. Nervous and defensive, Olly shifted upright in his chair and swallowed.

Sparkle continued to blink at him brightly and tapped his knee encouragingly. 'Darling one! I have to say I'm the *teensiest-weensiest smidgeon* disappointed. I was so desperate to hear your brilliant intellectual take on my novel and I'm sure all these wonderful people out here,' she stretched a graceful arm out towards the audience, 'were too.'

Olly felt his face burning beneath his hair. He had never felt so silly in his life. He cursed himself for not even reading the *Vixens* plot blurb. His mind had gone blank, there existed between his ears only a buzzing whiteness. He rummaged desperately for something with which to save himself. It seemed to him that his only hope was to sidestep the whole question of *Vixens*.

'Perhaps,' he gabbled wild-eyed, as Sparkle leant forward in an attitude of calm attention, 'perhaps you could tell us about your remarkable name.'

Sparkle clapped her lovely hands, sending several chunky, expensive bracelets slithering and jingling down her slender forearms. 'It's my porn name, darling.'

There was a shout of laughter from the audience at this. She had them eating out of her hand, Olly realised.

'Porn name?' he repeated in his best Lady Bracknell, hoping to steer the crowd back his way.

'Surely you know what a porn name is, darling?' Sparkle

reached out and slithered her fingertips over his knee. 'Name of your first pet and mother's maiden name. Sparkle was the name of my darling guinea pig and Champagne D'Vyne is my mother.'

There was a murmur of recognition among the audience at this. It was clear from the many fond, reminiscent smiles that Champagne was or had been quite a character.

A hand went up in the audience. 'Ooh,' exclaimed Jezebel, darting over in what might have been relief. 'A question already.'

The questioner was a middle-aged woman of judicial appearance. Her air was stern and intellectual and Olly's hopes rose that she would deliver a stinging criticism against a feckless life of glossy privilege. 'Do tell us how your friends the Princes are getting along,' she asked Sparkle in a voice positively dripping with hopeful sycophancy.

And after that, Sparkle was off. Olly felt at first sidelined then gradually invisible as she dropped names like bombs and delivered funny, clever, self-deprecating anecdotes that had the audience in stitches. He could only look on and marvel at her ability to work a crowd. There was no getting away from it, Sparkle D'Vyne was a sensation.

Towards the end, and with obvious reluctance, Jezebel managed to shoehorn a question his way. But Olly, embarrassed, humiliated and with a depressing sense of being hoist by his own arrogance, could only mumble in reply and give his questioner the most fleeting of glances. He took what comfort he could from the fact it was the friendly woman who, yesterday, had stuck her head through the tent flap and been snapped at by Jezebel. Her query was both insightful and appreciative. Thanking him for his answer, she said *Smashed Windows* was her favourite book of the year.

After the talk, the queues around Sparkle's table were at least four deep to Olly's one deep. Almost her entire stock of books was sold. Olly stared at the good three-quarters of his that remained and reflected gloomily that, despite confidently assuming the exact opposite would be the case, he had been outsold, outflanked and outperformed by a ditzy socialite who hadn't even written, still less read, her own novel. Almost the worst aspect of the whole thing was that she was impossible to dislike.

'Never mind, darling,' Sparkle shouted over cheerily as she signed the last *Vixens of Knightsbridge*. 'I'm sure they've all got copies of yours already!'

Olly was rather less sure.

'Some of them have several copies,' agreed his questioner from the audience, who now presented him with her book and asked for an inscription, 'To Jess'.

'Thanks for coming, Jess,' Olly wrote, hardly originally, but with great feeling.

'That was fun,' Jess observed to Ginnie as they left the tent.

Ginnie nodded absently. She had paid very little attention and almost everything had gone over her head. The tent, the people, the talking, none of it had seemed real. The only real thing was what she had witnessed last night, which endlessly replayed in her memory. Should she, Ginnie had spent the talk wondering, seek Mark out? It was starting to seem that unless she did, she would have no peace.

Jess, meanwhile, looked happily about her. She was enjoying herself; the talk had been fun and there was the party tonight to look forward to. What should she wear?

After negotiating Ginnie, apparently on autopilot, round a few especially crowded areas, Jess's speed picked up and she glanced around to make sure Ginnie was following her. In doing so her eyebeam swung across the horizon, and snagged on something. Something familiar, terrifying and completely unexpected.

Jess stopped dead in her tracks.

'What's the matter?' exclaimed Ginnie, jolted out of her reverie by the force with which she had just collided with her friend.

Her heart jumped as she saw Jess's terrified expression. 'Tell me!' Ginnie gasped. Jess seemed incapable of speech.

Then the spell broke and Jess began to gabble. 'Gin . . . it was him. I saw him. Those eyes.'

Ginnie shook her head vehemently. 'You can't have. How could he possibly be here?'

'He was . . . I swear it . . .' Jess's hands were covering her face as Ginnie hurried her to the nearest bar. The good thing about the festival was that you were never very far from one. 'The Boar's Head, Eastcheap' had hay bales for seats grouped around beer barrels sawn in half. Ginnie ordered two bottles of lager. Who cared if it was only half past ten in the morning?

'You can't have seen him,' she repeated to Jess, who looked grey with shock. 'How can you be sure? Did he see you?'

Jess shook her head. 'No, thank God.' She had ducked her head down just in time. 'At least,' she added, doubtfully, 'I don't think so.'

Just because she had not been looking at him, of course, did not mean he had not spotted her. Oh, why had she chosen this morning to wear an eye-catching neon coral sundress? There were eyes out there that she had no wish to catch.

Jess felt horribly jittery and unstable. Compulsively she knotted and unknotted her fingers. Her bottle sat beside her, untouched, an undisturbed slice of lime wedged in its neck.

But Ginnie, silent and incurious all morning, was now firing question after question. What was he wearing? Jess found it hard to remember. Fear had impaired her memory. There had been a crowd, a lot of people passing. The eyes alone were what had stayed with her. Eventually she could bear the cross-examination no more. She slapped the barrel-top and stood up.

'I've got to go, Gin. Come on.'

Everything was different now. It was as if the sun had gone in. It hadn't – it was shining as brightly as ever – but Jess felt cold inside. A heavy anxiety squatted in her stomach. She felt she no longer cared about anything, not even the party. What was seeing Ralph, compared with surviving? There was no doubting the murderous potential of those eyes.

'You can't go,' Ginnie objected, knowing she was repeating Jess's exact words to her yesterday. 'Not just like that,' she added feebly.

'Yes, I can. We both can. Why not? You don't want to stay. You told me last night. You've seen someone you didn't want to, and now so have I. Oh *God*, have I,' Jess exclaimed.

Ginnie was silent. She could hear, over the other side of the bar, the zoot-suited barman describing the pork scratchings; from some fashionable Scottish pig, apparently. Then, as an enormous noise burst suddenly from overhead everyone looked up. As if from nowhere a gleaming black helicopter appeared from over the tops of the trees.

The hysterical racket of the whipping blades heightened Jess's panic. 'So let's both go. Now.' She hopped urgently from foot to foot. But Ginnie remained seated, watching as the helicopter headed over the festival and started to descend near the house.

'Come on,' Jess urged agitatedly. Her eyes darted feverishly round, as if what had frightened her might at any time reappear. 'Come *on*, Gin. You were *desperate* to leave yesterday.'

Ginnie hung her head. 'Yes,' she agreed quietly. 'But now I want to stay.' Until Sunday at least, she was thinking. Until the Battle of the Bands.

CHAPTER 37

The helicopter was at a standstill now, its blades drooping over its gleaming black carapace. A man with emphatically dark hair and aviator sunglasses, his short, thick legs in jeans, was strutting across the lawn to the side of Wylde Hall. Wafting by his side was a thin and beautiful brunette exposing a largely flat chest and a lot of pale skin in a flimsy long red dress which clung to her bony frame. She carried a large and very shiny black bag and wore black high-heeled sandals with complex sculptural heels. The jewels on her wrist, neck, ears and fingers flared in the late morning sun.

Jude, watching the Badunovs' arrival from the distance of the knot garden, swallowed. That was serious jewellery. He could almost see the facets on those rings from here. A pair of huge men wearing earpieces followed, their dark suits straining over enormous muscles. They were carrying a collection of cases and boxes which they took into the Hall. Jude's eyes narrowed further. Which of those boxes had the jewellery in it? And how was he to find out, with two colossal Russian meatheads guarding access?

He watched as Jezebel, flanked by various festival munchkins, came across the lawn to greet the new arrivals; she was practically curtsying, Jude saw scornfully. He'd left her still compiling her dog disco playlist and now he could see the reason for the panic; peeking out of Daria Badunova's shining tote was the bony head of a tiny dog. There was a flash around its throat; Alexandr too apparently had a penchant for diamonds.

'Diamond Dogs' by David Bowie! Why hadn't he thought of that before?

The sight of the jewels – almost, now, in touching distance – sent adrenaline surging through Jude. He felt like dancing from foot to foot, like a boxer about to enter the ring. After months of planning and near-constant setbacks, the moment, along with the Badunovs, had arrived.

And if their bodyguards had as well, was that a problem? He cast an assessing look at the straining suit-backs of the huge and muscled escorts and forced down rising panic. They looked as if they bit pieces out of battleships for breakfast. Even Boz was no match for these two. They needed another change of plan. Jude corralled his rioting synapses and decided that if security was guarding the door, there might be a way in through the window. There had better be. There would have to be.

Guy was still sitting on the grass by Shanna's stall. His eyes were closed and his face tiptilted to the sunshine. He felt immensely satisfied. While Shanna-Mae was yet to surrender in any meaningful way to his overtures, she was treating him with much less scorn than before.

His makeshift battery had sent a charge of life not only through the ailing spray-tan machine but through his romantic prospects as well. His efforts, Heath-Robinson though they looked, had nonetheless been a resounding success and Shanna had been able to spray three clients in the time it took Guy to devise a way to rig the machine up to the engine battery. He had taken it out – Shanna, at the moment, didn't need the van to go anywhere – and it worked like a dream. Which was just as well; the lines outside the tanning booth were building up already and sales of Shanna's lotions and potions were brisk. Word about the Beauty Bus was evidently getting around.

And it was he who had made all this possible! Guy leant happily back with his hands behind his head and replayed over and over the glorious moment when Shanna had exclaimed to him, gorgeous eyes glowing with what might even have been gratitude, 'You saved me!'

'Gee, it was nothing,' had been the obvious response to this. Guy had never been one to shirk the obvious.

She had looked slightly shamefaced. 'You're all right, you are. And clever. Really clever. I'm sorry I was a bit rude when we met before, in that car park. I thought you were—'

'Just another posh idiot?' Guy prompted brightly.

A helicopter overhead had interrupted them at that point. Shanna had looked up, affording Guy the opportunity to admire her nose in profile and the way her hair fell down her back. 'I wonder if that's Boris Badunov. I heard someone say he was coming.'

'Who's Boris Badunov?' Guy and Rosie asked together.

Shanna stared at them. 'The oligarch? One of the richest men in Britain?' Her expression became thoughtful. 'Be good to get his wife pictured with Beauty Bus products.'

The name rang a vague bell, Olly thought. Hadn't one of the Guys gone out with one of Badunov's daughters? She'd kept an AK-47 under her bed, or something. Unsurprisingly, the relationship hadn't lasted.

'Got to go,' Shanna said, gesturing at the growing queue outside the Beauty Bus before returning her gaze to Guy. He watched her hesitate; she seemed to be weighing something up in her mind.

'Um, why don't you come back later and we'll go for a drink?'

Guy closed his eyes and saw stars explode. A date! He and Shanna, alone together. 'I'd love to,' he burst out vehemently.

'You too, Rosie, obviously,' Shanna added casually to her friend. 'We could go to that milkshake place you liked the look of.'

Guy sighed. So he hadn't quite got her to himself. Yet. But it was definitely a start.

More than a start. The moment he had seen her he had felt something switch on inside him. He felt warm and positive and loving towards everyone. A new sense of self-worth and usefulness filled him. She had said that he was clever! That meant more than any number of the A stars he most certainly would not be getting.

Guy had been too happy and busy over the last few hours to think about what would happen when, unavoidably, he ran into Tamara Wilderbeest again. Drawn into the all-consuming world of Shanna-Mae, he had completely forgotten Tamara existed, not to mention the rest of the Guys. But now, as he walked slowly away, they came back to mind, along with the realisation that Tamara might not be entirely happy at this abrupt transfer of his affections.

On the other hand, he had never made her any promises. They had just had fun together, that was all. Tamara had never really been his type, Guy rationalised. And while there had been intimacy, he was far from being the only one she was intimate with. Furthermore, he had always discouraged any suggestion they were an item. The more Guy thought about it, the more certain he was that Tamara would take the Shanna news on the chin and not worry about it.

* * *

The other side of the festival, Lady Tamara Wilderbeest was stalking angrily around. What she was trying to think of – still – was a way to punish Guy. So far she had come up with nothing. Normally, as nothingness was the usual content of Tamara's brain, this would be no cause for concern or even surprise. But now, forced to the unfamiliar labour of thought, it ached and protested at her attempts to make it form ideas.

A very loud pounding from outside now joined the pounding in Tamara's head. She was going past the Ital Freedom Fighters' Surf Shack. The freedom fighters were waving at her. 'Yo! White girl!'

It was on the tip of Tamara's acid tongue to tell them to fuck off. But then she noticed what she had not before, that there were biscuits at the end of their counter. Small, chunky biscuits that looked handmade.

She approached, smiling.

'Hey, yo, white girl, man,' said Freddie, looking her up and down. 'Where de other white girls, man?' He made a gesture with both hands, tracing the outline of a curvy body.

Tamara looked at them pityingly. You could tell they were Etonians a mile off. 'The others? Oh, you know. Around.'

Clemmie had peeled off ages ago. They had had a furious row and she had stormed off to inspect some Eighties power suits at a vintage clothes stall.

Tamara pointed at the biscuits. 'Are they . . . ?'

'Hash cookies? Well, there's hash in 'em. And some other good tings!'

'What things?' They had better not just mean eggs and flour.

Casper made a sign she understood. Freddie made another. Tamara whistled. 'They sound lethal,' she said admiringly.

'Wouldn't eat them all at once, put it that way,' Casper said.

Tamara smiled. Wouldn't it just serve Guy right if he ate one of these? Guy, so proud of never touching drugs of any sort. Well, he'd touch these all right. He'd be as sick as a dog for the rest of the festival and off his head into the bargain. The fat lady was unlikely to be impressed.

Jude was still trying to find the Hibbertygibberty Wood. It was taking longer than he had thought. The day was wearing on and he needed to get the other Geezers into position. But this bloody place was so confusing. He'd never been a great fan of the countryside. Too much green, too many trees and they all looked the same.

Every time he thought he had his bearings, he lost them again. Enormous coloured flags were forever looming in his sightline and distracting him. Plus oversized balloons and, most of all, bloody bunting. Jude felt that if he saw another string of triangular-shaped flags in faded florals, he'd throttle someone with it.

What was this vintage thing anyway? It had passed him by; he had been inside. Prison must be one of the few places on the planet uninfected by the trend for rose-print, polka dots and shrunken boiled-wool cardigans.

He did not want to Stay Calm and do any of the stupid things recommended on everything from T-shirts to toilet paper. He wanted to find some other criminals and do a robbery. But tree branches dangling with battered chandeliers and tin jugs of wilting peonies kept getting in his way.

And now someone on stilts was coming at him – *everyone* here was on bloody stilts – shouting through a red megaphone about a piece of performance art called 'How To Bake Your Trousers'.

Oh, where was the bloody Hibbertygibberty Wood? Now he had blundered into some sort of art area. Two women in long white dresses and Edwardian hats, dreamy expressions on their faces, were slowly kicking a football from one to the other under the gaze of an awestruck crowd.

Jude hurried away in the opposite direction. All this was getting on his nerves. And if it was irritating him, what it might be doing to Boz did not bear thinking about.

For the hundredth time, he ran through his mental checklist for the robbery. Not everything was entirely in place, but there were enough reasons for optimism. There was, as he had hoped, a window open in the Badunovs' bedroom. As well as a handy drainpipe beside it. Running the gauntlet of those boulder-like bodyguards would not, after all, be necessary.

Jude had also decided to stop worrying about where to hide the jewels. Perhaps he could, after all, just stuff them under Boz's hat. With any luck they'd escape with them immediately, although Frankie was proving elusive, not answering her phones. Jude was not panicking yet, but he needed to make contact soon. Frankie had to supply a fast driver and a fast, anonymous car. Otherwise it was going to be the pink limo, which couldn't manage over seventy and was far from subtle. Either that or some local bus.

But hang on! Jude stopped short, catapulted from his cogitations into the here and now. The answer to one problem at least was staring him in the face. He was walking past a cream VW van with 'Beauty Bus' painted on the side. Outside it was a table bearing a large collection of bottles and jars.

Jude felt a jolt of excitement. Why had he not thought of it before? Hiding rings and precious stones in make-up pots was an old jewel thieves' trick. You could smuggle them anywhere after that.

This lot on the table would be about enough, Jude calculated. They'd be breaking the haul up anyway; only the stones counted.

This was where George could finally make himself useful; he was an expert at this, working away at the clasps with a precision and delicacy belied by the huge size of his hands.

And then they'd just slip the sparklers in these pots. That Boz and George were dressed as women added an extra layer of cover. As it were. No one would ever think of looking at the beauty aids of a children's show. Even in a pink Hummer, if it came to that.

He strode up to the stall. There was no time to lose. 'Give me the lot,' he ordered the large girl behind the counter.

Shanna was affronted. Who did he think he was, this arrogant creep picking up her merchandise and regarding it with curled lip and assessing eye?

'That's my whole stock,' she pointed out. 'If you take it I'll have nothing left to sell.'

Jude took no notice. 'Put it in the bags,' he barked.

Shanna stood her ground and shook her head. She had customers coming back today, people who hadn't had the right money, or wanted more lotions, or whatever. She did not intend to let them down.

'You're telling me you won't sell your products?' Jude was incredulous.

'Not to you,' Shanna said firmly. Just what was going on here? This guy was slimy, no doubt about that. She had read all the biographies of cosmetics tycoons she could lay her hands on. People were always trying to steal their formulas. Her formulas were good and she was proud of them. If this guy intended to unpick her work in a laboratory, he had another think coming.

Jude could see that arguing was getting him nowhere. There was something immovable about this girl, for all her youth. He changed tack, cut to the chase and named a tremendous sum.

Still Shanna shook her head. 'I'm here to provide a service, not a takeover opportunity.'

Jude named an even bigger sum, everything, in fact, that was left of what Frankie had originally advanced him.

Shanna's head shook from side to side, more adamant than ever.

He could not, Jude saw, glancing at his watch, spend any more time on this. He had the Geezers to round up, to brief. Without another word he strode away. It was her decision. If she wouldn't sell it he would just have to take it by force.

He'd be back later.

CHAPTER 38

For Mark, the day had been an anti-climax. He had spent it searching for Ginnie Blossom in every festival nook and cranny, but without success. Once he thought he saw her from the rear, on the stall of a scented candle collective. He had rushed up; the woman – not Ginnie – had turned round and sold him a recycled jam jar of smelly wax labelled 'Gardenia and Bacon Sandwich'.

Mark's second disappointment was Spencer. He had been conspicuous by his absence the night before and drifted by to pick up his toothbrush just as Rob and Mark sat chewing brioches and drinking coffee.

Waiting, earlier, at the Brew Bar Boutique for the coffee to be ground then made using an oil lamp and a test tube, Mark had reflected that splitting the atom had been done with less fanfare. The brioche had come courtesy of a man in a tweed suit with a basket who cycled about the festival on a penny farthing.

When Spencer had arrived for his Colgate, Mark had been expecting jubilation. Spencer, surely, would be thrilled that he had returned to the fold and would play with the band.

But that the Mascara Snakes would ride again now seemed a matter of perfect indifference to the man once so determined to reunite them. 'OK,' was all Spencer said.

Mark was mystified. He pressed on. 'I want,' he said, 'to open the set with "Life is a Chocolate Factory Somewhere in the Milky Way of my Mind".' There had to be a reaction to this, surely. The song had never been Spencer's favourite.

'OK,' said Spencer again. 'Whatever.'

Spencer, Mark was forced to conclude, had other things in the Milky Way of his particular mind. It wasn't hard to guess what, or who. Spencer looked tousled and tired, but radiated an almost tangible sense of satisfaction and well-being.

'Where were you last night?' Mark asked.

'Dowsing my aura, mate.' Spencer spoke as if this were the most normal thing in the world.

There was a snigger from Rob.

'Doing what to your what?'

'My aura,' Spencer repeated. 'Rowan was trying to find out the size of it and what sort of shape it's in.'

'What's that about?' pursued Mark, as Rob snorted again. 'What happens?'

Spencer rolled his large and expressive eyes. 'So, mate, I get in the centre of a circle, yeah, and then Chris comes at me with the dowsing rods. All lovely jubbly. It's a big one, Rowan says, and very healthy.'

Should he, Mark wondered, be happy that Spencer now seemed to be as lukewarm about the Mascara Snakes as he had been on fire about them before? After all, it was the way out that he, Mark, had until recently been looking for.

Except that suddenly, it wasn't. He now felt – faintly but nonetheless definitely – disappointed. He realised that he wanted to walk out on a stage with the rest of them – Spencer included – and play a set. Wanted to stand before a microphone facing an audience, with the feel of guitar strings under his fingers.

But now there was just him and Rob. Half of the original line-up, and not the charismatic half at that. The chance had been missed, the opportunity gone.

Guy was on his way to meet Shanna-Mae. He had spent the day drifting and clock-watching, waiting for the longed-for hour to come. Never had time dragged like it had today. He had been round the festival several times but could remember nothing about any of it. It was all one noisy, crowded, colourful, smelly, hot blur. He had focused on nothing but the face of his watch as, with agonising slowness, the hands revolved.

Now his step was quick, his head was high and his whole being charged with purpose. Finally, it was time for their date. With Rosie gooseberrying, of course. But Guy had long ago resigned himself to that.

'Tamara!' Guy exclaimed, his voice high with panic. Even to his ears it sounded like a squeak. He had not seen her coming.

The shadows were deepening, eveningtide was fast falling and Tamara's silhouette as it approached him in its feather headdress and barely there bikini loomed threateningly against the blooming clouds. Guy braced himself for the first blast of what would surely be a torrent of fury. Somehow, he was sure, she had found out about Shanna.

The Wilderbeest eyes glinted. 'I've been looking for you,' she said.

Guy swallowed. He tried not to flinch as she came at him with both fists. But the expected blow did not fall and, instead, he found his arms full of rustling plastic. He opened his eyes to find himself holding a package containing some biscuits.

'Oh wow,' he said. 'Er, that's really sweet of you, Tamara.'

Tamara beamed. 'I saw them and thought of you.' Well, it was true in a way.

They gazed at each other. Tamara's gaze was unreadable. Then she smiled. 'They're kind of a goodbye present. I've found someone else.' Even to her own ears she sounded convincing; she had always been more at home with lying than with the truth.

Guy felt wobbly with relief. He wondered if he should try to seem upset. He couldn't, though. He had never been a good liar and he was so happy at the moment he could hardly stop smiling. 'Well,' he said brightly. 'That's good. I never really deserved you, Tamara. I hope you'll be happy.'

He wondered if, after all, he hadn't got Tamara wrong. Perhaps she was a kind and generous person underneath. Now he was, for the first time, really in love, he felt that the world was a wonderful place and everyone, even Tamara Wilderbeest, deserved the benefit of the doubt.

Tamara, for her part, gave him her best and most gracious smile, the one she used when the servants at Wilderbeest Towers were lined up for their small Christmas bar of chocolate. If her eyes remained icy and glittering Guy did not notice. 'No worries,' she said. 'Enjoy, yeah?' She dropped a light kiss on his cheek and sashayed off.

Guy stared after her, then blinked, rubbed his forehead and looked at the packet in his hand. Did he want to take a packet of biscuits on his date? He could always give them to Shanna, but was that appropriate, as they came from his ex? Guy decided that it wasn't and that he would leave them in the tent he shared with his mother. It wasn't far from where he stood now and his mother never even looked at biscuits, let alone ate them. It briefly flitted across his mind that he had not seen or heard from his mother for hours. But that had to be a good thing. She was clearly enjoying herself with this new friend of hers.

Sarah Salmon was feeling the heat. Not only the sort currently beating down on the tent village of the Wild & Free Festival, but professional heat too. Her editor had made no secret of his disgust at her lack of scoops. Of course the Badunovs were here, but, as the editor had not hesitated to point out, oligarch smoligarch, hardly front page stuff.

Adding to Sarah's problems was the fact that Dave Bishop, damn him, had drawn a complete blank in Wortley. There was clearly nothing going on between Nadia Ramage and James Dorchester-Williams. Nor had Sarah found out anything remotely scandalous from Victoria herself about her marriage. Nothing but James's unblemished track record as devoted father and hard-working director.

Sarah glumly poked her chopstick into a piece of sashimi. They were sitting at the festival outpost of a celebrated Shoreditch sushi bar which had only three seats and a seven-month waiting list. The festival version had six seats and no queue.

Sarah sent a swig of small-grower champagne after the sushi. Victoria had laughed hysterically at this label and asked if it was produced by midgets. Victoria's galumphing high spirits were grating on Sarah's nerves. She was clearly having the time of her life while, for Sarah, Wild & Free was an unmitigated disaster.

She was living in hope, nonetheless. She had instructed Dave Bishop to stay at Wortley for one more night. Victoria, meanwhile, was to come with her to the party in Wylde Hall. She had been beside herself with excitement to be asked and was already, thanks to the champagne, quite squiffy. The Symposium, Sarah hoped, might tip Victoria over the edge. With any luck she'd get so trollied she'd become the story herself. Sarah could take the pictures with her smartphone. Get the reproduction fee too.

Victoria lowered herself unsteadily down from the high stool. 'I feel a bit funny.'

'Have some more champagne!' Sarah immediately sloshed a foaming slap of wine into Victoria's half-empty flute.

'No, I'll go and lie down in my tent,' Victoria said firmly. It must be the sunshine and all the wine; she was not used to either. She needed a few hours of shade and quiet; there was also plenty of bottled water in the cool box. She was determined to be on form for the party.

Victoria made her way back shakily to her tent. The rose sprigs were revolving alarmingly as she entered, but at least it was private. She could lie here until she felt better.

She opened the cool box and pulled out a bottle of water. The sushi had been very salty. If only she had picked something sweet; even the tiniest bit of chocolate. Victoria could hardly remember the last time she ate something sugary.

What was that, sitting right in the middle of Guy's cowboy-motif sleeping bag? A bag of biscuits! Had Guy left them there for her? How considerate of him! Victoria slithered over the sleeping bags towards them on her stomach. They looked delicious. Thick, chunky. Chocolate chip? They were always her favourite.

Perhaps just this once she would let herself.

Seizing a cookie in each hand, she slithered back to her side of the tent. They crunched roughly beneath her eager bite. There was a slightly strange aftertaste, but Victoria overlooked this. Soon she had scoffed the lot.

CHAPTER 39

Jess had not wanted to go to the Symposium party. She remained desperate to leave the festival. But Ginnie, who had originally felt the same, now felt the opposite. They had both completely reversed their original positions. Why she was now so determined to stay, Ginnie would not say.

But Jess could guess. 'You think you've seen that headmaster,' she accused Ginnie.

'And you think you've seen that escaped criminal,' Ginnie riposted, equally exasperated. Then she had played her trump card by pleading a migraine and going to bed.

Jess did not believe for a minute that Ginnie was genuinely ill. Her friend had the constitution of an ox – 'as well as everything else', Ginnie was wont to sigh. And the timing was obviously suspicious. But Jess could hardly force Ginnie to get up, pack her things and leave. She had been conclusively out-manoeuvred.

With the result that she now faced an evening in which she either remained cooped up with a theatrically groaning suspected malingerer or went, as originally planned, to the party at Wylde Hall. Those two options at least had the benefit of being indoors, in an enclosed, protected space. Wandering about outside, Jess knew, put her at risk of encountering the mad staring eyes again – if, indeed, she had seen them in the first place.

Ginnie, she knew, doubted that she had. Just as Jess had doubted that Ginnie had seen her schoolteacher. Another complete reversal.

'How *could* he be here?' Ginnie had kept saying, echoing the words Jess had used about Mark Birch. But Jess knew what she had seen – and felt, like a bolt to her heart. One particularly frightening aspect to it had been the strange lack of surprise. It was as if, on seeing her old courtroom enemy, something as yet unacknowledged about the whole festival had come sharply into focus. A strange air of faint menace around the helter skelter and the revolving swings. Fairgrounds were always slightly creepy. But now she expected to encounter a murderer round every corner, the whole place seemed sinister to Jess.

Ginnie had disagreed. 'It's not creepy, it's lovely. And of course you're safe! Even if he was here, he'd never find you. There are thousands of people out there.'

Jess had called the police, but the sergeant had sounded doubtful. 'Oh, you're at that festival, are you?' he had said in his musing West Country burr. Jess could almost hear the reasons for not believing a word she said ratcheting through his mind. Drugs. Alcohol. About to go off his shift.

Even pointing out that she was a barrister cut no ice. The mere mention of London was enough to put his provincial back up and she suspected her hoity-toity official tones hadn't helped either. 'I'll send someone up,' was the sergeant's reluctant conclusion. 'But we're busy at the moment. Summer Saturday night, you know . . .'

'But this is a suspected escaped criminal!' Jess protested. 'An armed robber and murderer!'

'So you say, Miss,' came the weary West Country tones. 'But

we only have your word for it. You didn't go and accost him, did you? No witnesses, you say?'

Jess was forced to concur with all this. And as an officer of the law was clearly not coming any time soon – if ever – she had decided to go to the party in the end. She could have a fag on the way at least; rarely had she needed one more.

The woman with the clipboard had taken an age – on purpose, Jess was sure – to find her name on the list. Once admitted, she found the house, heaving with shrieking and giggling people, hard to recognise as the soothing and silent place in which she had first met Ralph.

And what would it be like to see him again? Her recent shock had changed her view of everything. She had thought some sort of spark had leapt between them, but that now struck her as embarrassing. What did she, a successful city career girl who had made her own way, have in common with some septuagenarian aristocrat?

Now, disenchanted and disengaged in her new white strappy party dress, Jess leant against the wall of the room which occupied the few inches of space between the edge of the crowd and the dreadful mural. For one usually the centre of any gathering, being a wallflower was an unpleasant experience.

All the same, she had to admit it was a fairly starry gathering. Close to where she stood, a well-known broadcaster was being fawned over by a short, busty festival official. 'Hashtag myhero,' she was saying. The broadcaster gave Jess a despairing look, and she giggled.

The flat, lonely feeling soon came back, however. 'No thanks,' Jess said, as a waiter came past with a tray of drinks. Alcohol wasn't going to help. Nothing was. Ralph neither, not that she could see him. Pehaps he hadn't bothered to come.

'I'm so *awfully* glad to see you!' First the exclamation from behind, obviously heartfelt, then suddenly Ralph was at her elbow. As the troubled blue eyes came into view, and the silver slide of hair, Jess felt her heart give a little jump.

'How are things?' she asked, reaching for the drinks tray as, with considerable difficulty, it made its return journey through the mob. Ralph seemed unaffected by the press of bodies, pristine in a baby-pink gingham shirt and white trousers, both pressed to within an inch of their lives. Male though he was, his fairness and pinkness made her think of a lovely rose.

'Things?' He regarded her disconsolately. 'They're awful. Badunov's ghastly. So much worse than I ever imagined possible. The price of everything, the value of nothing, that's him all over. Spent this afternoon pacing the basement planning his underground garage and gym complex. Helicopter pad on the roof.' Ralph frowned and shoved a long hand through his hair. 'I can't bear the thought of selling Wylde to such a creature. On the other hand,' he added as the thought struck him, 'we do have form in that respect.'

'Form?' Jess queried.

'Yes, the Elizabethan Sir Ralph de Gawkrodger, the one all us firstborn sons get named after, was an absolute thug himself,' Ralph sighed. 'He made a fortune out of the Irish wars and plundering Spain with Drake. He would probably have had a lot in common with Badunov.'

Jess chuckled and took a sip of wine. She smiled encouragingly at him. 'Surely you don't have to sell it if you don't want to.'

Ralph cast her a look; a hopeless flash of bright blue. He pulled a face. 'Realistically, what else can I do? I have no descendants.'

'None at all?'

'None, I assure you. Not even the usual sheep farmer in New Zealand who always appears at this stage.'

Jess snorted. Ralph was warming to his theme now. 'And so the question is, when given the choice between selling Wylde to someone with the money to keep it standing, even if converted to the very worst kind of luxury hotel, or holding on to it myself and seeing it rot and fall apart even as I rot and fall apart myself . . . well . . .'

'You're not rotting and falling apart!' Jess interrupted. 'You're in extremely good shape.'

She stopped, feeling this to have been rather a personal remark and more self-revealing than perhaps she had intended. She felt her face burn and saw Ralph's expression change. His gaze, still fixed on her, widened, as if something had occurred to him. Jess felt her heart turn over. She looked away, but not before she had noticed how suddenly charged the air between them had become.

Neither of them said anything for a few moments. The ebb and flow of surrounding conversations pressed in on them. Then Ralph spoke. 'I'm going,' he declared, 'to have a fag.'

'You smoke?' Jess said wistfully.

'I say, do you?'

Jess rummaged in her bag and produced her Silk Cuts.

'Come on then. No point trying to get over there,' he nodded to the distant entrance, 'we'll be trampled to death long before we get there. But there's a way up to the roof.'

'The roof?'

'Yes, it's rather nice. Good views.'

Quick as a flash he opened a jib door in the mural and nudged her through ahead of him. 'Come on. This way, through Princess Margaret.'

Elsewhere in the room, Olly was trying to remain optimistic. It was an uphill struggle, and had been ever since the Sparkle

D'Vyne encounter. Isabel had hardly been a comfort. While she had said relatively little, he sensed her relief that the shameless D'Vyne limelight-hogging had cut to almost nothing his time to talk about *Smashed Windows*. Isabel, at least, had not been embarrassed.

But Olly intended to reverse all his bad luck at the party. He was rubbing shoulders with some serious literary big beasts. But shoulders were where it began and ended. He couldn't seem to connect with any other part of them.

All around him he could hear people excitedly networking; the very air seemed to crackle with potential. You could, a tortured Olly felt, actually scent the future Oscars, the Booker prizes, the BAFTA-winning TV series, even the *Woman's Hour* serialisations. The people that fixed that sort of thing were all here. But he was just sinking without trace. Certainly he was sinking drinks. He had lost count of how many glasses he had lifted off passing trays.

A long arm was waving at him. Unsteadily. Tarquin Squint, too, had clearly been putting the hospitality through its paces. 'Oll! Come over here! Someone I wan' you to meet!'

Of the person next to him, clearly someone very short, only the top of a grey head was visible.

'Come and meet your heroine!' Tarquin boomed. 'Heroine, I mean Hermione, Grantchester!'

'Oh wow,' gasped Olly, feeling he had been rescued from the quicksand. He ploughed a determined furrow towards the much-garlanded author of *Nasty, Brutish and Short*.

Isabel, beside him, hurried after him as best she could. She was not enjoying the party but was determined to conceal it, less for Olly's sake than for her own. So far he had not even commented on her appearance.

This hurt as she had made, for her, considerable effort. There had been no mirror in the maids' room but the scrappy bathroom with its ancient, gurgling taps and flaking walls had a small looking glass blooming with mould and in this she had done her level best. The bigger mirrors, on the walls in the public areas on the way down, had confirmed her hopes; she looked, she thought, pretty good.

Her new dress was black and close-fitting with neat cap sleeves; it showed off both her elegant figure and dazzling red hair. She had bought pretty pointed silver slingback pumps; a rare frivolous touch in honour of their stately surroundings. But Olly had not so much as looked at them. Or her.

Ever since entering the party his chin had been up and his eyes eagerly scanning the horizon. He had already spotted, with mounting glee, a famous contemporary artist and a pop star turned speciality butcher. Particularly about the latter, Isabel found she could not share his excitement.

She had been compensating for this lack of attention by trying to concentrate on the house; in contrast to their horrible, poky room, the public areas were beautiful. They had come to this room through a Long Gallery whose elaborate plaster ceiling was a miracle of skill and invention and whose diamond-pane window bays were irradiated with rich evening sun. She would have preferred to stay out there than be in this great hot press of shrieking people. It made her nervous. But Olly always had to be where the action was.

'Are you all right?' Olly looked round at Isabel; there was, she saw, irritation in his eyes. 'Only you just squeezed my hand really hard.'

Isabel stared at him in despair. Did he really not understand?

Tarquin was still waving at his protégé but had changed arms to his drinking arm. As this held his glass he was now showering its contents liberally over his neighbour. 'Sorry, Heroine,' he was shouting, tugging off his tie and trying to dry her with it. 'Heroine! Heroine!'

This caused quite a stir in the crowd.

'Shit. He's poured wine all over H.D. Grantchester!' Olly snarled to Isabel. 'That's got me off to a great start.'

He barged up anyway, dragging his cringing fiancée. Perhaps it was drink, or excitement, or both, but it seemed to her that Olly had lost completely his gift for assessing a situation. Especially after this morning, when Sparkle D'Vyne had effectively wiped the floor with him, surely Olly realised he was going the wrong way about things? Watching him as he vainly sought a way in to talk about his book had been, for someone who loved him, painful to witness.

As was his behaviour now. Olly either could not see or would not accept that he was not wanted. It was, Isabel felt, putting it mildly to say that Tarquin's chucking cava over H.D. Grantchester had been a disincentive to further conversation.

The magisterial author had in fact turned her portly back on Olly. He watched disconsolately as she began to talk to Hermes Bugg, a stand-up comedian and author, as Olly had ascertained in a previous conversation, of a book called *Firing Cheeseballs at a Dog*.

Ignored once again by Olly as he desperately tried to break into the group, Isabel felt she could stand it no more.

A wave of frustration broke over her. She felt she could see the future, trailing after Olly to one literary festival after another. Sitting and watching as he discussed her painful past. Caring about her less and less all the time. It was clear that Olly had his sights set on horizons rather beyond Paradise Street, his job at the *Post*; herself, even. He had changed in ways beyond merely growing his hair all over his face and wearing jeans whose waistband hung down to his knees.

Well, Isabel had no intention of being a mere appendage. A plus one. A WAG and bag-carrier. She dragged the engagement ring off her finger. 'There's something I want to say to you,' she shouted, her voice thin and strained above the ever-increasing swell of voices.

Olly could not hear her. Someone was yelling to someone else at his rear. 'Darling! I've got a new career as a novelista! *Vixens of Knightsbridge* is my first masterpiece!'

Cold horror gripped Olly's spine. He felt that if he saw Sparkle D'Vyne ever again in the entire course of his life it would be too soon. But here she was, bouncy as ever, a vision of lissom blondeness in a black dress so tight you could practically see her kidneys. Plus the big black lenseless glasses, of course.

Olly's spirits sank further as he saw her being enthusiastically welcomed by Bugg and kissing H.D. Grantchester on both fleshy cheeks.

Isabel, ignored yet again by her fiancé, stared at the ring she held beneath the pads of her finger and thumb. She had meant to make a point only; to wave it at him and ask him if he remembered it, if it meant anything. Now it seemd her questions were answered. He was moving away from her, spun off by the eddies of people pushing and shoving. She was just about able to reach his jeans pocket, hanging off his bum, and shove the ring inside. Olly did not even turn round.

CHAPTER 40

James had decided to stay the night in the Stayhotel. It saved him a commute home and ensured he would be ready for whatever Rebecca de Sendyng had lined up in the morning. The fact that it also meant he could spend more time with Nadia was, he told himself, merely a bonus.

That Nadia was staying here too was just a coincidence, nothing more. Her family home was in the Midlands and she had a hotel room for the duration of the campaign. 'Room 101,' she giggled. 'Like in Orwell.'

James smiled. She was such fun. In the world of banking he met few women, and outside banking he met women like his wife. Nadia was a refreshing change. 'I know, why don't we have supper together?' he suggested casually, as if the idea had only just occurred to him and hadn't been, as was actually the case, bouncing about in his mind most of the day.

Nadia pulled a face. 'I suppose it would have to be here in the hotel. It might look funny otherwise. But I'm warning you, the restaurant's pretty terrible. I ate in it last night.'

James shrugged, as if none of this was of any consequence; as if the food was just fuel after a hard day's work and Nadia herself just a bit of company as they shovelled it down. But inside he was thrilled at her suggestion that it might look funny; a tacit acknowledgement, surely, of something slightly naughty, or at the very least unorthodox, in which they were both complicit. He also felt that however terrible the restaurant, he would rather be there with Nadia than in the number one restaurant in the world with anyone else. Including, though he stopped short of pursuing this thought to its logical conclusion, Victoria.

The hotel restaurant was called 'Encounters', which made James laugh, possibly too much. A skinny teenage waiter with flesh tunnels and a creased, tight and not-very-white shirt shuffled up to them at the Please Wait Here To Be Seated sign.

'Encounters' turned out to be a neo-Sixties affair with white blocky tables and low-hanging lights. The vaguely ball-shaped shades, made of complicated intersections of woven plastic, looked to James like vastly magnified dust mites.

Nadia honked with laughter when he pointed this out. Victoria never laughed this much at his jokes. And she picked from the menu fish and chips, which he found bewitching because it was the last thing his wife would dream of eating. 'I'll have the same,' he told the bored waiter, who inexplicably found his workplace much less amusing than they did.

James knew this was rash; fried food gave him indigestion. But in the company of Nadia he felt gay, incautious and thoroughly reckless. 'Oh, and a bottle of house white, please.'

'No, red,' corrected Nadia, to his relief. White wine, especially the sulphate-crammed stuff they no doubt sold here, gave him hangovers.

They chatted happily through the fish and chips and another bottle of Tasmanian Merlot and then ordered chocolate pudding, which Nadia also demolished with relish. James tried not to stare. He could not recall the last time he had seen a pudding-eating woman.

All too soon the evening was at an end. Nadia stood up. James blinked up at her as a heavy disappointment sloshed through his insides after the fish and chips and Merlot. 'You going? Don't want another drink?' It was hard to get the words out, for some reason. He could hear that he was slurring slightly. He had never been a big drinker, although he had drunk big tonight.

She looked at him, half-apologetically, half-anxious. 'I'd ask you for a nightcap but it's a bit risky. I mean, supper's probably OK.' She looked uneasily round 'Encounters'. 'But if someone sees us going into my room they really might get the wrong idea.'

He stared up at her. She looked, to him, quite distractingly beautiful. He was shocked, suddenly, by the force of the desire that rolled through him. 'You're a lovely woman, Nadia.'

Alarm jerked in her eyes. He ignored it. '*Really* lovely,' he asserted, thumping the table for emphasis.

She was edging away, as if he was a bomb that might go off. 'Er, it's awfully sweet of you,' she began with an uneasy smile. 'But for one thing I'm happily married and for another we're political opponents fighting for the same seat.'

With this last sentence she turned and hurried out of the restaurant.

James stared after her. Was it something that he'd said?

After a few minutes he stood up – more difficult than he'd thought – only to fall over his own feet and on to the floor, banging his head hard on the side of the table.

No one came to his rescue. 'Encounters' had only two staff and neither of them were in it. James sat up and rubbed the side of his temple.

It was as if the blow had brought him to his senses. He was a married man. A *father*. What the hell was he *doing*?

'Are you all right?' Nadia had come back again. She was peering down at him. 'I heard a crash.'

James looked back up at her through his mussed and dishevelled hair. He had never felt so embarrassed in his life.

'I'm pissed,' he said. He had always had a ridiculously weak head for alcohol. 'Three Pint Percy', they'd called him at university.

As Nadia looked down at him, her face a mixture of concern and what might have been disgust, James wanted to die of shame. He wanted to assume the foetal position and roll around in anguish on the floor.

What the hell had he been thinking of? If Nadia had responded to his advances, what then? Did he want a divorce?

No, he did not! Victoria had her moments, but she had been a good and loyal wife for twenty-five years. He loved her very much. As for Guy, his son, his only child . . .

Still on the floor, he stared around, gulping, opening and shutting his mouth like a fish.

Nadia was bending over him, gingerly patting his shoulder. 'Don't worry. We all have moments of madness. Especially in this stupid business.' She didn't sound especially convinced.

He made a determined effort to stand upright. 'I'm fine,' he muttered. 'I'll just go and get my key. See you tomorrow.'

'Yes,' said Nadia, doubtfully. 'You're sure you can get back to your room?'

He nodded hard, the movement sending his brain slamming painfully around his cranium. 'Of course I can. You should go. You don't want to be seen with me in this state.'

Nadia did not hang around to argue.

Lurching from side to side with his arms outstretched, using the walls of the corridors like ski poles, James pushed himself back to his room. Outside the door he fumbled for the card key he had just been given. He shoved it in the slot with a shaking hand.

The red light became green and he let himself in. As the door clunked shut, he leant against its inner side and felt a great sense of relief. Thanks to one sensible woman he had escaped disaster. It had been a crazy, combustible moment, but fortunately Nadia had thrown water on it rather than a match. He felt shattered but saved. And luckier – far luckier – than he deserved.

He must make the most of this second chance. Be a better husband and father from this moment on. A better human being. Maybe even a better prospective MP.

He still wasn't entirely sure he wanted the job, but perhaps he could do good things with it. Save the library, for a start.

He would start with a long hot shower; wash his past near-misdeeds right out of his hair. He ripped off his clothes and, naked, opened the door to the bathroom.

As yet another heavy door clunked shut behind him, James found himself thinking it was a strange shape for a bathroom. He was expecting a brightly lit box with mirrors and towels. But this one was thin with rows of doors stretching away down its length. Right opposite him was a framed print of a painting of a large red poppy. There was one just like it outside his door in the corridor.

Oh hell.

CHAPTER 41

'Sorry about the gloom,' Ralph said as he led Jess down yet another passage. 'One of my ancestors was in the Charge of the Light Brigade but now I go round turning off all the lights to save money. A different light brigade, I suppose.'

The route had been complicated, to say the least. They had come out of one door and in through another; up stairs, down corridors, through narrow passages and then suddenly out into enormous ornate rooms. Progressing speedily through the house, Jess gained an impression of impassive faces in heavy gilt frames, vast, carved marble fireplaces, gilded furniture, fluted columns marching down the centre of halls.

Now they were going up another flight of narrow, confined stairs; it was getting warmer and she sensed they were close to the roof. She was right, she saw, as Ralph, ahead, stopped and pushed at what seemed like a stiff, small door and disappeared.

Jess, reaching the threshold, looked out in wonder. After the darkness of the passages and the cool of the house, it was as if someone had taken the lid off a box. All was colour and warmth; a hot blue sky stretched above and a sea of grey lead spread all about her, punctuated by twisted Tudor chimneys which looked so small from below but were, up close, the height of a door and the thickness of a mature oak. The thin slices of brick were set beautifully, decoratively carved in places; Jess found it touching that so much care and skill had gone into something very few would see.

'Ah, but they did see,' Ralph remarked when she offered this observation. 'The Elizabethans were mad about roofs. They liked nothing better than partying on them. Having dinner on them, that sort of thing.'

'Sounds like fun.' Jess imagined gay blades in ruffs and ladies in farthingales giggling as they manoeuvred huge dresses up the narrow stairs. She bent to inspect an elaborate star-shaped badge stamped on a rectangular lead drainpipe.

'Clever of you to notice that,' Ralph said. 'It's the Order of the Garter.'

'Fancy putting that on your pipes.' Jess wondered what, given the chance, she would put on her own.

Ralph was laughing. 'It's a complete myth, this idea of the aristocracy being all good taste and restraint. My ancestors advertised their status in the most vulgar manner imaginable and at every possible opportunity.' He paused and his face fell. 'Which is why our oligarch friend will probably feel very much at home here.'

Jess gave him a cautious smile. 'But you're not selling to him.'

Ralph did not answer but crossed slowly to the turreted brick balustrade that stood chest-high at the roof edge. There was, to Jess, something defeated about the way he spread out his hands and leant over.

She wanted to go to him, comfort him. Fearful that her heels would make marks in the soft metal, she took off her party shoes and felt the roof leads warm her feet as she crossed to join him. A few weeds nodded from the wall and a lovely, obviously curious, pink rose had climbed all the way up from the ground and was now poking its gathered petal face over the edge, emitting waves of a rich and soapy scent.

Jess leant on the warm bricks, tucking her hands beneath her so as not to risk touching, as she longed to, Ralph's extended finger-ends. They seemed to exert a magnetic pull; and her own hands twitched in response. His signet ring glittered gold in the sun, the worn pattern just about distinguishable. Three chevrons on a shield.

Jess made herself look at the view. She was high up, higher than she had thought, and on the wide, green carpet of the park below, the festival spilled out before her. It was probably the only vantage point from which all that colourful chaos made sense. She could see what was impossible to work out on ground level, how it all interconnected. She could even see Genghis where, at this exact moment, Ginnie lay pretending to have a migraine and brooding about the headmaster.

From beside her, Ralph spoke. She was close enough to him to feel the vibrations of his voice. 'Not bad, is it?'

'Beautiful,' Jess agreed. More than beautiful. Utterly magical.

The sun, which on the roof was still warm and bright, had sunk low enough to leave the park behind the tents a vagueness of dark trees and shadows. The festival area was alive with lights; some faint, some dazzlingly bright, blooming in marquees and blazing on stalls so that even the coffee baristas resembled blacksmiths in Old Master paintings. Dotted around were flambeaux, ragged flames against the dark. There were braziers around tents, strings of coloured fairy bulbs everywhere; candles in the outdoor bars; chandeliers flickering in the trees. People drifted past in knots, their faces lit by all the different sources of light; dwellers in a happy fairy village.

Jess could hear snatches of music, talk and laughter. It

sounded spontaneous and cheerful; the steady thump of generators was like the beat of a heart. A midsummer night's dream, she mused. And she and Ralph an unlikely fairy king and queen, high enough above everything to see that while it was darkness on the ground, above the trees was still hot blue with the first and brightest stars appearing alongside an elegant sliver of moon.

Jess felt her heart fairly twist with love for the place. It energised her somehow, this sleepy twilight valley, in a way that all the brilliant buzz and rush of London failed to, especially recently. She had been wondering for a while about doing something different, writing a novel, say. But in the city the necessary energy and inspiration eluded her.

Here, at Wylde Hall, she felt at home. More than that, as if she had been meant to come here. Ever the hard-headed barrister, the tough city slicker, Jess rarely indulged her super-stitious streak. But now, looking down on the festival fairyland, she saw glimmers of a sort of destiny. In a sudden rush of insight she felt the great age of the landscape, sensed time passing, knew the insignificance and brevity of most things beneath that fast-disappearing blue sky. Life was precious and not to be wasted. It was hard, logician as she was, to escape the impression that this moment, on the roof, was an important one in her life, perhaps even a turning point.

She twisted round to Ralph, half-bursting with the urge to transmit all this, half-reining herself back. He might be charmed or he might simply think she was crackers. Or just another of the fortune-hunters he had fallen foul of over the years. In particular, she did not want him to think the latter. While it was true that she loved his house, she found the man, even after this short acquaintance, even more compelling.

Ralph met her eyes. He held them, along with his breath.

She looked so beautiful in her white dress, with the light breeze lifting her hair and the sun casting a golden halo about it. She seemed to him a vision, a goddess. A miracle.

Five seconds into meeting her he had known that she was absolutely perfect. For him, for Wylde, for everything. Of course, he had felt the same with all of his wives initially. But Ralph felt – hoped, anyway – that this time it was different. She, certainly, was different. The other wives had all raved about the house, but Jess was the first to really notice the details. Wylde seemed to spark something in her; she seemed to unwind and blossom within it. She had an empathy with the place the others had lacked, as well as a sharp intelligence, humour and sympathy. She had, in a word, class. If anyone could reverse the downward slide that was his house, not to mention the one that was himself, it was, Ralph was sure, Jess.

His gaze fixed to hers, he opened his mouth to tell her. But then he shut it again, remembering all the reasons why it was impossible.

The first downside was that there was no possibility she would be interested in him. She had youth, beauty, a high-octane job; why would she want to live in an old wreck like Wylde with an old wreck like himself? While he personally always fell in love instantly and unreservedly, other people were much more cautious. They went on dates to restaurants and the cinema, they got to know each other gradually, they proposed after years, not minutes. And for good reason, Ralph reminded himself; look, after all, where his precipitious past passions and instant proposals had got him. Six disasters under his belt and rampaging through his bank balance. He was hardly a good bet for anyone on the marriage front, let alone a woman like this, with the world – and its men – at her feet.

And then there was the house. It was almost certain to be

sold; what could he do to stop it? He was, in any case, caught between a rock and a hard place; a place about to fall down. If he refused to sell to Badunov, Wylde would simply fall to pieces. And, as the last of the line, he could not allow that to happen. Quite apart from the earthly ignominy, Ralph did not want, in whatever heaven or hell he ended up in, to run the gauntlet of furious ancestors waving their chainmailed fists at him.

In short, he had nothing to give her. If she married him, she would be marrying nothing. He would not even have a home. Or money. What cash he received from the sale would only just cover centuries of debt.

He glanced down. The sympathy in her eyes was leading him astray, reigniting the hope he was trying to smother.

But hope, in the end, had always burned brighter within him than anything else. That, presumably, was why he had made such a mess of things. The disaster of hope over experience.

And so Ralph, now, abandoned the struggle against the habit of a lifetime. Once again, while common sense advised against it, his heart urged him on, to enter the lists and ask yet another damsel for her hand.

He took a deep, fortifying breath. As perfect moments went, this one looked pretty good. Jess was still looking at him, her lips parted slightly in what looked like expectation. She had the face of an angel, Ralph thought. A beautiful black angel. He wished himself luck.

But Jess spoke first. 'You've gone purple in the face,' she said, concerned, and Ralph remembered to breathe at last.

He reached out and moved his hand on to hers. She did not, as he feared, pull away. He moved his head closer; he could see the flutter of her pulse under the dark skin of her neck. He breathed in her warm, spicy scent.

'I know this seems a little precipitous,' he said.

Jess looked over the wall. 'We're high up, you mean?'

Ralph cursed himself. It was coming out all wrong, this moment of supreme importance, this unrepeatable chance. The offer he was about to make must sound tempting and in no way allude to the mistakes and miseries of the past.

'And of course I'm completely useless and hopeless and have nothing whatsoever to give you, certainly no money and before long not even a house . . .'

Jess grinned. 'You're sounding irresistible.' While her tone was relaxed, a great excitement was gripping her insides.

Ralph hesitated before ploughing on. 'Ahem. But you do seem to me the most wonderful woman and I'd be terribly grateful if you might see your way to . . .'

As nerves got the better of him, he paused and swallowed. 'Yes?' gasped Jess.

'. . . thinking about possibly considering . . .' Ralph ploughed on, his voice tightening to a squeak.

'*What?*' She had both hands on his now, urging him on.

He cleared his throat and the sentence shot out. 'Becoming the seventh Lady De Gawkrodger?'

CHAPTER 42

Isabel was still fighting her way out of the party, still feeling frustrated and ignored. And while she blamed Olly's self-serving neglect almost entirely for her predicament, she knew she was partly at fault herself. She should have stood firm, followed her instinct and stayed at home. The memory of Olly's pleading weasel words, about needing her at the festival, wanting her support, made her furious. She hoped he would find the ring in his pocket soon, and that it would bring him to his senses.

She may as well, Isabel decided, simply go to her room, read and wait for him. But getting out was hard work. She twisted in the mass of bodies, shoving, gasping, and forcing with her shoulders, elbows, knees. She was literally fighting for her freedom.

But finally she was nearing her goal. The magnificent entrance was inches away; she could almost touch the carved swags of fruit and flowers. But then a sudden surge in the crowd propelled her backwards into the room again, swirling helpless as a leaf on the strong tide of humanity.

There was a ripple of expectation and excitement. 'The Badunovs are here!'

Forced in that direction, Isabel could just about see, entering the room, a beautiful woman with long, dark, centre-parted hair. Her thickly made-up face had a frozen, mask-like expression and her ears and neck blazed with diamonds, each one twenty times the size of that which had recently been on Isabel's finger. 'Talk about sparkling company!' someone said, as Isabel pushed past.

'THAT WAS MY FUCKING FOOT!' A red-faced blonde just inside the door with a mobile to her ear detached it to shout at Isabel. 'No, Dave, you can bloody well stay in Wortley. It might be that something's up. I can't find his bloody wife anywhere and she was supposed to be coming to this party with me. Hang on, Boris Badunov's just got here. I've gotta go, ring the paper, give the diary a few paras.'

Sarah broke off and shoved her glass right in the face of the harassed waiter heaving past with a bottle. 'Come on! That's just a thimbleful!'

The impossibility of moving in the crowd now obliged Isabel to listen to the blonde's roared potted history of the short man with the diamond-studded brunette. He was apparently a famous oligarch.

'His wife has made him come,' the blonde shouted. 'No, not the art collector, that was the last one. This one's into lit-glitz, hanging out with authors, buying literary festivals . . .'

The blonde's stentorian tones faded into the crowd. And the crowd was thinning. She was out! At last! On fleet, silent feet Isabel headed up the main staircase and along the red-carpeted guest bedroom corridor, past the glossy double white doors at which Olly had gazed so longingly when they had arrived. Isabel could now put the faces to the name-cards slipped into the little gold frames. They were all below her, red and shiny with heat and alcohol, at the party which, while it raged on the floor beneath, was all but inaudible up here. Dame Hermione

Grantchester, The Hon. Sparkle D'Vyne and, right at the end, Mr and Mrs B. Badunov.

Inside the room of Boris and Daria Badunov, Jude was replacing the picture over the fireplace. Everything had gone like clockwork. Below him, on the carpet, was the black leather chest that contained the key to his future. All their futures. Daria Badunova had not even bothered to lock it. The padded lid opened easily, revealing an Aladdin's cave of jewels that burst like fireworks on to Jude's feverish, greedy gaze.

For the moment, he exulted alone. Boz and Big George were elsewhere, dispatching the two bodyguards. It had, as Jude had anticipated, been easy work sending them upstairs with a Mickey Finn for the security detail. Bearing tumblers of vodka into which chloral hydrate pills had been slipped, the two cross-dressed gangsters, white gloves stretched over their enormous hands, had passed without note in the colourful party crowd.

Their reception upstairs had been better than Jude could ever have hoped. The two bodyguards, bored stiff and agonisingly conscious there was alcohol downstairs, had greeted Boz and George with delight. This was partly because of the vodka but mostly because they reminded them of their mothers. The four of them had danced a wobbly trepak and drunk to Mother Russia before the drug had taken hold and they had both collapsed on the floor. As Jude slipped inside to remove the jewel chest, George and Boz had grabbed the bodies and dragged them up a convenient nearby staircase leading to a cramped, deserted corridor. They were still up there, gagging and binding their victims as Jude slipped out now with the jewel chest under his arm.

Had he not been reeling under the weight of millions of dollars in gems, Jude would have punched the air. Never had he felt such triumph and relief. Finally, against all the odds, they had done it. The Diamond Geezers had pulled off their best and most audacious stunt yet!

As a movement caught his eye he turned, surprised; had Boz and George finished already? The expected huge and blocky frames of his brother gangsters, however, seemed to have shrunk into that of a slender red-headed woman in a black evening dress.

Isabel, for her part, was staring at Jude. She assumed, as he was coming out of their room, that he was some sort of aide to the Badunovs. Certainly he was glamorous: tall and high-cheekboned with floppy blond hair. Perhaps there was something groomed and Euro-exotic about his cool white shirt and loose, thin grey trousers. He wore white gloves, she noticed, which was odd, given the heat. And what his gloved hands were holding was a big black box.

She had been about to nod, say hello and pass on, but there was something disturbing in the quality of his stare. He had the long, yellow, assessing eyes of a big cat preparing to spring. Isabel felt sudden terror bolt up her throat.

She tried to hurry on by, but just as she attempted to, his free hand shot out and grabbed her wrist hard. Harder than anyone had ever grabbed her before. It was a grab that meant business; unpleasant business at that.

Her arm exploding with pain, her throat closing with fear, Isabel was yanked out of the corridor before she could make a single sound. She realised he was dragging her up the familiar dusty wooden steps to the horrid little room she shared with Olly.

Now they were in the dank upper corridor. And who was this? Coming out of a room beyond her own were two of the strangest figures Isabel had ever seen. They were huge and hulking and had big hands covered in white gloves. Their dresses were hideous and enormous. The hat worn by one had a brim almost as wide as the corridor. They were obviously men, and part of Isabel wanted to laugh. But a bigger part warned that there was nothing amusing about her situation.

'Let me go,' Isabel cried, struggling against the hand that held her.

But there was obviously no chance of that. Another hand – huge, gloved – now pressed over her mouth and pushed something into it. A gag. They tied it tight under her chin, it felt they were breaking her jaw in the process. She found herself thrown violently round and slammed hard against the wall. Her forehead rang with the shattering noise of impact. She felt something hard and metallic push between her shoulder blades; at the same time something was pulled over her head. A white cotton pillowcase. She stared at the threads, her insides liquid with fear. The certainty they were about to kill her broke over her.

Now she was being bound. Thin, tight rope cut burningly into her wrists.

'I do apologise,' one of them said – the blond man, she was sure. His tones were light, almost amused. 'But you came along at just the wrong moment.'

Isabel felt almost mad with terror. With the last of her strength and her only unbound limbs, she began striking out violently with her feet. Her pointed satin toe made contact with something hard and sinewy and a phlegmy howl of fury echoed round the corridor. Isabel's covered face exploded at the impact of a violent blow. She reeled, fell forward into nothing, then everything went black.

CHAPTER 43

Guy was in seventh heaven. He and Shanna-Mae were finally together. In the dark. Alone.

If, that was, you didn't count the thousands of other festival-goers in their immediate vicinity.

They had spent the evening walking round Wild & Free; Shanna and Rosie taking in the sights with the delighted alacrity of people who had been hard at work all day. Shanna in particular was fascinated by everything, and Guy found his own jaded cynicism melting under the warmth of her enthusiasm. 'It's so pretty,' she kept saying.

And it was, Guy had to admit. The sudden fall of darkness had transformed the daytime face of Wild & Free. From being loud, colourful and – as he saw it – painfully self-conscious, it had settled down to something more subtle, mysterious and romantic.

Fairy lights were everywhere, even on the people; cowboy hats were draped in small bulbs, as were dresses and tutus. Bright food stalls glistened with slowly revolving kebabs. Rows of sausages shone amid the browned edges of onions. Champagne corks popped in tented candlelit bars and pints glowed tawnily in glasses. Marquees were lit from within like lanterns;

dark figures danced against flashing colours to pounding music.

Shanna had been impressed by Petronella and the Fridge, even if, from Guy's point of view, what had once been one of his favourite bands now seemed just a whimsical woman singer with bare white legs and big white pants under a short white nightie yowling into a microphone to the accompaniment of an enormous guitar. No woman could compare to Shanna.

They had taken Rosie for milkshakes at a pop-up bar called the Hoxton Vitreous Enamel Workers' Canteen. It had up-ended vintage steamer trunks for tables and the milkshake menu had included lemon meringue and edamame bean. Everyone in it had been braying about their novels, but for once Guy didn't find this irritating. People could dream, couldn't they?

People could do all sorts of crazy things. Nearby, a man in a top hat on a unicycle had been juggling with flaming torches while, from a marquee entrance, came the cheerful noise of crashing drums and shouting youth.

The three of them had gone to watch. Some teenagers in striped T-shirts were just finishing their first song and looking delighted at their reception. 'We're the Sherbert Lemmings,' said the drummer in a Scouse accent. 'This is a really big thing for us. Thank you for coming to see us.'

'Aw bless,' said Shanna fondly.

As the trio made their way happily back to the Beauty Bus, three others, did they but know it, were heading in the same direction. Jude, Boz and Big George were hurrying to put the final part of their plan into execution.

Of course, ideally this would be a getaway car provided by Frankie. But Frankie remained unreachable. Either, Jude figured, she had abandoned all hope of the heist ever coming off. Or else she was dead. It happened, in their world. The implications for him were the same in either case. They would have to make their own way out.

Progress was slow and difficult owing partly to the heels on Boz and George's shoes not being designed for rapid progress through grassland. But the main reason movement was impeded was because all three insisted on having at least one hand on the jewels at any one time. As trying to escape with the jewel chest was inadvisable for obvious reasons, these were currently sagging heavily at the bottom of a pillowcase. It had been taken from the room where the bodyguards had been dumped, and where shortly afterwards they had bundled in the red-headed girl.

Boz and George were each gripping one of its corners while Jude held the neck. Bent and contorted in the various ways this required, they had looked such a strange group as they passed through the party that Jude had wondered whether carrying the Badunov jewel chest might have attracted less attention.

They had escaped without incident even so and now they were headed for the camper van full of beauty products. While there was a risk that the fat girl owner might be there, Jude did not see that as a difficulty. One mighty blow from Boz would take her out of the equation. She would, quite literally, not know what had hit her. Collateral damage was inevitable in situations such as this.

A middle-aged woman, quite clearly out of her head, was whirling round in circles singing 'I Feel Pretty'. She stopped and stared at the three of them. 'Want to dance?' she asked.

'Sure,' growled Boz, who had spotted an emerald of considerable proportions on her finger.

'Not with you,' the woman said, in precise cut-glass tones. 'You're a lady. I want to dance with him.' She pointed to Jude, who had spotted the ring as well. He hesitated, weighing it up. If he let go of the pillowcase, would the others escape with it and divide the bounty between them? Whoever claimed there was honour among thieves could not be further from the truth. On the other hand, there weren't many brains among thieves either, especially among these two. They needed him, Jude reminded himself.

With a warning glare at Boz and George, he stepped towards the woman and partnered her in a hasty waltz. She was heavier than she looked, sagging in his arms. They staggered around and she peered at him intensely. 'You're frightfully handsome.'

'Thanks,' muttered Jude, looking away hastily. Might she recognise him afterwards? He took her hand and, pretending to caress it as they turned, expertly prised off the jewel.

'My name's Victoria,' the woman said, as he brought her to a halt.

'Nice to meet you, Victoria. Why don't you toddle off to bed now?'

A trilling, girlish giggle greeted this. 'Oh no! I couldn't! I'm going to a party! Why don't you come?'

'No fanks,' Boz growled. 'Just bin to one.'

Still singing, Victoria twirled off, feeling prettier than ever.

Jude's hand was firmly back on the pillowcase now. 'Nice little mover, aren'tcha?' George cracked. 'Proper little Twinkle-toes.'

'Fuck off.'

'*LanGWIDGE!*'

'Got the ring?' Boz snarled. Jude opened his first; the emerald flashed in the limited light.

George was holding the pillowcase open. 'In 'ere then.'

Jude tipped it in with the rest. The three of them looked down at the mass of cut stones winking up at them as lovingly as parents might regard a newborn baby. 'Aw,' said George. 'Lovely, aren't they?'

Boz's alarming eyes were closed, his mighty nostrils straining wide and his huge chest inflating beneath his dress. 'Fucking love the smell, I do.'

'Of jewels?' Jude frowned.

'Of *money*.'

They set off again. That the festival was a noisy place was more than useful given the occasional great bestial roars of triumph from Boz and George. The pillowcase jerked violently from time to time as enormous, white-gloved fists pumped the air.

Jude regarded them with contempt. They quite clearly saw the job as over and done with. But for him it was never over until it was over. Until they had got the VW bus and were miles up the motorway. The bus would be reported missing, of course, but it would take some serious detective effort to link it with the jewel robbery. And by the time anyone did so, the stones hidden in their bottles would be far away. As would the three Geezers.

It had, Jude felt, all passed off perfectly, a textbook robbery which students of jewel thievery would be studying for years to come. He would, Jude congratulated himself, pass into history as one of the masters of the craft, and it would be one in the eye for that thing who had taken over their London patch. As well as vindication for Rich. Whose car, of course, he would be getting as a reward. A win-win situation, if ever there was one.

'Shaddup!!' he snapped at the others as they neared the place where the Beauty Bus was parked. Jude had found it without difficulty, having rehearsed the journey several times earlier in the day. Getting lost was not an option.

The bus, gleaming palely in the darkness, came into view behind the artisanal ice-cream stand. It would be the work of a few minutes to overpower the girl – if she was there. Boz's mighty hand over her mouth would ensure she wouldn't even scream. Ever again.

'Who's that bloke?' rasped Big George.

They were now feet from the Beauty Bus and Jude's hand clenched on the neck of the pillowcase. Immediately, both the others increased their grips.

Not one, but three people outside the getaway vehicle. One of whom, as George had correctly identified, was a bloke. Not just any bloke, either; but a tall, well-built bloke who, while clearly no match for Boz and George, was also, just as clearly, capable of making an unwelcome fuss.

Boz was flexing a massive gloved hand. The other still clasped the pillowcase. 'Come on then. Let's finish 'im off.'

Weary impatience filled Jude at yet another unexpected obstacle. He was almost tempted to let Boz off the leash. But it could get messy; actually, who was he kidding? If Boz was involved, there was no question that it would. Very messy indeed; the worst kind of mess.

'Hold on,' he cautioned the others, pulling them backwards into the shadow of some bushes and a large tree. 'Give it five minutes. He might go.'

But Guy, leaning against the warm flanks of the Beauty Bus, Shanna beside him, had no intention of going. Not now that Rosie was sleeping in the back like the child she had only just ceased to be and he finally had Shanna to himself. He spread out his long legs on the still-warm grass and felt utterly at ease.

'Look at the flowers.' Shanna gestured at the folded daisies. 'They've all gone to bed.'

In the shadows, Jude sighed impatiently. *Not the bloody flowers conversation.*

It soon moved on from flowers, however, and ranged far and wide. Olly had never had such a long talk with a girl before.

Perhaps with anyone, ever. As Shanna explained her – amazingly detailed and astonishingly possible-sounding – world domination beauty business plan, Guy felt a combination of admiration and desire to be part of it too. But he of course was destined for other things. He pushed away the thought of the A-level results, and his mother.

'Aw, *sweet.*' There was a sniff from where George sat in his dress, massive knees drawn up, mighty hands clasped round his vast and hairy calves. Jude glanced at him; he looked dewy-eyed. George caught the glance and his smitten expression changed instantly to one of glinting malevolence. 'So I'm a bit soppy? That a problem?'

'Not at all,' Jude assured him hurriedly. 'It's all quite . . . adorable. But we need to get them out of the way.' Time was running out. The alarm was sure to be raised by now. The police – albeit only the useless local ones – would be here soon.

But George had cocked his head and was gazing indulgently at the lovers again. 'Aw. Give 'em a few minutes. You're only young once.'

He had no choice, Jude saw. Boz's contribution to the debate, meanwhile, was a snore so rumbling and mighty it seemed to come from the bowels of the earth itself. He was stretched, massive and flat out, on the ground beside them, his skirt rucked up and his shoes half-off his mighty feet. One great, gloved hand still gripped the pillowcase, although perhaps not quite so tightly as before.

Jude's surveying glance, initially irritated, now widened into something more speculative and calculating. A plan was forming in his mind, one that the drawn-out tryst taking place before them might just facilitate. One which might just end with Boz's fingers being permanently loosened from the haul. George's too.

'You're right, George,' Jude agreed. 'All the world loves a lover, after all.' All the bloody world except him, he silently added. His only real love affair had been with cars.

It was a soft, warm night and the air was scented with grass and hay. The sky was almost dark now and the rich blue of the ripest blueberry. High up, big white stars burned passionately around a cool, reticent sliver of moon.

'They're so fascinating, stars,' Shanna remarked softly. 'I wish I knew more about them.'

'Me too,' whispered George dreamily from the darkness. 'Like stars, I do.'

Jude rolled his eyes and gritted his teeth. *Go to fucking sleep, George.*

'Some of them are very old, aren't they?' Shanna was still gazing at the heavens.

'They are, they are,' intoned George from the bushes.

They were indeed, Guy knew. Some had actually died millennia ago, but the distances were so huge the light from them was still travelling. He hesitated, about to say so, but then didn't in case Shanna thought he was showing off. Or, worse, just silly. He didn't want to spout clichés about what he suddenly, powerfully felt: a sense of how vast the universe was and how small he seemed in comparison. Shanna was obviously still uncertain about him, making this a fragile situation where the wrong word could destroy everything.

Shanna's forefinger rose upwards. 'What's that one called?'

'Orion,' Guy said instantly. The great constellation was wheeling into view above a shaggy row of trees. 'The Elvis of the night sky,' he added spontaneously. 'Looks like he's doing a hip thrust.'

'Oh *yes*,' Shanna exclaimed in delight. 'The disco king, definitely. The way he has his arms out.'

'Aw,' George sighed. 'S'lovely. Like watching some romantic film.'

'Isn't it?' Jude agreed through gritted teeth. *Just go to bloody sleep, George. Sleep! Sleep!*

If only he'd been able to slip the two of them a Mickey Finn as well. But even Boz and George weren't so dim as to fall for that. He'd have to do it by natural means. Jude yawned hugely, to encourage George. *Come on, George. Drop off.*

The plan in his head was complete now. Just as soon as they were both out cold, he would take the pillowcase and go. Leave them to the tender mercies of Fate, or the local police, whoever arrived first. He'd had, Jude felt, more than enough of both of them.

Guy and Shanna, leaning against the Beauty Bus, were looking at each other. 'You know a lot about stars,' Shanna said. His heart leapt at her tone, so unexpectedly admiring.

'I don't know much,' Guy claimed modestly. 'But I can spot the constellations. Like Gemini up there. And Taurus, and the Pleiades. And the big stars, Rigel, Aldebaran, Betelgeuse, Sirius.'

'That's pretty impressive. You're lucky. You must have been to a really good school.'

Guy considered this. He had never thought himself lucky. He had thought of school as a tedious obligation. This was the first time anything he had learnt there had come in useful. But wait, that wasn't true. The batteries thing. He'd learnt that at school as well, although his ultimate solution to the problem, connecting the spray machine to the engine battery and running it from that, had all been his own invention.

Mere feet away, in the shadow of the trees, Jude was holding his breath. George had stopped exclaiming and muttering encouragement. Was he finally asleep?

Jude's lynx eyes flicked over both his colleagues in the dark.

George's expression was beatific, as if even in sleep he was enjoying visions of perfect love, and his vast chest was rhythmically rising and falling. Boz lay where he had all along, snoring mightily and still unmoving.

It looked – it really looked – as if the moment had come. Drawing a deep, gathering breath, Jude moved fractionally, experimentally. Would they notice? No reaction from either of them.

And now for the difficult bit. Hands shaking, he reached out gingerly towards the two colossal bunches of fingers gripping the pillowcase. Starting with George, who had fewer digits and was therefore easier, he softly peeled them off, one by one. No reaction. Then, heart racing in his chest, Jude gently detached Boz. The littlest finger clung the hardest, but the material came free at last and finally Jude could feel what he had never felt before, the whole weight of the horde as it swung in the bag. It looked and felt as if a whole human head was in there. Jude gazed triumphantly at the lumpen sack, picturing rather than looking at the jewels within. No time for that now. He'd gloat later. When he was miles away.

CHAPTER 44

Jude glanced at the other Geezers. The two hands lately holding the pillowcase lay there quite helpless. Pale against the grass, palms upwards, thick, unconscious fingers curling in the empty air, like babies'. Aw, thought Jude, despite himself.

He moved his feet under him, preparing to push upwards. Cramp pulsed in his thighs. A kneebone clicked. Jude prepared to straighten, but then something shot darkly through the air. It had him before he knew it, a huge, hairy hand, complete with all its fingers. Jude's wrist strained and cracked in the mighty grip. 'Not so fucking fast,' said Boz.

George stirred. '*LangWIDGE!*'

Shanna's chin was still pointing at the stars, her eyes wide and her mouth slightly open. Her expression had lost its customary scepticism and was of a childlike wonder and abandonment. Guy followed her gaze. The stars seemed more enormous and brilliant than ever he had seen them; all that cold white light throbbing and winking at him from millions of miles and years away. As they had winked to Ulysses, Moses, Magellan and Marco Polo and countless nameless, toiling souls from the dawn of time until now.

Ulysses, Moses, Magellan. Guy was struck, for the first time, at the facility with which the names came to mind. Shanna was right. He really had been to a good school.

'Which is that?' she asked him next, pointing at the W-shaped constellation spreading out above Orion.

'Cassiopeia. The celestial pushy parent.'

Shanna shot him a look. 'You *what*?'

'Andromeda's mother,' Guy told her. 'Cassiopeia went around boasting about her daughter. Making sure,' he added sardonically, 'that she went to the most expensive school imaginable so she could go to the best university.'

'Well, what's wrong with that?' flipped Shanna immediately. 'Who doesn't want the best for their children? That's definitely the sort of mother I'd be.'

Guy felt a pang. There would clearly be a vacancy for the father of these children.

'It's not so much fun,' he offered hesitantly, 'if you're the child. I've got a mother like that, as you know.'

He braced himself, expecting Shanna to snigger, or say something cutting about the service station incident. But she said nothing. Her profile, in the darkness, looked contemplative. 'She just wants the best for you,' Shanna said.

'It's *not* the best, though,' Guy protested hotly. 'I always have to do what she wants.'

'Rubbish,' Shanna countered. 'She's brought you here, hasn't she? You've just told me yourself that she didn't want to; it was only because your dad couldn't.'

Guy was aggrieved. 'Whose side are you on? My mother was *horrible* to you in the petrol station.'

Shanna shrugged. 'I'm not taking that personally. The point is, your mother obviously adores you and you take her for granted. You don't realise how lucky you are to have someone who cares about you so much.'

He was about to protest again, but the urge died on his lips. She was quite serious, he could see. While it was not the first time he had heard such sentiments, it was the first time one of his peers had said it; someone whose opinion he valued. Guy could not quite let it rest, however. He made one final attempt to put his case. 'She's hell-bent on me going to Branston College.'

He had not expected her to have heard of it and was surprised when Shanna exclaimed in delight. Guy now discovered that Isabel, the woman he had met outside Branston all those months ago, was not only here at the festival too, but the great friend of Rosie's mother into the bargain.

'Small world,' he had to admit. But was it more than that? he wondered. Coincidence? Or Fate?

Their eyes had locked then, but Shanna was the first to look away. 'And are you going?' she asked. 'To Branston?'

She lived in the same town, Guy now knew. It was tempting to say that he was. But he knew, all the same, that he wasn't.

He didn't want to go to university. He wanted to do something practical, something with his hands, something that gave free rein to the inventive capabilities he felt sure were within him, but which had never had a chance to express themselves.

'Well, good for you,' Shanna remarked when he finally got all this out. 'You'd be wasted doing law or whatever. It was amazing, what you did with that lemon.'

Guy savoured her approbation. It was a delicious feeling.

'So what happened next?' Shanna asked.

He was lost. 'Next?'

'To Cassiopeia. The pushy mother.'

'Oh, her.' Guy cleared his throat. 'Well, all her boasting made the gods angry so they sent a sea monster to ravage the city . . .'

He could hardly see her now, but he could feel her admiration. It really was wonderful to know things, Guy had to admit. 'And Andromeda got chained to the rock to be sacrificed to the monster.' Guy paused and pointed upwards. 'She's just over there. *There*, see.' Realising his arm might not, in the dark, be visible to her, Guy softly took Shanna's fingers with his own and gently raised them upwards. The thrill of contact juddered round his entire body. He felt her fingers tense, then relax in his. He dropped his voice so it was only a murmur. 'But Perseus came to rescue her and they lived happily ever after.'

It was, Guy recognised, now or never. He lowered her hand, walked his fingers along her arm and moved his face towards hers. He felt a hot bolt of ecstasy as, in the dark, their lips touched and her mouth melted beneath his.

Guy felt a violent desire now possess him. Gently he pushed her backwards until she lay beneath him; he ground himself into her, softly at first, but increasingly insistently. He had assumed, at first, that her bucking beneath him and hammering on his back was encouragement. Now he realised it was the opposite. 'Get off me!' Shanna gasped, pushing him away with all her might.

Guy sat up and pushed both hands awkwardly through his hair. He felt thwarted and ashamed. He could not see her eyes but he could sense her cold stare.

'I don't know what you take me for,' she said crisply.

Guy's mouth opened, but then shut again. He had no defence. There was no excuse.

'Do all the girls you kiss usually just sleep with you?' Shanna inquired in withering tones.

'Yes,' said Guy honestly.

He had braced himself for a further blasting, so was surprised when she said, 'I'm sorry.'

'S'all right,' he muttered magnanimously.

'But I'm afraid I have self-esteem issues,' Shanna went on.

Guy nodded. Familiar ground, this. All the girls he knew had self-esteem issues.

'As in I've *actually got some*,' Shanna snarled. 'So you won't get your leg over me, caveman.'

The anguished Guy could see her, in the dark, standing up and dusting herself down. 'Go back to Mummy and leave me alone.'

The door of the Beauty Bus slammed. Shanna was in her citadel. As there was clearly nothing more to be done, Guy stumbled away.

In the darkness, the three Geezers stirred. Jude, now in a painful half-Nelson courtesy of Boz, was no longer in any hurry to leave. His fate, should Boz get him in that bus, did not look encouraging. He would have strangled him straightaway, indeed, had offered to. But then George had pointed out that Jude was the only one who could drive.

George stirred. 'Come on then. She's inside now. Let's do it.'

Unaware of the imminent danger to Shanna, Guy reeled across the parkland, cursing himself. He slapped his forehead hard, almost savouring the pain. He deserved it, and it was less acute than the pain in his heart.

He'd blown it, no question. What a bloody idiot. Everything had been going so well, and then he'd had to lunge in that stupid way.

And now, as Shanna had mockingly suggested, he had to return to his mother. And she would be furious with him, there was no doubt about that. He had not been in touch for hours. He pulled out his mobile, expecting page after page of anxious maternal texts. He was surprised to see that there was nothing.

Perhaps she intended a face-to-face interview. Guy groaned,

easily imagining the forensic questioning about what he had been up to. What would he tell her? That he had been with Shanna? His mother was depressingly keen on Tamara Wilderbeest, but he had less than no interest in that relationship. Biscuits or no biscuits.

He could just about see before him now, on the slight rise of ground by the yurts, the glowing pink and white sprigged tent belonging to his mother. She must be asleep; while the other tents had lights inside them, soft music playing and shadows moving around, Victoria's was dark.

Guy imagined, with a piercing pang of guilt, his mother going to bed alone, in a tent in a strange place. It struck him that he had never before seen things from her point of view. He had, as Shanna pointed out, arrogantly assumed himself to be the centre of her universe, and acted accordingly.

His mother, by contrast, had been heroic. Once his father had gone off to canvas at the by-election, it would have been simplicity itself for Victoria to announce that she was not going to Wild & Free and they were staying in London. He himself, Guy knew, broke arrangements all the time if it suited him, especially those with his mother. But Victoria had honoured the bargain and had brought him here despite her hatred of camping.

Only now, as he looked at the tent – the first his mother had ever put up, to his knowledge – did Guy fully appreciate the trouble she had gone to on his account. Plus, despite her obvious curiosity about his circle, she had had the grace to keep out of his way. You saw so many parents hanging out with their kids, embarrassing them . . .

Guy was now wondering whether the selfish and controlling one had been him, not his mother, all along. As he reached the little porch of Victoria's tent he vowed that he would appreciate her more from now on.

The tent seemed to radiate quietness and stillness. Guy was glad that his mother was sleeping peacefully and had not woken to find him absent. He opened the tent flap.

'Mum?' His tone was soft. 'It's me, Mum.'

He pressed on one of the little floral-sprigged pink lights that matched the tent. Victoria's sleeping bag lay smooth and unused. She was not there. And nor, Guy saw, puzzled, were Tamara's biscuits.

CHAPTER 45

On the third floor of the Stayhotel, Wortley-on-Thames, a naked prospective MP rattled at the locked door of his room. Shook the brushed steel knob with desperate violence. Threw himself against the door's impassive laminated fibre surface. For all this, it remained obstinately unyielding.

James looked down at himself in the wild hope of – what? Finding his card key shoved in his belly button? Some hope. Clearer even than the sight of his pendulous naked penis was the memory of the means of entry lying on the rumpled purple of the bedspread. Inside the room.

Downstairs, in the hotel's foyer, photographer Dave Bishop had decided to have one last look round before calling it a night and returning to London. He didn't care what Sarah Bloody Salmon said. There was nothing here for him.

Heavy biker boots rattling, Dave stumped past the men in crumpled suits who seemed always to be smoking at the entrance. He stomped across the reception area, where, also as usual, some crew-cut kid was spasming about in front of the Wii. He paused at the front desk, asked a couple of questions, nodded, went towards the lifts.

He knew where his quarry was. A couple of crisp twenties

waved yesterday at reception had ensured a flow of information. He had room numbers; he also knew, having just checked, that both MPs were in residence. 'Hammered, the guy,' the dead-eyed youth on the front desk had added, fingering his flesh tunnels absently as he spoke. 'Fell over in the restaurant, he was so pissed.'

That, Dave had to admit, sounded promising. A bleary-eyed MP shot through a crack in the door wouldn't rock the world but might be worth a few quid. He decided to start with James Dorchester-Williams. The lift door opened and he stepped inside.

The one thing that the City had taught James was to always have a plan. It didn't have to be a good plan. Just a plan, full stop. A plan was a bulwark between you and disaster. It bought you time, it gave you something to talk about. You could cover your bare arse with words, mask your embarrassment, hide your mistakes. Metaphorically speaking.

But in the harshly lit corridor on the third floor of the Wortley Stayhotel, there was nothing metaphorical about James's bare arse. It was there for all to see. And he didn't have any sort of plan to cover it.

Fortunately, no one had seen his bare arse as yet. But they would, and soon, if he didn't move it. He needed a plan.

Plan A was the welcome desk. It was there to help guests, after all. Welcome them, even. James thought of that bank of screens staffed by dead-eyed clerks, dealing with the queues in front of them with what seemed excruciating slowness. You could, James mused, stand in those queues for a long time.

Compounding the problem was the big foyer behind the queues, well lit by enormous glass doors. Doors you could see anything through. The foyer was always full of people too; the enormous Wii screen was a magnet for kids.

In short, someone like him, in his circumstances, might find the environment less discreet than was ideal. Plan A, James concluded, was inoperable.

Plan B was to go to Nadia's room and call for help from there. If he went quickly he might catch her before she went to sleep.

Obviously, it would be embarrassing. But could it really make things much worse? Following the scene in the restaurant, she thought of him as an idiot anyway. And it wasn't as if he needed to enter her room; all he would be asking was for her to pass him out a towel. And call the front desk for him.

It would help, of course, if he could call Nadia on his mobile and explain all this. If he had had her number, which he didn't. Although come to think of it, if he had his mobile he could call the front desk himself. But his mobile, James knew, was lying on his bed next to his room card. Inside his room.

The idea of somehow getting hold of Rebecca flitted in and out of his panicking mind. She was his agent, after all. Then he pictured her bulging eyes, bulging yet further with disgust. Her cutting, contemptuous tones. No. Anything but that.

The more James thought about it the surer he was that going to Nadia's room was the only possible answer. But – the thought hit him like a sledgehammer – what *number* was her room? How would he find out? He could hardly go, in his naked state, to the reception desk and ask.

Then it came to him, in a flash of pure inspiration. Nadia was in Room 101! 'As in Orwell,' she had said. As in *1984*.

The only remaining question was how to get, unobserved, to Room 101 with no clothes on. Presumably it was on the first floor. The lift was a bad idea; slow and heavily used. But there must be stairs somewhere, back stairs hopefully, that saw little use. Glancing down the corridor James was gratified to spot a pair of fire doors with a green staircase sign above them.

He could have done with a loincloth to cover his modesty, but his hands would have to do. Cupping his testicles, James headed towards the fire doors and saw that his luck was beginning to turn. A free-standing yellow plastic warning sign had been put out over some lino: 'Slippery When Wet'.

James seized it, folded it, and held the resulting plastic rectangle over his privates. It was on the small side for his equipment, but better than nothing.

Dave arrived on the third floor just in time to miss James's naked buttocks disappearing through the fire doors. He went to James's room and knocked. 'Room service,' he called, using the oldest trick in the book.

No answer. Dave was puzzled. Asleep? But according to reception, James Dorchester-Williams had only just gone to his room. So why was there no one home? Perhaps he was in the shower. Dave put his ear to the door and listened hard. He could not hear water.

And yet the hotel staff said both politicians were in the hotel.

A dirty excitement gripped Dave Were they *together*? In Nadia Ramage's room? His spirits lifted for the first time all day. All year, if he was honest.

James was hurrying down the back stairs with the sign held over his willy. To his vast relief he met no one for the first few flights. But just as he started the descent of the final stretch the fire door to the first floor opened. An elderly lady appeared.

James recognised her instantly. He had knocked at her door earlier that day. He'd remember that great cliff of lilac hair anywhere.

As she looked at him in appalled surprise, James began gabbling apologies, but she raised an imperious hand and cut him short.

'Didn't you come to see me today, young man?'

'I'm not sure . . .' James tried to fudge. Despite everything, 'young man' was gratifying.

'Yes, it was you,' she insisted. 'I never forget a . . .' Her eyes shrinkingly brushed his nether regions before closing tightly. '*Face*.'

'I'm most awfully sorry . . .' James began.

But the fire doors to the first-floor corridor were swinging agitatedly behind his putative constituent. He'd lost that one to UKIP, James guessed, reaching the ground-floor doors.

Inspecting his camera for roadworthiness, Dave was only half-listening to the lavender-haired old lady standing with him and a couple of teenagers in the lift. She had just got in, shaking with indignation and telling anyone not plugged in to an iPod (Dave, basically) about an unclothed man encountered on the staircase. 'And him an MP! Or trying to be!'

Dave suddenly tuned in. 'An MP?'

But the lift doors had opened at the ground floor and his informant shot off with surprising speed across to the welcome desk where she launched into vociferous complaint.

Dave rattled back into the lift and pressed the button for the first floor, electrified by what he had just heard. It couldn't possibly be true that the urbane James Dorchester-Williams was, at this precise moment, running buck naked around the Stayhotel with a cleaner's sign over what the old bat called 'his gentleman's area'.

Could it be true? What a photograph it would make if it were!

He had arrived at the first floor. The doors slid open and he stepped out, looking to left and right. The corridor was long and dimly lit and at first he could make out nothing but a greyish figure in the far distance.

Dave raised the camera with the magnifying lens and peered through it. Seeing that the figure's greyness was naked flesh, he felt, as he had never thought to feel again, a surge of pure adrenaline. Scrutinising the hair, the handsome profile scrunched in panic, he identified the figure as James Dorchester-Williams.

The prospective MP for Wortley – God bless him – was knocking frantically on one of the doors. Looking at the nearest number to him – 89 – Dave calculated swiftly that the door in question was either 101, or very near it.

The room number he had been given for Nadia Ramage.

Dave suppressed the manic urge to laugh, to punch the air. So it was true, all true! Oh boy. If this wasn't the money shot to end all money shots. He steadied the camera, held it to his eye, held his breath.

Oh my God. That sign. Slippery When Wet. He could see it through the magnifying lens. You couldn't make it up. But could you photograph it?

Dave sidled silently along the wall. He wasn't a small man, but he could make himself invisible when necessary. He was almost opposite the door now; he had a great side view of James in all his glory.

And now the door was opening! And yes, there she was. Nadia Ramage.

He had them both now, in the same frame. Dave's heart was thundering. His knees felt weak. Quick, now. Take the shot. Before he had a heart attack from excitement.

Bingo. Gotcha. Snap, went Dave. Zoom, zoom.

CHAPTER 46

Where, Olly wondered, was his fiancée? Isabel had been getting fresh air for a very long time. Or going to the loo or whatever she had said she was doing. He could not, now, remember.

Meanwhile, he was stuck with Sparkle D'Vyne and Squiz. Sparkle was recalling one of what were apparently many overdoses in the course of her distinguished social career and Squiz was hanging on her every word.

'Apparently my lips were bright blue. I can hardly bear to think about it. Blue's never been my colour . . .'

The room was swimming around Olly but thanks to the press of people there was no room for him to fall over.

'Excuse me,' he muttered, pushing past the lead singer of Bouillabass. Once he would have stopped; he liked French electropunk. But now he had to get to Isabel. Where was she? Nowhere to be seen, but somewhere, surely. A tall, pale, red-headed needle in a haystack of shouting literati.

Olly realised that he felt very drunk, but that with this state had come an odd clarity. His thoughts were moving much more slowly and focusing on areas he had not previously considered.

He felt detached from himself, almost as if he was watching himself from a distance. And what he was seeing was not impressive. If he was honest – and he felt able, now, to be honest – he looked like a pathetic attention seeker careering round a party trying to get a word in edgeways when it was obvious no one was interested.

Having admitted this to himself, Olly felt something like relief. He felt that he could finally drop the burden of pretence he had been carrying around since that awful interview this morning. He could admit that Wild & Free was not working out as he had hoped. He was not special here, that was the problem. He was a moderately well-known author, but so was everyone else. And some were more than well known.

Just from here, where he stood, he could see the Herman Munster-like frame of Jorgen Borgen, author of the celebrated *Oslo Slasher* series. And the wobbling cleavage of Fiona Whipple, creator of the *Sally Cupcake* novels, and the *Building Site Bakers* in the trademark hi-viz jackets and safety helmets that had made them a TV sensation. And over there was that vinegar-faced children's author Esther Quaid, whose *Little Charlie Star* series personally made him want to throw up, but which had entire shelves of Waterstones devoted to it. And earlier he had passed the grubby-looking S.T. Dawson, whose erotic *Mr Pain Needs A Secretary* trilogy had been the sensation of last summer. Who was *he*, in company like that? Who was he *kidding*?

Well, Isabel for one. With the benefit of his new, drunken detachment Olly could now see what he was putting Isabel through. It was as if a great shaft of light had shone in some previously ignored area of his brain, the bit that stored information about his fiancée. She had never wanted to come here. She had done it only for love of him. And what had he done? Ignored her.

'Ow,' said a well-known TV actress, as Olly trod on her foot.

Earlier this evening, he knew, he would have been all over her, praising her performance in the multi-BAFTA-winning *Paedos And Slags*. But now he merely apologised and tried to push on.

Now a blonde was in his way. Not one to make a bishop kick a hole in a stained-glass window, but one red-faced and inebriated and shouting into her mobile. Olly recognised her as Sarah Salmon the columnist and knew that he would formerly have tried to charm her too to get a mention in her largely incoherent but inexplicably influential column, full of ramblings and witterings about titled people he had never heard of. He ducked behind her, and passed on.

His eyes darted everywhere, searching for Isabel. He had to find her. He had lots to tell her. He was positively bursting with the things he wanted to say. Mainly, he wanted to apologise. He had believed many things for his own convenience. Convincing himself, for example, that Isabel wanted to come to the festival for fun. Only now did he remember that she had initially suggested he go alone.

And why? That too was obvious now. Because she had never got over the *Smashed Windows* business, of course. Not just the publication of the book itself, but the real-life events that were its subject. How could he have been so insensitive?

Olly wanted to kick himself, but there was no room to do so, and besides, plenty of people were doing it for him. He was stumbling over an unfeasible number of feet. His calves would be black and blue, which was no more than he deserved.

His own monstrous ego was at the root of it all. He'd been desperate for Isabel to see him addressing a rapt crowd at a literary festival. He'd wanted her to witness that public validation of his talent. And what had happened? He had been humiliated by Sparkle D'Vyne. He had deserved that too, he now accepted.

He had gone into the interview with entirely the wrong attitude. Arrogant, lazy, entitled.

Really, what a shit he was. He felt Isabel would agree with this assessment. Well, when he found her, he'd encourage her to let rip. Say exactly what she thought of him. Get it all off her beautiful chest. Then he'd take her back to their room, get their stuff and go. There was nothing to stay for here any more.

Having craned his neck a few more times, Olly remembered his mobile phone. He'd track her down that way. He reached for his back pocket.

There was something knobbly in it. Something small. Puzzled, Olly drew it out. The tiny diamond on the small ring glinted in the overhead light. He stared at it, wondering how it could have got there. Had he picked it up from the bedroom? Had she dropped it on the floor?

Then, somewhere in the back of his mind, came the tail-end of a distant memory. Earlier that evening, Isabel had been agitated, calling to him. Distracted by Sparkle D'Vyne, he had taken no notice. He now remembered the feel of her hand in his pocket.

He regarded the tiny circlet in horror. It was all too easy, now, to guess what it meant. That Isabel had had enough.

Panic swept Olly, followed by a backwash of self-pity. What if he lost her? What if there was no what if about it, he already had? He swallowed hard in a dry throat.

And then someone knocked him; the ring fell from his fingers. Instantly and completely, it disappeared. Aghast, Olly checked his shirt front to see if, by some miracle, it had looped on a shirt button. It had not. He could not even see the floor. But Fiona Whipple's cleavage was close by – had it fallen down there?

A scream rent the air. ' The *Sally Cupcake* author glared with two haphazardly mascaraed eyes. 'Get off my tits!'

Olly recoiled in horror. He hadn't thought through that aspect of it. He hadn't thought about anything beyond finding the ring. With the result that now, to judge by the censorious faces turned in his direction, he might be lynched for sexual assault. Almost definitely, Olly realised, as his eye met that of firebrand feminist cultural commentator Mairead Carp, whose *Masturbation Diaries* currently topped the charts.

There was only one thing for it. And he might find the ring while he was down there. Olly took a deep breath, sank to his knees and began to scrabble on the floor. As every conceivable type of shoe, from stilettos to Birkenstocks to brogues, to Dr Martens of clown-shoe proportions, now crushed or skewered his fingers and the backs of his hands, Olly assessed the likelihood of being the first ever literary festival martyr.

Misery swelled within him as he padded like a dog between crushed and soggy canapés and literary pairs of legs. He could not see the ring anywhere. Nor could he find Isabel. She, the ring and the future it represented, all seemed lost to him now.

Just what should he do now? His throat was hurting. His eyes burned. He wanted to howl with self-disgust. He had failed at everything. He was like the inflatable boy who came to the inflatable school with a pin. He had let everyone down, but most of all he had let himself down. What was there to do now but drink? Drink and drink until he dissolved in a pool of alcohol and soaked into the ground.

Victoria was having a simply marvellous time. Wild & Free was quite simply the best fun she had ever had. She'd been floating happily around the festival – it really had felt *incredibly* like floating – and everyone had been so friendly, she'd been filled with a huge, heart-bursting love for the whole of humanity. How had she never realised before how beautiful people were?

Every colour and sound had exploded within her as if she had never experienced colour and sound before. She'd had visions of flowers and fireworks and rainbows and all manner of things. Some deadening layer had been peeled off. She felt excited, exulting, full of energy. Alive for the first time in years.

She couldn't quite remember – was it possible she'd danced with a tree? Or a man dressed like a tree? And a frightfully dashing blond man who had been holding a pillowcase? And had she really gone down the helter skelter, screaming with childlike delight? And now, drifting around, she'd somehow floated into this simply *marvellous* party, a party, moreover, she had the faintest possible memory of actually being invited to! How wonderful of whoever it was to ask her! Was that *really* Mary Berry over there in the silver Doc Martens?

'That's an old trick!' she exclaimed gaily to the bleary-eyed young man whose hair hung over his face. He had, she noticed, very battered and dirty hands.

'What is?' asked Olly, regarding with suspicion this strange woman with her ecstatic expression and rolling, dreamy, unfocused gaze. He had never seen anyone so stoned in his life.

Victoria giggled happily. 'Taking two glasses so it looks as if you're taking one to a friend. Disguises the fact you're on your own.'

'I am on my own,' Olly replied stubbornly. 'And they *are* both for me.' Then he tipped both glasses down his throat in quick succession.

Victoria clapped her hands. 'Bravo!'

Praise, even from an obvious loon like this, had a positive effect on Olly. He felt better, if drunker than ever. The plasterwork on the ceiling seemed to be writhing. He lurched off, seizing another glass as he went. He was nowhere near drunk enough yet.

'Wait for me!' The madwoman was at his elbow. 'But aren't you an actor? I'm sure I've seen you somewhere before. Weren't you in *Paedos and Slags*?'

'No, *Gladiator*,' Olly replied facetiously.

The woman's expression had changed, he saw. From looking blissed out, she now appeared distraught. He had a feeling it wasn't anything to do with Russell Crowe.

'Are you all right?' he asked.

'Um, not really,' Victoria muttered through the hand now pressed to her mouth. What was happening? Was she going to be sick? She'd been feeling so wonderful, so happy, but now she felt terrible. Really terrible. Worse than ever before in her life. Nausea pressed in the base of her throat. The room was spinning wildly; it was frightening. She kept thinking it would stop, would stabilise, but it just kept moving. It was like being on a merry-go-round, except there was nothing merry about it.

Was it a hangover? Had she really drunk that much? She had never in her life drunk enough to justify how she felt now. And she had eaten the biscuits she had found on Guy's sleeping bag, anyway; they should have soaked up some of the alcohol.

'You look awful,' Olly said bluntly. The woman had gone absolutely ashen. 'Ish there anyone I can get for you?' Though God only knew how; he could barely stand himself. As had been the case most of the evening, the heaving crowd remained the only thing holding him up.

Victoria twisted her head slowly from left to right. The movement felt heavy and thick, as if moving through water. Everything which had been so bright before now looked blurred. Her ears buzzed and she felt as if someone had lassoed her skull and was pulling the rope very tight.

Most of all she felt horribly, horribly sick. Merely raising her head brought on a ghastly salival rush. Things were whirling around her, not gracefully and delightfully as before, but in a mad, sinister whirl. There were laughing, distended faces everywhere. Teeth, wild eyes, clawing hands. Whenever she shut her eyes the centrifuge in her mind, connected to her throat and stomach, seemed to double its speed. Her heart was thumping so violently hard she felt it might come through her ribcage.

With a mighty, determined effort, she tried to focus on Olly. 'Can you,' she said haltingly, 'take me back to my tent, pleash?'

Olly tried manfully to meet the gaze that was trying to meet his. 'Where ish it?'

Victoria tried to shrug; the resulting violent upward lurch of her entire body confused Olly. 'I don't know,' she slurred. 'But I really really need to shleep.' She stumbled suddenly and he caught her; utterly relaxed as she was, she was unexpectedly heavy.

She gave him, from the circle of his arms, a troubled smile and he realised he was stuck with her; he could hardly abandon her in this state. Somewhere at the back of Olly's alcohol-soaked mind gleamed the possibility of redemption if he assisted this woman. He could tell Isabel about it – she might be a tiny bit less angry about his behaviour in general and his losing the ring in particular. But it would probably be like tossing an ice cube into a volcano.

He stumbled out of the party with Victoria. He did not dare look up, so could only tell by the floors through which rooms he was, to all intents and purposes, dragging her. Oak boards gave way to black and white marble squares. There were steps, which he negoatiated gingerly. Finally, they found themselves outside.

He had a vague impression of tents with music playing and people lurching around excitedly with neon bobbly things on their heads. Maybe they were taking pictures with mobile phone cameras. There was a lot of flashing and neon, anyway, but that might have been his brain exploding. From time to time the ground reared up right in his face and he felt a distant blow to the forehead while, at the other end of his body, a dull pain burned at the front of his ankle. He had tripped over yet another guy rope.

Victoria was clinging to him when he wasn't falling over. She was looking around for her tent. It was somewhere about here, she was sure.

'Oh dear,' she said to Olly. 'I'm going to feel terrible in the morning.'

Olly did not want to even think about tomorrow. 'Did you shay you were near the yurtsh?' he asked as some large and rounded white forms loomed into view. 'Oh God,' he said, as he fell over yet another guy rope. A pink one, he realised as he picked himself up.

The woman had disappeared, Olly saw. She must have gone into one of the tents, perhaps into the very flowery one right next to them. Someone inside was talking loudly. 'Mum! For *God's* sake! I had no idea where you were! I've been worried *sick*.'

CHAPTER 47

Jess woke with a start and found herself staring up at three white chevrons on a blue background. Rather like a road-bend sign, but in a shield shape and hovering in the air above her.

Then she realised what it was, and where she was. In Wylde Hall, in Ralph de Gawkrodger's bed. The shield was his coat of arms. It was fixed to the inside of the top of a four-poster bed. So, presumably, one could wake up and remember who one was.

Or who one used to be.

Jess smiled, remembering the rooftop proposal. She had said yes instantly. Almost as instantly she had reassured Ralph that the imminent sale of his ancestral home could not have mattered less. She had felt a twinge of disappointment, admittedly. It would, Jess thought, have been lovely to wake up in this room, stare up at that shield, for the rest of her life. As it was, this first glimpse of it might well be the last.

Sic transit gloria mundi. The main thing was Ralph. If the choice was between a Ralph minus his landed estates rather than no Ralph at all, then there was no competition.

She twisted her head to the side. Ralph grinned from the next pillow along. 'That was marvellous,' he remarked. 'I haven't had sex for such a long time I'd quite forgotten what fun it was.'

Jess giggled. 'I agree.'

Ralph had, not to put too fine a point on it, been a revelation. He was not in the least inhibited. Far from it – he was one of those people, as Jess was herself, who threw themselves into lovemaking without any self-consciousness whatsoever. They were perfectly suited in that way as well as every other. The only doubt in Jess's mind was whether Ralph would be, as he claimed, happy to live with her in London. He struck her as a supremely un-urban creature.

'My flat's not very big,' she warned him.

'If it's got you in it, it's paradise,' Ralph assured her.

'But I won't be in it most of the time. I work very long hours.'

'Oh, I'll find something to do.' He had patted her hand. 'Go for walks and things.'

But Jess couldn't really see him happily roaming the crowded length and breadth of Upper Street the way he must roam the infinite green reaches of his ancestral park. She wished she could buy Wylde herself and give it back to him. But while she was well paid, her renumeration was not of a level to compete with an oligarch's.

She wished they had met before. She could then have helped him frame a financial rescue package, looked at ways of building Wylde into a business. But better to have met now than not at all.

'Oh, don't worry.' Ralph's bright blue eyes smiled into hers. 'Let's seize the day.'

He stroked her thigh. Her breath caught in her throat. What was it about his slightest touch that sent delicious shocks all over her?

'You're amazing,' she gasped. He knew just what to do and where to do it. While being married so often was obviously inadvisable, he had clearly learnt a thing or two about women.

'What's that?' A strange noise now broke into Jess's thoughts. Ralph, above, stared down at her. 'The same thing it's been all night.'

Jess shoved him off, laughing. 'Not *that*! I thought I heard something.'

'Just the earth moving, my darling.' And Ralph pulled her down again.

'There!' exclaimed Jess, popping up again, her eyes rolling round the room as she listened. Ralph immediately adjusted his position.

'Like that?'

'But, actually, I didn't mean *that*,' Jess explained, a few blissful minutes later. 'I meant that I heard whoever it was again. A sort of wailing.' She looked doubtfully at Ralph. 'Wylde's not . . . *haunted*, is it?'

That it might be had never occurred to her. The house, huge and ancient as it was, had felt so friendly. But Jess believed in ghosts. Perhaps living here might have had its negative aspects after all.

Ralph rolled off her. She was obviously distracted and he liked full participation whenever possible . . . 'Well,' he admitted reluctantly, 'there is supposed to be a White Lady. But I've never seen her, I can assure you.'

Not that it mattered now, of course.

He stroked her breast. Immediately Jess started up. 'I heard it! A scream!'

'No, you didn't,' Ralph insisted, covering her face with kisses. He might have heard something, even so. But he was determined to ignore it. Those stupid authors, he didn't doubt.

That was one aspect of Wylde he would not miss in the least: having to share his home with silly writers.

But the screams were loud now, too loud to ignore. The corridor outside rang with their echoes. Reluctantly Ralph threw back the covers. 'I'd better go and see what it is.'

Naked as he was, he swung himself out of bed. Five seconds later he was turning, with ever-increasing apprehension given the mounting hysterical racket, into the guest room corridor.

A spine-chilling sight met his eyes. A woman with hair down to her buttocks, her face a mass of raw and bloody flesh, stood at the end of the corridor, gesturing wildly, screaming in a guttural foreign language.

Ralph stared, more amazed than scared. So it was true. There was a White Lady of Wylde Hall. He had never believed it, never imagined, either, that she wore such frankly skimpy nightwear, let alone teamed it with feathered mules. She had very good taste.

Some of the silly writers, Ralph now noticed, were standing in the open doorways of their rooms. Either they wrote murder mysteries or writing gave you nerves of steel; they all seemed more excited than afraid. That bossy Dame woman, Ralph saw, was dominating the scene, resplendent in curlers and lashings of face cream, her bulky frame tucked into a lilac dressing gown.

'Ridiculous,' she declared in her fruity, querulous tones. 'You say she puts that on her face as part of her beauty routine?'

The question was addressed to Sparkle D'Vyne, who was lounging against her door frame in, Ralph approvingly observed, a rather smart leopard-print silk playsuit. She beamed and swished her mane of golden hair. 'Daria was telling me all about it at the party. Works wonders, apparently. And Alexandr gets to eat it in the morning.' Ralph, quickly putting two and two together, felt he did not envy Alexandr, whoever he was. He had thought Daria's husband was called Boris.

'Well, it's obvious the bodyguards have done it,' H.D. Grantchester pronounced. 'There's no sign of them anywhere. An open and shut *jewel* case, I'd say.' Evidently pleased with her quip, she turned on her tartan-slippered heel. The door of her room shut behind her, as if to clinch the argument.

Jezebel Pert-Minks now shot into the corridor wearing nothing but a small white towel. She was clutching three mobiles and wore a headset over her mussed-up hair. Her shouting into the phone rivalled the histrionic distress of the White Lady. Or rather the oligarch's wife, minus her jewels. Ralph had figured it out by now.

He raised his eyebrows and smiled encouragingly at Jezebel. 'My dear. Most unfortunate. I'll leave you to it then, shall I? In your capacity as festival organiser and all that?'

He hurried back to his bedroom.

'What's up?' Jess asked, concerned, from the bed. 'It sounded dreadful.'

'Oh it is, it is,' Ralph assured her. 'It's absolutely terrible.'

Jess raised an eyebrow. 'So why are you grinning like the Cheshire Cat?'

Ralph drew in a long, happy breath. 'If I may put it this way, I don't think it's terribly likely that our friend Mr Badunov will want to buy Wild and Free now. Let alone Wylde Hall. Now,' he added, his eyes gleaming as he approached the bed, 'where were we?'

It was, Ralph remembered as he pulled Jess to him once again, an ill wind that blew nobody any good.

In a room on the third floor of the Stayhotel, Wortley-on-Thames, a mobile phone was grinding itself round in circles on a table. Eventually the noise got through to James. He surfaced, slowly, from the unconscious. There was a ringing in his ears, as if something had just exploded. A sense of aftershock.

Where was he? He was hot and he felt sick. He raised his head, but it pounded with nausea, so he let it fall again to the flat polyester pillow. This was not home, with its goosedown.

The phone continued to ring, so with a groan and a great effort, he lunged in its direction and caught the receiver. 'Hello?'

'You fucking idiot,' said Rebecca.

It all came rushing back. The night before. Being naked in the corridor outside Nadia's room. Someone taking pictures. Pictures that must have hit the front pages by now. James gulped. He could almost see the grainy images with joky little exclamation marks in red circles over his rude bits.

Someone – Rebecca – was ranting in his ear, but James had tuned out completely. Jesus. Victoria and Guy. He imagined them looking at the papers, the colour draining from their faces. Victoria's hand clamping her mouth in disgust. Guy's eyes narrowing in contempt.

James gazed hopelessly, helplessly, round the room. Details previously unnoticed now seemed suddenly blazingly evident. The curtains had a horrible pattern on them, of flowers that bore no resemblance to anything that actually grew. They were thin and had been hastily yanked together; long rectangles of light flamed in the gaps and announced another hot, unforgiving day. He did not want to face it. He did not want to face anything.

Rebecca was still snarling out her anger, but he was not listening. She had always disliked him and was no doubt getting some self-righteous kick from all this. He laid the phone on its side and collapsed back on to the bed. But even from here he could hear Rebecca's tinny tones, ranting at the air.

He felt sick. So, so sick. Closing his eyes only made it worse. Oh God, he was in the whirly pit.

The phrase came back to him from long ago. From university. Spencer used to say it, when he'd overdone it on the lager. The thought of university reared up like a rip tide; a flood of regret now engulfed him. What a mess he had made of everything. And not just his own career and marriage, which was no more than he deserved. But Nadia's too, which she didn't deserve at all.

Regret now gave way to crippling shame. Nadia had left the hotel almost immediately after the nude scene. After calmly asking the photographer what paper he worked for she had turned to James and shrugged.

'Shit happens,' she had said, pressing back his stammering, horrified apology. She had added that she was going home, right now; she was pulling the plug on her election campaign. Her priorities had shifted; she wanted to be at home with her family when the news came out. 'It's all that matters in the end,' Nadia had said. 'Family.'

'Aren't you angry with me?' he had asked. He almost wanted her to shout at him. Rant and rave.

Instead, Nadia had turned on him a pair of eyes that were dark, sad shadows of the ones that had laughed and danced before. 'What's the point?' she had asked him. 'It's not just about me any more.'

His mobile rang. James stared at it, tight-throated with terror. Was it Victoria? Guy? Hand shaking, he picked it up.

'It's me again.' It was Rebecca, sounding predictably agitated. 'You put the fucking phone down on me.'

James sighed. 'There didn't seem much to say, really.'

'Well, there is. You should be thrilled.'

'*Thrilled?*' Even by Rebecca's standards – if that was the word

– this was amazing. From what twisted corner of policy initiative parallel universe did *that* come from?

'Yes, thrilled,' Rebecca repeated firmly. 'You've been unbelievably lucky.'

James's chest exploded in a violent cough. '*Lu* . . . ?' He couldn't find the second syllable.

Wheeling wildly through his distracted brain came the idea that she was making an existential point. His career and marriage may be smoking ruins but in a wider sense he had become more human.

'But the pictures . . .' he began.

'Haven't run.'

He had been standing up, half-pulling on his trousers. But now his legs gave way and he toppled on to the bed. '*Haven't run?*'

'They were stopped,' Rebecca said, going on to explain that the chairman of the newspaper company had been persuaded to pull them. He was a keen Party supporter and the scandal could cost the Party a key seat. The constituents of Wortley, it had been successfully argued, had already had one sleazeball MP to put up with. A second would be disastrous.

James did not flinch at the description of himself as a sleazeball. It was a tiny detail in a suddenly glowing and glorious canvas. Birds were singing in his ears and the hideous flowers on the curtains seemed actually scented and alive. 'That's incredible,' he said. 'An unbelievable stroke of luck.'

'For some of us, yes,' Rebecca returned crisply, adding that he, James, had been deselected with immediate effect – the official reason would be illness – and she had been asked to stand in his place. There was one day of campaigning left, after all. The party press machine was already lining up key interviews for her with the BBC.

James listened in awe, both of his ex-constituency agent's driving ambition and juggernaut efficiency, and of the benevolent Fate which had got him off the hook in so spectacular a fashion.

He felt an overwhelming relief. And ridiculously, childishly happy. His political career was in ruins, but his family life was intact and that, James felt, was all that mattered in the world.

'Good luck,' he said to Rebecca, and meant it.

He finished dressing with a singing heart. The bathroom resounded to his trilling as he shoved his mobile phone and wallet absent-mindedly in his sponge bag, and put his razor and toothpaste into his briefcase.

Now that there was no reason to stay here in Wortley, he was going to join his wife and son. At Wild & Free.

He left in the narrow cupboard the two suits by Tommy Masher of Savile Row, ditto the Hilditch & Key silk ties and Charvet double-cuff shirts. Let the skinny boy on the reception have them, with his compliments. James took the greatest delight in tossing out of the window every campaign rosette he possessed.

CHAPTER 48

Lorna Newwoman was under pressure like never before. She had not slept properly since getting to the festival and today was the Story Jam in the Hibbertygibberty Wood. She had gone to bed early in order to be rested and perform at her absolute peak. But the mosquito bites she had sustained during her encounter with Boz in the Hibbertygibberty Wood were now itchy fires all over her body. They had not aided restful sleep.

Nor had Buster and Django. Throughout the small hours the boys had repeatedly gone outside in order to wee against the tent. This had necessitated noisy and painful climbing over everyone else. Then they had started throwing things. Something heavy had flown through the air and hit her hard on the side of the ear. 'Just bloody well stop it!' Lorna roared, peeling Buster's sandal off her temple. 'I need to sleep, OK? I'm performing tomorrow!'

To her still greater fury, this outburst was greeted with angry voices from the surrounding tents. Voices telling *her* to shut up!

Lorna had simply roared back. She hated everyone in the surrounding tents. In particular she hated Tenebris for sleeping in the Westfalia and making her sleep in her own small and crappy tent. Tenebris' official reason was that he snored terribly and might disturb her. But this was the second night and she was yet to hear a peep coming from the van.

Once the shouting had stopped, the night was practically over. Accompanied by an orchestral swell of birdsong, rosy-fingered dawn began to touch the tops of the trees in the park, then spread a picnic blanket of golden light across the dew-beaded grass.

Bloody birds, Lorna thought, as she finally dropped off to sleep.

Alfie, however, was wide awake. All the yelling had woken him up and his rest had been fitful. Moreover, the shoe Buster and Django had thrown at Lorna had been intended for him. Most of the subsequent ones had hit their target. He had, Alfie decided, had enough. He didn't want to stay in the tent with them another minute.

Something in the birdsong called to him. He quietly unzipped the tent flap and ducked out. He was still in his pyjamas, an ancient and grey pair of Superman ones on whose account he had endured a lot of teasing from his cousins. The joke, if so it could be described, had turned on the chasm between the rippling muscles of the cartoon hero and his own puny and undergrown physique.

Sockless in his trainers, Alfie stepped slowly between the guy ropes and past the camper van in which Tenebris was sleeping. Alfie could see him inside, eyes closed, mouth open. The expression on his face was one of relief. Alfie felt he rather admired Tenebris for his courage in standing up to his mother. If only he had taken his sons with him in the van as well.

The façade of Wylde Hall, some distance away, now caught Alfie's eye. He paused to admire its gracious Tudor proportions, its barley-sugar-twist chimneys, its heraldic beasts against the skyline, its mellow red bricks being warmed by the first rays of morning sunshine. He loved old buildings, and stately homes in particular, although he knew better than to say so to his mother. Ever since arriving he had longed to have a proper look at Wylde Hall; now, it suddenly occurred to Alfie, with his mother asleep, was a perfect time to go and examine the place.

He walked towards it, through the silent tents, over the sparkling grass. It felt as if he and the Hall were the only ones awake – and that the Hall was awake, Alfie had no doubt. It looked so lively, its windows glittering in a friendly sort of way and its fancy chimneys twisted up like red drill bits to bore holes in the blue sky. Perhaps the holes that stars came through, Alfie thought.

There had been some wonderful stars last night; he had recognised Orion, and Gemini, the heavenly twins. He had not said so, though. Lorna wasn't interested in anything he was interested in: history and astronomy, languages and science.

He wound through the box garden and stared at the pillared entrance with the coat of arms at the highest point of the arched door. Chevrons on azure, he recognised, thrilled. Under a knight's achievement. Heraldry was another of Alfie's clandestine interests.

He pushed softly at the front door, which swung open. Looking inside, Alfie gasped. There were glasses everywhere, and paper napkins all over the floor, and platters that might have held canapés, and bottles stacked against the wall. But he took no notice of any of these. It was the tapestries he had noticed. Alfie had a special interest in tapestries.

He had seen pictures of tapestries in books but never a real one. These ones featured lots of bearded gentlemen wearing strange inflated shorts. Breeches, Alfie knew. And the huge things round their necks were called ruffs. His heart started to beat faster. He knew himself to be in the presence of something beautiful, old and valuable.

He dropped to his knees to examine the chequered marble floor. He could see tiny fossils in it, sea creatures from millions of years ago. He sat back on his heels and looked up; between the tapestries were pictures in gold frames, of more people in ruffs. The rising sun was throwing on the white walls sharp, criss-cross shadows from the mullioned windows. Alfie sighed in sheer bliss. He had never been inside anywhere like this before and he was wearing pyjamas, but he did not feel the slightest bit out of place.

He wandered on. All the rooms smelt of wine and the glasses and crumpled napkin theme continued. Already he had lost his bearings. This house was beautiful but it was also very big and it was difficult to remember what way he had come.

He paused before a portrait of a lady in a silk dress standing under an oak tree next to a gentleman in a fawn waistcoat. A small boy was standing serenely next to them, holding the lady's hand. Alfie envied the boy with all his heart. He felt that the house was like the one belonging to the lady in that book he had brought back from school once, the book his mother hadn't liked: *Great Expectations*. Miss Havisham.

Alfie didn't understand why his mother disapproved of Dickens so much. He loved Oliver and Dodger in *Oliver Twist*, Pip in *Great Expectations* and Esther in *Bleak House*. But his absolute favourite was *David Copperfield*.

Alfie felt a great sense of kinship with David, who, like him, had so many parental difficulties to overcome. It was David more than anyone else, even more than Miss Blossom, who had helped Alfie cope with his mother's latest name change. David had survived walking round Salem House with Mr Creakle's sign on his back saying 'He Bites'. And so Alfie had survived being rechristened Newwoman at St Stephen's Primary.

No one was around. Relishing the feeling of having the whole of this magical Hall to himself, Alfie drifted upstairs. He felt very small on the huge, wide staircase; smaller still in the wide, red-carpeted corridor lined with big white doors.

There was a sudden slam of a door. Alfie froze, and then looked around in panic as footsteps sounded behind him. There was a staircase to his left, a narrow one leading to the floor above. He ducked quickly round the corner and crept up.

What he found was a passage: gloomy, narrow and cold and lined with plain little doors. It had an unhappy atmosphere, Alfie detected. One utterly unlike the jolly, sated air of the rooms downstairs. The people who had lived up here were never jolly about anything, Alfie felt quite certain about that. He didn't like it and turned to go back down. But something caught his ear.

He could hear someone. Or something. Or maybe several things. A snickering, rumbly noise combined with a soft, animal moan. It seemed to be coming from a door at the end of the passage.

Alfie turned again and crept slowly down the passage, trying to detect which of the identical wooden doors concealed the source of the sound. He narrowed it down to three, then two, then one. Outside the door he put his ear to the wood.

How long she had been here Isabel was not sure. She had slipped in and out of consciousness. She lay on the floor between the beds. It was horribly uncomfortable, but as moving was agony she remained still and tried not to think about the dusty darkness beneath the bedframes. Would a mouse or big spider run over the pillowcase covering her head? The recent kerfuffle, however, seemed to have encouraged caution amid the rodent and arachnid community.

It seemed to her that never in her life had she felt so helpless. Why hadn't anyone come? What about Shanna-Mae and Rosie? Even the egregious Squiz? Surely, at some stage, they must notice she was missing and would come to the corridor to look for her?

Would *no one* come? She was in such pain. Her head throbbed and the heavy ache in her leg made her suspect that it was broken. But worse than all this was the ache in her heart.

Where was Olly? This question was the most miserable of all. When he found the returned ring, would he assume it was all over between them? He might instantly leave the festival, mad with grief. Or he might just stay where he was, at the party, concerned with nothing but his own advancement. To Isabel, unhinged with pain and panic, either scenario seemed possible.

Oh, she hadn't meant it!

Isabel squeezed her eyes shut as the tears flowed. Returning the ring had been a warning, not an ultimatum. She had been irritated, that was all; his behaviour at the festival had annoyed her. She hated the book and all it stood for and had not hesitated to make that plain. But how woefully insignificant the *Smashed Windows* business seemed, compared to what she faced now. Death itself, most likely. And it could have been avoided! If she had not – as surely it must seem – broken off the engagement, Olly would have come straight up here to find her. As it was, he probably couldn't bear to see where they had spent their last night together.

She strove to stop this horrid speculation, to get a grip on her panic, to think logically through what had happened. She had worked it out now, she thought. The handsome man with the box had obviously just stolen it from the room he was leaving. Presumably the people in the corridor were involved too; the Edna Everage dress was a disguise. As for the big men on the bed, they'd been here when she arrived: security guards, Isabel guessed. Certainly, that was what they looked like. Huge muscles, shaven heads. Possibly they had been stationed outside the room with the chest in. Had the blond man drugged them? She could not imagine how. But they had obviously taken something. They smelt heavily of drink and were very sound asleep, and as trussed as she was, as powerless. Should they wake up – and her hopes of even this were fast fading – they could do nothing to help either her or themselves.

Her initial fear that her assailants might return was now replaced by the more terrifying possibility that no one would. Ever. Had the three of them just been left here, to *die*? In this stinking, dusty, distant room in this forgotten, deserted passage? She had read of such things. People getting stuck in chests while playing hide and seek. Unable to lift the heavy oak lid. Suffocating, alone and unknown in a faraway upstairs corridor.

But she could not die. Not yet! Not while there was so much to do. She had plans. Work plans. Life plans. She had been getting married. She still wanted to. Even after all that had happened. Even after giving Olly his ring back.

Isabel groaned desperately through the gag. It felt as if it was all she could do. But her hopes that someone would hear were fast running out. She felt weak with pain and terribly tired, yet knew she must stay awake. If she slipped into unconsciousness, she might never wake up. With painful difficulty she twisted her stiff, tied, bloodless hands and pinched herself as hard as she could. And moaned again, as loud as she could.

She caught her breath. Had she really heard it? A rattle, at the door? Isabel's fear-racked heart jumped into her throat. Was it Olly, come to rescue her, at last?

The sticky, snickery rumble coming from behind the door was, Alfie was thinking, definitely a snoring sound. But the other was different; a cross between a groan of pain and a sigh of utter despair. As, once again, it rose to his ear, Alfie's entire small, sensitive soul rose in sympathy. Was someone ill in there, while someone else just slept? Before he could stop to think once, let alone twice, he had twisted the knob and pushed open the door.

It opened on a small brown room containing two narrow, old-fashioned-looking beds. Alfie stared, amazed. Not two people, but three. On top of each bed rose a great mound of dark-suited man. They had huge, craggy heads, very short hair and big muscles, like people in comics. They were both loudly snoring; their sucked and blown breath sounded like the crashing of mighty waves.

Between them, on the floor between the beds, was a lady in a black dress. She was lying with her leg in an awkward position. Alfie noticed it was bruised and bloody. It must hurt a lot, but he could not see the lady's face. She had a bag on her head, a pillowcase, it looked like. The *poor* lady. He had to help her.

He hurried forward the few steps to where he could crouch, seize the edges and pull it off. He felt her flinch with fear as he did so. Now it was off, Alfie gasped and stepped back, shocked at the gag beneath, the swollen bruise and still-wet blood beneath the wide green eyes staring at him with what seemed almost equal surprise. She had a lot of red hair, he saw. She was ginger, like him.

As the bag had come off, Isabel had expected to see either Olly's concerned face or Shanna with Rosie peeping anxiously over her shoulder. She stared, dazed with pain and disappointment, at this little ginger boy, his eyes burning with purpose behind his thick glasses.

'Don't worry,' Alfie said, more animated than he had ever been in his life. This pretty lady – this pretty *ginger* lady – needed his help. She was depending on him. On him, Alfie, shunned as useless by every other child at school. Mocked and bullied by Buster and Django, who said he was pathetic, a specky-four-eyes, weak, a cowardy custard and other terms too vulgar to repeat.

But where were all those people now? That, Alfie thought, jutting out his lower lip and stiffening his spine, was what *he* wanted to know.

Well, they weren't here, were they? There was *no one* else here of the faintest use. Even those big strong men were tied up and unconscious. So much for muscles, thought Alfie triumphantly.

He could help, though. He, Alfie Lintle-Newman-Newwoman. His narrow, skinny chest swelled with pride and determination. He may be feeble, he may be puny, he may have glasses and ginger hair. But he was, nonetheless, the knight in shining armour to this beautiful lady. He would not let her down.

'I'll be back as soon as I possibly can,' he gasped. 'You can depend on me!'

CHAPTER 49

It was a bright and lovely morning, full of birdsong. There were handfuls of dewdrop diamonds among the green grass blades. As well as Olly, who was out cold in the park, the already-hot sun turning his nose from white to red. He woke up, blinking through his hair. His fringe and his beard had grown so long that the front of his head now looked quite a lot like the back.

He felt sick and very hot and his head hurt. What had happened to him? Why was he out here and not in bed? Ebbing back, in shattered fragments, came memories of last night. He raised his hands to his face and groaned.

Isabel didn't want to marry him any more. He had lost the engagement ring.

And he had no idea – absolutely no idea – where she was.

Probably she had left the festival by now. He could imagine her, set-faced, getting on and off a series of trains. He could not blame her. If he was her, he'd dump him like a shot.

Scrunching his eyes against the pain that resulted from any movement, he raised himself to sitting and felt in his pocket for his phone. He dialled slowly, tongue poking between his lips with the mental effort. But both Isabel's mobile and – a long shot this, anyway – the Paradise Street house went to voicemail.

Sinking back against the ground, Olly abandoned himself once more to groaning self-pity.

'Mr Brown?'

The voice, which was a woman's, came from a long way above him. Olly tried manfully to open his eyes but the sun swung an agonising scythe of hot brilliance right into them and he had to shut them again.

The voice was not familiar. He wondered if it was the crazy woman from last night, the one he had helped back to her tent.

'Olls? If I may?' A giggle. 'You look so handsome lying there in your beard. Like Sir Philip Sidney. *Soldier, poet, scholar he . . .* how did it go?'

Olly had managed to lever his eyes open a slit now. The face was smooth and tanned and surrounded by bright blond hair. She wore heavily-framed, lenseless spectacles.

'Are you all right?' asked Sparkle D'Vyne brightly. 'It was so nice to do that thing with you yesterday.'

Olly groaned again. He'd forgotten about that, on top of everything else. He wished Sparkle would go away and leave him alone. She had trounced him at the talk; must she now come and dance on what almost literally was his grave?

But Sparkle did not seem inclined to go. 'Why are you on your own?' she inquired chattily. 'Where's that lovely girlfriend of yours? She seemed to be having a fabulous time at our talk. I kept looking at her, she seemed riveted.'

Olly wanted to say something cryptic, but found he lacked both the energy and the words. Frankly, he lacked everything. Self-respect. Purpose. Reputation. Isabel.

'She's dumped me,' he admitted.

Sparkle giggled. 'Poor diddums. Is that why you're lying around here? Letting your hot, anguished tears soak in the cold, unfeeling earth?'

'That sort of thing.'

'I'm sure it'll all blow over.' Her tone was indulgent; affectionate even.

'Are you?' He clutched at this straw of hope.

'Totally.' Sparkle sounded, as always, supremely confident. 'She's mad about you, anyone could see that.'

'Mad *with* me, you mean.'

Her warm sympathy was irresistible. In this hyper-self-conscious festival context, her Labrador bounciness was strangely endearing. He felt he rather liked being called Olls.

'Lover's tiff?' Sparkle settled herself on the ground beside him. 'You can tell Aunt Sparkle.'

Olly raised a hand to his head. All the alcohol had done something to his brain. Why else was he opening his heart to Sparkle D'Vyne? He could, this time yesterday, happily have murdered her.

Quite suddenly Olly found himself sniggering. He couldn't help himself. His laugh was high-pitched and silly. A ridiculous laugh for a ridiculous person in ridiculous circumstances. What else was there to do but laugh? 'Hashtag disaster,' he snorted, thinking of Squiz. 'Hashtag complete hash!'

Sparkle, sitting companionably beside him, smiled indulgently. She wore a short black and white check dress and a small black cardigan. Her feet in their ballerina flats waggled happily and her hair blew about in the breeze. She had started to make a daisy chain but the length of her nails was impeding progress. Olly stopped laughing. The daisies reminded him, with awful suddenness, of an afternoon on a sunny bank with Isabel earlier in the summer. Their last summer, as it turned out.

'I quite like real daisy chains,' Sparkle was musing. 'But I much prefer the ones that Tiffany make.'

'I wouldn't know,' Olly muttered, drowning in regret.

Isabel had placed a flower coronet on her head. 'How about this for a wedding tiara?'

'Awful business about Daria,' Sparkle said next.

'Who?' Olly muttered, still back in that lovely afternoon. *Oh Isabel.*

'Badunova. Boris Badunov's wife,' Sparkle continued conversationally. 'Had all her jewellery stolen during the night. All the bling that Boris had given her . . . oh, hello, little boy.' Olly heard her tone change and opened his eyes. A skinny red-headed child had appeared, his eyes agitated behind his glasses. 'Are you all right?' Sparkle was asking him kindly. 'Do you need some help?'

The child was muttering in her ear. He'd lost his mother, Olly assumed, noticing he was red-headed like Isabel. Would their children have been ginger too? He would never know now, of course.

He was interrupted by a horrified gasp from Sparkle. 'What? *What?* Are you *sure?*'

She had sprung to her feet. She had the child by the hand. 'Come on!' she urged Olly. 'This is a real emergency.' She tugged the boy's hand.

'He's lost his mother?' Olly was clambering to his feet with painful slowness, uncertain as to why he should be involved.

'No, he's found your girlfriend.'

'But . . .' Olly shook his head, confused. 'She's not lost. But she's gone home.'

'Have you talked to her?'

Rapid-fire questions from a sharply focused Sparkle were almost as bewildering as the questions themselves. 'Well, no. She wasn't answering her phone . . .'

'And that,' Sparkle said grimly, 'is because she's bound, gagged and possibly injured in the attics of Wylde Hall.'

CHAPTER 50

At first Guy had thought, unlikely as it seemed, that Victoria was simply hung over. But his mother never lost control to this degree.

He had laid her carefully down on her sleeping bag. 'Mum? Mum!' She had not stirred. He had slapped her cheeks gently. Still Victoria did not wake up. She just smiled and turned over on her side.

How on earth had she got hold of the stuff? Guy could not imagine. Of course, it was hardly difficult in a place like this. But it was impossible to imagine his mother asking for it. The only weed Victoria knew about was the type never tolerated in her flower beds.

The irony! His mother had insisted on coming with him to the festival because she did not trust him by himself, and she was the one behaving wildly. All he'd done all night was have a milkshake and see a few bands. And be sent off by Shanna-Mae with a flea in his ear.

It was now that Guy noticed the empty packet of biscuits. Tamara's biscuits, the ones she had given him. As a sudden, horrible suspicion gripped him, he snatched up the packet. There were a few crumbs and pieces left. He licked his finger, and picked up a few. There was no mistaking that dark and pungent taste. Anger tore through him like a flame.

Then he took his mother's pulse and performed a few simple checks. She seemed OK; she was breathing fairly peacefully. But she was unused to drugs and it was impossible to estimate the quantity she had taken. How many biscuits had there been? Guy screwed his face up, trying to remember. Four? Five?

He reached for his phone. He was taking no chances. He'd call the emergency services. And then he'd better tell his father. Probably all he would need, Guy thought, with all that by-election stuff on as well. But there was no question that he needed to know.

James was finally heading to the Wild & Free festival. He was not arriving in the way he had originally envisaged, in the family SUV on a boys' trip with Guy. He was on Shanks's increasingly exhausted pony, walking along a country lane.

His water had run out and so had his phone. But his heart was light and his spirits effervescent. He felt full of optimism and strength. That this was still the same day that had started so badly at the Stayhotel seemed unbelievable.

The weather was sweet and bright and warm. The sky was a fresh blue and the grass that rose gently either side of the road was an intense, glossy green. Birds trilled and swooped above and sweet, hot gusts of scent from the hedgerows caught his nose.

He had got here amazingly quickly. All the connections had worked. He had shot to Paddington from Wortley-on-Thames and got to Taunton just in time to get the local train to Simpleton, the town nearest to Wylde Hall and the Wild & Free festival. From here he was walking; there were no taxis at the station and ringing for one, the Simpleton station master had warned, often meant a wait of half a day.

James could not remember the last time he had been for a walk in the country, but he was going to be doing a lot more of this from now on. The road was as softly winding as one in a fairy story and the hedges he was walking between were so tall, so soft-looking, so plump, so full of colour, so abundant with flowers, so impossibly romantic. Beyond them, golden fields studded with hay bales rolled to a horizon of burning blue. Picturesque cattle and sheep stood placidly in the shade of great oak trees. Little winds winnowed paths through glossy grass. Birds sang, sun shone. The world was a beautiful place.

James felt, for all the sudden and violent end of his political life, utterly relaxed. That the Westminster nightmare was over was an enormous relief. He would have made an appalling MP; meeting Nadia had revealed that much.

He felt guilty about what had almost happened to her, but the bright side was that, in the end, it had not. As a result she would easily defeat Rebecca de Sendyng in the Wortley-on-Thames by-election. Rebecca had all the warmth and personality of an ice cube. Perhaps, in the end, he had done Nadia a favour.

Now it was time to do himself a favour. He must impress upon his wife that, having been up close and personal to both money and power, he wasn't really interested in either. Victoria had been barking up entirely the wrong tree. She had spent years furthering his career when it should have been the other way round. And that, James was quietly determined, was how it would be from now on. There had been a lot of time to think on this journey and he had put every second to good use.

It was obvious now – perhaps it always had been – that Victoria's slender, well-toned body contained if not a future female Prime Minister, then at least a CEO of a multinational. That his wife was wasted at home was one of the many things he would tell her when he reached her at the festival. Along with the fact that he loved her, of course. He hadn't said that in the past nearly enough.

So, James had concluded. If Victoria liked power, liked money, then let her go out and get it for herself. He'd be right behind her. Waving her off from the doorway as she stepped into her limo.

Because he, James, would be the family facilitator from now on. He no longer planned to spend all his son's waking hours at work. Guy would be off to university soon, or wherever else he was going. What time they had together was limited and precious.

He planned to enjoy himself from now on. Joy lent his feet wings. He sped on through the gates to the estate, noticing the stone-topped pineapples, the carved crests, the cherubs with little smiling faces. Go on, they seemed to urge him. Find Guy and Victoria!

Someone now loomed up before him, wearing a jester's cap and bells. 'Hello, hello, welcome to Wild and Free!' he exclaimed, capering around in the path in front of James . . . 'I'm Checkpoint Theo.' He flourished something brown and inflated on a stick. 'My bladder,' he explained with a bow. 'Tool of the trade.'

James looked at the welcome tents with their bunting and 'Welcome To Utopia' signs. He looked at the large black plastic dustbins with their signs saying, 'Cares. Woes. Hassle. Real Life. Work Shit. Please Dump In Here Before Entering The Festival'.

How many other people had had as much hassle to get rid of as he did? He could be here all day, dumping it.

The jester was back in his face. 'Day ticket?' he demanded. 'Or are you staying till tomorrow?' As James hesitated, Theo, who wasn't as laid-back as he looked and in addition was on commission, switched into hard sell mode, listing the various attractions.

'. . . Strictly Come Dad Dancing, that's, like, a competition for, you know, how dads do embarrassing dancing at parties . . .'

'No thanks.'

'No worries.' Theo consulted his iPad. 'Um, well, if you're more of the academic type,' he looked James doubtfully up and down, 'there's a contemporary thought workshop in the old bakehouse, it's called Kitchen Think . . .'

James shook his head.

'No worries. Then there's Battle of the Bands . . .'

'Battle of the Bands?'

Theo's smile was derisory. 'Amateur rock competition. Old guys with guitars, mostly. Very old guys, some of 'em . . .' He went on in this vein, squinting at his screen all the while. James half-listened politely, until a name caught his ear, shot into his brain and exploded.

'*What* did just you say?'

The jester's cap and bells shook. 'The Upward Mobility Scooters. Yeah, amazing, isn't it? They're all over eighty, they've formed a band and—'

'No, no, the ones you mentioned before them,' James said urgently. 'What did you say they were called?'

Theo looked even blanker than seemed normal. 'Did I mention someone else? The chap hoppers? Lord Edgware and the Bullnosed Morrises?'

'No, you said some old college band with a funny name . . .'

The jester's rings rattled. 'Oh yeah. The Eyeliner Worms or something. No, rewind. Mascara Worms.'

'*Worms*? Not Snakes?'

Theo was flicking the screen of his iPad. His fingers were tanned and had ankhs and crosses drawn on them in biro. 'Oh yeah. Snakes, you're right. Apparently they were a college band about a thousand years ago . . .'

James stared indignantly.

'But they've got together and come here just to do the competition. Kinda gets you here, doesn't it?' He thumped his bare torso in its hi-viz jacket.

'Your heart's on the other side,' James told him. A tremendous excitement gripped him from the feet upwards.

He wanted to cheer and leap about, to punch the bright and sunny air. His wife was here, his son was here, and by the most incredible, unbelievable stroke of luck, his old friends from college were here.

It was if all the most important pieces in the jigsaw of his life had miraculously slotted back together in one place.

'Hey! Not so fast!' Theo was capering after him up the drive making a 'money' gesture with the hand not holding the bladder.

'Oh, sorry.'

'No worries.'

As James paid the entrance fee – an astonishingly large amount – there was a wild whooping of sirens, a roar of heavy engine and a screeching of tyres. They both stepped aside as an emergency ambulance, blue lights flashing above its neon green hospital livery, turned into the drive.

James watched as it roared between the sunny trees, scattering the birds. In the midst of all that was pleasant about life, it was an unwelcome reminder of the alternative. 'Looks like a bad start to the day for someone.'

'Some woman OD'd on hash cookies.' Theo shook his head and his bells rattled.

'Kids, eh?' James said.

'Nah, mate. She was about fifty.'

CHAPTER 51

'*I'll* organise the festival next year,' Jess promised her future husband from where she sat in the steaming bathtub in the cupboard in the corner of his room.

Jess was serious. She already had ideas about how Wild & Free could be improved. A tad less irony, she thought. She had as much a sense of humour as the next woman, but it was all so ironic at the moment it wasn't ironic at all.

Now, obviously, was not the time to discuss all this with Ralph. Having obtained leave from the Badunovs to get dressed before they all discussed the robbery further, he was currently hurriedly throwing on some clothes.

Jess had offered to face Boris Badunov too, but Ralph had declined. 'I can cope, my dear.'

'But he might try to get you to hand over some of your portraits in compensation or something,' Jess said as Ralph let himself out of the room. She was, she realised, feeling proprietorial about the house and its contents already.

Ralph stuck his head back through the door. 'He's more likely to try and stop me ringing the police,' he said dryly. 'From what I hear, some of those jewels had a most questionable provenance.'

Jess sank back into the water, grinning. It was bewildering, the speed and drama of this change in her circumstances. Twenty-four hours ago she had been resigned to a lifetime alone. Now she would have a coat of arms! What would Ginnie make of it? Jess wondered gleefully.

Then her smile snapped away. Ginnie! It was, Jess was suddenly, guiltily aware, a horribly long time since she had been in touch with her. Ginnie would have spent the night alone, no doubt worrying where she was. She really must go and see her, Jess decided, rising from the foam.

She dressed hurriedly in last night's white dress, now decorated with grubby smudges from the floorboards, and left the room. Downstairs, she passed quickly behind the workers clattering bottles in black binbags and putting glasses back into boxes. She met no-one's eye. Let them think what they liked.

She strode out of the hall and through the festival. Over the glittering grass she went, past the many-coloured tents, admiring the sun-gilded tree-tops and the shimmering leaves. She gazed up at the blue wash of sky and felt the birdsong swell in her ears.

It was a *beautiful* morning. Despite almost no sleep, Jess felt completely energised and refreshed. A sort of inner brightness was filling her, an excitement, a spirit of generosity towards the whole world. She felt as if she owned the place – which, as things had turned out, she very soon would.

She was no longer afraid of *anyone*, in particular men with mad staring eyes. One of the many things she planned to tell Ginnie was that she completely agreed with her on that front. She had been imagining it. Tall, proud and as gloriously conspicuous as you like, Jess strode purposefully towards Genghis.

But when she got there, full of excitement, Ginnie was not in. Jess was immediately fearful that her friend had given up and gone home. Spotting, on Ginnie's bed,, a small white note, Jess's heart thumped. But it was not what she feared.

Gone to the Story Jam. Gxx

She might as well, Ginnie had decided. After a long night rattling around – a fiftful breeze had sent the wind chimes wild – in what suddenly seemed a very large and empty Genghis, even the thought of an amateur children's story-telling competition seemed attractive.

She had by now walked around the festival so many times that even she was starting to tell the difference between the endless identical Indian street food stands. Or the equally numerous upcyclers and furniture editors with their graffiti lampshades and denim whatnots.

The Story Jam made professional sense anyway. Children, after all, were her business. Or had been. Ginnie had used her long, dark night in Genghis – although actually it had been quite bright thanks to the party going on in 'Attila' next door – to reflect on her future. She had come to the conclusion that she needed to move on, perhaps move away from Chestlock altogether. Her sighting of Mark Birch, singing softly outside the camper van, had made it plain how much she needed to.

As retro pop had boomed from Attila, Ginnie had thumped her embroidery-ridged ethnic pillow. She had cursed her own soft heart and hopelessly impressionable nature. She still loved him, more madly than ever, despite what he had done to her. Only by removing himself from his vicinity would she ever get over him.

Their rehearsal slot was at lunchtime and Mark, on the Big Top stage, felt exasperated. None of it was working out as he had hoped. Singing with Rob had lulled him into a false sense of security, or at least into the assumption that they'd sound quite reasonable together at the Battle of the Bands rehearsal, with Spencer in the line-up and all their guitars plugged in.

They sounded even worse than he had originally imagined.

Partly this was because Spencer was not concentrating. Physically, admittedly, he was up on the stage, microphone arranged at a Liam Gallagher-ish angle. But that his mind was not on the job in hand was obvious. As was the reason.

Rowan was standing at the back of the Big Top in her breast-clinging velvets, hands on her thighs and swaying with suggestive abandonment to whatever risible excuse for music they were managing to produce.

Even so, the lead singer's inattention was not the most serious problem. It was their lack of a drummer that was the real disaster. Spencer had been every bit as groundlessly optimistic as Mark had been fearful about filling up the hole with the famous 'clever guitar work'.

The lack of a rhythmic frame for their songs rendered what had already been pretty poor stuff into meaningless mush. Having just seen Lord Edgware and the Bullnosed Morrises in action, Mark no longer felt they would actually come bottom. But second bottom was definitely the best they could hope for.

What made Jimmy's absence still more glaring was the presence of an actual drum kit at the back of the stage; it belonged to the Upward Mobility Scooters but they had sportingly left it for the use of other groups. Lord Edgware and the Bullnosed Morrises had used it and the Mascara Snakes could also have availed themselves if anyone could have been spared from the guitar or vocals line-up. As it was, in both these respects, they needed all the help that they could get.

Mark groaned and looked again at the set list. Perhaps if they just sang something simpler? 'Jonathan Livingston Scargill', for instance, had complex riffs and bombastic bass chords which none of them could do any more. And 'Berlin Wallpaper' required a heavy, pulsing drumbeat and skittering cymbals whose absence could not, as Spencer insisted, be compensated for by foot-stamping, which made them look like some kind of world music collective.

He had to do something. It would be a disaster whatever happened, but he was in it up to his neck now, Mark recognised. And people were actually coming to see them: all those kids who had listened to Rob and himself. Not to mention – dreadful, wonderful possibility, this – Ginnie Blossom.

Had he really seen her, though? The idea was so far-fetched, and yet she had seemed solid and real enough. More likely it was just longing, the power of suggestion on his sun-fevered brain. He had not seen her again, for all his searching, and another night had dimmed, not the memory, which was as bright as ever, but the possibility that it was true.

'Look, guys,' Mark said, hoping that adopting Spencer's vernacular would help make his case. 'What about doing "Life is a Chocolate Factory" instead of "Scargill"?' So far, all his old prejudices apparently intact, Spencer had still refused to countenance it.

Spencer shook his head again, but Mark had already started to strum the chords. Rob stepped up to the mike and joined in, and even though Spencer – rather childishly, in Mark's view – was putting petulant fingers in his ears, Rowan, at least, seemed to appreciate it. She was standing, eyes closed, hair swishing, at the back of the tent next to the mixing desk where appreciative roadies were watching her swaying rhythmically and rubbing her thighs.

Mark, encouraged, reached the end of the first verse. But here he was stopped, as it were, in his tracks.

'Stop it!' Spencer yelled. 'I bloody hate that song. Soppy crap.'

'No, it bloody isn't,' Mark snarled back. That was it. He'd had enough. Again.

He slipped his guitar strap over his head and walked off the stage. 'You can stick it,' he yelled at Spencer, 'where the—'

'Baby!' interrupted a low, soft voice. It was chastising, yet indulgent. Turning, Mark saw that it was not, as he had supposed, aimed at him.

Rowan had stopped swaying and rubbing. Her hair had stopped swishing and her eyes were open, staring straight at her lover. 'Baby!' she cooed at Spencer. 'That's such a cool song. I totally dig it. Can't we hear the rest of it?'

Mark, storming towards the tent exit, now turned to see Spencer's former furious expression turn to one of blinking, drooling adoration.

'Sure, baby,' he said in high, eager-to-please tones. 'Sure we can.' He picked up his guitar, grinned and glanced from Mark to Rob. 'Guys? A one, a two, a one two three four . . .'

CHAPTER 52

The Big Top was a busy place. People were constantly entering and leaving it, but none James recognised. The striped red and white tent flap lifted gently, invitingly, in the breeze. Were the Mascara Snakes behind it, in there?

By the guy ropes, James hesitated. He felt both wildly excited and cripplingly shy.

He warned himself not to expect too much. In all probability, Theo had got it wrong. You only had to look at him to see how full of crap he was. Take what he'd said about the other bands. The Bullnosed Morrises, or whatever. And those old people. Eighty-something rockers. The Upward Mobility Scooters. Yeah, right.

But now the flap of the tent wobbled and buckled and eventually lifted, and a group of ancient gentlemen slowly emerged. They wore black leather pork pie hats and round blue John Lennon glasses. With them was an equally venerable woman in skinny jeans. 'Look,' she was berating one of the men, 'it's like Ray Davies says. If you can't sort your middle eight out after a fortnight, you need to see a psychiatrist.'

'Is that what Ray Davies says?' quavered another of her bandmates.

'Typical,' croaked another. 'Whippersnapper. What does he know about rock and roll?'

Now the flap moved again and a number of elongated young men in Morphsuits, top hats, monocles and co-respondent shoes emerged, blinking, into the light. If anyone anywhere was called Lord Edgware and the Bullnosed Morrises, James had to accept, it would be this lot.

And now, through the open flap, James could hear something, the jangle of guitars within. A song he recognised even though three decades had elapsed since last he heard it: 'Life is a Chocolate Factory Somewhere in the Milky Way of my Mind'.

For a moment, leaden with emotion, he could not move. Then he waited to hear the drummer come in, just to compare, to see if the new guy was better than he had been. He waited and waited. They had evidently rearranged the song. The drummer was coming in later.

James himself could wait no more. He raced to the flap and dived in.

'Jimmy! Jim!' Mark almost fell off the stage, such was his excitement.

Enfolding his old friend in his arms, looking into his eyes, Mark felt thirty years just disappear.

'You recognised me!' James tried not to show he was a hair's breadth from bursting into tears.

'Well, I wouldn't have,' Mark admitted, 'if I hadn't seen you on the telly a couple of days ago. By-election, was it?'

James raised his eyebrows. 'Oh that,' he said.

'Yes. That. So how d'ya get on? Did you win?'

'Long story.' James looked towards the stage and the drum kit. 'So who's doing my bit?'

'No one,' Mark assured him. 'You're here just in time. It was sounding bloody awful.'

The timing was unbelievable, Mark thought. The rehearsal had reached the point when not having a drummer was being keenly felt by Rob and Mark. Spencer, meanwhile, was keenly feeling only one thing that anyone could see.

'You don't have anyone on drums?' Jimmy's eyes widened. 'But there's a kit.' He could see the sticks on the snare. His fingers itched. It had been a long time.

Spencer had caught up with developments now. The prospect had briefly torn his attention from Rowan, even. 'Mate!' He was clapping Jimmy on the back. 'You came, after all!'

James was puzzled. 'After all?'

Mark joined in. 'I phoned. Your wife. About the festival. Months ago.'

James shook his head. 'She didn't mention it.'

Somewhere in his mind, a cog now meshed with a gear. Had there been a reason for this non-mentioning? He recalled the purge of his rock memorabilia. An invitation to play that had not been passed on. Just before he stood for a by-election.

He felt a powerful rush of annoyance. He reined it in, however. What did it matter? And Victoria would be too busy pursuing her own agenda from now on to interfere with his any more.

'Can I borrow your phone?' James asked Mark. Thanks to his own flat mobile, Victoria and Guy were still unaware that he was here. The idea was delightful. What a surprise they would get!

His wife went to voicemail but Guy answered.

'Dad? Jesus, Dad, where have you been? I've been trying—'

James exploded down the phone. 'I'm here! At Wild and Free! Can you believe it! I'm about to hit the drum kit! Come and watch!' He sounded like a teenager, even to himself.

But the real teenager on the other end sounded flat. 'Didn't you get any of my messages?' asked Guy.

'No, but I'm *here*!' Why didn't Guy understand? 'At the *festival*!' James repeated. 'Where are you? We can meet up now.'

'No, we can't.'

'Why not?'

'Because I'm in hospital with Mum.'

CHAPTER 53

It was early afternoon and Lorna Newwoman was in the Hibbertygibberty Wood. The Story Jam was about to start. She was behind a clump of rhododendron, breathing deeply and visualising, preparing for the performance of her life.

She could hear the audience gathering, chattering. Babies were crying. Kids were screaming. Parents were shouting. They had better calm down, Lorna thought grimly. She had no intention of yelling over all that.

Peeping out from behind a frond she noted that Tenebris and the boys were in the front row as instructed. Alfie, Lorna saw, looked irritatingly calm. Almost pleased with himself, which he had absolutely no right to be, having given her the fright of her life earlier that morning. With typical self-centredness he had chosen today of all days to wander off from the tent in his pyjamas, meaning that Lorna had been quite unable to polish the dynamics of her performance of *The King Who Couldn't Wee*.

Tenebris, meanwhile, had scoured the festival, checking all the Lost Persons Totems. But no small ginger boy was in evidence at any of what he secretly thought of as startlingly and – given their purpose – unsuitably priapic papier-mâché poles.

Fortunately, just as Lorna threatened to lose altogether what passed for her rag, Alfie was spotted rushing between the tents. He had the most ludicrous cock and bull tale about finding someone bound and gagged. Alfie, his mother thought, had a great deal to learn about how to construct a convincing story.

Lorna had not yet seen the terrifying Boz, but she had heard him. He was based behind another set of bushes deeper into the Wood, along with a couple of other people – probably the men who had turned up to collect him the day before – who were presumably part of his act as well. They seemed to have a great many artistic differences. Certainly, there was a lot of shouting.

Pixie, the festival assistant charged with overseeing the competition, was darting about nervously. As before she had a clipboard almost as big as herself, hundreds of lanyards and the usual half-dozen or so mobiles. 'Have you heard about the robbery?' she asked Lorna, her bug eyes wide with excitement.

Lorna listened with satisfaction to the tale of the looted gems. What did people expect if they wore tiaras to festivals? She hated the rich. They were leeching scum and deserved all they got. Or lost.

'Good news that the police are here, though,' she observed to Tenebris. With regard to Boz, certainly, it made her feel moderately less in danger of her life.

Tenebris stared. 'You're always saying they're pigs and fascists.'

Lorna glared at him.

Now, backstage – or rather backbush – she awaited her moment. The list of other acts she had finally yanked out of Pixie's shaking grip had not seemed to constitute much of a threat. There was *Tummy Train*, which warned of the dangers of junk foods. And while she had been initially concerned about *Big Butts Are Best*, it turned out to be an eco-homily about rainwater harvesting. Only *The Storyteller's Stinky Underpants* by the Rogues and Vagabonds Theatre Group seemed to be anything to worry about. And that was for reasons that had nothing to do with the story.

Out in the front row, Tenebris sat cross-legged and very uncomfortable. The ground was stony and he was being eaten alive by midges. And next to him were Buster and Django, who, if they weren't eating dirt, were hitting each other.

As usual, Tenebris utterly lacked the strength to upbraid them. It wasn't that he didn't recognise that his sons were badly behaved, more that he could do absolutely nothing about it. While horribly aware, everywhere he went, of disapproving glances from other parents, Tenebris had now ceased to respond to them. Even to acknowledge them. What was the point?

'Feel free to tell them off,' he had invited one particularly tutty, disapproving mother who had been shoved aside by Django in the stampede for some free balloons advertising 'Professor Arsenic's Madlab'.

The woman had looked disgusted. 'I'm afraid I wouldn't feel comfortable disciplining other people's children,' she had sniffed, keeping her eyes unwaveringly on Tenebris as if to commit his description to memory for the future use of the social services.

Now Tenebris brightened as a woman entered the audience area. And not any woman either. An *amazing* woman. In glorious and triumphant contrast to the downtrodden dads like himself and the boil-washed, lank-haired, make-up-free mothers who had otherwise assembled, she looked part of an altogether more sophisticated, exciting and glamorous world. She was tall and black and wore a short white lacy dress to stunning effect. She stood for a few minutes, an elegant dark flamingo, looking around, apparently searching for someone.

Tenebris yearned to catch her eye. For reasons he didn't quite want to think through, but were to do with the life he might have lived and the woman he might have lived it with, he wanted to leap up and shout, 'Pick me! Pick *me*!'

He saw her face light up with delighted recognition and gazed as she picked her way along one of the freestyle, haphazard rows to sit down next to a pretty woman with shoulder-length brown hair who gave Tenebris's goddess a strained smile. But then her face changed utterly, to happy amazement, as the goddess started on what was evidently an extraordinary piece of news. Tenebris watched wistfully. How he wished he was the recipient of those confidences!

'He's asked you to *marry* him!' Ginnie could not believe her ears. 'Blimey. He's a fast mover, I'll give him that.' Behind her amazement and delight swirled a backwash of pure envy. In all the years she had known Jess she had never seen her eyes shine like this before, never seen her so blazingly happy.

Jess giggled. 'He says that there's no point faffing about at his age.'

Ginnie smiled. 'It's wonderful news, Jess. I hope you'll be really happy.'

Jess squeezed her hand. 'I will. And you will be too. We have to get you back in touch with this headmaster.'

'Oh,' said Ginnie, glad of the distraction. 'It's starting!'

A short woman holding a clipboard now appeared from the bushes at the side of the stage. She was greeted with some dutiful whoops. Django threw a pebble. It was beginning, Tenebris recognised with a sinking heart.

Behind a rhododendron bush some twenty feet away, Jude glared at Boz and Big George. They glared back. Stalemate had been reached. After all they had achieved, with their haul quite literally glittering at their feet, was this, Jude asked himself angrily, how it was all to end?

They should have been miles away by now. Not squatting here in the dusty bushes, with pairs of enormous women's shoes, Boz's much-crumpled hat and George's battered wig scattered around them.

The jewels which remained in the pillowcase they were still all holding should now be safely swimming in face cream. They had been so close, Jude groaned silently. Everything had been ready. Only the timing had gone wrong.

Well, if you didn't count the half Nelson business. Fortunately Boz had eventually bought the story that he had only been moving the jewel sack from a muddy patch.

They had been, the three of them, on the point of jumping the Beauty Bus when Jude's sharp ears had caught the unmistakeable sound of a police siren. Many police sirens. From that moment on, escaping from the festival by camper van was out of the question. Escaping by anything, for the next few hours at least. That the police would search all exiting vehicles was more than likely, and there was an obvious risk, especially in the context of a recent jewel heist, of them recognising Boz and George.

'So it's back to Plan A, lads,' Jude instructed, as cheerfully as he could manage. In the face of Boz's murderous nihilism, being upbeat was less a moral imperative than a sensible safety precaution. 'Back into the wood.'

The glint in Boz's eyes was like the edge of a knife. 'Not that fucking kids' competition?'

'LangWIDGE!' scolded George.

'We've got to do the show,' Jude explained patiently. 'There'll be police all over the festival soon. The last place they'll expect to find a jewel gang, not to mention escaped criminals, is performing at a Story Jam in the Hibbertygibberty Wood. And these bushes are perfect for hiding the stuff. Just give it to me and I'll put it under these leaves . . .'

He tugged at the pillowcase but George and Boz continued to hold fast to their sections.

'You get your thievin' hands off it,' Boz growled.

Jude looked offended. 'My hands aren't any more thieving than yours.'

'Stop bleedin' arguing,' instructed George. 'The tension's getting to us all,' he added pacifically, knitting his massive craggy brow. 'We've got to think of a way out. Literally.'

Jude dredged up his most convincing tone. 'We've got to go through with the show.'

'Do me a favour,' snarled Boz disbelievingly. 'Think I can't work it out, do you?'

'Work out what?' Jude returned, his clear blue eyes innocent.

'What you're planning. That me and George go on stage and do all the farting and whoopee cushions crap so you can sneak off with the swag.'

Jude, who had actually never thought of this, tried his best to look shocked. 'I would never do that,' he said in wounded tones. *But now you mention it . . .*

There was silence, as each of the three of them reverted to suspicious glares directed at the other two.

Eventually Jude sighed. 'You can hardly take the swag on stage with you, Boz.'

Boz's great square white teeth showed in a snarl. 'You want to bet?'

'It's a good idea,' Big George now put in unexpectedly. 'You take it on stage, Boz. Over your shoulder, like Dick Bleedin' Whittington. That way we can all keep an eye on it.' He turned his huge head to Jude. 'It's not as if he's gonna run off with it through the bleedin' audience, is it?'

'. . . can you welcome Lorna Newman . . .'

'Newwoman!' roared Lorna from the bush at the side.

'. . . welcome Lorna New*woman*, performing *The King Who Couldn't Poo.*'

Lorna bounded on, overhyped on adrenaline and coursing with anger. 'Wee!' she bawled at Pixie. '*The King Who Couldn't Wee!*'

'Oh my God!' Ginnie gasped behind her hand to Jess 'So that's why she's here. To perform her masterpiece.'

Jess grinned. 'You know it then? Quite a title.'

'I had to read it out to the school,' Ginnie groaned.

Jess's eyes widened. 'What? How come?'

Someone was glaring at Ginnie from along the row. A woman in glasses with wobbly white arms, her frizzy hair secured with a staked leather clasp, was gesturing at her to be quiet. 'I'll tell you after.'

The woman with frizzy hair now directed her fury at someone jostling along the row behind. If people couldn't turn up on time, she was heard to mutter, they should not come at all.

Mark Birch, the recipient of these attentions, blanked them. He'd had enough of being told what to do. He'd had enough, full stop. Just when everything seemed to have finally fallen into place, just when Jimmy had turned up out of the blue at the exact moment he was needed, he'd had to go haring off to the hospital. Poor sod, Mark thought. He hoped Victoria would recover. She'd never been particularly nice to him, but Jimmy was obviously devoted, so there had to be some good in her.

The news about Jimmy's wife had been the final nail in the coffin of the Snakes reunion. None of them had felt it would be appropriate to play a concert after that. So now what?

Going to see Lorna Newwoman perform at the Story Jam would normally be the last thing on Mark's list. But it might, in some vague way, help Alfie. And, given the Chestlock connection, there was a very slight chance that if Ginnie really was here, she might be there. Although now he was here, and looking around, he could see that she wasn't. And probably never had been.

This festival was one of the strangest, most frustrating experiences of his life. And the most extraordinary aspect was the now-you-see-her, now-you-don't game with Ginnie Blossom. He must finally accept, Mark told himself, that he had imagined it on both occasions. It would drive him insane otherwise.

He took a deep breath and stared at the grass between his knees. Perhaps he really should go home now. The band thing was never going to work and he was just kicking about, wasting his time.

A voice now caught his ear; an unmistakeable, strident voice. A gimlet-eyed woman had appeared on what passed for the stage. Mark's spirits slumped. Lorna Newwoman was about to give her all.

He resigned himself to listening. But then another voice caught his ear, one that could not have been more different. It was soft and warm and low and it was coming from the woman sitting in front of him. A strawberry blonde with creamy skin. An absolute knickerbocker glory of a woman.

Mark shook his head and rubbed his eyes. Ginnie's head was mere inches away. He had always thought of her hair as brown, the colour of glossy milk chocolate. But the sun – or something – seemed to have lightened her hair, and this close, closer than he had ever been, he could see that it was composed of an infinite number of colours. There were threads of red in there, of gold, of black.

She had taken off all the make-up from yesterday, he saw as she turned her profile towards her friend. He felt a dart of pleasure and relief; the natural flushed peach of her skin was, after all, far lovelier than any imitation. And her cinnamon sprinkle of freckles would be invisible under thick foundation; the sweeping, eminently kissable tip of her nose upstaged by a bright slash of lipstick, or eyes bristling with mascara. She was perfect just as she was. Perfect for him.

It was in that moment that Mark knew. His every fibre thrilled with the certainty of what he was about to do. Ask her to marry him, right after this show. He was going to get down on his knees, right here, in public, in the Hibbertygibberty Wood. It wasn't the perfect moment, not in any sense of the word, but they were indisputably both present, which was an improvement on recent circumstances.

He had no idea what she would say.

Well, he did. Almost certainly it would be a no. But at least she would know, whatever she thought of him, however angry she still remained, that he loved her.

As she moved he watched the light shift in her hair, skimming across the ripples and waves. He closed his eyes as its scent wafted towards him; clean, warm, peachy, like a rose in full summer. He breathed in. He was lost. He would never forget this perfect moment. Whatever happened next, he would always have this.

CHAPTER 54

Tenebris, in the front row, was torn exactly between wanting to sink into the ground with shame and wanting to gaze forever on the heavenly visage of the black goddess in the white dress. Apart from a few unavoidably strident anthropomorphic grunts he was managing to tune Lorna out almost entirely. He kept his eyes firmly turned from the stage, desperate not to advertise the connection between them.

His cover, however, was merrily being blown by Buster and Django, whose contribution to the performance was a mixture of obscene heckling and joining in with the more explicit parts. Alfie, meanwhile, just stared, his face purple with embarrassment. Tenebris sympathised passionately. What must the object of his adoration think?

Heart in his mouth, he stole a peep. The goddess and her friend were laughing, and Tenebris felt joy sweep through him. That was all right then. Everything was all right. So far as Tenebris was concerned, Lorna's entire appalling performance – the whole effortful and exasperating business of coming to the festival, even – could be justified by that one beautiful smile.

'You were right to come here, Gin,' Jess was sniffing, wiping eyes wet with mirth. 'I wouldn't have missed that for the world.'

Nor me, Mark sighed, smitten, behind. *Nor me.*

Pixie was walking across the stage clearing, juggling her mobiles, slithering with lanyards, clapping with difficulty around her enormous clipboard.

'. . . thank you, Lorna Newman.'

'New*woman*!'

Pixie ignored this '. . . and so, without further ado, Thieves and Vagabonds and *The Storyteller's Stinky Underpants*!'

More whoops. Relaxed after the hilarity of the last one, warmed by the joy of her friend, Ginnie clapped enthusiastically as the new act came on.

But then she felt the body beside her suddenly stiffen. She heard Jess gasp. One of her friend's thin dark hands fumbled for Ginnie's, seized it and clung mightily on. 'Oh God,' Jess whispered through chattering teeth. 'It's *him*!'

'But it's a woman,' Ginnie returned, puzzled. A strange woman, admittedly. The figure on the stage was hugely tall, its vast frame draped in a hideous pink nylon dress, its lack of feminine grace somehow only accentuated by the flounces edging the skirt and neckline.

She had enormous feet, Ginnie saw, and shoulders of extraordinary width beneath the dangling brim of a battered pink hat. Over one of these shoulders was flung a grubby white sack, like a pillowcase, Ginnie thought. One massive fist gripped its neck and it sagged as if it had something heavy in it. What that might be was as yet unrevealed, its role in the drama clearly still to come.

'Not a woman!' Jess gasped. 'He's in drag. Look at the *eyes*!'

Ginnie looked at the eyes and immediately saw what was meant. The sheer menace they emanated was terrifying. They had looked frightening in the paper, but in the flesh they were unforgettable. Her disbelief gave up and died. It *was* him. The escaped criminal. The desperate man on the run. Jess had been right, after all.

'There are police here,' she hissed to her friend. Jess's hand, in her own, was shaking. She could feel, beside her, the terror-rigid frame. 'Don't forget that.'

Jess was looking about her in panic. 'Not *here*, though. And I know he's going to see me. Any minute.'

He really might, Ginnie saw. The mad eyes were sweeping the audience, rolling round all the faces. Daring, it seemed, anyone to recognise him. But it made no sense at all. An escaped criminal, drawing attention to himself with a huge plasterboard toilet? 'Why is he doing *this*?'

'Isn't it obvious?' Jess gasped, hysterical. 'Who's going to think it's really him? Who'd look for him *here*?'

She had a point, Ginny conceded. Competing in a children's storytelling festival *was* an ingenious disguise. No one would expect to find a killer in such a context. How *creepy*, though. How horribly, coldly calculating.

'I've got to get out of here,' Jess was muttering frantically. She had, Ginnie could see, utterly abandoned herself to panic. 'He'll kill me if he sees me. Shoot me on the spot. I was the prosecuting barrister, remember.'

'Yes, but that's your *job*, Jess,' Ginnie reminded her in a low voice. 'You were only doing your job. He *should* be locked up. He looks,' she said shuddering, 'like a complete psychopath.'

Hot fingers gripped her arm. 'That's *exactly* what he is. You don't want to know what he does to people, Gin. Some of the pictures we had to look at during the case . . .'

'Yes, yes, all right,' Ginnie interrupted hastily. In spite of her best efforts not to, she could imagine.

'Sit down!' she hissed. It was obvious to her that keeping still was the only safe option. But Jess, whose nerve had utterly snapped, was already rearing up in panic. In her haste to get away, she now tripped over the cantankerous frizzy-haired woman, who exclaimed, loudly and intolerantly. 'Oh for God's *sake* . . .'

'I'm so sorry,' Jess apologised.

Mark, trying his best to divine the cause of all this sudden agitation, now saw the figure on the stage suddenly stop dead. Quite a strange figure; a big man in drag, hat and all, his vast and unusually muscular arm extended in the act of pumping a whoopee cushion. The audience was tittering. Then the hat fell off and there was a burst of collective laughter. And, from the row in front of Mark, a scream.

The shaven head with its enormous jaw now turned with slow, steady menace on the powerful sinews of its neck. It seemed to Mark to be staring, with great mad black eyes, straight at Ginnie. The great form bent slightly, as if coiling to spring. An endlessly long black arm unfolded and a huge, scabbed and hairy hand pointed in their direction. A bitten-nailed finger extended, dropping the white sack it had gripped so hard until now. The bag hit the rough earth with a clinking sound; the neck opened and something brilliant spilled out. Something which shot dazzling light into the sun, something glassy and shining and beautiful.

The audience gasped. George, beside it on the stage, gasped. Backstage, Jude gasped.

'Jewels!' shouted Buster and Django. 'Real jewels!' They burst forward as one, into the clearing, and grabbed the sack before George could so much as move.

Unaware of any of this, Boz was making rapid, deadly progress through crowds which parted before him like a Red Sea of festival parent-wear. His entire focus was on one woman. One woman he had vowed never to forgive and to kill on sight, if ever he saw her. 'You!' Boz roared mightily at Jess. 'You!' Then, as Jess and Ginnie clung to each other, and Jess screamed, he sprang.

Tenebris Hasp, on the front row, had been watching the drama unfold. He sensed before it happened that his goddess was in serious danger. And so when Boz turned, pointed and leapt, Tenebris was ready.

He may be half Boz's height and a third of his weight, but he had selfless courage and hopeless infatuation on his side. As well as a decade's worth of repression and humiliation. He may be weak, henpecked by Lorna and routinely belittled by his sons. He may be a mouse, but by God, he still had a roar in him.

And he was going to save Jess, whatever it took. And so, as Boz leapt, Tenebris leapt too.

But too late. With one mighty, swinging arm, Boz swatted Tenebris as if he were no more than a fly. As Tenebris crashed to the earth, Boz thundered past him, towards the women struggling to escape.

Mark, however, was not too late. He too had shot to his feet and now hurled himself before Ginnie and Jess at the exact moment Boz burst upon them, nostrils flaring, eyes blazing, his massive teeth gnashing and emitting flecks of spittle. It was the last thing Mark knew.

And just as everything went black for Mark, a great shouting and barking of dogs announced the arrival of the Somerset police. The less perceptive element of the crowd cheered, some still half-imagining this to be part of the act. But one look at the blackly furious face of Boz, struggling in the firm grip of four officers at once, suggested very definitely otherwise.

In the ensuing excitement and chaos there were many voices raised.

That of Lorna Newwoman, demanding to know who had

won the Story Jam competition. Those of the policemen trying to catch Buster, Django and most of all the jewels. That of George, roaring furiously as he attempted, despite the restrictions of his clothing, to stop Jude dashing for the pink Hummer without him.

Boz, Jude was thinking. Bloody, bloody Boz. Always the weakest link in the diamond necklace. The worst and most surreal aspect of the surreal bad luck that had persistently dogged this whole enterprise.

Jude was sweating as he rarely did; his heart thumped with the unaccustomed effort of running. He was, he knew, running the wrong way. He should be going towards the police, not in the opposite direction. But George, hot in his pursuit, was between him and the long, protective arm of the law. Jude had no intention of risking a close encounter with his erstwhile accomplice.

There was no brotherly love in George now, that was for sure. Bad luck was certainly not going to wash as an excuse. Who the kids were who had stolen the jewels Jude had no idea, but that George believed he'd put them up to it he'd gathered from the furious bellows behind. Big George was beside himself. And for the object of his ire, as Jude knew, that was a lethal situation.

He could see George's point. Not only did he stand to lose a fortune, but face among the international criminal mastermind fraternity. It was the latter, Jude knew, that George would find hardest to overlook. He may have scruples about swearing, but it was forgiveness Big George had real issues with. He bore grudges. Violently. And for years.

Jude willed his legs on, stumbling and swaying over the slippery grass. He could almost feel Big George's meaty breath on his neck, feel his knife-blade sharp on his face. He no longer wanted the Ferrari; that, Jude thought, was a distant dream. Perhaps it had never been anything else. Not that it mattered now. He merely wanted to survive.

He could not go on, even so. He was slowing down; his legs were heavy and dragging. Every sinew in his body was screaming at him to stop; his heart, meanwhile, felt about to burst in his ribcage.

Jude paused, turned, and between great, ragged, gulping breaths watched Big George, in his wake, tripping and falling over the grass in his ridiculous, huge high heels. His wig had slipped sideways over his furious face and he was holding up his skirts to expose massive knees, hairy calves and – unexpected touch, this – a pair of Union Jack boxer shorts.

Jude clocked the policemen rapidly gaining from behind and hoped this image of Big George would sustain him when, as was now clearly inevitable, he returned to being a guest of Her Majesty.

CHAPTER 55

It was unlike Rosie to be so forceful, but she had no intention of taking no for an answer.

'Go on, Shanna. Ring him.'

They were setting out the Beauty Bus stall. Revellers from any number of possible raves the night before were reeling blearily past, blinking in the bright light of morning. Shanna paused in her careful arrangement of the various bottles and surveyed the small, indomitable figure of her friend. 'I'm not being told what to do by someone in a nun's dress and orange Crocs,' she pronounced haughtily. Some of Rosie's experiments in the Great Big Dress-Up Marquee were more successful than others.

She looked back at her bottles on the counter, arranged in diamond patterns across its width. Yesterday it had been one continuous wave; Shanna liked to ring the changes.

'That bloke never came back,' she remarked. Then, as Rosie looked puzzled, she added, 'You know. That rude one in the suit who wanted to buy all my stock.'

Rosie put her hands on her ecclesiastically draped hips. 'Don't change the subject,' she said sternly. 'Ring Guy now.'

Shanna tossed her mound of golden syrup hair. 'I don't see

why I should. He treated me disrespectfully.'

'Well, I'm sure he's sorry now,' Rosie said sensibly. 'He must be. He was nuts about you. He's probably kicking himself.'

Shanna, now arranging the lemons into an artistic pyramid, paused to consider this. If she was honest with herself – and Shanna prided herself on always being so – she was slightly beginning to wonder whether she had over-reacted. Guy had backed off immediately; it wasn't as if he had forced himself on her. He had looked, more to the point, genuinely sorry.

It wasn't just the fairness of it either. She missed him, and the limbo of not knowing what to do now was frustrating as well as worrying. Would he get back in touch, or had she scared him off for good and would never see him again? The latter scenario seemed the most likely, Shanna felt, recalling her sharp words and angry gestures with something very close to regret. She gazed at the lemons, remembering what he had done with those as well.

'*And* he saved you when the spray machine broke down,' Rosie now pointed out, as if Shanna needed reminding.

Shanna stopped piling lemons. Great businesswomen, she knew from her research, as well as her own instincts, were not only honest, they were also able to admit when they were wrong. But this was not a business matter, even so. This was something else altogether.

'Yay!' said Rosie, seeing Shanna reach for her phone.

James had lost track of the dramatic twists and turns of the day. He was worn out by the emotional highs and lows. It seemed to him that he had lived many lifetimes, not just one, in the course of the past few hours. The power of Fate, and of the impassive might of unexpected events, impressed itself on him as never before. It seemed to him incredible that he had ever felt, in the past, the least bit in control of anything. Life was a fragile ship, tossed on the stormiest and most violent of seas.

After being woken up in the Stayhotel by a furious Rebecca, he had made the long, hot journey, by train and on foot, to Wild & Free. Here, out of the blue, he had been reunited with the Mascara Snakes. But then he had discovered Victoria was in hospital. That had been the worst thing of all.

Then had come the drive through unfamiliar countryside – cruelly beautiful given the circumstances – to an unfamiliar hospital. Then the waiting in the corridor under the strip lights, staring at the hospital lino, looking up as occasional cleaners went past, or orderlies pushing trolleys.

Victoria was more or less all right, thank God. But all the staff said Guy had been right to bring her. Given the heat, and Victoria's excited state, the dangers of dehydration had been as serious as the consequences of what she had taken. She was about to be discharged, and then they would all go home.

James had, as he'd promised he would, updated Mark, Spencer and Rob after arriving at the hospital. Rowan, Spencer proudly reported, was asking the Morrigan, who was apparently a Celtic goddess, to intercede for Victoria. James was touched. He had met Spencer's latest flame only fleetingly, but she had seemed very positive and genuine. She had told him that Spencer was moving into her covenstead in Leicester with her after the festival. It had to be love, James thought. Spencer had never, to his knowledge, been north in his life.

There had been less opportunity to catch up with Mark, James reflected. Or Rob. But there would always be next year. They would meet up then, if not before. The Mascara Snakes reunion would happen. The world was not going to get away with it that easily.

It was a comfort to feel, beside him, Guy's shoulder, thigh and elbow pressing into him as they sat in the hospital corridor with its fizz of strip lights above and its slick shine of lino below. And in-between the smell of gravy and an ever-passing procession of motley personnel in blue cleaners' uniform or hospital scrubs.

Shanna, beside Guy, squeezed his hand and Guy squeezed hers back. While last night had been miserable and this morning even worse, it had nonetheless been one of the high points of his life to get her text – *I'm sorry. Where r u? Want 2 c u* – and subsequently to see the double doors further down the corridor swing open and Shanna appear.

The magnificent Beauty Bus, Guy knew, was currently parked amid a sea of much less interesting vehicles in the hospital car park. Next to Shanna, in a nun's outfit, sat Rosie, although it was, Guy felt, only a matter of time before she was whisked away to hear confession. Several people already had stopped and directed her to the hospital chapel.

How would his mother react to Shanna, though? Guy fretted. He was bursting with good intentions towards Victoria; would never again take her for granted, would befriend her on Facebook, Twitter, whatever she liked. But the likelihood that she would disapprove of the other most important woman in his life threatened all his other noble resolutions. And there was no way, whatever she said, that he was going to Branston College.

Now, as his mother appeared from the ward and walked slowly round the nurses' station, he felt a pull of apprehension beneath his relief.

James, too, felt a cold wave of worry mingling with his joy. Victoria looked pale, but cheerful enough. Yet there was something hesitant about her; the shock, he guessed, of finding herself ill. Victoria was *never* ill.

How, he wondered, would she react to all the plans he had

made for her? He longed for her to fulfil her own potential instead of endlessly micro-managing his life and Guy's. James swallowed, collected himself and grasped his son's hand hard as they both stood up. Whatever lay ahead, he loved Victoria. He would look after her; he would never let her down.

He saw her staring up at the strip lights. She'd have noticed the décor, of course. Winced at the pattern and colour on the nylon bedscreen. No Buzzie Omelet here.

Had he known it, Victoria's thoughts could not have been further from Buzzie Omelet. She was still absorbing what had happened to her. The doctors had all told her that she'd made a good recovery and no harm, after all, had been done. So why, Victoria wondered, did she feel so – *what*?

Different was the only word for it.

The inside of her mind had been like a washing machine on the final spin. Churning madly, full of wild impressions. Snatches of music, colour, light. People speaking, shouting. Engines roaring, sirens screaming. She felt hot and sick. Then – nothing. And now the noise had stopped and she could see clearly. She felt strangely serene. She was absolutely sure of one thing.

She had been an *idiot*. What had she been *thinking* of?

How could she have pushed Guy in the way that she had? Forced James? It was all so clear now, so pin-sharp and bright. She had made her husband and son obey her will. Do what she wanted. And they had done so, to make her happy. She had never cared or even thought about what might make *them* happy.

Could they forgive her? Could she forgive herself? And, having forgiven herself, could she give herself the chances that she had never allowed herself before?

Such as – the idea had struck Victoria like a thunderbolt –

instead of James standing for Parliament, standing herself. Taking a degree herself – she had never been to university – instead of forcing Guy to.

There was a lot to talk to James about. What would he say? He, after all, would have to support her. But after all she had put him through, would he want to? And if Guy hated her, who could blame him? She had sought to dictate not only his choice of university, but his choice of girlfriend. In the past few hours, many things had made Victoria blush, but the memory of her obsession with Tamara Wilderbeest more than most. The very same Tamara who, according to Guy, had been responsible for the biscuits that had made her so ill. She would no longer meddle in her son's love life, Victoria had decided. He was much more sensible than she was.

She blinked as, now, she saw them coming towards her. James was so handsome! Guy was so tall! Both so healthy, so perfect just as they were, just to look at. She was so blessed, so lucky, so sublimely fortunate. How could she ever have expected, have wanted, any more?

'Darling!' James was uncertain how to interpret the strange expression on his wife's face.

'Mum!' exclaimed Guy, equally awkward.

As they stared at her, fearful and hopeful, Victoria smiled. But not at either her husband or son. 'Hello,' she said, extending a hand to Shanna-Mae. 'It's so nice to see you again.'

Guy's glance met his father's, full of relief. One down, Guy thought. Now there was only the thorny subject of technical college to go. But that could wait. There would be time for all that and more.

As Shanna-Mae's eyes, wide with surprise, met his, he grinned at her. Things were looking up. Things were going to be great.

They were almost out of the hospital when a trolley being pushed by two green-boiler-suited ambulancemen rolled past them, followed by a pretty, if obviously anxious, brown-haired woman. James's eye dipped automatically to the body on the trolley and gasped as – just about – he recognised the bruised and battered face. One eye was entirely closed beneath a shining purple hillock of bloody bruise. The nose was a mass of blood and the mouth twisted and swollen. James guessed that several teeth were missing. Mark's hair was full of dirt and grass.

'*Mark!* Jesus, mate. What the hell's happened to you?'

Mark, inert against the pillow, squinted up with his one good eye. 'Believe it or not, mate,' he began, forcing the words out as best he could through his split, swollen mouth, 'this happened to me at a children's storytelling competition.'

James shook his head. He had obviously misheard. 'I just thought,' he said to the pretty woman, 'I heard him say it happened at a *children*'s competition.'

Ginnie nodded. 'A jewel-thief murderer on the run knocked him over. It's true,' she added, as James stared at her. Who was this crazy woman? Pretty, yes, but obviously mad.

The ambulance drivers both now decided the unscheduled pause was over. 'Come on, sunshine. Let's get you to the doctor.'

As the wheels began to turn over the shining lino, Mark raised his head fractionally. 'Ginnie's going to marry me,' he called, pointing a bandaged figure at his companion.

'Congratulations!' called James. What was the point of trying to make sense of it all? He may as well go with the flow.

'I'll send you an invitation,' came Mark's strangled tones.

'Great. And let's get Spence to organise the stag night,' called James, as the trolley went round the corner.

Oh dear. Was that one step too far? James cast an apprehensive glance at Victoria. She was laughing.

EPILOGUE

Twelve months later

It was *brilliant*, Mark thought, to be up here on stage. Seeing the split beam of spotlights through smoky gloom. Hearing the echo and thrash of guitars, the crash of the drums to the rear.

'Life is a Chocolate Factory' sounded even better than he had imagined through the huge Big Top speakers. Even the gaffers were looking appreciative as they stood about, beer bellies swelling under black T-shirts, tattooed arms folded. The mixing desk, way over at the other side, raised the occasional approving thumb as some tricky harmony came off rather better than anyone expected.

Everything, in every sense, had come off better than expected.

Mark now spotted Ginnie. She was standing next to Jess, Rachel and Ralph in the semi-darkness at the back of the tent. The usual feeling of happy goosebumps erupted all over him. He had been concerned that the loud noise might be bad for the baby but Ginnie said she doubted it could do much harm, just this once. It was such a happy occasion, the pheromones would be worth having anyway.

Last night he and Ginnie had been looking at the heavens. An enchanted evening had deepened into a bewitching night.

They had watched the brilliant stars until they faded into a dawn radiant with pink fire and birdsong. It had, Mark thought, been like watching the beginning of the rest of his life.

'I want to call him Orion,' Ginnie had said, softly touching her belly. 'Do you think that's a bit much?'

'Yes,' Mark said immediately, then paused. Was it really a bit much? Was anything a bit much if it made Ginnie happy?

Certainly he would have thought so once. But that uptight, irascible person had gone forever. And while Mark would never be a trusting soul exactly, he was a good deal more tolerant. Were outlandish children's names so bad? His new intake last September had included a Rain, a Blue and an Octavian. Which was practically Orion, except longer.

Jess, next to Ginnie, let a long, low breath out. She could relax now. The first Wild & Free under her watch was a success. Which was a small miracle, given the pace and complexity of the past twelve months.

Her whirlwind marriage to Ralph, although low-key, had nonetheless taken place in the mediaeval estate church and thus revealed the full extent of its rotting condition. Getting a church roof appeal off the ground had been Jess's first job as lady of the manor; her second to organise Mark and Ginnie's nuptials.

After a working honeymoon spent touring the stately homes of England with particular reference to their commercial outlets, Jess had thrown herself into getting the festival off the ground. She found not only that she had a flair for it, but that she loved it. The literary aspect was her particular passion and interest, and in this she had been helped enormously by Olly and Isabel. Having recovered, both physically and mentally, from their respective traumas of last year, they had been glad to come back and take a leading role in events.

Jess had worked hard to achieve this, making Olly the main

literary link and ensuring he had the pick of the interviews. H.D. Grantchester had not been asked, but Sparkle D'Vyne had. She had shown an unexpected talent for social reportage: 'The Great Festival Heist' her celebrated and sparkling account of the previous year's diamond-studded fiasco, had won awards for *Vanity Fair* and there was talk of a film. Jess, always on the lookout for publicity, hoped it would prove to be more than talk.

And perhaps that would not be the only film. The past twelve months had also seen *Smashed Windows* optioned; Olly was currently working on the screenplay. Isabel, too, was dominating the screen; the small one in her case. Her series about *Shakespeare's Women* on BBC Two had been an enormous hit and Jess had been quick to spot an opportunity. For Wild & Free, Isabel had reshaped her TV material into a series of popular lectures; online booking had been oversubscribed three times. Even the Master of her own college and his wife had had trouble getting tickets, but Jess had swiftly stepped in to sort this out. There they all were now, dancing around in the mosh pit. The Master of Branston, with his youngest daughter Violet on his shoulders, looked happy but surprised, as if unable quite to work out what he was doing here.

James, behind his wall of sound, was watching for his wife. Victoria had promised to be there as soon as she could but her town hall meeting had probably overrun. She found it hard to tear herself away; no one had ever enjoyed being a local councillor more. Ultimately – and fired by the example of their new close family friend Nadia Ramage, MP for Wortley-on-Thames – Victoria had her sights set on Westminster. James had not the slightest doubt that she would get there. But she was taking it slowly and steadily; as the whole family were, in every sense.

He sucked in his cheeks and did his best Animal-from-the-Muppets impression for the benefit of the cameras. The reunion gig was being filmed and recorded for a DVD that was the centrepiece of the new business James was helping Rob with. Last year's truncated Wild & Free, with its cancelled Mascara Snakes reunion, had been the start of a new life for everyone. Except for Rob.

Mark and Spencer had returned from the festival with new relationships, if in Mark's case a few bruises as well; and James had taken his own life – and wife – in hand. But Rob had simply been obliged to swallow his frustration at having to go home early not having played a note with his old band. He had quietly packed his monobrow and returned to provincial accountancy.

Except that he hadn't, Mark, James and Spencer subsequently discovered. The effect of Wild & Free had been to reveal to Rob that he wanted something rather more out of what remained of life. With the agreement of his wife he had cut loose and launched a website resource specialising in linking up former student bands who had lost touch with each other over the years.

Bands Reunited, as the service was called, aimed not only to help estranged rockers rediscover each other, but to point them in the direction of studios, recording facilities and anything else they might require. Including, of course, the chance to perform live in public at the Wild & Free Festival's Battle of the Bands, now sponsored by Bands Reunited. The response had been enormous, too much for Rob to handle alone, which was where James came in. He and Rob had just launched the special Bands Reunited record label on which the winners of the present competition would release their first album.

It was amazing, James thought, how things had turned out. How one short festival could affect so many lives.

Mark could see both Alfie and Lorna dancing happily around in the mosh pit with Tenebris and his sons.

Buster and Django, in the end, had turned out to be much less daunting a prospect than they had looked when first arriving at St Stephen's. Ginnie's gentleness, encouragement and persuasion soon had them eating out of her hand, revealing that, under all the pent-up aggression, they were bright, even endearing boys. What they had really needed was a regular school day, it seemed.

Alfie, too, had changed almost out of all recognition. He had grown and filled out, and his confidence had soared. He was also absolutely obsessed with heraldry and his mother, to the school's secret amazement, had not sought to block this interest or any other. Alfie had, as a result, presented several talks to the school on the subject of knights, battles, the Order of the Garter and all the excitement and general violence of the Middle Ages. Far from making him an object of derision, these had inspired his classmates to come to school with wooden swords shoved in their bookbags in readiness for the Battle of Crécy or Agincourt at breaktime, with Alfie always either Henry V or Edward III, depending on which conflict was in the spotlight.

But the real Newwoman–Hasp-related miracle was that Lorna, who had reverted to Newman just when everyone had got used to Newwoman, seemed, so far as one could tell, quite normal these days.

As in not normal.

'Not normal?' Ginnie had queried, when first Mark had floated this idea.

'As in not normal for Lorna, but normal for sane humanity. Tenebris is good for her. Now she's finally seen what a good thing she's on to there.'

Tenebris, with his calm good sense and understated ways,

was certainly half the reason. The other was Jess who, with her uncanny ability to spot potential in the most unlikely people, had given Lorna the annual four-month-long job of curating the amateur storytelling competition at the Wild & Free Festival. As a former competitor, Lorna knew the score better than most; knew, too, exactly what facilities were needed to improve the whole operation.

As a result, a proper stage had been built – by Tenebris – in what was still called the Hibbertygibberty Wood because no one could think of anything better. And because Lorna, with whom people were reluctant to argue even now, declared herself fond of it. But the Wood itself was much improved; the bushes nearest to it cleared to minimise mosquito nuisance. And there were copious quantities of free anti-insect cream on hand to tackle any that remained.

This latter was supplied, in her trademark labelled pots, by Shanna-Mae, ever quick to spot a promotional opportunity. She was back this year with an entire Beauty Marquee. Guy, when he could get away from his practical engineering course, was on hand to help when any of Shanna's no-less-than-four spray-tan booths, all going great guns round the clock, developed problems. It was suspected among the staff, including Rosie, that Guy pretended there were problems just so he could fix them. He and Shanna may have been together twelve months now, but he was clearly not resting on his laurels.

Spencer, at the front, was in his element, dancing about, dodging the plugs and amps as Rowan, hair swinging, waved at him with both arms extended from the mosh pit, revealing the dragon tattoo which matched exactly the one on Spencer's bicep. 'The dragon,' Spencer had earnestly explained to Mark, James and Rob before they had gone on stage, 'represents the earth energies in all cultures.' He had wanted to dowse everyone's auras for luck, but unfortunately – or fortunately – there had not been time.

Rowan's wheeling, dragon-tattooed limbs now delivered a glancing, if accidental blow to Lorna, who just smiled and didn't seem to mind at all.

Having delivered the final line of 'Life is a Chocolate Factory', Spencer punched the air and the crowd in the Big Top were whooping and whistling and applauding even before the last note had died away.

Of course, the Upward Mobility Scooters had almost certainly won this first Bands Reunited-sponsored Battle of the Bands. Their tribute to the Stones, 'Gimme Sheltered Accommodation', had caused near-riots of audience appreciation. But, as Mark, James, Rob and Spencer were aware; and Jess, Ralph and Ginnie were similarly conscious; and Lorna, Tenebris, Alfie, Buster, Django, Sparkle, Olly, Isabel, Shanna-Mae, Rosie, Diana, Richard, Violet, Victoria and Guy knew too, there was always next year.

Want to know where it all began?

WENDY HOLDEN

Gifted and Talented

Welcome to Branston College. We are an academic institution in the heart of an ancient university town . . .

Diana is starting a new life as gardener at Branston, a challenging restoration project which allows her to indulg a love of delphiniums beneath the disconcerting gaze of dishy but remote Richard, the recently widowed College Master.

A new term brings new students, among them It Girl Amber, darling of the gossip columns and dead ringer for inclusion in the university's notorious elite society. As lustful teenager and crabby tutors run riot in Diana's garden, her peaceful haven is trampled, and then a blast from the past threatens to ruin a new romance. Can anything save Diana's hard-won happiness, let alone her herbaceous borders?

Acclaim for *Gifted and Talented*:

'A warm-hearted page-turner' *Sunday Times*

'A fun yet touching tale about class and privilege' *Good Housekeeping*, Book of the Month

978 0 7553 8527 0

headline
review

WENDY HOLDEN

Marrying Up

Scheming social climber Alexa is a class-hopping cruise missile. She's aimed at the very top of the gold-digging tree. But will she get the title, towers and tiara of her dreams?

Beautiful, penniless student Polly is in love. But is there more to dashing vet Max than his animal instincts?

Passionate love, eye-widening snobbery and more-than-naked ambition abound in this tale of contemporary Cinderellas.

Praise for *Marrying Up*:

'A brilliant juicy Cinderella tale ****' *Heat* No. 1

'This fabulously witty story of love, social climbing and downright snobbery is a riot of a read *****' *Closer*

'Pin-sharp social-climbing comedy' *Grazia*

'Social snobbery and bare-faced ambition . . . a modern fairytale that chimes perfectly with our post-Wills-and-Kate world' *Glamour*

978 0 7553 4264 8

headline
review

WENDY HOLDEN

Gallery Girl

Alice loves art, but her gallery-owner boss Angelica is interested only in money. Alice also loves her boyfriend, but he's interested only in his career. Bad boy billionaire artist Zeb is interested in Alice, but then he's mainly interested in sex. Meanwhile, shy-but-brilliant painter Dan scrapes a living holding village-hall drawing classes. When bored rock wife Siobhan joins one, things get colourful.

Will life for any of them be picture perfect? Or will they all make exhibitions of themselves?

Praise for *Gallery Girl*:

'Wendy Holden is a brilliant writer . . . Great fun, filled with sparkling dialogue, witty asides and a fast-paced narrative. A real treat' *Daily Mail*

'Witty, raunchy' *Grazia*

'Wendy Holden on form is a thing to behold' *Daily Mirror*

'Holden's trademark satire here acquires an extra bite' *Guardian*

'A fabulously frothy tale of a woman drawn into the glamorous, sex-fuelled world of contemporary art' *Good Housekeeping*

978 0 7553 4260 0

headline
review